THE DANCE CARD

JOHN R. FEEGEL

AVON
PUBLISHERS OF BARD, CAMELOT, DISCUS AND FLARE BOOKS

Designed by Francesca Belanger

AVON BOOKS
A division of
The Hearst Corporation
959 Eighth Avenue
New York, New York 10019

The Dial Press edition contains the following Library of
Congress Cataloging in Publication Data:

Feegel, John R
    The dance card.

    I. Title.
PS3556.E32D3   813'.54   80-24011

First Avon Printing, May, 1982

To forensic pathologists—
who do more and make less than the others.

1 Peachtree Street traffic in Atlanta was heavier than usual. On good days Twig Stanton, M.D., could make it to the Hyatt Regency in under five minutes; but with a convention in town he knew he would have to move slowly with the crowd and wait for the lights. He hated using the blue light on his dashboard, thinking it made him look more like a cop than Atlanta's chief medical examiner; and above all he wanted the medical examiner's office to look neutral and civilian.

Twig Stanton went to medical school at Johns Hopkins. His father, who'd been a general practitioner, had said that a Hopkins man was too good for pathology, but Twig had found internal medicine and surgery boring. For his pathology residency he chose the Massachusetts General Hospital, and after a few weeks of bullet holes and homicide investigations with the Boston P.D., Twig was hooked. Cancer and its cure would have to wait for someone else.

His mother had named him Clarence. Twig had been her maiden name. In college he decided to shorten his name to C. Twig Stanton, which he thought had a more sophisticated ring. Later on, when his work brought him into daily contact with tough city cops, he dropped the initial. Two last names made him sound very southern, which was fine, since he had been born in Raleigh and spoke with a soft Carolina accent. The only time the name sounded ridiculous was when he was paged in airports by a nasal female.

Two-sixty-five Peachtree Street NE came into view as Dr. Stanton eased his new Oldsmobile around the corner. The blue dome of the satellite bar on top of the Hyatt Regency Atlanta threw back the sharp rays of the morning sun. Stanton glanced at the clock in the dash: 10:07 A.M., a hell of a time for a jumper-suicide. Suicides were usually discovered when a family resumed a routine from which the victim had chosen to absent himself—dead in bed

1

when everyone else got up for work, dead in the garage when somebody tried to drive downtown, dead in the bathroom when people got home from the office. There was a time and circumstance for every style...a pattern.

"Forensic pathology," Twig Stanton would lecture his students, "is the science of pattern injuries. Look close enough at the wound and you can figure out what happened. The burn on the inside of the motorcyclist's leg; the bumper fractures of the auto-pedestrian victim; the powder stippling of the close gunshot wound. Pattern injuries. That's what it's all about." A few of them would listen, but at that stage in their medical training they were more easily fascinated by brain surgery, vaginal deliveries, and the emergency room. Forensic lectures were only bread on the academic water, but he believed that if he preached to fifteen hundred medical students over ten years, one or two of them would choose the M.E. office as a career, and that would keep the meager staff alive. So far he'd been right.

Dr. Stanton rolled into the curved driveway of the hotel and stopped behind the two Atlanta police cars partly blocking the exit. One of them had its blue lights blinking, needlessly attracting a crowd. He flipped his keys to the doorman.

"Try not to steal the radio."

"No chance," the young man said in a soft Hispanic accent. "This place is already crawling with cops." He tossed his head toward the revolving door and the activity in the lobby.

"Uh-huh," Stanton said. "Add me to the list."

Dr. Stanton walked briskly into the hotel lobby. Ordinarily the medical examiner's office wouldn't send a pathologist to a routine suicide and hardly ever would the chief show up; but another jumper at the Hyatt Regency was enough to attract Twig Stanton's attention. First of all, he had been making a private study of why people check into a plush downtown hotel and then leap into the lobby from the upper floors. Second, Stanton knew that the hotel would come to a standstill until the body was removed. As chief medical examiner he could authorize the removal of the crumpled body before the police investigation had been completed. And third, the place was crawling with pathologists for the annual joint meeting

of the American Society of Clinical Pathologists and the
College of American Pathologists—a golden opportunity
for the Atlanta medical examiner's office to look good.

The lobby was spacious and beautiful. The floors faced
inward, giving the guests a breathtaking view of the lobby
below from the glassed-in elevators. The hotel had almost
a thousand rooms in twenty-six floors towering above the
lobby. Vines and plants clung to the balconies of the upper
floors, giving the place the look of a modern-day hanging
garden.

A graceful metal sculpture reached skyward to the fourteenth floor, changing shape when seen from different levels. Standing on a stem of stainless steel, it lifted its gold
and silver arms upward like a flower and transformed the
indoor canyon into a galley. So far none of the jumpers
had managed to land inside the metal sculpture. (The Parasol Bar had not been as fortunate. It occupied a prominent
corner of the lobby and its petallike roof of sculptured iron
and glass, suspended by a single cable, provided an attractive target for anyone choosing the direct route down.
The medical examiner's records showed that more than
one had tried this way to crash the party.)

Stanton walked quickly toward the crowd near the airline information booth and saw the body of his newest
statistic sprawled behind it. The police had roped off that
corner of the lobby, and a maid had brought a sheet for
cover. Blood soaked through, turning it into a macabre
flag for the viewers to comment on. Without apology, the
medical examiner elbowed his way through the knot of
people, some of them no doubt doctors. Twig had received
a program for the convention weeks before. The educa-
tional talks and workshops were arranged so that no one
could attend them all, and prudent conventioners studied
their programs in advance, reserving seats in those ses-
sions that interested them most. Dr. Stanton had promptly
lost the program among the papers on his desk.

Stanton approached the nearest uniformed officer and
reached for his identification folder.

"It's okay, Doc," the policeman said, lifting the rope to
admit him. "I remember you from the slides you showed
at the police academy."

"Oh, thanks," Stanton mumbled. He was both pleased
and disturbed to be recognized. His work required a good

public image so that Fulton County would continue funding his department without wrangling; but on the other hand, as the man with the proof of death in every Atlanta murder case, he could easily become a target for some disgruntled relative of a defendant. It was safer to be unknown.

The police photographer flashed another shot of the body; he'd finished his ID pictures but waited to see if Twig would ask for more. Two detectives stood near the body, interviewing a bellhop. Stanton joined them before approaching the body.

"Mornin', Doc," the bigger detective drawled, dismissing the bellhop. He was Shelby Baines, forty, permanently assigned to homicide, and counting the days to retirement.

"Mornin', Shelby," Dr. Stanton said. They shook hands and exchanged glances.

"They sure like this place," Baines observed. He glanced around the spacious lobby. The Hyatt Regency called it an atrium.

"We've had a bunch, haven't we?" Stanton remarked. His slow North Carolina attitude blended easily with the big Georgian detective's personality. "I've been going over some of those cases."

"The attraction must be the way the lobby looks when you get up there," Baines said, glancing toward the top floor.

"The architect should have thought of that when he planned the place," Jimmie Butts, the other detective, added. He was in his late twenties and, compared to Shelby, a rookie.

"Want to look at him now, Doc?"

"Might as well," Stanton sighed. He glanced at his watch. "I've still got cases in the morgue to get done. The irony is that after I get them cleared out, I'm coming back to the Regency."

"Here?" Butts asked, interested. Young detectives try to be interested in every irrelevant detail. Remembering details later tends to impress their senior partner. Jimmie Butts had already learned that.

"Uh-huh," Stanton said. "There's a convention of pathologists here this week and I want to catch some of it."

"Nice of them to schedule the meeting right in your backyard," Baines said.

"I guess if you live in Atlanta, more things are apt to happen than if you're the pathologist in Nosebleed, U.S.A.," Stanton agreed.

"We've already met him," Baines said lightly.

"Who?" Stanton asked.

"Your pathologist from Nosebleed, U.S.A.," Baines said. "Only the place is called Poplar Bluffs, Iowa."

"That's him over there by the officer at the rope," Butts said, pointing with his pencil.

"What the hell are you guys talking about?" Stanton growled, expecting a punch line.

"That guy identified the body for us," Baines said. "He came in just after we did. They body wasn't even covered. He took one look at the dead guy and made him."

"Said he knew him years ago," Butts added. He flipped his little notebook open and scanned two of the pages. "His name is Edward P. Adams, and he's a doctor."

"Who?" Stanton asked. "The dead guy?"

"No. The pathologist over by the rope," Baines said. "But the dead guy is a pathologist too."

Twig Stanton's interest soared. "Really? Who is he?" He walked to the body and stopped to raise the sheet from the bloody head. The exposure of the dead man evoked a soft gasp from several of the ladies behind the rope.

Detectives Baines and Butts joined him at the body. "The name we got from Dr. Adams was George I. Toll, M.D.," Baines said. "You know him?"

Stanton stared at the blood-spattered face. He shook his head slowly without speaking. Toll was dressed in an ordinary shirt, dark trousers, and plain black shoes. He did not look particularly prosperous. Stanton estimated he was in his forties. His brown hair was matted with blood and brain that oozed from a massive skull fracture.

"You don't see many suicides among pathologists," Stanton said. "Especially high jumpers." He dropped the corner of the sheet on Toll's face and glanced at his hands to see if they were bloody. They were still clean.

"According to the desk clerk," Baines said dryly, "he checked in yesterday. He listed Haiti as his home address."

"Haiti? How does this other guy know him?" Stanton asked, glancing in the general direction of Ed Adams.

"He said they were in the Navy together," Butts said.

"Well, that ought to make your identification easy."

"We'll fingerprint him at your place," Baines said, "but there was no doubt in Dr. Adams's mind when he eyeballed him."

Stanton glanced at Adams. He wore a dark blue three-piece suit with a narrow black tie tied in a fifties knot, brown shoes, and white socks. His wife wore a light green dress from J. C. Penney and, as she would probably put it, sensible shoes. The Adamses had finished talking with a uniformed officer and stood silently, facing the body. Maude Adams held her black shiny purse in front of her pubic area and Ed folded his arms across his chest.

"Maybe I should have a word with this Dr. Adams," Stanton said. "Maybe he can supply a motive."

"Why not?" Baines agreed. "But so far it looks like a routine suicide. Don't you think so?"

"From what floor?" Stanton asked, craning his neck to look upward.

"We don't know," Butts said. "There were no actual witnesses to the fall. I mean, he didn't hang onto one of the balconies and attract a crowd, or nothing like that."

"He had a room on the twenty-sixth," Baines said. "He checked in alone, but we haven't seen his room yet. I want to clear the body out of the lobby first."

"Was Dr. Adams able to give you any more information about him?" Stanton asked.

"Not really," Baines said. "Adams said he hadn't seen the guy in years."

"But he recognized him at first glance, sprawled across the floor of the hotel," Stanton said, stroking his chin.

"Dr. Adams strikes me as that kind of a guy," Baines said. "Y'know, one of those guys that can tell you what's in their pockets without looking?"

"They made us do that at police academy," Butts volunteered. "Hell, I never knew what was in my pockets or what I ate for lunch yesterday."

"An organized mind," Stanton said. He glanced at the two detectives as Baines nodded in agreement. "That's what it takes."

Jimmie Butts glanced at the crowd. Two ambulance attendants waited at the police rope. One of them shifted his weight from foot to foot and glanced at his watch. He apparently had better things to do than stand around the

Hyatt Regency lobby, waiting for the medical examiner to clear a suicide.

"Is it okay to move the body?" Butts asked Dr. Stanton.

The medical examiner glanced at the form under the sheet. "Yeah," he said softly, "let's move him over to the morgue."

Butts waved his hand. The attendants moved under the rope, bringing a portable stretcher that looked clean enough for cardiac surgery. Their movements were crisp and professional. They were trained to work in full view of the public, and could move the messiest body without embarrassment or exposure.

Shelby Baines motioned to Dr. Adams to join them. At first the Iowa pathologist pointed to his chest and mouthed, "Who, me?" but then quickly scrambled under the rope. A nod from Detective Baines cleared him past the uniformed officer. Dr. Stanton watched Dr. Adams approach with hurried little steps.

"This is Dr. Edward P. Adams, Dr. Stanton," Baines said. "Dr. Stanton is the chief medical examiner."

"Dr. Stanton?" Adams said. "I'm pleased to meet you. I'm a pathologist myself. Poplar Bluffs, Iowa." He shook the medical examiner's hand enthusiastically.

"In Atlanta for the convention?" Stanton asked, filling in, and reclaiming his hand.

"That's right. Not my idea, you understand," Adams said. "But the medical staff at the hospital back home entered into this damned fool agreement with the state licensing board and HEW to send all of the hospital-based physicians—y'know, the pathologist and the radiologist?—off for a meeting or two. They said it was to keep us up-to-date. I call it a waste of time."

"Continuing medical education is popular these days," Stanton said, evaluating Dr. Adams's every movement. He had already classified Adams as a bug that inhabited small hospital laboratories in obscure towns across America, endlessly examining gall bladders and appendices. For Stanton that was a far cry from the practice of medicine. He had once estimated that he could stand that kind of pathology for about a week. A week would have been too long.

"Seems to me," Adams continued with his next breath, "if these fellows spent part of each day reading their basic textbooks, they'd stay about as up-to-date as anyone could expect. I brought my Boyd with me."

Stanton's mind flashed to an ancient copy of *Textbook of Pathology* standing at the end of his bookcase in medical school. Adams was no doubt thinking of a newer edition.

"Detective Baines says that you recognized the body," Stanton said.

"Yes, sir, I did," Adams replied, watching the ambulance attendants lift the body and sheet to the stretcher. "A terrible thing. Terrible. Did he fall?"

"We don't know very much about the circumstances surrounding his death, Dr. Adams," the medical examiner said.

"Ed," Dr. Adams offered.

". . . er, Ed," Stanton said. "But how did you come to know Dr. Toll?"

"I met him in the Navy. Oh, I didn't know him all that well, you understand. More like a transfer period. It was at Key West, Florida."

"When was that?" Stanton asked.

"April ninth, 1961," Dr. Adams said, rolling his eyes backward to sharpen his memory.

"Were you both pathologists at the naval hospital in Key West at that time?" Stanton asked.

"Well, something like that, Dr. Stanton," Adams said precisely. "Actually, I was the pathologist assigned to Key West, but they sent Dr. Toll to relieve me on some temporary duty. Least, that's how it appeared to me."

"Why was that?" Baines asked.

"Well, they sent me a telegram," Adams continued. "Right from the Navy Bureau of Medicine in Washington! And it said I was to expect this Commander George Toll, show him around the place, and then report to Boston for further training."

"Where did Dr. Toll come from when he reported to Key West?" Stanton asked.

"Darned if I know," Adams said. "All I know is he flew in there, full of Navy spit and polish—ribbons on his chest—that sort of thing, and said he was Commander George Toll. Not *Dr.* Toll, you understand, but *Commander* Toll." He paused to sneer slightly for Dr. Stanton. "I don't know if you were in the service, Dr. Stanton, but that's not the way two pathologists say hello to each other."

"Uh-huh," Stanton said. "Was that the only time you met Dr. Toll?"

"Yes, sir."

"And you remember him?" Baines asked skeptically.

"I'll remember you too, sir," Dr. Adams said proudly. "Your name is Detective Shelby Baines, right? And this young man is Detective Jimmie Butts. Remembering names and faces comes easy for a pathologist. Right, Dr. Stanton? We are what you might call masters of detail."

Twig Stanton, a master of disorganization and office clutter, found himself mentally saying, "Oh, dear. Oh, dear." Stanton sometimes had trouble remembering his own secretary's name, although she had been with him for over five years.

"Was there anything unusual about him when he reported to Key West?" Baines asked.

"Oh, my goodness, no," Dr. Adams said disapprovingly. "When I saw him that day in Key West, he was Regulation all the way." He glanced at the shrouded form on the stretcher as it left through the crowd. "I don't know what could have happened to him to make him do a thing like this."

"He jumped," Jimmie Butts supplied.

"He certainly did, Mr. Butts," Adams agreed. It was obvious that, given the chance, Adams and Butts could sharply disagree.

"You say that Dr. Toll was in Key West on special assignment?" Stanton continued.

"That's the way it seemed to me," Adams said. "I don't know what it was, though, because they never did send me back there. After Boston they sent me on to San Diego, California, for the rest of my time in the service. Of course, it was only a few more months."

"Then how do you know that Dr. Toll stayed only a few weeks in Key West?" Baines asked.

"I called down there from the naval hospital in Boston to arrange for the transfer of some books that I had left behind. You see, I had expected to return, and only took my W. A. D. Anderson for my daily reading."

"And Dr. Toll was gone?" Stanton offered.

"That's right," Adams said, acknowledging Stanton's perception. "Commander Toll, they informed me, had been reassigned."

"Did they say where he had been sent?" Stanton asked.

"No," Adams said. "But they shipped my books and notes to San Diego without any trouble."

"And you never saw or heard from Dr. Toll again?" Baines asked.

"No, sir, I did not."

"Thank you, Dr. Adams. You have been very helpful to us," Dr. Stanton said. "Are you staying here at the Hyatt Regency?"

"Just for the convention, of course," Adams said. "I've got to get back to Poplar Bluffs and my laboratory."

"I'm sure they miss you," Stanton purred. "I may contact you again before you check out."

The police photographer had been waiting patiently a few steps away. Dr. Stanton had not asked for any additional shots, but the man had taken a couple as the body was removed anyway. "Excuse me, sir," he said to Detective Baines, "you want any more pictures?"

Baines glanced around the scene. "You got one of the blood and brains on the floor?" He pointed to the place where the body had been.

"Yes, sir," the photographer said. "Right after they picked him up."

"Okay," Baines said. "I think that's about it for here."

"I'll shoot the routine shots—dressed and undressed, at the morgue," the police photographer said. "And by the way, it's probably none of my business, but who's the other guy photographing this scene?"

"Where?" Baines and Stanton said simultaneously, looking in different directions.

"Up there," the photographer said. He pointed to a corner on the fifteenth floor overlooking the Parasol Bar. As he did, a man in his shirt-sleeves took one more shot with his 35 mm, realized he had been spotted, and stepped back out of sight.

"I thought he was somebody assigned to get some high-level views of the scene," the police photographer said. "He used a telephoto lens. I figured he was working with the medical examiner's office."

"Maybe the newspaper?" Dr. Stanton asked.

"He had better equipment than any newshound I've ever known," the photographer said. "There was another guy with him too."

"Check them out, Jimmie," Baines said. "That looks like fourteenth or fifteenth floor to me."

Detective Butts looked at the glass elevators and felt his stomach quiver. "Can I walk up?" he asked.

"Might as well," Stanton said. "The man just entered the stairwell on that floor. By the time you get up there, he'll be long gone."

2 Twig Stanton did have a lot of work to do at the morgue, but he was in no particular hurry to face it. He wanted to let the body of George Toll reach the Fulton County morgue, be photographed, undressed, rephotographed, fingerprinted, toe-tagged, weighed, and measured before he showed up to start the autopsy. To kill some time, he decided to have an early lunch at nearby Pittypat's Porch. The restaurant and its Deep South menu would have suited Twig Stanton perfectly if it wasn't always filled with tourists.

The TV in the bar offered the noon-hour news as he entered, even though it was not yet twelve. The commentator, a young black woman, announced that the Middle East remained unsettled, that the leader of some obscure African nation had just made an outlandish statement about the Queen of England, and that an average share on the New York Stock Exchange had dropped a few cents in moderate trading. Then without warning she began to read a bulletin:

This, just in. At the Hyatt Regency Atlanta, a short time ago, a prominent pathologist leaped to his death into the lobby. The doctor was attending a convention sponsored jointly by the College of American Pathologists and the American Society of Clinical Pathologists. The case appears to be a suicide, although further investigations are continuing. An autopsy is scheduled for later this afternoon. [Pause] The name of the dead man is being withheld pending notification of next of kin.

The newscaster looked into the camera and held a serious expression as the scene dissolved to an ad for a laundry product.

"Goddamn," Stanton muttered to himself. "They got that out fast enough."

"Pardon me, sir?" the bartender asked.

Dr. Stanton shook his head. "No, nothing, thanks," he said. He turned from the bar and marched out the door. Since he hadn't cleared the body or a press release, he was anxious to know if the story had been reported from his office.

His rising anger was not evident in his driving, except for impatient horn blowing and uncharacteristic muttering at red lights. He wheeled into his assigned space, slammed the door, and entered the side door of the medical examiner's office. His secretary was a precise, menopausal woman who had been married to a cop about twelve years before.

"Libby," Stanton said in a tone that broadcasted a warning, "who gave out the news clip?"

"What news clip?" she asked.

"The noontime TV. They had a blurb on about the pathologist that jumped inside the Hyatt Regency. Hell, I haven't seen him with his clothes off yet."

"Well, it didn't come from us," she said. "Maybe it came from the morgue boys—or the drivers?"

Stanton paused to consider those possibilities. "I'll check on that, but God help them if they are giving out information about new cases without clearing it with me. I pay them to move bodies, not to talk about them with the news."

Libby smoothed her hair to make sure that every strand was pulled back tightly in place. "They came in the receiving door about fifteen minutes ago. They called me when they got here. I don't think they've even had time to undress the body yet."

"Did the police photographer show up?"

"Not as far as I know," Libby said. "But maybe he went directly to the morgue through the back door."

"He knows he's supposed to log in up here." Stanton would not tolerate people wandering around the medical examiner's office, even if they were police personnel.

"Uh-huh, but how many of them do?" she asked with a helpless shrug.

"Libby," Stanton announced firmly, "we've got to get back to some basic discipline around here. Get out the memo file and put it on my desk. I'll review all the office directives right after I go down to the morgue and make sure that none of our boys were involved in that news release." The chief medical examiner accepted his secretary's nod of approval and walked toward the door leading to the stairs and the morgue below.

The medical examiner's office was located on Coca-Cola Place behind the Grady Memorial Hospital. (Coke had been invented just down the street.) Since many of the homicide cases died in the Grady emergency room before being transferred to the M.E.'s office, the location was reasonable. It was a modest but functional two-story building, with drive-in accommodations in the rear for the dead, and a set of steep front steps for the living. The body-storage morgue, dissection room, and anatomy laboratories were on the ground floor and, for security reasons, had no windows. The second floor was all office spaces. With just under a thousand autopsies a year the facility was small, and very active. It also served as a training facility for investigators, police, and forensic-pathology residents from Emory University.

Dr. Stanton opened the morgue door and found the room in total darkness.

"Bubba?" Stanton called into the silent room. There was no response. The doctor paused for a moment. He groped along the cool, tiled wall, found the switch, and filled the room with light. The corpse from the Hyatt Regency was still on the ambulance cart, but the sheet had been removed and thrown on the floor. Stanton went closer and looked at the body of Dr. Toll once more.

The clothing had been methodically cut along the front of each trouser leg, and the pockets removed. The breast pockets of Toll's jacket had been slit and the shirt pocket was torn along one side. The garments had been intact at the hotel.

The chief medical examiner's blood began to boil. First the unauthorized press release to the TV newswoman, and now destruction of the clothing before the police photographer had arrived. He found himself shouting for Bubba Hutcheson, the head morgue assistant; but again, there was no response.

Stanton moved around the morgue and dissection room, shouting Hutcheson's name and slamming his palm onto the stainless-steel table. The pain in his hand snapped him back to reality and he lowered his voice. He refused to believe that Bubba Hutcheson, after so many years of faithful service to him in the morgue, would permit the mutilation of Dr. Toll's clothes, and leave the body out of the cooler, uncovered and abandoned. Bubba was home-grown and took his work seriously. He had joined the county hospital system as a sweeper and had risen from house-keeping to chief assistant in the morgue. Some of his drinking friends joked that he had not progressed at all, but had been assigned to work with dead bodies because he was a terrible sweeper. But Bubba Hutcheson was proud to be the chief assistant to the medical examiner.

Dr. Stanton strode to the big meat-locker door of the walk-in cooler, still grumbling. He threw it open with a grunt, anticipating the escape of cold and unpleasant air.

"Jesus Christ!" he said softly.

Bubba Hutcheson sat on the floor in front of him, tied to the two ambulance attendants, back to back. Their eyes begged for help as the men shouted against their gags. One of the ambulance drivers had a cut over his right eye and blood ran down his face, soaking the gag, and dripping onto the front of his white coat.

Stanton tried to pull the gag from Hutcheson's mouth but it was too tightly tied behind his head. Each of the men had his feet tied together, his knees drawn up, and his hands tied behind his back. The doctor went to the morgue table in the other room and returned with a scalpel. He cut the gags from their mouths as skillfully as a surgeon removing a brain tumor and then severed the nylon cords that bound their hands and feet.

"God, Dr. Stanton," Bubba said, almost breaking into tears, "it was awful."

"What the hell happened?" Stanton asked, still cutting.

"We were jumped," said the attendant who was bleeding. He put his hand to his laceration as soon as it was freed, and looked at the blood on his fingers.

"Here, let's get out of this body cooler," Stanton said. The men struggled to their feet, helping each other, and went into the main dissection room where the body of Dr. Toll still lay.

"Christ! Look at what they did to the body," one of the attendants said, pointing to the slashed garments.

"Who were they? Where did they come from? What's this all about?"

"I don't know, Dr. Stanton," Bubba apologized. "I was alone here in the morgue, cleaning up? Y'know?"

"Yes, sure, Bubba," Stanton soothed. "Are you hurt?"

"Naw, I ain't hurt," Hutcheson said, "but they hit Morgan here in the face with a gun." He pointed at the injured ambulance attendant.

"But, why, Bubba?" Stanton persisted. "Who were they?"

"Two big guys, both of them," the other attendant said. He glanced quickly at Hutcheson, and resumed his description. "They had on dark blue suits."

"They looked like FBI guys to me," Morgan said.

"What do you mean, 'FBI guys'?" Stanton asked.

"Oh, you know," Morgan said. "They looked big, and tough, and well dressed and..."

"...polite, but no bullshit," the other attendant continued.

"They both had guns," Bubba confirmed.

"What did they want?" Stanton asked.

"They wanted to know if we took anything off this dead guy," Morgan said. "Right, Castner?"

"What do you mean, 'took anything off him'?" Stanton asked.

"I don't know, Dr. Stanton," Hutcheson whined. "I just don't know." The experience had obviously traumatized him.

"They knew what they were after," Morgan said. "They searched all of us and when I tried to stop them, one of them hit me with his gun."

"I thought we were going to be killed," Hutcheson said.

"Were they after jewelry or something?" Stanton asked. He looked from face to face and then at the body of George Toll.

"They went through his wallet," Morgan said. He pointed at the money and cards scattered over the top of the morgue desk. "If they wanted his money and credit cards, they were right there. But they didn't take nothing."

"Well, what did they say?" Stanton insisted. "They must have said something. Maybe that would tell us what they were looking for?"

"They only asked us if we were the ones that picked up the body at the Hyatt Regency," Castner said.

"And they especially wanted to know if the cops took anything off the body at the scene," Morgan added. He had taken a clean compress out of one of the morgue cabinets, and held it to his eyebrow.

"We showed them the property list," Castner said. "Y'know, the one we got the cops to sign? I showed them it was blank. That proved the cops didn't keep nothing. But then they shoved us around and searched our pockets. They started in on the body after they tied us up in the icebox."

"This is the goddamnedest thing I ever did hear of," Stanton mumbled. "We had a typewriter stolen from the lab one summer, and some of you guys have always been nicking the pure alcohol, especially around Christmas, but I don't remember anyone ever coming down here to rob a body."

"One time a family said we took some lady's ring, remember?" Hutcheson said.

"Uh-huh," Stanton acknowledged. "And that was when we started listing the jewelry as 'yellow metal with clear stone' instead of 'gold and diamonds.' As it turned out," he explained to the attendants, "the woman had pawned her ring to buy wine, but the family insisted that she never took it off. Let's see what Shelby thinks about this." He pushed the intercom button on the telephone and picked up the receiver, dialing two digits.

Libby answered immediately. She always answered quickly when she knew he was upset.

"Yes, sir?"

"Libby, get me Detective Baines, will you? He may still be at the Hyatt Regency."

"Are you psychic?" Libby asked playfully. "He's on line four, calling you."

"Perfect," Stanton said. He punched the blinking button for line four. "Shelby. I'm glad you called. We've got the damnedest thing over here."

"Well, you're not the only one. You know that jumper from the Hyatt? Well, we just went up to look at his room."

"And?" Stanton prodded.

"It's a hell of a mess. Somebody's been over it with a fine-tooth comb. They went into every drawer, every

pocket of his suits, tore through his luggage, and even cut
the backs out of pictures hanging on the wall."

"No shit?" Stanton asked. "Well, they hit us too, Shelby.
Two guys jumped the ambulance attendants and my man,
Hutcheson, right after they got back with the body, and
gave them a going-over. They tied them up in the cooler
and cut the pockets out of the corpse's suit and shirt."

"What were they after?" Baines asked.

"I can't tell," Stanton said. "But it sure as hell wasn't
money or credit cards."

"In a way I'm glad to hear about them hitting the
morgue like that," Baines said.

"Glad! Why are you glad?" Stanton asked.

"Because we weren't sure this pathologist didn't ransack his own room, like some crazy," Baines explained.
"I mean, what the hell, if he's loony enough to jump into
the lobby of the Regency, who knows what he might do to
his room? Like the numbers in the bathroom."

"What's that?"

"The bathroom in his hotel room. Somebody wrote 'two-
five-oh-six' on the mirror.

"Is that his room number?"

"Naw. He was in two-six-ten. Damn, I wish Butts had
found that guy with the camera. I wonder why they didn't
search him in the hotel room."

"How about—these guys attack him in the room, he
breaks through them as they crack the bathroom, makes
it out the door, and falls over the balcony?" Stanton suggested.

"Or gets pushed?" Baines asked slyly.

"Just what I need—another homicide." He paused to
look at the men in the morgue. They hung on every word,
waiting for him to get off the phone and explain everything
to them. "Did you check out room two-five-oh-six?"

"It's vacant. And it was empty yesterday too. The toilet
didn't work. The hotel plumber says it was stopped up with
a Kotex. You think it was a big clue?"

"I'd better say no, Shelby, 'cuz if I say yes, you'll find
the damned thing and want me to blood-type it."

"Look," Baines said, sounding serious again. "I'm going
to put a burglary detail on Dr. Toll's room and go over
every inch of it. I don't like the looks of this thing. And
in the meantime I want to talk to your morgue men."

"Be our guest, Shelby. We've got nowhere to go. I'm going to delay Dr. Toll's autopsy until we get some of this stuff straightened out."

"See you in a while," Baines promised as they both hung up.

Twig Stanton faced the perplexed morgue assistants. Morgan removed the compress from his eyebrow when Dr. Stanton attempted to look at it.

"You'd better go over to the E.R. and let one of the interns clean that cut and put in a couple of stitches," he said.

"I'm going to go too," Castner said. "I want them to check me over and give me something for my nerves. Those two guys scared the shit out of me. I mean it."

"Yeah, you're right," Stanton said. "All three of you might as well go over and get checked out."

"Not me," Hutcheson said. "I'll calm my nerves with some Johnnie Walker this evening."

"But it's Workmen's Comp.," Stanton teased.

"Don't make no difference," Hutcheson said, smiling widely. "Them boys in the Grady E.R. can find somebody else to learn on. Not me. I've been around here too long for that."

3 In Catholic college circles Georgetown University was considered reasonably conservative. It was founded in 1789 and boasted of being just about as old as the federal government. In fact, it wasn't always easy to determine which of them exercised the greater influence over the lives of the people in Washington, D.C. Some say that during the Kennedy administration there were so many Catholic college graduates in Washington Georgetown became the seat of the invisible and intellectual government while the White House was surrendered to the tourists. That is probably an exaggeration; however, the influence of the Georgetown School of Foreign Service on the State Department over the years should not be underestimated, and the constant flow of attorneys from G.U. Law into the agencies cannot be ignored. In Washington, D.C., there are at least two powerful forces at work and they are not always pitted against each other. One of these forces is certainly Georgetown University. The other may be the federal government.

Father Terrence P. O'Connell had accepted an emeritus position in the history department to avoid being put out to pasture at the Tertian Retreat house in Warnersville, Pennsylvania. He was neither senile nor embarrassing, although his seventy-four years made everyone, including his boss, the Jesuit Provincial, wonder how long he would last. His field had been international law, but there was no emeritus position available either at the School of Foreign Service or downtown at the Law School. Consequently, Father O'Connell had searched old Healy Hall on the main campus until he discovered a cubbyhole large enough to hold his modest collection of books, and promptly moved in.

Father O'Connell had promised his lifelong friend, Father Higgins, head of the history department, that he would stay out of the way and not attempt to teach history,

learn history, or even comment on history. Father O'Connell
was content to have been history.

His emeritus position gave him time for his other interests. It was claimed that he could read fluently in nine
languages, and that he could speak at least four. Some of
the reading languages were ancient, of course, but nonetheless his linguistic abilities were legendary. For this
reason younger members of the Jesuit community simply
assumed that Father O'Connell spent his time reviewing
Coptic verbs or translating obscure Greek works. The Reverend Terrence O'Connell, S.J., did nothing to refute these
myths.

Father O'Connell had waged a quiet but effective cam-
paign by mail on behalf of John F. Kennedy. He had written to thousands of influential Catholic professional men
around the country, and had urged them to openly throw
their support to the young senator from Boston. O'Connell's
years in international law had brought him into contact
with representatives of many foreign governments, and
he was not too shy to call in these chips as well when it
seemed appropriate to do so.

Later, political analysts were able to assess O'Connell's
quiet efforts on Kennedy's behalf, and to rank it favorably
with some of the larger campaigns. Some quipped that
Father O'Connell would be named an ambassador-at-
large, if not the President's man in the Vatican after the
election was over. That appointment, of course, did not
occur. Instead Father O'Connell either fell or was pushed
into bad company. Not that he was easily scandalized or,
for that matter, adversely influenced. His strength of character and loyalty remained beyond question. That was
probably why President Kennedy had secretly appointed
him his personal link to certain clandestine activities of
the CIA around the world.

O'Connell's appointment was so carefully drawn that
his name never appeared in any of the official registers.
Kennedy never paraded the crafty Jesuit in front of the
American people for fear that the lunatic fringe would
become even more hostile to his administration than they
already were. As a result John F. Kennedy had arranged
with the Jesuit Provincial in Baltimore to maintain Father
O'Connell at light duties at Georgetown, but available for
instant consultation. Colonels, generals, and admirals had

inherent conflicts of interest, some of the civilian advisers warned the President. One reminded him that you do not ask an Air Force general *if* a place should be bombed, but only *how*. In O'Connell, Kennedy felt a confidence that the ranking men in uniform could not match. As an expert in international law and foreign affairs, Terrence O'Connell could serve as an adviser where others failed, and as a priest he could function as a confidant at a level other advisers could not approach.

Father O'Connell served as a go-between and contact with several of the Cuban Catholic hierarchy exiled in Miami. Kennedy relied on the priest's estimate of the response that an invasion by expatriates could expect from anit-Castro forces in their homeland. O'Connell insisted that the response would be far weaker than the CIA professionals predicted. He based this assessment on his judgment that many of the exiles, while shouting loudly and waving fists in Miami, did not represent the rural poor. Castro might have been a gangster, but when compared to Batista he would seem a saint to these poor farmers, Communist or not. O'Connell had advised John Kennedy not to expect a popular uprising in response to a return of a small band of disgruntled men who had been expelled from Havana.

Only two men knew how much Father O'Connell's advice influenced the President, and one of them was assassinated in Dallas. The other one became an emeritus professor of history at Georgetown University.

Father O'Connell sat at his cluttered desk and wondered what he might have seen through the window of his office if he had not built a bookcase in front of it. He sighed, and continued to stare at his telephone. The loss of the view was a small sacrifice, he mused. And after all, one had to have books.

There were three telephones in the office, and the one that now occupied his mind was usually kept in the desk, where not even the wires could be seen until the drawer was unlocked and opened. He tapped his pencil impatiently. Then, as if prodded by the stick, it rang. He picked it up before it could ring again.

"This is the watchman," Father O'Connell said. He hated codes and all this cloak-and-dagger stuff that the Company insisted on.

"This is a visitor," a male voice said.

"Did you find the dance card?" O'Connell asked. He moved to the edge of his chair and began to make an endless coil of telephone wire around his bony fingers.

"That's negative, sir."

"Negative?" O'Connell said loudly. "How can you say negative? It's got to be there."

"We made a thorough search. It was not in the room."

"What about the carrier?" O'Connell asked. "Maybe it was on him somewhere?"

There was another pause, which Father O'Connell did not miss. "We checked the carrier quite thoroughly, sir."

"And?"

"Also negative."

It was O'Connell's turn to pause. There was something wrong here, bullshit code or not. Father O'Connell was used to listening to the hesitant and furtive confessions of college boys expressing their guilt about French-kissing and masturbation and a rare, off-campus piece of ass. At least he was used to that in the fifties. Lately they didn't come into the booth anymore, or if they did, it was to confess feelings of social injustice and lack of charity.

"Did anything go wrong?" Father O'Connell probed. "I mean, nobody got hurt or anything, did they?"

The telltale pause returned and stayed a little too long. "There was an accident," the man said at last.

The priest threw his eyes heavenward, uncoiled his fingers from the telephone wire, and made a rapid sign of the cross.

"What do you mean, 'accident'?" he asked.

"You want me to . . . tell you . . . over . . . the phone?"

"Well, not every detail, but you can end the suspense and tell me something. What went wrong? You know as well as I do this phone is probably clean. This code stuff is a lot of—"

"Okay," the man interrupted. He did not care to get another of Terrence O'Connell's lectures on the system. It was something that you believed in or you didn't. He did. O'Connell didn't. At least not anymore.

"Well, it goes something like this." The man paused to shrug at his partner standing next to him, half in and half out of the phone booth. "We made it to the carrier's room.

The directions were very accurate, by the way."

"Yeah, yeah, go on."

"And we found the carrier at home, just as planned. We made a reasonable offer to the carrier but the carrier did not cooperate by surrendering the dance card."

"Did he say he had it?" O'Connell prodded.

"Negative. He gave us a complete denial. He even told us he didn't know anything about anything. All lies. It was plain."

"So what then? You hit him or something?" The Jesuit offered the most innocuous difficulty he could hope for.

"We made the grab. And there was a struggle," the man minimized. "The carrier regained his liberty, temporarily, and..."

"Well, come on."

There was another pause.

"A struggle occurred," the man said, "the results of which were not totally satisfactory."

"You got away clean?"

"Not exactly. That's a yes and a no, if you know what I mean." The man was reluctant to explain the details to Father O'Connell. Neither of the men was happy working with the aged priest. Both of them thought he was senile, but orders were orders.

Everyone wished that the Bay of Pigs affair was over, and according to some, after so many years it was. But Terrence O'Connell, S.J., was an unusually patient and thorough man. For him a project was over when *all* of the details were taken care of, and in this case there were things left undone. Father O'Connell was personally willing to do so, but he knew he was seventy-four. He vowed that if the Lord gave him a few more years, he would use them to complete his assignment.

O'Connell assumed a hushed voice that forbade the unspeakable. "You didn't...you didn't shoot him or anything like that. There were strict orders not to cause him any bodily harm. That was made very, very clear to both of you before you went down there. Wasn't it?" He was lecturing college boys again.

"Yes, Father," the man said, responding to the tone and his mental image of the aged and angry priest.

"Then what in God's name happened?"

"He came out of the hotel room like a bull. He hit me in the face and jumped Clyde before we could get a hold of him. He was a lot stronger than we thought."

"So, what then? Couldn't you subdue him?"

"No. What happened was we tried to grab him but he fell over the railing."

"And escaped?" O'Connell asked.

"The railing was on the twenty-sixth floor, Father."

The mental scene puzzled the Jesuit for a moment.

"He fell straight into the lobby," Hardy said. He paused to let the Jesuit consider that.

"God have mercy on his soul," Father O'Connell said softly.

"We followed him to the morgue," the agent said. "There were too many cops to check him again in the hotel lobby, but we got some good pictures of the investigation."

"Quietly, I hope." Father O'Connell had visions of the whole affair showing up in *The Washington Post*. Georgetown University would love that, he mused, and so would the Provincial.

"Oh, yeah. We shot the pictures from way up above them. They didn't see us at all."

"But all you got was garbage, right?" Father O'Connell asked.

"Oh, probably. Except for one guy."

"One guy? Who?"

"Well, you know, the hotel was crawling with pathologists."

"Yeah. Their convention. That's why Commander Toll was supposed to be there." The priest instantly regretted the use of the carrier's name over the phone even though the Company checked it every week for him.

"Well, one of them walks out of the crowd and identifies the body laying there in the lobby."

"No kidding?" O'Connell tossed that one around in his mind for a moment or two. "Did he look like a pathologist?"

"Yeah. A real duck. We got his name and stuff from the hotel people."

"You said you went to the morgue."

"Yeah," the man continued. "We wanted to check him out again. We knew the dance card wasn't in the room."

"And?" the priest asked suspiciously.

"We got the jump on the ambulance drivers and some

clown in the morgue and cut Toll's clothes up. He was clean."

"Swell," O'Connell said sarcastically. "And now the morgue personnel know that there was a search and that you two guys were after something."

"We didn't have any choice," he explained. "We weren't sure if they took the dance card off the carrier and put it somewhere, or if it was still on him. It was a calculated risk."

"You didn't find it," O'Connell offered.

"Right. But nobody in the morgue got hurt. I guess we might as well head back home."

"Back?" O'Connell yelled. "What do you mean, back?"

"We haven't got the dance card, so there's nothing to stay around here for," the man explained. "Besides, it's liable to get a little sticky when they find those morgue guys."

"Look, you two," the priest said slowly and carefully, "I don't want you on this assignment any more than you want to be on it. But let me tell you something. That dance card is still somewhere down there. There is no question about your coming back right now. Do you understand?"

"What do you want me to do?" Hardy asked.

"Hang around. Bird-dog it. You probably won't get a chance to comb the room again, but you can wait and see what *they* turn up."

"We did the room very thoroughly," the agent said. "The dance card is not there."

"Okay, so he swallowed it," the Jesuit offered lightly. "But wherever it is, we have to find it. If that information falls into the wrong hands, it'll be on page one of every newspaper in the country."

"What else do you want us to do?" Hardy asked.

"Wait for the autopsy. Maybe you can recontact the man in the morgue and ask him what they found. At least we'll know the cause of death—for our records. And let's check out that other pathologist."

"Okay, watchman. I'll stay on it. But don't get your hopes up."

"I wish you had my confidence," the Jesuit said sweetly. "I'm going to come to Atlanta myself. I don't like the way it's moving."

"But..."

The priest hung up without another word. He slid the drawer in, locked it, and held his chin in his hand.

In Atlanta the agent stepped out of the phone booth and looked at his partner. He shook his head slowly and helplessly. "I don't know about that priest," he said.

"Why did you tell him that Dr. Toll fell?" Clyde asked.

"What did you expect me to tell that crazy bastard? That he slipped when we held him over the railing?"

"But that's what happened, Hardy."

"Yeah, but he would have blown his stack and got us transferred to Chile. You know how he is."

"Somebody ought to tell him what the dance card is really worth," Clyde said. "Come on. Let's get out of here before anybody asks us who we are."

The two agents walked out of the main entrance room of Georgia State University and onto Decatur Street. They were only a few blocks from the medical examiner's office and downtown Atlanta began to feel very small.

4 Most Navy doctors are more physician than sailor. That was never true of Commander George I. Toll. Dr. Toll was Navy ROTC in college and Navy scholarship in medical school. He interned and took his pathology residency at the U.S. naval hospital at Jacksonville, Florida. In his off quarters and summers George beefed up his qualifications by taking short courses in diving, underwater demolition, celestial navigation, and other sea scout adventures that did not impress many of his medical associates. One of them cynically observed that all George needed was an anchor tattooed on his arm. In fact, one weekend in San Diego he tried to get one, but the tattoo parlor was closed. By the time it reopened, he had sobered up.

The briefing for his temporary duty at the naval hospital in Key West started at Bethesda in January of 1961. George Toll had made commander by then, and found himself among a rather select group of career Navy medics and hospital service personnel who had been quietly collected from all over the world for a hush-hush assignment. They were housed separately on the grounds at Bethesda, and each of them was given a closed-door interview with the old man himself. Each of them was told that there was an element of risk involved in the project and that only volunteers would be exposed to possible combat situations. They had the chance to back out quietly, and a couple of the older doctors did. They saw no reason to get involved in something crazy so close to retirement. But something crazy was just what Commander George Toll wanted.

Scuttlebutt had it that the project had to do with some mysterious fleet rendezvous in the Mediterranean, and that there was going to be an invasion of the Middle East. The more cynical and better informed among them announced that whatever it was, it was going to happen in Southeast Asia. As proof they offered the theory that French Indochina was a powder keg with Communist and non-Communist forces shooting at each other every other day.

When the group was finally selected and the pep talks about secrecy and national security had been delivered, they settled down to serious briefing. Several hundred brave Cuban soldiers had volunteered for training in Guatemala, Panama, Louisiana, Florida, and as close as Fort Meade, just outside Washington, D.C. The operation had begun before the election of President Kennedy and ran smoothly under the eye of the CIA, although plans for an actual invasion of Cuba had been delayed until Kennedy was securely in office. Incredibly, Eisenhower had not told Kennedy about the plans for Cuba until they drove to the swearing-in ceremony, top hats and all. Kennedy, however, was probably no more surprised by all this than George Toll, who'd always thought that Cuba was just a handy place to keep Havana. He had no real conception of what had happened in Cuba or who Castro was, and at the time couldn't have cared less. Any adventure would beat looking down a microscope in a Navy hospital.

Trinidad, a city of twenty thousand inhabitants and located on the south coast of Cuba, was originally selected as the invasion site. While it was not exactly a coastal town, it had an airfield that could be used to land the anti-Castro air force loaded with supplies and equipment that would be needed after the city was taken. In addition Trinidad was protected by a ring of mountains into which the invaders could escape if anything went wrong. The CIA and the Joint Chiefs of Staff were very happy with it, but Kennedy, persuaded by his own advisers, changed the target to Girón; and Girón would have to be approached through a swamp after a landing on the beach and Bahía Cochinos. The world would quickly learn that Bahía Cochinos translated into the Bay of Pigs.

George Toll took the whole plan seriously because it was Navy, but others began to lose confidence when several news leaks hit the papers. After January 10, 1961, when *The New York Times* described the anti-Castro force that the U.S. had been training in Guatemala, Navy doctors more sophisticated than Commander Toll pointed out that the CIA was involved and that strictly naval traditions might not be followed. Toll eventually found it easier to dislike and distrust these CIA men who offered discourteous advice to senior naval officers.

It was a bright tropical morning in Key West when Commander Toll arrived to relieve Lieutenant Commander Ed Adams as pathologist. The beaches and the clear blue waters surrounding the little island gleamed in the Florida sun. From Front Street the whole world seemed to be at peace. Dr. Adams had anticipated some sort of an explanation about his sudden reassignment, but he was disappointed. Commander Toll arrived in sharply pressed whites, greeted him with a salute and formal handshake, and gave the astonished Iowan his orders. Later Ed Adams said that he had felt like he had been invaded and captured and that he was being sent to Boston as a POW.

During the Bethesda briefings Toll had been led to believe that he would see action. He had assumed that he would be put in charge of an emergency laboratory or blood bank on board a carrier or at least a destroyer. He found out the carrier *Essex* was involved, and the helicopter landing ship *Boxer* was in the area with a thousand battle-ready Marines on board. Destroyer escorts and submarines were assigned to guard duty, but the actual "invasion fleet" consisted of five liberty ship-freighters and two old infantry-type landing crafts. The U.S. Navy was assigned to an observer's role, despite the eagerness of many of the ranking officers present to participate actively.

One hour after Adams's departure Toll was authorized to open his own orders. He was ready to throw his clean white cap on the deck, scrambled egg and all, and stomp on it when he learned he had been appointed chief of the morgue service.

"Morgue supervisor!" he had said aloud behind Ed Adams's desk. "What the hell is this whole Mickey Mouse operation about?" he asked the empty room. He was ready to pick up the phone and call Medical Operations at Bethesda to ask to be relieved when he came to the last paragraph in his sealed orders:

No communications are authorized or permitted regarding these orders. Further details forthcoming verbally via properly identified personnel. Said personnel not Navy.

George Toll reread the paragraph and swore quietly to himself.

The next morning the lab secretary came into the inner office to announce that a man named James R. Fahey had arrived. She explained that the man refused to state his business and that he seemed quite insistent. Dr. Toll had a good idea what the man represented even if he didn't know who he was. Fahey was shown into the pathologist's office without delay.

James R. Fahey was almost typecast for his part and Commander Toll had a difficult time repressing a smile when they met. Fahey was six feet, two hundred pounds, white, athletic and in his late thirties. He wore a black straw business hat, a dark blue Palm Beach suit, and lightly tinted glasses that made his eyes hard to follow. His lips hardly parted when he spoke and his back teeth remained clenched at all times.

George Toll stood up when the tall civilian entered the room and extended his hand. "I'm Commander George I. Toll."

"James R. Fahey," the man said. They exchanged a brief handshake and when his hand was free again, the man reached into the inside pocket of his jacket. For an instant Dr. Toll thought that the man might produce a gun from a shoulder holster. These were crazy times and Toll regretted the flash of paranoia.

"I am an agent with the Central Intelligence Agency," Fahey said, holding his identification folder closer to the pathologist.

"I thought you guys always claimed to be librarians or agriculture inspectors," Toll said, laughing a little to relieve the tension that had quickly built up in the room.

"There's no need to be covert in this situation, Dr. Toll—or do you prefer Commander Toll?" The agent took the chair to the right of the pathologist's desk and took off his hat.

Toll shrugged slightly. "Take your pick. The Navy says Commander. The other doctors say doctor more often than not. But what about you? Do I call you agent or something like that?"

"Jim will do just fine."

"Okay, and I'm George, if you like."

"Thanks, but my father was a physician and even my

mother referred to him as 'the doctor.' So, if you don't mind, I'll find it easier to call you Dr. Toll." He smiled slightly and gave an impression that at one time he might have been human.

"Was?" Toll asked.

"He died when I was in high school. Heart attack. Worked all the time. But maybe it was the best thing for me. Up till that time I thought I wanted to be a doctor. But when he dropped dead in the garage one night, getting ready to go out and see some ungrateful bum in the rain, I decided it wasn't worth it."

"Gee, that's tragic," George Toll said. "That happens to too many hardworking doctors." It did not happen to very many pathologists.

"I went to law school instead," Agent Fahey said.

"And then into the CIA?"

The mention of the CIA snagged James Fahey back to reality. What little warmth he had shown was suddenly withdrawn. "I'd like to explain to you why I am here, Dr. Toll."

"And explain to me why I am here," the pathologist added.

The agent looked at the doctor with moderate alarm. "Weren't you given the preliminary briefing at Bethesda?" he asked.

"Yeah. I got all that. All that invasion stuff. They told us about the anti-Castro air force." The pathologist made a face that said he didn't think much of a few poorly equipped B-26's, even if they were called a whole air armada.

The stare from Agent Fahey could have frozen water in a glass. He offered no reply. His silence forced Dr. Toll to continue.

"Okay. So a lot of Cubans have worked themselves up real tight for this affair. I'm sorry," George Toll said. "But what pisses me off is that I volunteered for this fiasco and all I get to do is sit behind this desk. Why didn't they leave Ed Adams on the job?"

"Who?" The agent frowned. It was his job to know all of the participants in his sector, and his designated sector was the naval hospital at Key West. He was not familiar with Ed Adams's name.

"Ed Adams. He was the Navy pathologist that I replaced. He could have counted dead bodies just as well as I can."

"Counted dead bodies?" The agent was visibly shocked.

"Hell, yeah." Commander Toll threw his order envelope on the desk. "Take a look at that set of orders," he said. "They must have been cut by my worst enemy."

"I'm familiar with your orders, Commander." The agent said *commander* as if it were a disease.

"Oh, yeah," Toll said. "I forgot. I suppose you're the one that is supposed to show up and fill in the blank spots?"

"Exactly."

"Well, okay, then. Let's have it. Tell me that I get to go on the invasion." He searched the agent's blank face for some sign of hope. There was none.

"Your assignment is here, Doctor."

George Toll continued to search the agent's implacable face. "But—I'm assigned to the morgue."

The agent nodded. "I know," he said flatly.

Commander Toll stood up and walked around his desk, his hands clasped behind him. He thought about the time he had invested in those extracurricular Navy activities and wondered why he had bothered.

"You have a very important assignment," the agent said.

"Oh, I know that," Commander Toll said. "Every time there's a war, somebody has to count the bodies and identify the dead. I know that's important. Hell, I took a short course in disaster identification at the AFIP in Washington a couple of years ago."

"Where?"

"The AFIP," Toll explained. "That's the Armed Forces Institute of Pathology."

"Like the FBI academy at Quantico?" the agent asked.

Dr. Toll squinted at the agent. There was no hope. "Yeah," he said, "they're just about the same."

"Your assignment involves more than body identification."

"It does?" There was hope in Dr. Toll's heart again.

"Yes. Considerably more."

Commander Toll stopped pacing and sat on the edge of his desk. He gestured with both hands to encourage full disclosure.

"That's all I can say about it at this time," the agent

said professionally. "I have a strict time schedule to follow
on each portion of the plan that I am authorized to disclose."

"When can you tell me?" Commander Toll asked.

The CIA agent looked at the pathologist sympathetically. He knew that this Navy doctor was not used to
working in the dark and that any decisive word would
help. He remembered that from the psychology courses the
Company included in his training. They had taught him
how to be content without a goal in sight. The agent remembered how difficult that had been. He knew it was
harder for a mere Navy commander-pathologist.

"After the fifteenth of the month," the agent said.

"The fifteenth? Is that D-Day?" Toll asked anxiously.

The CIA man put a finger to his lips. "Shhh," he said.
"You have to know some things very quietly and other
things not at all."

"Are they going to bring the wounded in here?" Toll
asked. He was becoming more excited now.

"Maybe some of them."

"And the others?"

The agent hesitated. "There are other designated areas.
Homestead Air Force Base, for instance."

"In Miami?"

"South of Miami."

"But all the dead ones will be brought here?"

"I don't think that we can plan on 'all' of anything going
any particular place, designated or not."

"But the bodies will be brought here to Key West,
right?" Toll persisted.

The CIA agent nodded. It was clear to him that the
preservation of Commander Toll's goodwill was important
to the success of the operation in his sector, and tidbits of
information would keep this Navy pathologist contented.

"By and large," the agent repeated.

"So I was right," George Toll said heavily. He stalked
to his side of the desk and slumped in the swivel chair.
"The grave patrol."

"Look," the agent said, getting up and putting on his
hat. "It's a little early in this mess to get upset. Your job
will be explained to you in a few days." He paused for a
moment as if he were thinking of something.

Commander Toll frowned. "Are you expecting a lot of casualties?"

"Not so much that," the agent said. "It will be more of a distribution problem. And we'll have to be careful of the politics."

"Politics? What politics?"

"Later, Dr. Toll," the agent said, opening the door to leave. "Everything in due time."

"Sure. Treat me like a mushroom."

"A what?"

"A mushroom," Toll said. "Y'know. Keep me in the dark and feed me horseshit."

The CIA man gave a polite smile that almost showed his teeth. They were still clenched. "Oh, by the way," he said, leaving.

"Yes?"

"Don't try to leave the hospital grounds. It might prove embarrassing for all of us."

"You mean I'm a prisoner?" Toll asked incredulously.

"Well, *prisoner* is a harsh word, don't you think, Doctor?" The agent grimaced and looked at the ceiling for another choice. "Let's just call it *restriction*."

"Son of a bitch," Commander Toll said tightly.

"Adiós," the agent said. He offered another small, sweet smile.

5 On Wednesday afternoon, April 12, 1961, John Fitzgerald Kennedy walked into the State Department auditorium for his weekly press conference. He looked good and stood tall. His back was not bothering him as much as it had during the previous few days. He paused for a moment alone with his press secretary before he faced the assembled reporters.

"Cuber, Cuber, and more Cuber," Kennedy twanged. "Eichmann went on trial yesterday in Jerusalem and the Russians have just sent some Major named Gagarin into space today, and all they want to hear about is Cuber." The President searched Salinger's face, but there was no hope. It would be Cuba.

In his reply to the first question thrown at him the President said, "The basic issue in Cuba is not one between the United States and Cuba. It is between the Cubans themselves. And I intend to see that we adhere to that principle, and as I understand it, this administration's attitude is so understood and shared by the anti-Castro exiles from Cuba in this country." He ruled out an intervention in Cuba by United States armed forces under any conditions.

Some of the newsmen bought the President's remarks on face value because, like converts to an evangelical sect, they wanted to believe. The *Jornal do Brasil* applauded the young President's statement and said it showed that the United States was beginning to understand Latin American psychology.

At Base Trax, high in the Sierra Madre in western Guatemala, incongruously facing the Pacific rather than the Caribbean, the training activities were beginning to look more professional. The original plans to train the men into a guerrilla force had been abandoned and a CIA man, known only as "Frank," had managed to mold them into an invasion unit. Through Frank they suddenly got beds, uniforms, new weapons, and adequate ammunition. A kitchen was built and, along with additional barracks, an electrical plant. The influx of this equipment and the arrival of additional American advisers made the hopes of the exile volunteers soar. They were confident of the full support of the United States even though the President and the State Department were forced to issue cover stories that denied all involvement.

Frank knew that at full strength La Brigada would number no more than nine hundred men. A few of the volunteers were professional soldiers but most were students. Others were professional men—doctors, lawyers, businessmen, fathers and sons; several Catholic priests—each of them dedicated to the liberation of his homeland from Castro and his Communists. The CIA had advised their leaders that thousands of homeland Cubans waited for their arrival to rise up in a spontaneous effort to reclaim their country. In their hearts each of the volunteers believed this was true. What they had not heard was the negative appraisal of the situation that Terrence O'Connell had offered.

In January the paratroopers had left the Sierra Madre for a new training site in the plains near San José. The new camp was so infested with snakes and ticks that the place was quickly called "Garrapatanango," or "Base of the Ticks." Even these pests could not dampen the excitement. These Cubans were *free* and they were going home! By the end of the training, the force was reassembled into one unit and the frustration of continually postponed target dates began.

Finally D-Day was announced. It was to be Monday, April 17, 1961.

Bill Peterson rolled over and put his hand on the ringing telephone. It was the morning of Saturday, April fifteenth—Olympics Day in Key West. Peterson had been looking forward to sleeping late, then watching his son run in the relays. He couldn't imagine who'd be calling so early, but sat up and put the phone to his ear and listened.

"What the hell do you mean, 'a B-twenty-six'?" Peterson yelled. "You're out of your mind. We don't keep any twenty-sixes around here. We—"

He stopped talking and listened carefully. His new tone

of voice told his wife that someone of superior rank had
come on the phone to continue the conversation.

"Yes, sir," Peterson said. "I'll be right there." He hung
up and stared at his bare feet.

"What is it, honey?" she asked. She put her hand on his
back reassuringly.

"I don't know," he said wearily. They had been to a
party at the NCO club the night before and she had let
him make love when they got home even though it was
very late. After all, the parade didn't start until ten thirty.

"You've got to go in?" she asked sympathetically.

"Uh-huh." He stretched and yawned. He shook his head
vigorously, but the fog did not immediately clear. "Some
crazy bastard just landed a B-twenty-six on our strip and
it's full of bullet holes."

"Bullet holes?" She sat up quickly, suddenly wide
awake. "Oh, Bill," she said, troubled. "Is it real bad? I
mean... are we in another..." She was unable to say the
words. She had worried through Korea with him away,
and had tried to be a good Navy wife.

"No, honey," he said, holding her in his arms. "It's nothing to worry about. The lieutenant says that the plane is
Cuban."

"Cuban like Miami or Cuban like Cuban?" She was
well aware of the constant flow of anti-Castro articles in
the south Florida newspapers, and worried that Havana
was only ninety miles away.

"No, Cuban Cuban," he said. "But the lieutenant says
it's hush-hush." He pushed her away gently and smoothed
the hair from her forehead.

"What have you got to do?" She looked worried. He was
beginning to dress without his usual morning shower. To
her that meant he was in a hurry.

"They want me to check it over, fix it, and get it the
hell out of here as soon as I can." He rummaged through
the second drawer for clean socks.

"In the laundry basket in the closet," she prompted.
"But if the pilot was being shot at, he may not want to
leave right away."

"Honey. I just fix planes. I work for the U.S. Navy,
remember? I'm not one of those CIA characters and my
name is not Julio Perez." He raised his hands helplessly.
His wife interpreted the gesture to mean that he

couldn't find clean socks and threw back the sheets to get up.

"Relax. Relax," he said, nudging her back into bed with his hip. "You look better in bed." He held up the socks triumphantly.

"Who's Julio Perez?" she asked, readjusting to the warmth of the bed.

"Nobody. What I meant was, I'm not some crazy Cuban exile who's just itching to go back and get killed. I'm from Bangor, Maine, remember?"

"Uh-huh." She smiled devilishly. "Remember the Maine." She pulled the covers over her head as he pounced on her and began to tickle. After a few moments of play he closed the bedroom door and locked it. He had enough seniority to be a little late.

At the airport the Immigration and Naturalization officials had hustled the two "defectors" to a quiet room, but not until the reporters had had a good look at them. Interviews were promised but indefinitely postponed as rumors of a Cuban war flashed along the news wires. Within an hour telephones were off the hook in Miami, Washington, and New York, probing, explaining, dodging, and denying. If it had been staged to be confusing, it was a temporary success.

In Miami, almost simultaneously, another B-26, also showing bullet holes and also bearing Cuban insignia, had landed. The pilot wore a baseball cap, dark glasses, and a T-shirt. He had only time enough to light a cigarette and show himself to the reporters before the "immigration officials" swept him away to parts unknown.

One of the reporters noticed that a machine gun on the Miami B-26 was taped shut. He may have thought this was peculiar for a plane that had just survived a bombing run over Havana. But of course he didn't know how annoying the dust had been in Nicaragua. It would take him a few days to add that much up.

For the moment the "Cuban pilots" were defectors from Castro's air force. That was the story the reporters were told by tight-lipped American civilians in business suits. And if they didn't like that story, they could write their own. Several of them did, eventually.

At the naval hospital Commander George Toll took the news at breakfast with a shrug. What the hell, he reasoned, there were no dead bodies on the B-26, so why should he care? The officers' mess served respectable steak and eggs.

Later that day in Washington, D.C., there was fur in the air. Saturday plans all over suburban Virginia and Maryland were suddenly canceled. Whatever it was that was bugging the boss was enough to cause pale green Fords to speed along the Potomac toward CIA headquarters. The dogwoods had started to blossom and the drive along the George Washington Parkway was otherwise pleasant. Spring in Washington can be lovely.

Allen Dulles waited in stony silence as a small cadre of alert and worried men took seats in the small conference room adjoining his office. Two were still absent when he began to speak. Several more were away on urgent assignments in New York, Miami, Key West, and points south.

"I presume, gentlemen," the director began with painfully precise diction, "that you are aware of the B-twenty-six incidents." He adjusted his pipestem, curing some minute difficulty, and then searched their faces, one by one.

The nearest agent broke the awkward silence. "We were all briefed on the plans, sir," he said rather weakly in spite of himself.

"And you were given to understand that these 'exiles' were to pass as defectors from Castro's air force?" Dulles prodded.

There was a grunt of assent from the group.

"Then why in the ever lovin' hell," Dulles said, leaning forward and lowering his voice to a rasp, "didn't somebody have brains enough to brief our beloved ambassador to the United Nations, Adlai Stevenson?" He waited a moment for a reply that did not come and then turned around, throwing his hands in the air.

"Mr. Schlesinger went to New York last week, sir," a senior agent said.

"Swell," Dulles said, turning quickly to face the perplexed man. "And you may know by now, *if* you read newspapers or watch television, that Adlai Stevenson has just put his lifelong reputation for impeccable honesty on the line by demonstrating to Castro's ambassador, Raúl Roa, that these planes came straight from Havana..." He paused to give each man a moment to appreciate Stevenson's delicate position before adding, "...like an imported cigar."

"How did he do?" an agent asked from the end of the table.

"How did he do?" Dulles shouted. "Stevenson did just fine. Just fine. After all, he wasn't lying when he told Roa that the planes weren't ours. The poor son of a bitch was simply led down the primrose path. Hell, he probably believes the planes are Castro's even now!"

"How's the press taking it?" an agent asked.

"We may have fooled *The Tampa Tribune,* but I don't think anyone else really bought it," Dulles said. "Roa is running up points by the minute in New York. Stevenson will have it all handed to him in a neat little package. Our esteemed ambassador to the U.N. will be pissed off at us, gentlemen, and I want you to think of some way to smooth his feathers."

"Maybe he'll get the hint from Roa's accusations and back off a little," an agent suggested.

"Hell, man," Dulles said, "he's already quoted the President's promise that we won't be involved in Cuba, and he's called for the planes to be impounded!"

"Impounded?" the agent asked. "You mean the B-twenty-sixes?"

"Hell, yes, the B-twenty-sixes," Dulles said. "But what's worse, Salinger's been forced to deny all knowledge of the bombing of the air bases on Cuba. How long do you think that story will fly?"

"Until Monday morning, I hope," a senior agent said softly. He opened his hands in front of him and looked at them carefully. They were empty.

The Liberty ships waited for the Brigade at Puerto Cabezas, Nicaragua. The troops had been transferred from the Guatemalan camp by air, using Retalhuleu as the jumping-off place. The ships were old and rusting. They carried only 50-caliber machine guns for deck defense, and Brigade officers worried that even these meager weapons had not been properly positioned. Other officers pointed out that the U.S. air cover would make the machine guns superfluous anyway.

Spirits remained inexplicably high as the men set about refurbishing the aged transport ships and loading their supplies on board. The winches and the hoists strained and shrieked with the load and the rust, but, item by item, the equipment for the invasion was lifted aboard and stowed below. The leaders of the Brigade were so confident of a successful landing that no one gave any thought that most of the supplies needed on the beach were loaded onto the *Barbara J.* Later, when both the *Rio Escondido* and her rusting sister ship, the *Houston,* were burning helplessly in the water off the Bay of Pigs, a better plan of distribution would be discussed.

The landing craft were fourteen-foot, open boats with outboard motors and no protection at all. But the troops knew that with the U.S. Air Force and the U.S. Navy behind them, fourteen-foot open boats would do just fine.

The U.S. Navy stood well offshore, out of sight. The commander-in-chief, Atlantic (CINCLANT), had received carefully worded instructions to stay invisible. At least six destroyers and the carrier *Essex* were authorized to convoy the invasion force and to stand by, offering an air evacuation route if everything failed. Not one of the men who would be landing in Cuba had any idea that the big guns on the American destroyers and the planes on the *Essex* would play no part in the invasion.

6 On Key West it was business as usual. It was Sunday. The shrimp boats chugged through the harbor to disgorge their catches from the night before, and tourists stopped in the street to photograph Hemingway's old house on Whitehead Street. The house was set back about a hundred feet from the gate, in a corner lot that supported palms, palmettos, and banyans. Hemingway had built the first swimming pool in Key West and could often work comfortably next to it. He had correctly prophesied that the completion of the overseas highway from Miami would allow every tourist who could drive a car to invade Key West and destroy its isolation. By 1961 they had driven him elsewhere and everywhere, in search of life, in search of himself.

By the time the Cuban exiles would reach the Bay of Pigs, Hemingway would be preoccupied with other things, including shock treatments at the Mayo Clinic. The end of April would see the Brigade's efforts end in failure, and in July Hemingway would join many of the invaders, but not in his beloved Cuba. In Ketchum, Idaho, he would blow his head off with a double-barreled shotgun.

Commander Toll looked out of the hospital laboratory window and surveyed the activity in the courtyard. A small group of Cuban volunteers had been assembled at Boca Chica Naval Air Station, housed temporarily in a small barracks near the hospital. Toll was impressed by their determination if not by their youth. Ironically, none of them would leave Key West until the invasion was over.

Toll turned from the window and walked into his office. A corpsman had brought him the Sunday *New York Times* from the hotel newsstand. The pathologist opened it on his desk. The headline read:

CASTRO FOES BOMB 3 AIR BASES;
2 OF RAIDERS FLEE TO FLORIDA;
CUBA IS MOBILIZING, BLAMES U.S.

Below the headline there was a picture of the B-26 that had landed in Miami the day before. The pilot of the plane was shown below the picture as he prepared to talk with immigration officials. His name was not given. The lead article by R. Hart Phillips was datelined Havana, April 15. It described raids on three Cuban military air bases by B-26's of the type Batista had purchased from the United States.

Fidel Castro was quoted as saying that the planes in the raids had been supplied by the United States government and that they were not defectors from his own meager air force.

The plane in the *Times* photograph was numbered 933, and on the tail, the authorities in Miami proclaimed, was the Cuban star and the initials *F.A.R.* for Fuerza Aerea Revolucionaria. The president of the exiled Cuban Revolutionary Council in New York said markings clearly identified the planes as defectors from Castro's air force, but Dr. Raúl Roa, the clever Cuban ambassador to the U.N., observed that anyone could paint an airplane.

There was a knock on Dr. T_ll's door.

"Come in," he shouted.

The door opened and James R. Fahey entered. He carried a folded, bulky newspaper under his arm.

"Oh, I see you already have the paper," the CIA agent said. He looked generally pleased with himself and the world.

"Mm," Commander Toll said. He gestured toward the soft chair in the corner. "I guess it's started, huh?"

"I only know what I read in the papers," Agent Fahey said, smiling. He sat down and opened his copy of the *Times* in his lap.

"Those B-twenty-sixes sound about as phony as three-dollar bills," the pathologist said. "I don't know how you guys can expect anyone to believe that these pilots were defectors from Castro's air force when you don't put them on television and let them tell their stories."

"That's because you've been briefed on the operation and you know there's something coming off. If you were a housewife in Peoria, you'd buy it."

"If I were a housewife in Peoria, you could tell me the planes were part of the military escort for the Russian cosmonaut!" Commander Toll said. He folded his hands

behind his head, sat back in his swivel chair, and wondered
about Gagarin and his trip around the world.

"We only need the story for a couple of days," the agent
said. "It's a diversion."

"I don't know about you guys," Commander Toll said,
smiling. "You fly a B-twenty-six in here half shot up, and
then you hide it where nobody can see it."

He walked the doctor through the door of his office and
down the corridor of the small hospital to the exit. They
crossed the courtyard, ignoring the young Cubans who
were doing exercises, and headed for a Quonset hut. It had
been painted gray, like everything Navy, and it bore a
serial number on the door. There was no guard on duty.
The agent took a single key from his pants pocket and
unlocked a padlock on the door.

It was dark inside the Quonset hut until the agent
threw the switch. Several overhead lights flooded the
room. The hut was empty.

"The skating rink?" Commander Toll asked.

"No, Dr. Toll. This is to be your workshop." Agent Fahey
threw his arms to the right and left to demonstrate the
expansiveness of the facility.

"To do what?" Toll asked cautiously.

"To receive bodies, if any, from a certain clandestine
military action and to assist one or more agencies of the
United States government in disposing of these bodies
with a minimum of embarrassment and exposure."

Commander Toll looked at the CIA man and then gazed
around the room. "To do what?" he asked absently. His
heart felt heavier. He was to be the morgue supervisor
after all.

"Can you keep a secret?" Toll asked in theatrical whisper. "I really don't know anything about pathology." He
paused to gauge the reaction from the CIA man. There
was none. "So why don't you ask Allen Dulles to transfer
me to the hospital ship in the invasion force?" Commander
Toll asked.

Agent Fahey's eyes became very narrow. He liked jokes
only when he was able to control them. "What hospital
ship?" he asked.

"Oh, they always have a hospital ship. Y'know, a big
white ship with a red cross painted on the side? And then
the guy in the submarine sees it through his periscope and

gives his exec a look?" He made a small circle with his thumb and index finger and squinted through the hole at Fahey.

"There is no hospital ship," the agent said flatly. He continued to stare at the pathologist.

"No?" Toll asked. "Well then, how 'bout getting me transferred to the carrier? There is a carrier, isn't there?"

The CIA man became deadly serious. "The U.S. Navy will not be participating in the invasion. At least not directly."

Commander Toll sensed the grim tone immediately. He had touched a nerve. "Then how do the exiles get to Cuba? Swim?"

"They will be provided with suitable transportation," Fahey said. "But we have received clear instructions to maintain a low visibility. You may have read the statements of our ambassador to the United Nations?"

"Mr. Stevenson will think of something," Commander Toll said. "He's a clever guy."

"Clever, but not dishonest."

Commander Toll gave a shrug and said nothing.

"Mr. Stevenson, like so many other public officials, suffers from a handicap: his work requires the truth," Fahey said.

"But you guys can go underground and deny everything," Toll said. "Stevenson has got to sit up there in New York and listen to those Russians mouth off about everything that happens all over the free world."

"That's true. And it's unfortunate." The agent paused in his absentminded reading of the pathology titles that lined the shelves and turned to face the doctor. "I would not have designed the system to work this way." There was a chill in his voice that reminded the Navy pathologist of a Marine colonel with cirrhosis he had once examined at Bethesda. The colonel had lost almost all of his men at Tarawa. He had been a captain then and had fought his way onto the beach alone.

Commander Toll decided it was time to change the subject. The agent was beginning to twitch.

"How about my briefing?" the pathologist asked, smiling.

"That's why I came over here this morning, Doctor. I

called the BOQ and they said you had already reported to the hospital lab."

"Well, Cuba or no Cuba, this is still a Navy hospital, and I'm the TAD pathologist."

"Very admirable, Dr. Toll, but I want you to remain free from routine hospital duties so that you will be available for our...special project."

"Which is?"

"Come with me, Commander Toll," the agent said, extending his hand to touch the pathologist's elbow. "I'll show you around. Dr. Toll, you were handpicked for this highly sensitive assignment and—"

"Highly sensitive, my foot!" Toll snapped. "You're going to bring in a bunch of battle dead, and I get to identify them. Isn't that about it?"

"That is, uh, partly correct, Dr. Toll." Agent Fahey nodded his head slowly. He knew that a gentle approach would keep this pathologist on the team while a more direct attack might lose him.

"Shit, the Navy has got body-ID teams already, Mr. Fahey. They don't need me to do this. Hell, they've been tagging bodies for years."

"Sure they have, Dr. Toll. And they've been doing a marvelous job of it too." His tone was sweet enough to put Commander Toll on guard.

"Okay. Drop the other shoe," Toll said.

The CIA agent sighed. Lowering his voice, he became almost intimate. "The President of the United States," he said gravely, "has issued certain guidelines that will govern many of our actions, Commander Toll."

"Thank God for Jack Kennedy," Toll sighed.

"This operation was not begun under Mr. Kennedy," Fahey said softly.

"Oh?"

"It was planned under Mr. Eisenhower and had other features characteristic of that period. But with the election the Company was forced to bide its time until the plans could be reviewed by the new group at the White House— if you know what I mean?" Fahey raised his eyebrows encouragingly.

"I heard about the election, Mr. Fahey," Commander Toll said sarcastically.

"We would have been a little more 'prepared' for this operation had Mr. Nixon won."

"You weren't too sure of Mr. Kennedy, huh?"

"The change of parties generated a certain atmosphere of uncertainty within our organization."

"But you're sure of Mr. Kennedy now?" Dr. Toll asked.

"I am personally. But I don't think that the advisers he has collected around him see eye to eye with everything we want to do in the Western Hemisphere. Hell, some of these new guys in Washington think we owe the whole damned world a living, and if you let them run it, they'd give it all away faster than you and I could keep it secure." He paused to savor his own remarks.

"I know what you mean," Toll said. "You spoke of 'receiving bodies'?"

"Some of the men will be killed. We have to expect losses in every operation."

"Uh-huh."

"And we have made provisions for the recovery of selected bodies and their transportation by air to Boca Chica and then to this hut."

"Why 'selected bodies'?" Toll asked.

Agent Fahey looked at the commander for a moment, measuring the doctor's ability to receive classified information. Fahey did not believe in the public's right to know or, for that matter, the First Amendment, when the subject approached national security. But he did accept the training principle that said professional men worked more competently when they knew the objective.

"It has been decided that the Cuban dead will be interred in Cuba," Fahey said. "That is, after all, their homeland. They will be given hero's graves and the places will serve as shrines to the Cuban people. They're very religious, you know." He lowered his voice again although there was no one else in the Quonset hut. "Mostly Catholics, we think."

"I see." Commander Toll was trying hard to recall what he'd once learned about psychiatry.

"Okay," he said. "So, if you bury the Cubans in Cuba, who's left?"

Agent Fahey resumed his eyebrows. He looked at his shoes and took three deliberate paces away from the pathologist before wheeling around to face him again.

"Commander Toll. You are a bright young man. You are no doubt reasonably well read in current events. You do, after all, read *The New York Times*."

"Sundays."

"Yes, well, we are in a sensitive position here. This operation has received extensive support from the prior administration and—"

"Eisenhower?"

"Among others. And abrupt changes in plans or tactics cannot now be allowed to jeopardize everything. We are sympathetic with Mr. Kennedy's position, and we are under direct orders to support the President at every stage of the operation. However..."

"However?" Commander Toll said encouragingly.

"There are certain facets of this program that are irreversible. You understand?"

"Not really, I—"

"I'll put it to you straight, Commander Toll. President Kennedy has issued orders to the Agency strictly forbidding the direct use of U.S. military personnel in this invasion."

He marched back to the Navy doctor and stood close. There was a faint odor of coffee on his breath.

"But there's Navy activity all over this base," Toll protested in a hushed tone.

"Of course. And there will continue to be. We have a whole task force standing by off Nicaragua right now, ready to escort the invasion force to the south coast of Cuba."

"That's not involvement?" Toll asked.

"That's not *direct* involvement, Commander. The presidential prohibition was carefully worded to permit the operation to go forward, but reserving a position of denial for the White House. That way we can say to the Russians and the Communist Cubans, we were not directly involved." The agent paused for a contented smile.

"And the bodies?" Toll prompted.

"The bodies, Commander, will unfortunately be our own military personnel."

"But you said—"

"I said there were certain facets of this operation as *originally* conceived and developed that would not permit complete changes. As a consequence there are several key members of the primary invasion team who cannot be replaced with Cuban exiles at this late date."

"So U.S. military will be directly involved in the assault after all," Toll said.

"In a word, Commander Toll, yes. It is unavoidable at this time. There is no way to train a sufficient number of Cuban pilots, demolition experts, frogmen, communications men, and others to replace the Americans who are, at this moment, deeply committed to the success of the operation."

Commander Toll looked puzzled. He was not sure how far he should push this Mr. Fahey. He had already been made a virtual house prisoner by non-Navy personnel, and the secrecy surrounding the B-26 at Boca Chica told him that the CIA boys were in charge. Even Rear Admiral Plowman, the Commander of the naval air station, had refused his calls when he tried to check out the assignment.

"The President is going to allow that?" Commander Toll asked at last.

"The President will be carefully advised," Agent Fahey said with a smirk. "He may not be *fully* advised, but he will be carefully advised."

"I see."

"And, of course, each of the American military personnel who takes part will be stripped of all identifying insignia, papers, and dog tags. They will be issued uniforms similar to the members of Brigade two-five-oh-six, and if captured they will testify that they deserted the United States Armed Forces and volunteered to join the Cubans."

"What's the Brigade two-five-oh-six?" Toll asked.

"That is the name chosen by the Cuban exile force for its invasion group. The name comes from the serial number of one of their men who was killed in a training exercise in the mountains of Guatemala."

Commander Toll gave a low whistle. "You mean there are that many of them?"

"Probably not, Commander Toll. They started the serial numbers at twenty-five hundred, so we really don't know how many they finally recruited. Even I don't know the strength of the force." He frowned with that admission.

"How will you find these Americans if any of them are killed?" Commander Toll asked.

"We have issued each of them a small brass plate, like the ones the coal miners carry when they go underground. But there is nothing on the plate but a number. The plate cannot be connected to any American force if it falls into Communist hands."

"But how will you know them on the scene? I mean, will you have to go through the pockets of all the dead men to pick out the ones with brass plates?"

"It is safe to presume, Commander Toll, that the other members of the invading force will know who is who. There are special members of each battalion who will be responsible for the identification of the battle dead. Our job is simply to provide a place for them to go with any American casualties. Wounded will be brought to this hospital, where a special area has been cleared. A handpicked group of doctors from Bethesda will treat them as required. Other casualties will be flown by helicopter to the carrier *Essex*, where preliminary or minor treatments will be given." He paused to savor the precision of the plan in his mind. "All the dead will be brought here, to you."

"Uh-huh," Commander Toll grunted. "And what am I expected to do, resurrect them?" He attempted a smile but it froze halfway when the agent continued to stare at him inflexibly.

"Commander Toll," he began, "I thought I made it clear to you that the official position of the White House and the State Department in this matter is that there are *no* Americans directly involved."

"You guys want me to change them into Cubans?"

"Your job," Fahey said, "will be to examine the bodies, confirm the identification of each man—we will provide you with full dental records and fingerprints—catalogue their fatal injuries for the records—sealed records, I might add—and prepare them for interstate transportation to their home bases."

"When some guy who is supposed to be assigned to a Navy demolition crew in Rhode Island turns up full of Cuban bullets, isn't his mama going to wonder what happened?"

"He will not be full of Cuban bullets," Fahey announced flatly. "You will see to that. I am sure that as a board-certified pathologist you are well qualified to discover and document other types of pathology and other causes of death suitable for the adult North American male?"

Dr. Toll squinted at him and tried to piece it all together. "Phony autopsies and phony death certificates," he breathed.

"Ahhhh. So quick of you to hit on a plan like that!" the CIA man said facetiously. "I couldn't have explained it better. Except..."

"For?"

"One minor detail." Fahey held up a bony finger in front of his face. "The autopsy report you send with the body and the death certificate you complete will be, as you put it, 'phony,' but you will also maintain a factual and accurate record as well."

"Who gets that?" Toll asked.

"I do," Fahey said, holding out his hand. "I will get every copy, every note, every specimen, and all recordings connected with each body you examine. Understood?"

"Understood. And the wounds or injuries?"

"Our military embalmers will take care of those details, Commander Toll. Where there are obvious wounds or injuries, such as the loss of a limb or whatever, you will simply invent a traumatic incident that matches the anatomy. Of course, these traumatic events will be 'accidental' and in no way connected with a hostile military operation."

"Of course," Toll repeated.

"We will provide you with a set of death certificates for each state so that they can be promptly filed when the man is returned to his home base, wherever it may be. You will sign them all, using your right name, identifying yourself as a Commander, U.S. Navy Medical Corps, but leaving the place of the examination blank. It will be typed in later."

"What if I am asked about all this later?" Toll said. "What will be my cover story?"

"There is no cover story, Commander," Agent Fahey said. "What you are going to do here will simply never have existed at all. You and the other members of this special medical team will be reassigned throughout the Navy, and your records will reflect temporary but very normal tours of duty at Boca Chica. Since all of you are career Navy men, we have the highest degree of confidence in your abilities to remain silent."

8 By Tuesday morning there was no longer
any need to keep Dulles under wraps, and
the President summoned him and the operations chief to his office. The CIA chief
and Dick Bissell arrived in the same car
and went into the White House by the side
door. It was exactly 6:00 A.M.

The President was already pacing the Oval Office. He
paused at one of the windows, his hands clasped behind
him, as the two men entered, shut the door quietly, and
emitted a simultaneous, "Good morning, Mr. President."

The young President turned carefully.

"Let's have it. How bad is it?" He stared at Allen Dulles
first.

The director looked at Kennedy for a moment and flexed
his jaw. The muscles of his face became prominent. Bissell
caught the mood of his boss and froze. He knew that in a
confrontation he could not survive. Sacrificially, he jumped
in with both feet.

"The landed troops have sent back very favorable reports," he said, a little too rapidly. "They have established
a beachhead and have knocked out several Russian-made
tanks."

Dulles and Kennedy continued to look at each other,
eye to eye. Dulles had served two previous presidents as
head of the OSS in World War II, and as the architect of
the CIA. An early-morning meeting with John Fitzgerald
Kennedy was not awesome to him. Yet he knew that a
personal attack, while probably justified for many reasons,
would not benefit his beloved Agency. He pulled his battered pipe out of his jacket pocket.

"May I?" Dulles asked.

"Yes, sure, smoke it, Allen," the President said. "Be
comfortable. Sit down, sit down."

Allen Dulles had already loaded his pipe in the car. He
now paused to light it.

"They lost two of the transport ships," the case officer said, still trying to break the tension.

"We know all that," an impatient voice sounding much like the President snapped from the corner of the room behind the two visitors. Dulles and the CO wheeled around to see who spoke and recognized the President's brother, Robert.

"Good morning, Mr. Attorney General," the CO said.

"Mr. Kennedy?" Dulles said, greeting Bobby with a superfluous question.

"One of your men gave us almost hourly phone calls all night long," the President said. He sat behind his desk and spread his hands in front of him. Dulles thought that he looked unusually tired.

"They needed those planes," Allen Dulles said between puffs. Everyone watched as he managed to light the pipe, using two wooden matches burning together.

"Look—" Bobby Kennedy said, charging over to the side of the desk and turning to face the CIA men. "Don't start a lot of crap about those planes. First you fly two B-twenty-sixes into Florida and expect to fool the whole press corps with some cock-and-bull story about Castro defectors, and then nobody briefs Adlai Stevenson. If anybody got our asses into that crack, it was you."

"We were informed," Dulles said testily, "that Mr. Stevenson had been thoroughly briefed on the operation by State. Evidently that information was incorrect. Or else..."

"Mr. Stevenson is being quite honest, I think," John Kennedy said. "Somebody screwed up. Nobody told him about the air support or the use of the Navy. And now that these things are coming to the surface, he'll have his ass handed to him by Roa and the Russians." The President sat back in his chair and looked at the ceiling.

"I think we're still clean as far as the Navy goes, Mr. President," the operations chief said. He glanced quickly at the director to see if he had spoken too soon. This wasn't a league in which he felt comfortable. Allen Dulles did not return his glance.

"Good," Bobby said. "We're all grateful for small favors."

"They went in before dawn?" the President asked.

"For the first time in United States military history," Dulles said stiffly. He was correct, of course, and all of them knew it. There had never before been a night invasion with American forces involved. The Joint Chiefs of Staff had accepted the plan only after it was made clear to them that the President would never approve a daylight assault on Cuba with U.S. Navy ships visible for photographs. By attacking at night, the admirals could pay lip service to Kennedy's orders to stand fifty miles offshore, and offer escort duty much closer to the beach, using the darkness to sail out of sight before dawn.

"Without air support," Dulles said softly, "we have a better than average chance of getting our asses shot off down there. Castro's air force was not destroyed on the ground by our first attacks, although we caught him completely off guard. We got maybe forty to fifty percent of them."

The attorney general nodded, and threw a glance at his brother.

"The rest of his planes chewed up the landing forces," Dulles said with the slightest smirk. "They sunk the *Rio Escondido* and the *Houston* right offshore."

"The men got off," the CO said.

"But they got strafed on the beach," Dulles added dryly. "Castro's B-twenty-sixes and T-thirty-threes owned the sky."

Robert Kennedy squinted and thought for a moment. "Does Rusk know all of this?"

"By phone. An hour ago," Dulles said.

"But those are not new planes," Bobby asked, his tone indicating the answer. "Those are the same ones we sold Batista."

"Right," Dulles said. "The tanks are Russian. The planes were ours." He puffed on his pipe and the bowl made a slurping sound.

"What about the tank crews?" Bobby asked suspiciously.

"Mostly Cuban, we hear," Dulles said. "But you know as well as I do that the Cubans can't run new tanks by themselves. If we knock enough of them out, I'll bet we turn up a Russian or two."

"The Russians would deny them, of course," the CO added.

"I don't know," Robert Kennedy said softly. "They're in the same bind as we are." He glanced toward his brother as he continued. "You guys come up with a couple of Russian prisoners, and they might just jump right in," Robert Kennedy said. "Wouldn't they almost have to, Allen?"

"I suspect they would," Dulles replied. "But I don't think there is much danger of any Russians being taken prisoner."

"How about Russian bodies?" Robert Kennedy asked.

"We will include the bodies of any foreign nationals that we consider 'embarrassing,' in our Key West plan," Dulles said.

The attorney general looked at each of the CIA men before speaking. "I thought that plan was only a contingency to be used in the event of an unavoidable American casualty."

"*That* event has occurred," Dulles said flatly. He poked at the upper crust of ashes with his finger. The fingernail came back soiled with additional gray soot that no longer looked out of place.

"I suppose that couldn't be helped," Robert Kennedy sighed. "I only wish we could have honored the President's wishes and kept all of our men out of this."

"Some of the unit leaders were indispensable," the CO said. "If we had had more time, we might have been able to train enough exiles to—"

"We've been over that ground before," the President said. "I thank you both for coming and am confident that you are both aware of my position in this matter." He extended his hand to the CIA men, shaking Dulles's a little more firmly and for a longer time.

"One last thing, Mr. President," Dulles said, still holding the President's hand. "I would be remiss in my duty as CIA director if I did not tell you that the men now on the beaches in Cuba will not survive without air support."

John Kennedy continued to stare at Allen Dulles, and took back his hand. "I appreciate your candor, Mr. Director," the President said. "I will take that under advisement."

Robert Kennedy glared angrily at Dulles for his remark, but the director could afford to ignore the little brother.

"Today, Mr. President, is a new day," Dulles said, getting in one more shot.

"Thank you, Mr. Director," Kennedy said. "Stay in touch."

The invitation to leave the Oval Office was unmistakable. The CIA men shook Robert Kennedy's hand without enthusiasm as he walked them to the door. The President remained, standing alone behind his desk. He was quite aware that it was a new day, and he knew he too would have to face it.

Outside the office door Allen paused for one last futile attempt to light his pipe.

9 The invasion ground to a halt. A few nearby towns and crossroads had been taken, but casualties were heavy. From offshore CIA advisers continually promised support even though the rebel leaders knew it was too late. The final promise was to evacuate the men from the beaches but the leader of the invasion refused, smashing his radio in defiant contempt. They would, he vowed, prefer to die on their native soil.

In Washington, at CIA headquarters, concern was approaching panic levels. One last attempt had to be made to change the President's mind. Planes were standing by on the *Essex*, ready to be launched at dawn. Without control of the sky even an evacuation would be a bloodbath.

The President had to make an appearance at a White House social affair that evening. For an hour and a half he danced around the ballroom to the music of the Marine Band and mingled cheerfully with the distinguished guests. He was Jack Kennedy at his best. Just before midnight he and several others excused themselves and returned to his office, where a top-priority meeting of the CIA and the Joint Chiefs was already in progress.

The principals included the operations chief, Secretaries Rusk and McNamara, General Lemnitzer, Admiral Burke, McGeorge Bundy, Vice-President Lyndon Johnson, Arthur Schlesinger, and Walt Rostow. Many of the civilian advisers arrived in white tie and tails, giving the meeting a ridiculous tone.

The CIA deputy director for the Cuban operations made a last-ditch argument for air support. He told the President how desperate the situation had become and how low the Brigade was on ammunition and supplies. The almost hopeless situation was corroborated by the military advisers, and there was no difficulty in convincing the general and the admiral of the importance of air and sea support. The civilian advisers, however, remained unalterably opposed to further involvement. A few wanted to offer ships to evacuate the beachhead, but none of them would agree to the aggressive use of U.S. military forces.

John Kennedy knew he was doomed to criticism whichever way he went. He glanced at the clock. It was after one o'clock on Wednesday morning. If any effective action were to be taken, it would have to be authorized immediately. A B-26 would take hours to make the run from Nicaragua.

"I'll go along with the idea this far," he announced. "I'll allow six jets to fly over the Bay of Pigs area for one hour at dawn."

The admiral glanced at his watch as the CIA men nodded approvingly.

"These jets can fly support for the B-twenty-sixes coming in from Nicaragua, but—" The President paused, his finger poised in midair. "*But,* gentlemen, let me make this perfectly clear. These Navy jets are *not* to seek out air combat or ground targets."

"And if they are fired upon, Mr. President?" someone asked.

The President paused and pursed his lips. "They may defend themselves and the B-twenty-sixes from air attack. But nothing further."

"That means the Castro planes will have to let the B-twenty-sixes fly through or risk taking on our jets in a dogfight," a civilian adviser said, losing himself in the crowd.

"That's exactly what it means," John Kennedy said. "But it may give the men on the ground enough time."

"To do what, Mr. President?" the CO asked.

"To evacuate," Kennedy said. "They have got to understand that this is a single effort. There will be no continuing air support after this mission."

"I'll see that the instructions are flashed to the *Essex* immediately," the admiral said.

"And I'll notify the exile air force at Puerto Cabezas," the operations chief added.

"Gentlemen," the President said wearily, "it's almost two A.M. Thank you for coming."

10

Nine of the original B-26's had already been shot down or were unable to fly, and their exile pilots not in much better shape, when news came through of the support flights ordered for dawn. The remaining pilots were less than enthusiastic. So far their flights had been nearly suicidal. The B-26's were unprotected against Castro's odd assortment of fighters; and with missions around the clock the exile air force was decimated by fatigue. An argument over the promised jet support erupted as soon as the dawn raid was announced. Some of the Cuban exile pilots, already feeling betrayed by the lack of fighter support, refused to fly. Immediately four American advisers, technically civilian pilots under contract to the CIA, volunteered to fly the missions. They were assured that a presidential order had been issued authorizing Navy jet support from the *Essex*. They were to rendezvous off the Bay of Pigs, and then proceed inland to bomb designated targets.

The four American fliers, two in each B-26, looked confident as they took off for the three-and-one-half-hour flight to the Bay of Pigs. With U.S. Navy jets defending them, they had high hopes for the mission. They knew that Castro's poorly trained fighter pilots would be no match for the Navy combat teams. It promised to be a glorious day over Girón.

The two lead B-26's approached Girón as dawn broke. So far they had been unopposed. A few miles behind them exile volunteers piloted two more B-26's. One of them developed engine trouble and was forced to return to Nicaragua, but the other one flew on alone.

Suddenly Castro jets appeared and began to attack. The American pilots radioed the coded distress signal to the Navy jets.

"Mad Dog Four. Mad Dog Four. May Day. May Day,"

the pilots shouted. The exile pilot, several minutes away and still out at sea, could hear them plainly.

There was no response from the Navy jets. They were still on the flight deck of the *Essex*. Somehow the time difference between Cuba and Nicaragua had not been considered. The B-26's were over their targets a full hour before the Navy jets were even launched.

The Castro jets had another field day. One B-26 began to burn, and crash-landed at a Castro-held airstrip on a sugar plantation. The other B-26 crashed into the sea, killing everyone on board.

The lead exile B-26 pilot continued on to his target. The Castro jets were apparently preoccupied with the other two bombers. He located the Castro artillery concentration in front of San Blas, and came in low for two heroic passes. On the first run he strafed with machine guns, and on the second he scored a direct hit with two napalm bombs. The psychological effect on the Castro troops and artillery was devastating, but his plane was badly damaged by intense ground fire. One engine went out, and later he would count thirty-seven bullet holes in his fuselage. Despite this damage he flew the B-26 at wave-top level, all the way back to Puerto Cabezas, and landed safely. His were the last shots fired by the Brigade air force.

The Navy jets remained on the carrier *Essex*. Without the promised air support the supply ships canceled the unloading. The ground forces were now doomed.

At six o'clock a C-46 flew into a liberated airfield near Girón and unloaded several hundred pounds of rockets, ammunition, communications equipment, and messages. Before leaving Nicaragua, the pilot had been told that his mission was particularly important—he was to receive wounded men and selected others. On board, a civilian adviser explained the mission further.

The CIA man in charge of the airfield sensed increasing panic among the men standing guard. When the C-46 landed, they formed an armed ring to isolate the transport plane from everyone—Castro forces and exiles alike. It had been assumed that a rush by desperate exiles, eager to be evacuated, might occur, and the agent in charge had given orders to shoot any unauthorized man that tried to get near the plane.

A Jeep roared onto the field as the last of the explosives and equipment were being unloaded, and a swarthy, middle-aged man got out. The driver stayed behind the wheel. The man wore camouflaged fatigues, the sleeves cut off above the elbows. He was unshaved and his eyes were red. He walked toward the transport plane's open door, but was stopped by a tall man with a carbine.

"What do you want?" the man asked, threatening the visitor with his weapon. The visitor was unarmed.

"I am Dr. Carlos Pardo. I am a medical officer. Who are you?"

"I am David," the man said. There was no hint of a Cuban accent in his speech.

The "first name only" was instantly familiar to Dr. Pardo. He knew no additional explanation, rank, or identification would be given.

"Is this plane available for the evacuation of my wounded?" the doctor asked. He tried to look beyond the American with the carbine, but David blocked his view of the loading hatch.

"No, Doctor, it isn't," David said.

"But I have several very badly wounded men in Girón," Pardo pleaded. "They will die if they do not get to a hospital."

"I am sorry, Doctor. This plane is taken."

"Taken?" Pardo asked. "Taken by who? Taken for what?" As he spoke, an Army truck drove up and stopped nearby. Two men resembling David got out of the cab and established guard positions. Dr. Pardo stared at them silently. The back of the truck opened and several men jumped out. They paused and then assisted several other men, all in camouflage uniforms, out of the truck. Pardo could see that these men were wounded. Some had slings, one had a bandage around his head, and one was on a stretcher.

No one spoke as the group headed for the C-46. The wounded men were helped into the plane before the other men returned to the back of the truck. They worked as a well-trained team, forming a guard unit going and coming from the truck to the plane.

"Who are these men?" Pardo asked, astonished.

"They are men," David said flatly.

Dr. Pardo glared at the CIA officer. "I told you I had

many wounded men in Girón. They need to be on this plane!"

"This plane is not avilable, Doctor," David said inflexibly.

Confused and not believing, Dr. Pardo turned and saw the armed team move several black zippered body bags out of the truck and into the belly of the plane.

"But these men..." Pardo began, becoming angry. "They are loading dead bodies into the plane!"

"Doctor, I will have to ask you to leave now," David said.

"No!" Dr. Pardo said. "I am not going to leave here until I talk to the Brigade officer in charge of this plane. You are not a Brigade officer. You are one of *them*." He pointed at the other men loading the bodies on the plane.

"Doctor," David said through his teeth, "get back in your Jeep and return to your duties. There is nothing I can do for you."

Dr. Pardo attempted to force his way past the CIA man. David brought his carbine across the doctor's chest and hit him on the shoulder. The doctor's arm went numb with pain. The CIA man reversed his weapon and put the muzzle under the physician's chin.

"Listen to me, Dr. Pardo," David said, using a hushed tone that forced the exile medic to listen carefully. "I will not hesitate to blow your fucking head off and shoot your driver right where he sits. Do you understand?"

"But my wounded are—"

"Get into that Jeep and get your ass out of here," David said. "Now!" He pushed the muzzle of his weapon against the doctor's neck brutally.

Dr. Pardo stumbled backward, grabbed for his injured shoulder, and ran to his Jeep. "I'll see about all this," he shouted. "I will go to Brigade headquarters and tell them what you are doing here." There were tears in the doctor's eyes from the pain in his shoulder and from his rage as he ordered his bewildered driver to go.

David watched as the Jeep sped away. He turned and silently caught the eye of the officer in charge of the loading. "Have we got them all?" he asked.

"As far as I know," the man responded.

"Okay," David said, heading for the plane. "Signal the others and let's get the hell out of here."

The other officer spoke a few words into a hand-held radio unit and watched as a dozen or so men sprinted from the main building of the airfield. The engines of the C-46 began to whine, then sputter, and then roar as the pilot readied the plane for takeoff. The men running for the plane had a general resemblance to each other. They were all a little older, well built, white, grim-faced, and silent. Had they spoken, there would have been no Spanish accents.

They scrambled aboard and closed the door of the bulky transport plane. The pilot revved the engines and turned immediately onto the runway. The gentle wind was favorable to him and there was no tower to clear. The sky was his to claim.

The plane roared down the runway and leaped into the air at the first instant the proper speed was reached. It headed for the nearby trees, clearing them by only a few feet. The pilot banked sharply when the beach came into view and skimmed along the water. So far there were no Castro jets in sight, and no hostile ground fire was received. Men below them waved and others continued to work with the dwindling stacks of supplies scattered along the beach. Near them a small pennant marked a spot where the bodies of the frogmen had been stacked. The spot was bloody, but the dead frogmen were gone.

A few miles offshore the C-46 pulled up and headed for the clouds. There was still no one in pursuit. The pilot flew a southwesterly course for about fifteen minutes before turning in a slow, wide circle for the northeast.

11

On Key West Agent Fahey alerted Commander Toll and brought him to an isolated hangar at the end of a runway at Boca Chica. The C-46 had made the ninety miles without incident or detection by Castro forces. On approach the plane had been guided in without delay, acknowledging in blind code. The plane was then directed to the open hangar, where a squad of Marines stood guard.

Fahey flashed his ID wallet at the first Marine and drove the gray Navy sedan into the hangar. The CIA squad on board had already begun to unload the body bags. The wounded men were put in ambulances and driven away toward the hospital. The naval hospital at Key West had been built originally as a Marine hospital in 1844. By 1942, after several more buildings had been erected, the hospital had expanded to 290 beds. In 1961 few of the beds were in use, and many wings were totally empty—an ideal spot for the quiet treatment of the CIA men returning from a battle in which they had never officially served.

Commander Toll looked at the activity inside the hangar and was amazed. The men in the camouflage fatigues worked with silent efficiency. The nonwounded men gathered in a tight group at the far end of the building and talked quietly with a man in civilian clothes. The man with a clipboard seemed to be debriefing them.

Fahey and Dr. Toll approached the collection of body bags. "These are your patients," Fahey said. "There may be a few more later, but that's it for now."

The CIA man called David waited to be recognized. Agent Fahey knew he was there, but ignored him for several moments. The pathologist did not know it, but he was standing between an agent from the Clandestine Services and an agent from Operational Services. They were aware of each other, however, and that was sufficient. Finally

Fahey turned toward the operations division "animal" and spoke to him.

"Yes?" Fahey said haughtily.

"David," the operations man said, identifying himself. He came to attention, but did not salute. "I have certain items for you if you are in charge of this phase." He pointed at the body bags with a thrust of his head.

"I'm Fahey. I'm in charge of this phase." Agent Fahey continued to stare at the hard man in fatigues. He didn't understand the animals and he really didn't care to. His job was cerebral and clean—Clandestine Services gathered information for use in the best interests of the United States with little or no discovery of the activity. The operational agents, on the other hand, were given specific targets and objectives with little explanation of why it was to be done. Their job was to blow a particular powerhouse, sabotage a selected chemical plant, eliminate a certain foreign military officer, and always to deny all association with the Agency if caught.

David held a small cloth bag suitable for a half a pound of tobacco or a bottle of Crown Royal. It was purple and closed by a tightly drawn yellow cord. He offered it to Fahey.

Fahey looked at the bag before accepting it. For an instant he thought it was someone's head, and that the operations agent was playing a crude joke on him.

"What is this?" Fahey asked.

"Brass plates," David said without emotion. He gave Commander Toll a quick glance and returned his attention to Agent Fahey.

"This is Commander George Toll," Fahey offered.

"It's a pleasure, sir," David said, shaking the pathologist's hand. He displayed instant military courtesy and protocol without a salute. "I am called David."

"I'm happy to meet you, Mr....er...David," Commander Toll said awkwardly. He had never before been introduced to a man in military fatigues who had only a first name and no visible rank or organization.

"Some of them still have their ID plates on them," David explained to Agent Fahey. "These were taken off a couple of the frogmen by the burial team before we got to them. I guess they didn't understand what they were supposed to do."

"Do you?" Fahey asked.

"Me, sir?" David asked. "Oh, yes, sir. I think I do." He gave a quick smile and then got rid of it when Fahey maintained his deadpan expression.

"Are you on loan from the military or...?"

"I'm regular Agency, sir," David said proudly. "Of course, on this assignment I haven't got my full ID..." He paused, wondering if Agent Fahey was seriously challenging him.

"No, David, that's all right," Fahey said. He knew better than to provoke an animal.

"I can give you a number to call in Washington, if you want," David persisted.

"That's okay, David," Fahey said, smoothing it over. "Here, let's get the doctor started." He took Commander Toll by the arm and turned him toward the bodies on the floor.

"Is this all of them?" Commander Toll said, counting the bags on the floor. "Where are the medical records?"

"The medical records?" David asked.

"He means the dental charts and the identification packets, David," Fahey said. "I'll have them brought to your morgue. I had them all flown in from Washington."

"But how did you know who was going to be killed?" David asked simply.

Agent Fahey looked at David with feigned contempt. "I had the ID folders for *all* the agents involved flown in. Not just the dead ones."

"I guess we've all got one of those ID folders on file somewhere, huh?" David asked.

"Most of us, anyway, David," Fahey said. "I'm sure there's one for you."

"Charts of my teeth? The whole works?" David asked, fascinated.

"Maybe even more," Fahey said. "Ever break a bone? Had your appendix out? Got any scars or distinctive moles? All that information is filed in your identification file. Makes life easier for guys like Dr. Toll, here." He placed his hand on the pathologist's shoulder and gave it a small squeeze.

"You guys think of everything," Toll said flatly. "You keep physical files on each other so that some pathologist can identify you after you're dead, and then you deny you know one another anyway."

"*We* acknowledge each other, Commander Toll," Fahey said. "It's the Agency and the government that is sometimes forced to deny us. Right, David?"

"Right." He looked at Agent Fahey with a stony expression. He was never sure what these guys from the clandestine section were up to. A remark like that reminded him to be careful.

Dr. Toll looked at the line of body bags. Each bag was about seven feet long and was closed by a double zipper that started at either end and met in the middle. The zipper tabs were now wired together with a breakable seal, like a boxcar. The bags were rubberized plastic, but one of them oozed blood anyway.

"This operation will be a little different than your usual autopsies, Commander Toll," Fahey said. Agent David looked at the two men with obvious surprise at the remark. He suddenly realized that it might not be his business and looked away toward the group of men still talking with the civilian.

"If you don't need me anymore, Mr. Fahey," David said, nodding toward the debriefing group.

"Huh? Oh, yeah, David. Thanks a lot," Fahey said. "I'll take it from here." He waited a minute until David walked away and then continued with Dr. Toll. "I know a little bit about how you pathologists like to work."

"Oh?"

"I was—how would I put it?—briefed in Washington."

"Uh-huh." Dr. Toll was immediately suspicious. These CIA civilians had claimed control over the Navy and now one was crowding the practice of pathology. What next? Toll asked himself.

"I am told that you like to spend several hours on each body, making detailed studies and completing exhaustive reports," Fahey said calmly. "But, you see, we do not have that luxury today." He gestured toward the body bags.

"We have a lot of cases to do, as far as I can see," Toll said.

"Yes. Of course. But your job here is a little different than you are used to."

Toll continued to smell a rat, but did not want to push

the agent too fast. "So what do I do? Start on them here in the hangar?"

Agent Fahey gave a little laugh. "Oh, heavens no, Dr. Toll. Nothing that crude. We will transport all of them to your morgue hut. You will find every instrument you need there."

"But it was almost empty when we looked at it before," Toll said.

"I have had it stocked. But everything will be returned to me for shipment back to Washington."

"I understand. Is that the only 'difference'?" Toll asked suspiciously.

Agent Fahey paused. "Not exactly. The problem is one of time, Dr. Toll. You will have to start on these cases as soon as possible and complete them without delay. They must be ready for transportation by tomorrow morning. Sooner if possible."

"Nonstop?" Commander Toll asked. "All these autopsies, back to back, with no break?"

"Back to back if you wish, Commander Toll," Fahey said. "But it was suggested to me that you could do them simultaneously, if you wanted to?"

"Alone?"

"The Agency has supplied a few volunteers to assist you. However, you must understand they are not used to this kind of work and may not be as efficient as you would like them to be. They have received a minimum of instruction on autopsy technique," Fahey said smugly. "Not enough that they will be able to make correct diagnoses or make meaningful mental notes."

"They've been cross trained?" Commander Toll asked.

"You know about that technique?" Fahey seemed surprised.

"Sure. It's a good way of keeping something quiet when you need help from other guys. You train him backwards and give him phony information. Then when he assists somebody who knows what to do, the helper comes away with the wrong conclusions. That's the way they use electricians at some of the top-secret atomic-energy installations. Those guys know how to do their own little job perfectly, but they have got a totally screwed-up idea of what the whole plant does. Right?"

Agent Fahey glanced left and right quickly. Dr. Toll

was beginning to recognize that quirk as a sign of Fahey's anxiety. "Not exactly, Dr. Toll," Fahey said. "But you understand that you are not to explain anything to these assistants or to correct any observations they may make in the course of your autopsies."

"I understand. I'll keep them as dumb as you guys have made them," Toll said. "Just as long as they help when I need it."

"They will respond to your every wish," Fahey promised.

"And you? What will you be doing all this time?"

"I will coordinate the records," Fahey said. "I have also received selected training for this project. I'll be there to assist you in the identification and your dental comparisons."

"Are you a dentist?" Commander Toll asked.

Agent Fahey flashed his eyes from left to right. "No. But I think I will be able to help you. I'll also keep notes as you go along. Weigh organs. Measure things. You know what I mean."

"Sounds to me like you took the short course in disaster identification at the AFIP," Toll said.

The mention of the abbreviation for the Armed Forces Institute of Pathology, located at Walter Reed Army Hospital in Washington, D.C., caused Agent Fahey's eyes to roll. The AFIP was the consulting agency for all of the pathologists in the Armed Forces, regardless of branch. It had an impeccable reputation for diagnostic consultation and offered "short courses" to military and civilian pathologists throughout the year.

"Our relationship will be more cordial, Dr. Toll, if you will stop asking me questions that I have no intention of answering." There was nothing friendly about the agent at that moment.

From time to time associates had accused Dr. Toll of being imprudent, but never stupid. He knew when it was time to back off and play the game straight. Fahey's tone made it clear that this was probably one of those times.

"I guess I'll head over to the morgue hut now," Toll said. "There are probably things I'll want to set up."

"David will drive you," Fahey said. It was more of a command than an offer. He turned and shouted to David.

The man in the camouflage fatigues responded immediately.

"Yes, sir, Mr. Fahey?" David said.

"Drive Dr. Toll to the morgue hut and let him in." He handed David the keys to the hut. "Use the Navy car. And after you let the commander off at the hut, I want you to come right back here. Do you understand?"

"Yes, sir," David said, the football player receiving instructions from the coach.

"I have some details to attend to here, but I'll want to join Commander Toll shortly." He turned to the pathologist, satisfied with the arrangements. "There is one other thing that I would ask of you."

"Yes."

"After David drops you off at the morgue hut, please don't try to leave that building or communicate with anyone. The phone has been connected to a special switchboard for the next few days, and we have posted a few men in the area. For security, you understand."

"Oh, yes," Toll said flatly. "I understand."

Agent Fahey knew that Dr. Toll did not really understand, and that lessened his anxiety.

Fahey looked at David and Toll with a half smile that told them they should be leaving. "I'll see you at the hut, Dr. Toll," he said.

"Right," Toll replied. He turned to leave with David. "Don't forget to bring the bodies."

"Trust me, Commander," Fahey purred.

Dr. Toll glanced over his shoulder at Agent Fahey and said to himself, "I wish I could."

12

The morgue hut had been fitted with five portable operating-room tables and lights. Most of the equipment was better suited for battle surgery but was adequate for autopsies. As he entered the hut and looked around, Dr. Toll assumed Agent Fahey had developed a connection with an Army field hospital somewhere. In fact, the equipment had been requisitioned for a "field exercise" in North Carolina and was, on paper at least, being used at that moment somewhere west of Fayetteville. Fahey and his friends had a winning way with official government forms.

The tables had been assembled along one wall of the hut. The overhead lights were on and the room was as bright as any brain surgeon could demand. Instrument tables had been set up at one end of each table, and two attendants busied themselves with stainless-steel tools and blank body diagrams. Each of them came to attention when Commander Toll opened the door. He wore his khaki uniform with appropriate Navy insignia, while the two assistants were dressed in orderlies' whites and aprons.

"As you were," Toll said mechanically. The men smiled and continued to adjust instruments on the trays, oblivious to Navy protocol.

"We're almost ready for you, Commander," one of the attendants said, continuing to work.

"That's fine," he said, walking to the nearest table. "Looks like you've got everything shipshape." On the instrument table in front of him there were three Bard-Parker scalpels with number 21 blades. Evidently someone knew what they were doing. No surgeon would have chosen a blade as large as a 21, but that was exactly what a pathologist needed. The table also held a few rat-toothed clamps, a pair of curved scissors and a pair of straights, a long and a short pair of forceps, and a Stryker head saw.

"My name is George Toll," the doctor said, offering his hand to the assistants, one at a time.

"Yes, sir. My name is Abbott," the first assistant said.

"And I'm Costello," the second man added.

"Oh, shit, more of that stuff?" Toll said. "For a moment I thought you guys were real."

Abbott shrugged and gave a helpless look. "We all have our assignments, Commander. Costello and I have been training for this job for quite a while, and those are the names that they gave us." He paused self-consciously. "I hope you'll understand."

Abbott seemed to be in his late twenties, Costello a few years older. Both of them were white, blue-eyed males with average builds and no recognizable accents, although occasionally Costello's nasal tones made Dr. Toll think of a med school classmate he had known from Chicago. Whoever had trained the two men had done a good job. They knew how to assist without intruding.

"We have a set of whites for you over here, Commander," Abbott said, pointing to a corner of the hut where a screen, a table, and a cot had been set up. There were coffee and cups on the table, and the cot was outfitted with a blanket and pillow.

"Swell," Toll said. "How about gloves?"

"Seven and a half or eights, sir?" Costello asked quickly. He held up a pair of surgical latex gloves in each size.

"Eights," Toll said. He walked to the dressing corner and began to change. "What's the cot for, battle fatigue?" he asked, struggling into his scrubs.

"We don't know how long this activity will take, sir," Abbott said, glancing at Costello.

"Well, neither do I," Toll said. He pulled the white scrub shirt over his head. "But I guess we're stuck with it until we finish."

"Yes, sir," Abbott replied. By his tone and his demeanor, Toll had Abbott identified as a military man, probably of noncom rank, but his branch did not come through. He was not yet sure about Costello. He could be straight Agency.

A truck stopped outside, ran its engine for a moment, and then went silent. Abbott and Costello looked at the door. The object of their special training had arrived. Agent Fahey stepped inside, followed by two young men in camouflage fatigues carrying a body bag.

"Ah, there you are, Commander Toll," Fahey said, "dressed and ready for action." He turned slightly to speak to the two soldiers. "Put them down in a row along that wall," he ordered sharply. Fahey pointed to the floor opposite the tables. The two men obeyed without comment, and left the hut to get another body.

Fahey looked around the hut and winked at the assistants appreciatively. "Good work, men," he said. "Have you met Abbott and Costello?" he asked Dr. Toll.

"Abbott and Costello," Toll said sarcastically. "Why not Laurel and Hardy?"

"They're off on another assignment," Fahey said without smiling, and Dr. Toll really couldn't tell whether or not he was serious.

"I think we received our whole shipment of equipment, Mr. Fahey," Abbott said.

"Uh-huh," Fahey replied. "Including the special diagrams?"

"Right, sir," Costello said. He held a clipboard with standard AFIP autopsy diagrams attached. Some showed the front and side views of the head, while others displayed the chest, abdomen, and extremities of an average male in the so-called anatomic position.

"I was a little worried about getting them," Fahey said, directing his remarks to Commander Toll.

"Oh?"

"You probably recognise most of this stuff as Army issue," Fahey explained.

"I'm Navy," Toll said.

"Yes, of course, Commander," Fahey said facetiously. "But you can appreciate that the autopsy diagrams and some of your peculiar instruments are not supplied with the standard Army field hospital. I had to shop around to collect all of this stuff myself." He smiled, apparently pleased with his efficiency.

"Looks like you got it all together," Toll said. He turned away from Agent Fahey and watched the body detail carry in another lifeless bag. They had started at the front end of the hut and were working their way toward the back. Neither of them spoke or looked around.

Agent Fahey carried a black leather briefcase that bore no initials or markings. He walked to the coffee table in the corner and put the briefcase down. He motioned for Dr. Toll to join him and began to unpack individual files.

"The dental records?" Dr. Toll asked.

"Right. I already pulled the identification files for six of the men. These are men who were known by the time they were loaded into the C-forty-six. I'll match the others as we go along." He suddenly looked toward the two men near the bodies. "Keep them all facing the same way," he shouted. "Heads out, feet toward the wall. Got it?" There was no reply, but the men nodded.

"Do you have some special way you want the autopsies done, or...?" Dr. Toll smirked. He knew what lay in front of him and he was ready to begin. Fahey had already warned him that a few more bodies would be brought in from the destroyers or from the beach, if any were located before the Cuba operation closed down. There were twelve bodies in the line already.

"Abbott and Costello have been trained in a certain routine," Fahey droned. "If you wouldn't mind, I'd like to let them set it up their way. I'm sure you'll find it satisfactory."

"If it's good enough for the AFIP, it's good enough for me," Toll said lightly.

Agent Fahey's eyes flashed left and right. He turned toward the two assistants and shouted, "Put the first five on the tables." Abbott and Costello leaped into action. They approached the first bag, unzipped it, and threw back the upper flap. It was the body of a paratrooper. His eyes and mouth were still open and his camouflage uniform was soaked with blood. There was an oval, high-caliber entrance wound in the middle of his throat, and a massive exit on the back of his neck. Pieces of muscle and spinal cord protruded from the jagged wound near the base of his skull. Dr. Toll would have a tough time inventing a cause of death that would satisfy his next of kin, if any.

The two attendants began their routine. One held the corpse's stiffly curled fingers while the other pressed their tips against a pad of black gelatinous ink. Then, without speaking, the pad was put aside, the excess ink wiped away, and a paper strip was pressed against each finger. The paper strip was marked right and left and had a square for each finger. Costello held it in a curved metal scoop that gave each finger something smooth and firm to press

against. In a few seconds they had produced an acceptable
set of fingerprints from the paratrooper's dead hands.

Abbott hovered over the face for a moment with a Polaroid camera and adjusted his height for focus. He flashed a
single view of the face and waited for it to develop. He put
the photographic waste material into a special red plastic
bag for security, and placed the picture near the fingerprints. In the meantime Costello had indicated the neck
wounds on the first diagram after measuring them carefully. He used a metal tape measure that sang when re-
tracted to identify how far above the heel the entrance
wound was located. On another diagram he sketched the
uniform and made a list of the clothing along the left margin.

Abbott held a small green plastic bag for his partner
as Costello went through the man's pockets. He produced
a crumpled handkerchief, a cigarette lighter, a crushed
pack of Marlboros, and a small pocketknife. There was no
money and no wallet. Then, searching in an area near the
belt where tailors used to put watch pockets, Costello found
a hard metal plate. He took a Bard-Parker 21 and made
a slit in the cloth along the bottom of the plate. Costello
glanced at the plate and handed it to Agent Fahey.

"Hank," Fahey said, reading the simple inscription to
Commander Toll. He picked through the files under his
arm and found Henzler's.

"That's it?" Toll asked. "This guy goes into an invasion
with only a little brass plate saying, 'Hank'?"

"Would you prefer name, rank, and serial number?"
Fahey asked, handing the pathologist Hank's identification folder. In the upper right corner of the folder it said:

HENZLER, HENRY R.
CAUC. 37
CONTRACT—VOL.
PARENT SOURCE: ARMY
DATA: 82nd AIRBORNE
HANDLE: HANK

The printing was in computer lettering and the file was
slim. Toll opened it without waiting for further permission
and saw a standard U.S. Army dental chart and a routine
medical record. Attached to the inside cover was a head-

and-shoulders photograph of Henzler as a combat paratrooper.

"I think you'll find enough medical information in that folder to identify him, Dr. Toll," Fahey said. "If you have any doubts as we go along with these cases, let me know and I'll make arrangements to have the fingerprints processed by teletype in Washington."

"You have friends at the FBI too?" Toll asked.

"We have contacts at the FBI," Fahey said. "I'm never sure which of them are friends."

"I know the feeling," the pathologist mumbled.

Abbott and Costello stripped Hank of his uniform and shoes, wheeled him to the first table, and lowered him onto it. Henzler's wound dripped blood on the floor; Costello wiped it up with a khaki-colored towel, leaving Abbott to push Henzler into position for the autopsy.

Dr. Toll took a step closer to the table and the body, but Agent Fahey touched him lightly on the arm. "Wait," he said softly. He nodded toward the attendants.

Abbott took a position on one side of the table facing Costello on the other. Abbott picked up a scalpel and Costello took a long pair of forceps. Then, as if going through a rehearsal, they paused to glance at Agent Fahey. The go-ahead nod was given and Abbott made a sharp incision in Henzler's chest. He began at the left shoulder, came across the chest, and turned his blade sharply upward toward the right shoulder. He had quickly carved a V in Henzler's chest with one professional motion. Costello took the point of the V in his forceps and felt the small, stainless-steel rat tooth bite into the skin. He pulled the skin upward as Abbott continued his incision along the midline of the abdomen, deftly jogging to avoid the navel and ending just above the pubic hair. Then, with alternating cutting and holding, the two men quickly cut the chest to the ribs and laid aside the broad flaps of skin, muscle, and fat. The joints between the clavicle and the breastbone were skillfully severed by Costello's scalpel blade as Abbott ran the Stryker saw along the ribs. With a minimum of wasted motion the two morgue attendants had opened Henzler's chest and abdomen, exposing his internal organs.

"Somebody trained those two guys really well," Toll observed.

"I wish I could pass along the compliment to him," Fahey replied.

Costello stationed himself at the head of the table and parted Henzler's hair at the rear of his head with the handle of his scalpel. When he had formed a part, he turned the instrument around and incised the scalp from ear to ear. The skull immediately came into view. Costello cut the scalp from the bone by severing the wispy fibrous attachments. Then he pulled the scalp flaps forward over Henzler's face and backward toward the base of the skull. There was hemorrhage in the upper area from the massive gunshot wound.

With the skull exposed like part of a garden statue, Costello again picked up the Stryker saw. He made a rapid saw cut around the skull, leaving a notch at the front and back for stability. This was a tradition among professional morgue assistants, but surprising coming from Costello. Funeral directors had complained that a single saw cut around the skull without a notch left the head unstable for viewing at the wake. Without it one last kiss on the forehead was likely to shift the skull beneath the skin, a shocking sight for the next of kin.

"We're ready now, sir," Abbott announced in Dr. Toll's general direction.

The pathologist approached the table solemnly. In his training no autopsy had ever been approached lightly or with disrespect. "Thank you, gentlemen," Toll said. He began his dissection with the heart.

Abbott and Costello, in the meanwhile, knowing that there would be a brief period of time in which the pathologist would prefer to inspect the body organs and spaces by himself, had turned their attention to the second body bag. With repetitive precision they collected the face Polaroid, fingerprints, and brass plate from one of the frogmen. On his brass plate it said simply, "Bill."

Record keeping became Agent Fahey's job. He carefully collected the photographs and the fingerprints, marked each of them with the dead man's code name, and reserved them for the file. In fact, as any scrap of paper became available, Fahey either filed it or placed it in the red plastic bag. Commander Toll assumed that the contents of the red plastic bag were headed for supervised destruction. Fahey would personally see to that later.

Henry Henzler's internal organs were essentially normal for his age. The rifle bullet had destroyed his neck and his upper spinal cord, killing him quickly and allowing only a small amount of blood to be gasped into his lungs as he died. The inhaled blood gave the cut surface of the spongy lung tissue a leopard-spotted appearance as Dr. Toll made long, routine slices through these organs. There were dark pigmentations from the dusty air that Henzler had breathed over a lifetime. Agent Fahey incorrectly identified the black material as evidence of the man's cigarette smoking, but since the men had agreed neither to ask questions nor offer explanations during the autopsies, Fahey's error went uncorrected.

Dr. Toll again directed his attention to the paratrooper's neck, carefully examining the edges of the entrance wound. He continued his dissection by lifting the flap of skin at the top of the chest, and cutting beneath it.

"This was at close range," he said absently. His comment quickly brought Agent Fahey to inspect the wound.

"Why?" Fahey asked, searching for a clue.

The pathologist stared at the agent for a moment before answering.

"Powder stippling," the pathologist said. He pointed to a series of small black dots imbedded in the skin on the front of the neck.

"That means it was close, huh?" Fahey asked. Behind him Abbott and Costello had stopped their work and came to see what the pathologist had found.

"The powder behind the bullet hits the skin within eighteen inches or so from the muzzle and makes these individual powder markings," Toll lectured. "Now it's not correct to call it powder burns, although that's pretty much what it is. Some call it powder tattoo."

Fahey felt the presence of the two assistants behind him and turned. "Carry on with the other bodies, you two," he barked, and Abbott and Costello scurried away immediately. "And, Dr. Toll, please remember our agreement. No questions asked, no answers given."

"Sorry," the pathologist said, laughing.

"Please don't misunderstand, Doctor," Fahey continued. "I'm as interested as anyone could possibly be. But if we are going to control our information"—He lowered his voice to a whisper and threw his head toward one of the assistants—"we'll have to play it by the book."

"I understand," Dr. Toll said just as quietly. "I'll try to watch it."

"And let me suggest something more to you," Fahey said, still using his whisper. "If you're going to get through with these bodies before dawn, you'd better simplify your method."

"How so?"

"You're doing an excellent and thorough job, Doctor. Any university would be proud of you. But we have as many as twenty cases to clear out."

"Twenty?" Toll gave a low, half-whispered whistle.

"I anticipate a few more from the hospital," Fahey said.

"So you suggest I cut and run?" Toll asked.

"In a sense, yes. You may want to concentrate on the main areas of trauma and curtail your examination of the noninvolved organs. That's the only way I can conceive of you finishing at all."

The pathologist leaned on the dead man's shoulder for a moment and thought about Fahey's suggestion. Blood ran from his rubber gloves and made crude palm prints on Henzler's skin.

"I guess you're right," Toll said. "But what about the reports? Are we going to use recordings, or what?"

"The reports will be made in outline form as you finish each case. You let me know when you are ready, and I will help you complete them. You may make any drawings or diagrams that will help you fill out the reports, of course."

"But I'll never get to see the final reports to correct them, right?"

"That's correct. All of this material, including your notes, photographs, and whatever, will be immediately classified as top secret."

"And I'm not cleared to read it," Toll said.

"Ironically, that's correct, Dr. Toll." Fahey almost smiled. He leaned closer to Dr. Toll, but avoided touching Henzler's body. "Maybe we could start with this case?" He was speaking softly again. He showed the pathologist the report form.

"You mean now? Kind of a report-as-you-go?" Toll asked.

"If you don't mind, Commander," Fahey said. "I think we can take care of this report without any problems. I mean, I'm no pathologist, but it looks to me like we have a gunshot wound of the neck."

"Front to back, large caliber, probably at close range," Toll added. He watched as Fahey entered the diagnosis and comments on the report form.

"Anything else?"

"You mean pathologically?"

"Yeah. What else did this guy have?"

The pathologist glanced at his dissection board again. The internal organs were partly cut and lying on top of one another. Dr. Toll raced through the mild pathological conditions the organs displayed to him. He frowned for a moment and made a sudden, clean slice through Henzler's brain. It was normal, as he expected.

"Nothing, really," Toll said at last. "He was in pretty good shape."

"Want to say normal and let the clerks fill in the report with some textbook descriptions?"

"Clerks at the AFIP?" Toll asked wryly.

"Expert clerks, Dr. Toll," Fahey replied. He tapped his ballpoint against the clipboard in his hand. "Twenty cases, remember?"

"Okay," the pathologist said, surrendering. "Put down, central nervous system: normal; heart: minimal coronary artery disease—up to ten percent; lungs: aspiration of blood, mild; liver: normal; kidneys: normal; GI tract: normal. That ought to do it, if you want to skim."

"Think of it as assisted reporting," Fahey said. "Now what about the cover story for the folks back home?"

Toll looked at him blankly.

"Something for the death certificate," Fahey whispered insistently.

"What would turn you on?"

Agent Fahey looked at the pathologist impatiently. He was sure that as the work progressed, Toll would become more cooperative. The training psychologist had instructed Fahey that Toll, at least at the beginning, should not be pushed. The Commander was Navy, not Agency; a doctor, not an agent.

"Think of something that will sell," Fahey said. "Not too exotic. Let's see...he was a paratrooper, right?"

"If you say so," Toll replied.

"How about a report that says he fell out of an airplane and broke his neck?"

The pathologist shook his head. "No dice. He'd have fractures of his legs, back, and liver. Besides, what will we do with the neck wound?"

The agent thought for another moment. "How about a training accident. You know those towers where they lift a guy up on his parachute straps and then let him drop?"

"But Hank here is an expert paratrooper. What would he be doing up one of those training towers?" The pathologist began to wonder how much help he could really expect from this agent.

"Sure he's an expert," Fahey said, warming up to his new idea. "He's up the tower training someone else and he falls off, landing on a stake or something like that. The stakes goes right through his neck. How's that sound?"

"Sounds fishy to me," the pathologist said. "Wouldn't there be witnesses?"

The agent frowned. "Yeah, maybe you're right. Got a better idea?"

The pathologist studied the corpse for a few minutes. "Okay. It's a freak accident. A fall, if you like. But not from a plane or a tower. That would be too high and he would have to break too many other things. Let's make him a low-level fall. Like the second floor of a barracks."

"A barracks? A barracks where?" Fahey asked.

Commander Toll spread his arms widely and innocently. "Hey. My job is diagnosis. *Your* job is cover story and circumstances. Why not put him on temporary duty somewhere? He gets a little drunk and falls out the window, landing on an iron fence. The upright fence picket goes through his neck. How's that?"

"Will it wash?"

"It will if you keep him on base somewhere," Toll said. "I mean, if you put this accident downtown in some American city, you're going to run afoul of the local medical examiner. He would have investigated the case and kept records."

"We'll make them all occur on military posts," Fahey agreed. "And I like your fence idea." He began to write an explanatory paragraph on the form. "Fell from barracks window," he murmured as he wrote. "Impaled on fence post.... How drunk was he?"

"Oh, put down three-two-five," Toll said.

"Could he walk at three-two-five?" Fahey asked.

"Oh, yeah, but not too well," the pathologist added. "About well enough to roll out a barracks window."

"Okay, then. That'll take care of case number one," Fahey said. "I'll start a North Carolina death certificate on him."

"Why North Carolina?"

"The Eighty-second Airborne is there," Fahey said. "I'll research the point and give him an acceptable temporary duty station. We don't want him home based. Too many friends. Too many questions."

"Uh-huh," Toll said. He looked at the body on the next table. Abbott and Costello had already opened the head, chest, and abdomen. They were now busy with the fingerprints on number five. "You know, in some hospitals the pathologist would quit if you asked him to do more than one autopsy a day?"

"But not medical examiners," Fahey said.

"No, you're right there. The ME's are generally forced to crank out the volume. But nothing like this!"

Fahey allowed the doctor to study the assistants for a moment. "What about body number two?"

"Well, he's obviously got a bullet wound of the chest. Front to back, through and through." The pathologist walked to the second table as he spoke. The agent joined him at the opposite side of the table.

"What can you do with him?" Fahey asked.

Commander Toll pushed the heart and left lung to one side and scooped out the blood that filled the chest cavity. He adjusted the operating-room light and left a bloody handprint on the handle. "Ahhh," he said. "We're in luck."

Agent Fahey was pleased to hear the doctor use the *we*. "What did you find?" he asked. He looked into the chest cavity but was unable to appreciate what the pathologist had found.

"The bullet went clean through," Toll said. "It found an intracostal space fore and aft."

"What does that mean?" Fahey asked.

"The bullet entered his chest in front and exited in back without striking any bone."

"So?" the agent was puzzled.

"So I can cut the wounds out, dissect the lungs into mincemeat, and call him a heart attack."

The pathologist stood back, mentally admiring his morbid creation.

"What about the scrapes on his hands and feet?" Fahey asked. "And that scar in his thigh?"

"We'll make him a heart attack while swimming. The scrapes on the hands and feet look like barnacle injuries to me, so you'd better think up some seaside resort for him. The scar in the thigh looks like an old gunshot wound. Let's leave that one alone. He's probably explained the thigh wound a long time ago, and too many will remember it."

Fahey looked into Bill Douglas's folder and smiled. "You're pretty sharp, Doc. The guy was a frogman. The scrapes are probably from something underwater. The thigh wound was acquired in Korea."

Commander Toll chuckled. Maybe this agent could be manipulated after all. Toll now knew the man had been a frogman in the invasion. The more details he knew, the safer Dr. Toll felt. He had already seen Abbott and Costello cut his wet suit off. But if Fahey wanted to attribute his deduction to the pathologist's expertise, who was he to argue?

Dr. Toll picked up the pace set by the two assistants and rapidly supplied both real and false diagnoses for each of the remaining bodies. For the B-26 pilots he invented high-speed automobile crashes. Fahey supplied the details. Joe Gorsuch, fatally burned when a tank blew up, became a victim of a hangar fire at MacDill Air Force Base. The engineer, shot in the liberation of the Girón airfield, became a hunting accident while on leave in western Colorado. The town Fahey selected was so remote that there was no coroner or doctor, and the local probate judge would be satisfied that the man had been on leave from the Air Force.

And so it went throughout the night. Commander Toll performed quick but accurate autopsies, dictated the essential findings to Agent Fahey, and then joined him to invent a plausible "accident" to explain the death. The proper death certificates were filled out and placed in each man's folder for transmission with the body and filing in the county of the accident. The accident scenes were not actually re-created except to file the appropriate "reports" with the local military police. Burying fake reports in military files was anything but difficult for Agent Fahey and Company.

A Russian adviser, shot while his tank was being knocked out, was something of a problem. Fahey came up with civilian clothes that would defy even experts from a crime lab, shoved a crumpled receipt from a mission soup kitchen in Detroit into a pocket. The receipt bore the name of John Smith and the date was carefully blurred. The Russian's body was then packaged for immediate shipment to a back street in Chicago. The theory was that the medical examiner's office in Chicago was unlikely to conduct a thorough investigation; but since no records on Mr. Smith existed in the U.S., he could have been jumped just about anywhere.

Thanks to Fahey's marvelous dental charts and medical records, all of the bodies were identified. Every man was sewn closed by Abbott and Costello after the internal organs were replaced. No tissue specimens were saved and no microscopic slides were prepared. In those cases where Dr. Toll was required to alter the appearance of gunshot wounds, the whole area was excised, minced, and scattered throughout the abdominal cavity. No one, including another expert pathologist, would be able to identify a single wound.

Finally near dawn the last body was finished. The four men were weary beyond feeling. Agent Fahey surprised everyone by producing a bottle of Johnnie Walker Black from the depths of his briefcase and passing around medicinal shots in paper cups. The drinks were taken numbly without smiles. The first round as a salute to the dead men, the second as a toast to themselves.

"A job well done," Agent Fahey said, lifting his cup in praise.

"Thank you, sir," Abbott and Costello chorused.

"Let's hope it works," Commander Toll said. His eyes ached and his legs felt like pillars of stone.

"It will work, Commander," Agent Fahey said grimly. He frowned at the pathologist to remind him to avoid further comments in front of the assistants.

"All that's left is to arrange the transportation, I take it," Toll said.

"It's all arranged. I have a crew arriving shortly to load the bags for transfer to Boca Chica. They'll be airlifted from there." Agent Fahey squinted at the assistants and received assuring nods and grunts. Code names had been dropped and real names had been attached to the foot end of each bag. The time had come for the military men to return to the realities of ordinary life, if only as corpses.

"How about this wreck?" Dr. Toll asked, looking around the hut. It would have been difficult to perform one autopsy without leaving a minor mess, but this many had created a disaster.

"Abbott and Costello will see to that, Commander," Fahey said. There was a good-natured groan from the assistants. "After a short but well-earned rest, of course," the agent added generously.

"They yank all the equipment?" Toll asked.

"Down to every last used scalpel blade," Fahey said. "I'll take the papers and the records, of course."

"And what do I get?" Commander Toll asked, sipping the last of his Scotch.

"You get the warm thanks of the Agency and several other representatives of the federal government," Fahey said. "You may not receive any visible sign of that appreciation for a while, under the circumstances, but the time will come. I understand that you will be given a temporary duty for rest and to minimize your contact with the outside."

"Like where?" Commander Toll asked cautiously.

"I believe, Dr. Toll, that you are about to enjoy a brief cruise in the Pacific," Agent Fahey said.

"The Pacific?" Toll asked, obviously surprised. "And what if I don't want sea duty at this time?"

Agent Fahey smiled sweetly. "Why, Commander Toll. I believe you will find a request for sea duty signed by you in your personnel folder in Washington. It's been there for months."

"A forgery," Toll hissed.

"Unthinkable!" Fahey replied. He turned to the two assistants, bestowed a small smile on them, and then nodded his head to send them back to work. They responded without hesitation. The Navy pathologist stared at Agent Fahey. He was afraid that he had underestimated the agent and his Company. It had been said they were capable of anything. Commander Toll wondered if he was about to find out.

"It occurs to me," Dr. Toll said, "that other than your

two henchmen, you and I are the only ones who know what
went on here."

"No, Commander," the agent said smugly. "As you
yourself observed, Abbott and Costello have been cross
trained and will be reassigned. In point of fact, *only* you
and I know what went on here."

"Uh-huh. And if you became dissatisfied with me, I'd
be just one of your pawns, right?"

"We'd never become dissatisfied with you, Doctor,"
Fahey protested innocently. "You're on the team, so to
speak."

"So to speak," Dr. Toll repeated softly. He paused for
a moment, hoping that Fahey would find reason to do
something else. Dr. Toll needed a few minutes. "Would
you excuse me, Mr. Fahey? Even pathologists go to the
bathroom."

"Oh, yes, of course," Fahey said graciously. He stood
up, took his files, and joined his two assistants. Commander Toll noticed that when Fahey and the assistants
were alone, they were much more chummy than when he
was present. Dr. Toll suddenly felt uncomfortable and un-
safe. He made his way to the far corner of the hut. A small
toilet room, obviously abandoned for several years, had
been partially refurbished for the operation. He entered,
pulled the string to light the unshaded light bulb, and
locked the door. He reached into his underwear and withdrew an index card and a ballpoint pen. Dr. Toll sat on
the toilet and stared at the ceiling. Then with a concentrated effort he began to write. Using his smallest pen-
manship, he carefully printed the code name, the real
name, the actual wounds, and the phony diagnoses for
each case, adding, as best he could, whatever salient military fact about the body he could recall. When Toll was
a resident, the dictating equipment broke down so often
that he developed an unusual talent for short-term reten-
tion of autopsy details. Right now his memory was dulled
by fatigue but sharpened by anxiety, breaking about even.

He wrote quickly, conserving space on the card but
cramming it with as much as he could remember. Too
much time in the toilet would arouse Fahey's suspicion.
He had no watch to glance at, but he knew he was dangerously close to running out of time. Shadows and footsteps approached the door but retreated when he flushed

the toilet. He stuffed his notes into his underwear along with the ballpoint pen and rejoined the men in the room, feeling much more secure. That index card may have been the shortest insurance policy ever written.

13

Over the next several days President Kennedy announced personal responsibility for the failure of the Bay of Pigs, but continued to deny the direct involvement of U.S. military forces. Conscience dictated the former policy, while world politics required the latter. Fidel Castro had, of course, recovered a couple of the dead American B-26 pilots whose planes had crashed too far inland to be retrieved by the CIA body teams. The recovery of the Russian officer from the tank, however, and a hastily drawn deal between the CIA and the KGB prevented the Cuban leader from making any embarrassing announcements. It also prevented John Smith from making it to Chicago.

Commander Toll returned to Bethesda, Maryland, and began to get things together for his Pacific assignment, whatever that would be. Until it came through, he had freedom of the base. On the flight home he'd finally found some time to think. He realized he could have paid no attention to the clandestine instructions he received, for all that was really needed for that assignment was a pep talk on national security and a guidebook to pathological lies. In his heart he wasn't convinced that Fahey and his men would be able to carry the masquerade off; but his own part in it was over, at least, and he hoped he would never hear from any of them again.

Commander Toll entered his room at the BOQ and locked the door. He glanced around the room for signs of changes since he had been gone. Everything looked secure. He walked to the window and glanced across the broad green lawn of the naval hospital. It was a fine spring day and life was beginning to reemerge in Maryland. Across Wisconsin Avenue and through the trees he could see part of the National Institutes of Health, still under construction. He pulled the shade down, turned on the ceiling lights, and opened his suitcase. Inside he found his usual

93

sloppy array of underwear, socks, khaki shirts, and personal effects. George Toll was not a neat packer.

He took his shaving kit out of his bag and unzipped it on the desk. In the bottom of the kit there was a new bar of Lifebuoy soap, still in its box. Toll had Scotch-taped the dance card inside the cover, then glued it. The doctor now split the edge of the soap box, opened it flat, and slowly peeled the tape from the cardboard, taking special care not to damage his message. Then from his pocket he removed a new roll of Scotch tape he had bought that morning.

The pathologist quietly removed the large center drawer from the desk and placed it on the bed. Kneeling under the desk, he was able to tape the card to the bottom part so that it would be totally hidden when the desk drawer was replaced. As a temporary hiding place it would do.

After he replaced the drawer, he took out a single piece of Bethesda Naval Hospital stationery. He used a ballpoint to write his short message:

TO: Agent James R. Fahey
         Central Intelligence Agency
         Washington, D.C.

FROM: George I. Toll, CDR, MC USN
         BOQ
         U.S. Naval Hospital
         Bethesda, Maryland

RE: Recent Social Event

Enjoyed the dance and meeting your friends. Glad they all made it home safely. I will probably never see any of them again, but I will remember them for a long time. To jog my memory, I will keep the dance card in my scrapbook, very safe and very sound. I look forward to my Pacific cruise. If I were to have an accident, all of my personal effects, including the dance card, will go to a lawyer in Chicago, with a letter of explanation.

As long as I am happy in the Navy, your social club

will rank high on my list of interesting acquaintances.

Love and kisses to Abbott and Costello.

Commander Toll folded the memo, wrote the same vague address on the envelope, and attached a stamp. The return address was his own. The pathologist mailed the envelope from the hospital lobby and went to the executive offices to check for an assignment.

A civilian secretary was on duty in the outer executive office. She was young, reasonably pretty, divorced, and occasionally sleeping with the boss. She was carefully made up and wore a single string of imitation pearls across her light wool sweater. The tips of her shirt collar pointed from the neck of the sweater. The desk prevented Dr. Toll from admiring her skirt and legs. She looked up from a letter she was editing as the doctor approached.

"Yes, Commander?" she said, smiling.

"I'm Commander George Toll. I'm here on temporary assignment and I'm expecting new orders. Is there any news?" He was pleased to see that the door to the old man's room was closed. He stood close to her desk, but was careful not to touch it.

She flipped through a small stack of letter-sized papers at one side of her desk.

"These just came in. They are the lastest assignments, Commander Toll," she said. "I don't see anything here for you. Did you have any idea of..." She paused, letting her sentence trail off as she came to a telegram at the bottom of the stack. "Wait a moment," she said.

Commander Toll craned his neck awkwardly to get a look at the telegram, but she pulled it out of the stack and read it silently.

"Is that for me?" Toll asked.

"Just a moment, sir," she said. Her expression had frozen. She continued to look directly at the Navy pathologist as she stood up, reached behind her, and opened the door of the executive officer.

"I'll be right back," she said. She disappeared into the office, leaving George Toll to stare at the pictures of old Navy doctors and even older ships on the walls. He wondered why the Navy thought John Paul Jones's battle on the high seas was appropriate for the waiting area of a hospital office. But then, he mused, what in the Navy is appropriate?

They didn't keep him waiting long. In less than two minutes the door opened and a full captain emerged. Commander Toll had never met the man before, but he had reason to. The civilian secretary stood behind the captain, trying to see around the man's bulk. The captain was in shirt-sleeves, his tie loose, obviously interrupting something else to speak to Commander Toll.

"Commander Toll? I'm Captain Whiting. Good to meet you." He extended his hand to the pathologist.

"Thank you, sir."

"Suzy has just given me this telegram," the captain said. "It's about you."

"Me, sir?" Toll asked.

"Yes. It's a little unusual, so I thought I'd handle it myself. Cut the red tape, and all that."

"That's very thoughtful of you, sir," George Toll said cautiously.

"The telegram is from the Office of the Secretary of the Navy," Whiting said. He pronounced the words in capital letters.

"Yes, sir?" That was the closest that Toll dared come to saying, So what?

"Well, Commander Toll, I have observed that a communication from the Bureau of Personnel or perhaps from somewhere within the Bureau of Medicine has been sufficient to work a transfer in the past." He handed the telegram to Commander Toll, and waited as the pathologist scanned the few lines it contained.

"The message, Commander Toll, says you are to report to the U.S. naval hospital on the island of Guam, utilizing first-class travel 'as convenient,' and authorizing all naval installations on route to provide you with 'every courtesy.' And it's signed on behalf of the secretary of the Navy."

"Does that mean I can get a per diem travel advance?" Toll asked innocently.

"It means, Commander Toll, that you can probably run down to the Washington Navy Yard and requisition a destroyer, if you like," Whiting said, enjoying his joke.

The pathologist looked at the captain for a moment, wondering what it was all about. He knew that the CIA had influence, but this was more than he had anticipated. Returning from Key West, he had been provided with a seat on a Navy transport plane. Standard treatment, nothing more. But now suddenly the red carpet was being rolled out for him.

"The telegram doesn't give any reason for the transfer, sir," Toll said, handing it back to the captain. "Can you see anything on it that I'm missing? I'm not used to this sort of thing."

The captain glanced at the message and smirked. He pointed to a small coded subscript in the left lower corner and showed it to Commander Toll. "See this?" he asked.

"Yes, sir."

"SECNA VPREF," Whiting said cryptically.

"Which is?"

"It's used to identify a special preference of some ranking official in the government. In this case, the secretary of the Navy. But it could actually be someone higher pulling rank."

"Sir?" Commander Toll tried to sound confused. He knew it did not pay to let other career Navy men think you had political influence. Political favor was usually granted, but the stigma would follow a man throughout his entire career, and be noted in his personal record, like illegitimacy.

"Like someone in the President's office? Or the vice-president?" Whiting suggested. "They wouldn't sign their own requests. Anything coming down from that high up would be signed by the secretary of the Navy. Usually the man named in a message like this knows more about it than the hands it passes through." The captain eyed the commander with suspicion and admiration.

"I really have no idea, Captain," Commander Toll pleaded. In his mind he concluded it had to be Fahey. Who else?

Captain Whiting held up his hand. "That's all right, Commander, I'm only an internist in a career sailor suit. There's plenty about this job I don't understand and a lot more I never ask questions about. Another three years and I'll have my thirty and that will be that."

"Yes, sir," Toll said blandly.

"And after that it's back to some place like Mann, West Virginia, or Biloxi, Mississippi, to run a small, afternoon-only practice listening to hearts and farts. Oh, excuse me, Miss Cavanaugh," he said without apology.

The civilian secretary took the cue and scurried off down the corridor, her stack of personnel actions still in hand. "Check with me for any travel arrangements you need, Commander," she said over her shoulder.

The captain leaned closer to Commander Toll. "Play it for all it's worth, Commander," he said. "I don't know what you did to make somebody upstairs this happy, but like everything in this Navy, it won't last. Next week they'll have you swabbing the head."

"Yes, sir, thank you for the advice." He stepped sharply back and threw a surprisingly well-executed hand salute.

Captain Whiting tossed the salute back and winked, like an old-timer is supposed to do, and disappeared into his office. Commander Toll turned and left the personnel building as quickly as he could. On his way back to the BOQ, he passed the mailbox and thought of his letter to Agent Fahey. For the first time since leaving Key West, Dr. Toll thought he might have misjudged the CIA man. He knew there was no way to get the letter back again. Had he known the Agency would treat him so royally, he would not have sent the dance card announcement to Fahey. But then, staring at the mailbox and considering all the angles, Dr. Toll made up his mind that he had done the right thing.

Dr. Toll walked to the annex that held the Officers' Club. It had a beautiful bar and a respectable dining room. It may not have been the finest in Washington, but by Navy standards it was well above average. He ordered a Scotch on the rocks from the bartender and carried it to a phone shell just outside the door in the hallway. He opened his wallet and fished deeply among the credit cards, finally producing a small card, worn smooth from carrying and faded from disuse. It was the telephone number of a Navy nurse who lived off the base in a nearby apartment.

The number rang only twice before she answered.

"Is this Pam Fisher?" he asked.

"Yes, who is ... George!" she said, recognizing his voice. "When did you get back?"

"A little while ago. What are you doing? What are you doing tonight?"

"Nothing, nothing," she said, answering his questions. "Actually, washing my hair and nothing."

"I want to buy you a drink and then take you out to dinner."

"Oh, great," she said. "You'll have to tell me all about New London?"

"About...?" He paused, a little confused. Then it all came back to him. The night before the departure to Key West she had asked him where he was going. He had said something about a short course in emergency medical problems on submarines in Connecticut. "Oh, that," he said, recovering. "It was boring. All about how to pack a guy in ice bags and give him antibiotics if he gets an acute appendicitis. I knew all about it anyway."

"So did I," she said.

"You did? How come?"

"I remember seeing all that on an old midnight movie on the television. The sub rests on the bottom, and some destroyers drop depth charges all over the place while the corpsman packs the patient in ice and mops his brow for the rest of the film. Or did they give him ice cream?" she asked, trying to remember.

"Either way, it's a lot of crap," Commander Toll said. "Can I see you?"

"If you can stand wet hair, you're on."

"I'll be right over." Dr. Toll hung up the phone and finished his drink. He returned to the BOQ and showered before changing to a fresh uniform. He looked good in his full uniform and he enjoyed wearing it, even though he always felt that it buttoned awkwardly. He paused at the door of his room and adjusted his cap. Convinced he was the best-dressed naval officer in Washington, he opened the door and reached for the light. Suddenly an uneasy feeling came over him. The dance card was still taped to the underside of the desk. Would it be safer there or should he take it? Fahey would not have had time to get the memo even though by then it had probably cleared the hospital mailbox. But if Fahey sent someone to search his room just on general suspicions, they might find the card and its protection would go up like smoke. He stood in the doorway and thought for a moment. There was no sense taking chances. For a while the card still belonged with him. If they got him, they got him, and it might as well be card and all. For now, they would not be interested in his dance card or his dancing partners. He went back into the room and removed the drawer noiselessly. He picked at the Scotch tape and succeeded in peeling it off without harm to the card. It was clear that the card was not going to be his handiest possession, and that he'd have to find a better place to keep it.

George Toll thought of Henry Henzler's body as he read his name. He wondered if he had already made it back to North Carolina and whether the locals were buying the accident story.

"Oh, well," Toll sighed aloud, "that's Fahey's problem now." He stuffed the dance card into his right pants pocket and headed for the officers' club to find a taxi.

The ride to Pam Fisher's apartment took less than ten minutes, and if Toll had had any doubts about whether the public was falling for the government's line about the invasion, the taxi driver set him straight.

"They had the right idea, if you ask me," the cabbie said. "Shit. We should have sent in a bunch of Marines with 'em, taken over the whole fuckin' island, and kicked Castro's ass the hell out of the place. And the Russians with him." The taxi driver was warming to his point of view.

"It's the next apartment house," Toll directed. "But maybe you're right. Maybe we should have done more down there." He gave the driver three dollars.

"Done more? What do you mean, more?" the driver said, astonished. "Hell, Commander, we didn't even put a single man ashore!" He shook his head sadly.

George Toll stared at the cabdriver as he counted the change.

I've got to hand it to you, Jim Fahey, he thought. You're fooling all of the people part of the time, and that's a great American tradition.

Commander Toll knocked on the door of apartment 520 and waited. Pam Fisher was standing on the other side of the door, counting to ten. (She was from New England, and her mother told her never to pick up the phone on the first ring or answer the door immediately—it was some-how unladylike.) On ten...eleven...twelve, Pam opened the door and threw her arms into the air.

"George!" she squealed. "I'm so happy you're back." She put her arms around him and kissed him on the lips.

He was still kissing her as he put one arm around her waist, picked her up easily, carried her inside the tiny apartment, and kicked the door shut.

"Your hair's still wet," he said, putting her down. She was just five feet tall and size three.

"Uh-huh," she said. "It'll be dry in a jiffy. Let me get a towel. You can make some drinks." She moved toward the bathroom. She was wearing a ratty bathrobe that made her look sloppy and cute at the same time.

"Best idea I've heard all day," he said. He took off his cap and jacket and put them on the back of the chair. "You want Scotch?" He walked into the kitchen and opened the refrigerator for ice. The ice tray was encased in a thick layer of frost and had to be wiggled free.

"No," she called from the bathroom. "I want a rum and Schweppes. I'm rushing the summer."

"It's barely spring."

"I know, but I'm sick of this damned Washington winter. Tell me all about the submarines."

"They're long and gray and they go under the water," he said. He looked in the cabinet above the stove and found a bottle of Scotch and a half-full bottle of light Bacardi.

"Really?" she said sarcastically. She came out of the bathroom wearing a towel on her head. "I thought they had stripes and looked like peppermint sticks." Pam Fisher was about twenty-eight years old. After high school in Boston she had thought about becoming an airline stewardess, but her need to care for other people led her to become a nurse. She had spent one year at St. Elizabeth's in Brighton, but living at home or anywhere near her mother became impossible. Her father, a drug salesman for Smith Kline & French, had left after resigning himself to his inability to correct his wife's alcoholism, and had never come back. He called Pam from time to time, whenever he was lonely in some motel room alone on his route in northern New England, but she knew he could never re-create anything in Boston for her. The Navy had offered a reasonable alternative, and the assignment to Bethesda had been a dream.

"Okay. Here's the real scoop on subs," Dr. Toll said. He came out of the kitchen with a drink in each hand. "They are cramped and uncomfortable and the men have to sleep in shifts because there aren't enough beds to go around." He handed her the drink and kissed her again.

"They must be pretty fancy submarines," she said, taking an extended sip.

"Why?" he asked. He glanced around her apartment. It was a mess, but by her standards, not too bad.

"Because as soon as you left, two federal gumshoes showed up to check us out. Y'know. 'Routine questions, ma'am.'"

"How did they put us together?"

"You answer that one," she said, squeezing her hair in the towel in big handfuls. "I don't think they were interested in me."

"What did they want to know?" He took his drink to the window and looked out, trying to appear unconcerned. In the street there was no one in a trench coat leaning against a Paris lamppost, smoking a Gitane. It was almost disappointing.

"Oh, they asked me how long I had known you. Where we met. Whether our relationship was only social. Pretty nosy, if you ask me."

"And you told them?" He continued staring out the window. Commander Toll hadn't expected the security checks to extend to occasional girl friends, but after meeting Fahey, why not?

"Sure, I told them," she said. "It doesn't pay to give a couple of feds in dark blue suits a hard time when they want to know about somebody else who's also career Navy. Y'know what I mean?"

"Yeah, honey, I know damned well what you mean, but I'm not sure I like it."

"You're not pissed off at me, are you, George? I mean, you know those two guys could find out the first day of my last period if they really wanted to. So why string them along? Why not lay it all out, make it easy for them, and run up some Brownie points like a good Navy nurse?" She came over behind him and put her hand in the back of his neck. She smelled like a fresh bath rather than the perfume department of Garfinkel's and he liked that.

"Who were they, FBI?" he asked, turning around to face her. He liked the way she felt when she stood close to him.

"They had those wallet-flipping ID cards. I really didn't

read them. I mean, what's the difference? They could be Navy Intelligence, FBI, National Security. Who cares? Try to duck them and they bug your phone. How can you win?"

"That doesn't mean we *have* to give in to them," he said softly. "If we give up our personal lives without a fight, they'll have it all." He slipped his arms around her and held her close to him.

"Oh, come on, George. What's the big deal? You wanted to take a couple of days off in New London looking at submarines, and two goons drew the assignment of checking you out. It could have been worse. You could have been sent to that Bay of Pigs affair and got killed." She twisted slightly and broke away from him, reaching for a pack of cigarettes on the messy coffee table. She put her drink down on a ring that had dried there previously.

George Toll studied her as she lit the cigarette. How could she know? How could she know without asking about all of it? And if she really knew, why would she go on about the submarines and New London? Did she pick up the Bay of Pigs from the newspaper like the cabdriver? What the hell, everybody was talking about Cuba.

"Did those two feds tell you anything or did they just ask questions?" he asked casually.

"No, nothing. They just leaned on me for our personal info. They seemed satisfied when I told them I'd slept with you. Those guys are like parochial schoolboys when it comes to asking the hard-on questions. Especially to a female."

"Come on," he teased. "Even if they didn't give a shit about what we do here, you would have found a way to tell them."

"George!" she squeaked with delight. "You make me sound like an exhibitionist, or something."

"Well, maybe not an exhibitionist," he said, crossing the room to sweeten his drink with a little more Scotch, "but you sure as hell don't mind telling people about your escapades in this apartment."

She smiled comfortably. "Telling is half of the fun."

"Uh-huh." He took a long pull on his drink and studied her again. Given the wrong information, she could be very dangerous, he decided.

"Be practical, George. If they just tailed you for a couple of days, they'd probably find out more than I could tell them anyway." She danced mischievously toward the bathroom, threw off the towel, and began to attack her hair with a comb and brush. "And who could care? The submarines?"

It made him breathe easy to hear her refer to the submarines again. He had planted that cover story with her on the spur of the moment when he realized that he had no ready-made excuse for his assignment to Key West. Sometimes the quick stories survived longer. The long ones tend to have too many details and each one was a threat to exposure.

"Where do you want to eat?" he said, raising his voice over the roar of her hair dryer.

"How much money have you got?" she shouted back.

"Enough."

"Someplace downtown, then," she yelled. "I'm sick of the hospital and I'll positively throw up if you take me to the Officers' Club again."

"Nobody likes a puking nurse," he said, but not loud enough for her to hear him clearly.

"A what?" she yelled.

"I said, how about the Market Inn?"

"Okay with me, but I'm really not in the mood for seafood."

"A steak?" he yelled.

"Great. Where?"

"Oh, we could go over to..." He was shouting when she switched off the dryer. He lowered his voice in midsentence. "...the Sans Souci. The food is great there, if you don't mind the French."

"I can't stand the French, but I don't mind French cooking." She had not closed the bedroom door, hoping he would watch her dress. "It could be worse," she added.

"Like what?"

"You mean, like what's worse than French?"

"Uh-huh." He stayed in the kitchen making another drink. He promised himself that he would buy her another bottle of good Scotch, and wondered who else was sharing this one.

"Oh hell, lots of things," she said. "Like Cuban."

He was stunned by her remark. That was the second time she had referred to something Cuban.

"Like Cuban food," she repeated. "I hate it. It's full of garlic."

Commander Toll sighed with relief. He was sure she was too stupid to cover a slip of the tongue so smoothly.

"I don't think Cuban cooking would be too popular in Washington tonight anyway, Pam," he said lightly.

"Why not?"

"Kennedy has banned Cuban cuisine from the White House while he's eating crow."

"I'm ready," she said, rushing out of her bedroom. She wore a medium-length black dress that moved expensively and made her look delicious. "Are you?"

Toll finished his drink in one long gulp and put the glass down without taking his eyes off her. "No," he said, "and you're damned lucky I'm not. If I were *ready,* you'd have to shower and change again before we went out to eat."

She came over to him quickly and pressed herself against him. She kissed him lightly on the lips. "I'm not that hungry anyway," she purred.

The dawn broke through the rain and threw soft gray light into Pam Fisher's bedroom. Most of her clothes were on the floor. Her bed was also a mess. She'd helped a Navy pathologist attack the bedding in an assault dedicated to their total satisfaction. At last, their passions exhausted, the sweetest sleep of all had come to claim them.

George Toll's hairy legs stuck out from the lower end of the crumpled blanket. He slept facedown and hugged the pillow with a childlike grasp. Pam slept on her side, facing away from him, the gentle curve of her hip outlined by the sheet.

The air was suddenly stabbed by the unpleasant whirring of a sick alarm clock, missing its bell. She reached out instinctively and slapped it into silence. She sighed deeply and wondered if another day could be survived. Suddenly she was aware of the man in bed with her and was pleased. She rolled over to face him.

"Hey, sailor," she said softly. She ran her fingers along the depression in his back.

"Mmmmm," he said appreciatively. "I'll give you exactly one hour to stop molesting me."

"An hour's too long."

"How 'bout twenty minutes?" He reached for her and pulled her close to him.

"I'll lose my job," she whispered. Her breath was stale but not offensive.

"You're on duty?" he asked painfully.

"Uh-huh. And I've got a crusty old admiral on my ward who's fallen in love with me. It will break his heart if I'm late with his pills."

"I'm going to break his heart," George said. He turned to face her and felt his morning hardness brush against her tenderly. She quickly yielded and accepted him eagerly. She ignored the slight soreness from the night before and tried to make his body a part of her own again.

In exactly twenty minutes they were again satisfied; she twice and he once. He dozed off, savoring the stolen minutes as she eased herself out of the bed almost without motion, and tiptoed to the shower. When she emerged, dried and powdered, her makeup applied and her hair half brushed, he was in a deep sleep. She knew he had no morning duties. He had told her so the night before.

She watched him sleep as she put on her uniform. He was partly exposed and that excited her a little despite the generous passion they had so recently shared. She considered waking him and then decided to leave him a note that said she would wait for his call, sometime during the day.

It was ten thirty when he awoke, realized whose bed he was in, and read the note propped against the little clock. He rolled onto her side of the bed, enjoying the smell of her hair on the pillow. He thought about lying there all day, waiting for her to come home, throw off her uniform, and jump on him, naked and hungry again. Then, as quickly as the fantasy had entered his mind, it disappeared and was replaced by more difficult thoughts. He knew he had to follow up on his temporary orders to Guam and make the necessary arrangements. Red-carpet treatment or not, he would still have to wade through the quicksand of Navy bureaucracy before he could enjoy the trip.

Commander Toll leaped out of bed and showered quickly. He needed a shave, but he could not bring himself to use the razor on the rim of the tub. Tub razors in women's bathrooms are always for shaving legs and armpits. The blades get to be a year old before anyone changes them. He put on his uniform and searched his pants pocket for the dance card. It was still there. Pam Fisher was not the type to search a lover's pockets. He inspected his face in the bathroom mirror and decided he could survive the short walk to the hospital.

He let himself into his darkened room, turned on the light, and dropped his cap on the bed. He tugged at his tie, and began to unbutton his day-old shirt when a white rectangle on the floor caught his eye. It was an envelope, facedown. It had apparently been slid under the door during the night. He stopped undressing and picked up the envelope. As he turned it over, he recognized it was his own, addressed to Mr. James R. Fahey, % the Central Intelligence Agency, Washington, D.C.

It had been diagonally stamped, "Addressee Unknown."

Commander Toll sat on the edge of his bed and inspected the envelope carefully. There were no marks to suggest that it had been opened. The stamp was canceled and postmarked Bethesda, Maryland.

He turned the envelope over in his hands several times before opening it. Inside he found nothing more than his own short note to Agent Fahey. There were no additional marks on the note. It was folded exactly as he had mailed it. He stared at the note and then inspected the front of the envelope again. He felt the hair on the back of his neck move and a chill run through his cheeks. But then he thought it through. Why not? he reasoned. The post office has simply been instructed to deny the existence of the CIA and to return all mail to the sender. So this letter made it to a night postal clerk in Bethesda who whacked it with a purple "addressee unknown" stamp and round-tripped it to the hospital. A night hawk in the hospital saw the rank on the return address and slipped it under the door. Better yet, Fahey and his friends had not heard about the dance card at all.

George Toll smiled at himself, tossed the letter on the desk, and continued to undress. He shaved and changed to a clean uniform. He had not eaten and decided to walk over to the Officers' Club snack bar. On the way he passed a house phone and called Pam's ward. The ward clerk said that Lieutenant Fisher was busy with a patient, but that she would accept a message.

"Tell her the commander is alive and well," George said.

"Commander who? Is he a patient up here?"

"Just tell Lieutenant Fisher the treatment worked."

"Is that on the patient's chart?" The clerk was becoming more perplexed. "Hello?"

George Toll smiled contentedly to himself as he put the receiver on the hook. Sometimes he was convinced that the Navy had been organized solely to provide entertainment for practical jokers. Any other reason would have to bring tears to a grown man's eyes out of frustration and silent anger.

At the Officers' Club an aged black attendant in a white coat was carefully pressing plastic letters onto the felt board that would become the menu for lunch. Commander Toll stood behind him, quietly watching the menu unfold like a dietary anagram. He paid no attention to the burly man that approached him from his right.

"Oh, Commander Toll," Captain Whiting said. "I was just going to call you."

"Yes, sir," George Toll said, smiling happily.

"About your orders. Forget it."

"Sir?"

"Whoever you charmed at NAVSEC to okay a jaunt to some soft tropical island for you, has backed out. I got a phone call this morning followed by a hand-delivered message from the secretary's office, the subject of which was you." He thumped his stubby index finger on the pathologist's chest.

"Is there something wrong, sir?"

"Wrong?" the captain shouted in a harsh whisper. "You're damned right there's something wrong. Your travel orders have been canceled and they want me to hold you here at the hospital until somebody from downtown can get over here. I tried to find you earlier this morning, but..."

"Did they say who was coming from downtown, sir?"

"No, they didn't," he sneered. "But it's somebody big enough to have the secretary's office pissed off. And let me tell you something right now, Commander. When they're upset downtown over something we've got out here, we don't like it. Do you read me loud and clear?" He continued to glare at George Toll.

"Am I under house arrest, sir?" Toll tried not to sound testy. The captain was obviously in no mood for argument.

"No, Commander," he said impatiently, "you're not under house arrest. Just hang around. The *Man* wants to see you and that ought to be enough."

"Yes, sir."

The captain glanced at the snack bar. The steward had completed hand-lettering the menu. He pushed George Toll's arm toward the snack bar with all the exasperation of a loving but offended headmaster. "Go ahead," he said, softening a bit. "Get your lunch and then come over to my office. There just can't be anything good about this. And they didn't even say what you did. That's the worst part of it." He paused to look at George Toll again. "Say, where was your last TAD? You're just back from somewhere, aren't you?"

"Yes, sir," Commander Toll said, wondering if he should try the New London story on the captain. "But it's classified."

"Classif—" The captain caught himself in midsentence and bit his tongue. As personnel officer he had been told some of the story concerning the new officers who had arrived on TAD to receive special instructions on some top-secret project. He had signed them out in blank to several senior officers in the Pentagon, and he was experienced enough not to inquire further. He squinted at Dr. Toll and began to nod his head slowly as if to say he partially understood. Of course, he didn't at all.

"I have a number you can call downtown if you care to inquire further about my previous assignment," the pathologist said. "I'm sorry, sir, but it is the answer that we were instructed to give if anyone such as yourself asked about it."

The captain shook his head. "No, thanks," he said. "I've had all the telephone conversations with downtown I care to have for one day. Thank God it's Friday." He turned away from the commander and walked on.

Commander Toll went into the snack bar, ordered the special, and carried it to an empty table in the corner. He was the first customer for lunch and the place was practically empty. He picked at the braised beef cubes on overcooked noodles and pushed the parsley aside with his fork. "Hardly anyone eats the parsley," he muttered to himself, remembering a question a carrier pilot had asked him about "parsley and pussy."

A classical snafu, he assured himself, and thought that if he intended to remain in the Navy as a career medical officer, he would have to learn to smile on such occasions. He forced a private, tight-lipped grin and half expected his face to crack.

The aged snack bar attendant approached him in a measured snail-pace. When he got to the commander's table, he stood there silently, waiting for the officer to invite him to speak. He had worked for the Navy all of his life, and for him waiting was more than mere protocol.

After a moment Commander Toll realized that the old man had not come to adjust something on his table. "Yes? What is it?" he asked.

"Excuse me, sir," the man said. "Captain Whiting's office called for Commander George Toll."

"Yes, I'm Toll."

"Pardon me, Commander, but the captain says you are to report to his office right away."

"Thank you. That's fine," Dr. Toll said. He rose, dabbed himself with his napkin, and gave the attendant a half dollar. He was anxious to discover what the hostility was all about and just whose toes he might have stepped on. Wild thoughts raced through his mind and disappeared. . . . Maybe the whole CIA plot was uncovered and they're rounding up everyone who was involved . . . Maybe the Navy found out what he had done in Key West and was upset about the duplicity of it all. . . . Maybe Agent Fahey had fallen from grace with the government . . . maybe . . . maybe.

At the captain's office the young secretary, face expressionless, nodded toward the door and told him that "they" were waiting for him.

He walked into a room that was a small museum of naval memories. The walls were covered with framed photographs of ships, groups of men in naval uniforms, certificates, and citations. The captain sat at his desk, his hands folded in front of him. The papers on the desk were arranged a little too neatly. Behind him in the corners, the American flag and another one, too tightly furled to be recognized, gathered dust and history. The wall facing the desk held a few rows of books with dull covers. The windows looked out on the well-trimmed back lawn.

There were two leather chairs in front of the desk facing the captain, with polished wooden arms and straight unyielding legs. A man was seated in one of the chairs, his back to the door. He was smoking a cigarette and he did not move when Commander Toll entered.

"Come in, Commander Toll," the captain said. "Sit down." He pointed to the other empty chair in front of his desk.

"Thank you, sir," George Toll said. He tried to sound confident. He walked closer to the desk and turned to face the civilian in the chair.

It was James R. Fahey.

"Hello, Commander," Fahey said wearily. He offered a limp hand and did not get up.

"Mr. Fahey," Dr. Toll acknowledged. He shook the agent's hand more forcefully than he intended and quickly relaxed his grip when Fahey did not respond.

"The captain has graciously consented to our using his office," Fahey whined as George Toll sat down. The CIA agent threw a sudden glance at Captain Whiting and waited for a response. The gesture was so severe that the pathologist was compelled to look at the captain. For an instant the captain looked at Fahey. His face flushed slightly. Whiting stood up self-consciously.

"Well," the captain said lightly, "if you gentlemen will excuse me, I have several important things to attend to."

Commander Toll felt slightly embarrassed for the captain. The agent frowned, pursed his lips, and flapped his hands weakly. Fahey was clearly in charge.

"Thank you, Captain Whiting," Commander Toll called after him as he left his office. "What's this all about, Mr. Fahey?"

"You tell me." He took a long puff on his cigarette. He held it between his thumb and fourth finger. George Toll had only seen that done in foreign movies.

"Beats me. I arrived back here and Captain Whiting showed me a telegram from the secretary of the Navy's office. It was like I had suddenly inherited the whole Navy. He said I could write my own ticket to Guam or someplace out in the Pacific. And then this morning, poof, I'm shit on the stick." He held his hands in front of him, palms up. "What's the deal?"

"When we finished our little 'party' in Key West, Commander Toll, I made it very clear to you that I was to be the custodian of *all* of the reports. That included the notes, diagrams, and everything else connected to that operation. Do you remember that?"

"Yes, sir?"

"Then you are probably as surprised as I am to learn that a certain document—admittedly of unknown content and questionable importance—has escaped this security plan." He continued to stare at the doctor. His cigarette had burned dangerously close to his fingers and he half rose to butt it forcefully in the captain's clean ashtray.

"Pardon me, sir?" Commander Toll asked blandly.

"Oh, shit, George," Fahey said, slumping in his chair again. "Let's not play games. Tell me about this goddamned dance card."

"The what?" Commander Toll's eyes widened with a guiltless expression that was too innocent to be convincing.

"The dance card, Doctor, the dance card," Fahey rasped. "Do you think we get our mail through a slot in the door marked 'CIA secrets only'?"

Toll looked at Fahey with an astonished expression he could not hide. He slid his hand over his right thigh and felt the outline of the card in his pants pocket. He instantly regretted the move and studied Fahey's eyes to see if the agent had followed him or read his mind. There was no change in Fahey's expression. He looked very tired and somewhat exasperated. He had apparently not had many restful nights.

"I...er...sent you that letter because I was concerned about my personal position in this whole matter, Mr. Fahey," Toll said, trying to regain his composure and confidence. Inside he could feel his heart pounding and his mouth had gone dry.

"Why should you be concerned about *your* position?"

"I'm not used to this sort of thing, Mr. Fahey. I'm a doctor, not a spy. All that stuff we did in Key West made me very nervous." There was a dull ache in the back of his throat and he found it impossible to swallow.

"But it went according to plan, Commander," Fahey reassured him. "Everybody went to the place we selected for him and no one questioned any of our cover stories. At least not yet." Fahey seemed slightly more relaxed, talking about the successful operation.

"It's not over," Toll offered. "The Brigade is being captured by Castro and put into prison."

Fahey brushed the remark aside with a flip of his hand.

"We have already started negotiations to buy them back."

"Buy them back? Castro has them up for sale? Like slaves?"

"Not exactly like slaves, Commander. More like war trophies. He knows they are no good to him dead, and he knows that their relatives in Miami escaped with a shitload of Batista money. Most of them are doctors and lawyers and businessmen. Or at least so they all say. What will happen, we understand, is that the President will appoint a blue ribbon committee to negotiate with Castro, and then offer to buy the captives with medicine and farm machinery."

"Well, it's way out of my league. All I worry about is pathology."

"And you do a good job of that too, Doctor. I know. I saw you in action." He paused to smile at the commander softening a bit during his explanation of the ransom maneuver. "Now, what about this thing you call the dance card?" Fahey held his hand out like a teacher waiting for an errant pupil to spit out his gum.

Commander Toll shook his head. "It was all a lie, Mr. Fahey. There is no dance card. I only said that to make you think I had something you couldn't get to. I thought it would keep your boys from coming after me in the middle of the night."

"I don't believe you, Commander," Fahey whined.

"Really. It's the truth."

"Commander, you are interfering with a highly sensitive operation. It may be *very* dangerous for you."

"I don't know what scares me more about you guys, Fahey," Dr. Toll said. He got up and walked into the middle of the room. "I don't know whether your promises or your threats carry greater weight. Talking with you is like trying to stuff a cloud into a plastic bag." He slipped his hand into his pants pocket and fingered the dance card again.

"If you cooperate, you have nothing to fear," Fahey said. He reached for another cigarette and lit it with a small silver lighter. Dr. Toll recognized the lighter as one of those little ones that operate sideways with a flick of the thumb.

"And what if I don't?" The doctor hunched his shoulders and stood that way for a moment in the center of the office. He looked at his foot and traced the pattern of the rug with his shoe.

"Lots of bad things could happen, Doctor." Fahey puffed deeply on his cigarette and exhaled the smoke in a long, thin stream.

"You mean, I wind up in the Potomac some night?"

"Oh, come on, Commander. We don't murder naval officers. Give us more credit than that, for heaven's sake."

"It is said that you do a pretty good job on selected civilians."

"Things can't always be as neat as we'd like them to be," Fahey admitted icily.

"It sounds like I'm safe as long as I stay in the Navy."

"That may be an oversimplification, Commander, but it does present a modicum of truth." The agent allowed himself a comfortable smirk. "But," he added slowly, "we...are...going...to...get...that...dance...card."

"Mr. Fahey, I am going to tell you just once more and then I am going to end this conversation," Toll said forcefully. "I do not have any dance card or any other information that belongs to you. And what's more, you no longer have any letter of mine. So as a commissioned officer in the Medical Corps of the United States Navy, I am going to refuse to answer any more of your questions until you press formal charges against me and provide me with counsel."

"You're making a mistake, Commander."

"Maybe," George Toll said, walking toward the door. "But this is still America and what's more, if I did have some top-secret information, I'd hardly be so stupid as to give it to you or keep it in a place where you could find it." He reached for the door and opened it, half expecting Agent Fahey to jump out of his seat and grab him.

The CIA man remained seated and continued to enjoy his cigarette. He was a better poker player than to show his hand too soon.

When Commander Toll returned to his room in the BOQ, it was obvious that someone had gone over it expertly. Expert enough, in this case, to leave several signs that the search had been done, and clever enough to put almost everything back in place. Fahey was already sending him silent messages. Toll knew this would not be the last visit he would receive.

14

The Navy cooperated with the CIA and kept Dr. Toll carefully watched at the hospital complex in Bethesda for several months. He was barred from the medical library and forbidden to attend professional meetings. He was excluded from the brilliant lectures offered by the Armed Forces Institute of Pathology at nearby Walter Reed. His intellectual exile was more than frustrating. Captain Whiting repeatedly told him that he was not under house arrest, and that formal charges had not been preferred against him. Nonetheless Toll's requests for leave and for permission to travel were invariably denied.

The newspapers and magazines were filled with stories about Castro's negotiations with the United States to exchange the 1,199 captives from the Bay of Pigs invasion for agricultural tractors, food, and drugs. Castro called his demands an indemnity for partial damage to his country caused by the invasion and became infuriated when the thirty-million-dollar ransom was denounced as a tribute by several members of Congress. Kennedy tried to convince the American public that the attempts to raise the money were entirely private and in no way connected with the government. The Logan Act forbade private citizens to negotiate with a foreign government, so a committee of prominent citizens was formed. They included Dr. Milton Eisenhower, Eleanor Roosevelt, and Walter Reuther. Another committee representing the families of captives opened an office in New York on Madison Avenue and by June of 1962 had gathered some fifty-two sponsors from the arts, business, labor, education, and religion. They included Cardinal Cushing, Archbishop Pike, and General Lucius Clay. Even Jackie Kennedy's sister made the list.

By the time Castro had held his mass trial of the prisoners, and imposed fines, the ransom demand had grown to sixty-two million dollars.

Neither the CIA nor the Navy could prevent Commander Toll from reading the conflicting reports, appearing daily in the American press. He was aware the captives were being held, without toilet facilities and medical attention, in the cramped cells of the Castillo del Principe, an ancient fortress constructed by the Spanish in 1794. He knew what the outcome would be if the ransom was not paid soon.

"You are killing those men in Castro's dungeons," James Fahey told Dr. Toll during one of their lonely meetings.

"I have nothing to do with it," Toll repeated.

"You have withheld vital information and breached your security oath. You should be dropped into the Cuban prison by parachute. It would be a fair exchange for your treason."

"If I could free just one man by surrendering the information you think I have, I'd do it," Toll pleaded. "But I don't have any dance card." Surrendering of the card at that late date would probably accomplish nothing more than getting him court-martialed and charged with a high crime against the United States. It certainly wouldn't free any prisoners.

The surprise searches by unseen CIA agents had failed to recover the card. He had kept it in almost constant motion, hiding it in unexpected places around the hospital complex at Bethesda, and sometimes in his anxiety and frustration wishing that it would be discovered. But invariably, whenever he looked for it, it was still there, undisturbed, mocking him, protecting him, demanding more and more of him.

Months later, after many meetings with Fahey and other agents, held both at Bethesda and at a place in downtown Washington unknown to Commander Toll, the pathologist was summoned to Captain Whiting's office again. The captain, as usual, was not present. Agent Fahey, appearing somewhat more frustrated, was alone. He looked tired. It was now December of 1962. Some of the prisoners had already been returned to Miami. The newspapers hinted that the rest of them would arrive before Christmas. The ransom had apparently been paid; the civilian committees claimed success; the government issued denials of formal participation; the drug manufacturers reaped enormous tax benefits on the "donations" and a pledge that future VA contracts would be exclusively theirs.

"This will be your last chance to cooperate and redeem

yourself, Commander Toll," Fahey told him. "The exchange has been successfully negotiated by Mr. Donovan, a New York lawyer. The prisoners are coming home to Miami." Fahey knew that Donovan had organized the OSS in World War II, but chose to characterize him simply as "a New York lawyer."

"That's wonderful," Toll said genuinely.

"It may not be wonderful for you."

"Why? What have I done to be involved with the prisoners' release?"

"You have continued to withhold the dance card, Dr. Toll. Your persistent failure to cooperate has left us no choice than to brand you as a dangerous person—one who has continually demonstrated an attitude that runs contrary to our national interests." There was a hint of a smile on Fahey's rigid face, but it was not friendly.

"You mean I'll be kicked out of the Navy and tried for treason?"

"Oh, no, Dr. Toll. There's not a chance of that. In fact, we *prefer* that you stay in the Navy. It will make it much easier for us to monitor your activities and, shall we say, 'influence' your future assignments around the world?" The smirk had overcome the frozen face and now mocked the pathologist.

"I could resign," Toll suggested.

"Certainly. And that would make things easier for us. We can be more straightforward with civilians."

"Like a sudden accident?"

"It could be arranged. After all, even battlefield injuries can be reported in such a way that they are accepted by home-based medical personnel as various forms of training accidents."

"I'm aware of that, Mr. Fahey. And I'm not sure I'm proud of my part in that masquerade."

"But you did a *brilliant* job, Dr. Toll," Fahey beamed. "Every single one of your autopsies were accepted by the families of the deceased without question. We are deeply indebted to you." Fahey rubbed his hands together enthusiastically.

"Indebted enough to call off your dogs?"

"Certainly—upon receipt of the dance card. And not one second sooner."

The Navy pathologist stared at the CIA man in silence. Fahey was a ruthless agent for a part of the government Toll had never really comprehended. He could not be sure what Fahey and men like him saw as their true cause. Each of them would claim to be defending the United States, and some of them would ultimately give their lives for it, but it was clear to George Toll he believed in a totally different government than they did. This was equally clear to Fahey, for both of them saw themselves as patriots, each loyal to the United States.

"Okay, level with me," Toll said. "What is going to happen to me?"

"Actually, nothing is going to happen to you." He paused to choose his words carefully. "It's more like— things are going to happen *with* you."

"How so?"

"I have reliable information that the United States Navy has several assignments for you. Very unusual assignments, I might add."

Dr. Toll's mind flashed to the recent heated exchange between Kennedy and Khrushchev over the Cuban missile crisis and the successful earth-orbit flight of John Glenn. Very unusual assignments are immediately available to the Navy and other highly secret branches of the government.

"You're going to make me an astronaut?" Toll quipped.

"Hardly. I don't think you're the type, Dr. Toll."

"A U-two pilot, then?"

"You can joke about this if you wish, Doctor, but until we recover that dance card, we do not intend to let you out of our sight."

"You've done that already. I've been an illegal prisoner of this damned hospital for too long. My family must think I've deserted them."

"You don't have any family, Commander," Fahey announced flatly. "We've checked all that out. Including, I might add, your only Uncle Page in North Carolina."

"How is Uncle Page?" Toll asked. "The last I heard, he was an assistant in the anatomy department at the university."

"He died." Fahey gave no hint of sympathy.

"You mean your...?"

"We had nothing to do with it." It was clear from Fahey's tone that had Uncle Page possessed anything "they" wanted, they would have had a lot to do with it.

"How did he die?"

"Stroke. In a whorehouse. I think the medical examiner called it a ruptured berry aneurysm."

Toll nodded his head knowingly. "Good old Page. Active to the end."

"And since you have no real family, you leave us no alternative. We have only you to pressure."

"You did a good job on Lieutenant Fisher."

"The nurse?" Fahey shrugged. "We didn't hurt her."

"You poisoned her mind against me and finally had her transferred."

"She could have been useful."

"She tried," Toll conceded. "She's too honest to be an agent."

"Sleep with someone else," Fahey suggested, waving his hand.

"I might have been in love with that girl," Toll protested. "You had no right to interfere. I've tried calling her, but you've got her so spooked, she won't even talk to me."

"You're only in love with medicine and maybe the Navy."

"But that's *my* business, Fahey. You guys go too far."

"Only as far as we need to, Commander."

"I can take whatever you have to hand out."

"Sure you can. All of us can. To a point. And we are going to see where your breaking point is."

"You are."

"We are." Fahey stood up and walked toward the bookcase. He read a few of the Navy-oriented titles and frowned. He could not understand how a four-striper could limit his reading to ancient sea battles and texts on naval engineering. For him the world and the knowledge it contained was far wider in scope and aimed at only one goal: the security of the United States in a world filled with enemies. There were no private lives, no love affairs, no government careers, more important to him than that goal.

He turned to face the Navy pathologist once more. "I have taken a personal interest in your medical career, Dr. Toll."

"Oh?"

"I noticed you wrote a paper, a few years ago, on cancer of the breast."

"It wasn't much. We were studying the effects of some hormones on dogs."

"But!" Fahey interrupted. "It shows you have an appreciation for research."

"I'm really more of a practical pathologist than that. The dog research came early in my career."

"Oh, yes. I'm quite aware of that. You later showed great promise as a hospital man interested in patient welfare and that sort of thing."

"I'm a doctor, Fahey."

"Yes, indeed. That's why I had our men in the psychological division assist me in the design of your itinerary. Your first assignment, I believe, will be to a minesweeper squadron somewhere off Alaska."

Dr. Toll winced. "I've never seen myself as a seagoing sailor. Especially off Alaska in midwinter."

"Neither did my psychologists. In addition, you will not directly participate in the medical care for any of the men in the squadron. Instead you will be concerned with relatively basic astronomical observations while on board."

"Why? I was never very good at astronomy."

"I know, Dr. Toll. It was one of your worst subjects. Once we've shown to what extent we can control and modify your behavior, you will eventually be reasonable in your attitude and acquiesce to our simple demands."

Toll's anger began to surface despite his self-control. "But I told you I don't have your goddamned dance card!"

"I simply don't believe you. Oh, you have managed to elude our searches and have by now found a safe place to deposit the card, but I'm confident that we can change your mind. In the end you will beg us to accept the dance card, if only to return to the things you enjoy doing."

"I can learn to live with sea duty," Toll said through tightly clenched teeth.

"Of course you can. But when you do, I will arrange for an appropriate transfer."

"Like what?"

Fahey rolled his eyes toward the ceiling and raised his shoulders helplessly. "Like any number of places. Midway Island, perhaps? You're probably aware that Midway is a charming little spot in the Pacific. One point nine square miles, I think. And I understand the Navy medics draw straws at Pearl Harbor to see who goes there. The loser going, of course."

"Midway is all Navy," Toll retorted.

"Uh-huh. That makes control easier. There's absolutely nothing for you to do there. I'll see to that. And there are no women there, either."

"And if I survive Midway?"

"There's the Harold Lee Holt Telecommunications Station of Exmouth, Australia. I hear the black flies there are marvelous conversationalists."

"Where is that again?"

"In northwesternmost Australia. It's run jointly by the Aussies and the U.S. Navy. Some of your medical colleagues have begged for transfer after only two months at dear old Exmouth. I understand there's no one else there. Not even kangaroos."

"I might learn to love it."

"And after that there's the weather observation station at Iceland? They tell me it's overcast twenty-four hours a day and that there is a constant forty- to fifty-knot wind with a chill factor of thirty-five to forty degrees below zero in winter. You won't even get into Reykjavík to drink booze with the natives, which seems to be their national pastime."

"I could study Icelandic." Toll was determined not to give in, although the station assignments sounded like the ends of the world to him.

"Or volcanoes, if we were to allow that sort of thing."

"But you won't."

"No. Your assignments are designed to be a careful study in intellectual deprivation. After one or two of them you might even be willing to *invent* a dance card to get us to call the whole thing off."

"So I could quit the Navy and take my chances."

"Better yet. Our 'accident' division is quite expert, Doctor. Give those boys a few months to work on you in civilian practice and you'll end up identified as a pervert, a dope addict, and an incompetent doctor out to maim the entire countryside with his bungling malpractice."

"You're a son of a bitch."

"I know, Dr. Toll, I know," Fahey seemed pleased by the unofficial title.

The pathologist turned away from the CIA agent and stared out the window. He watched the medical personnel and patients strolling along the well-manicured walkways on their way to interesting and meaningful things to do. He would have volunteered to assist in the performance of a routine urinalysis if it meant getting away from Fahey and Company. He's insane, Dr. Toll thought. Maybe he could be reported. But to whom? Who would do anything about it? Fahey had the whole damned Navy cooperating with him. No one would give him a chance even to file a complaint against Fahey; and an investigation would probably be just what the CIA wanted. It would give them a chance to enlist all of the Armed Forces in their plan to destroy one pathologist. He clenched and unclenched his teeth and made fists so tight his fingernails cut into his palms. Finally he turned to face the implacable Fahey.

"Well?" the agent asked.

"Pack my seabag, Fahey. I'm going to outlast you bastards."

Fahey showed no sign of disappointment. He had known all along that Commander Toll was not going to give in that easily. The psycho boys had assured him of that.

"I hope you live long enough to regret your choice, Doctor." Fahey said *doctor* as if it were a disgusting word. He walked quickly to the door and slammed it as he left.

Everyone remembers exactly where he was when President Kennedy was shot in Dallas on November 22, 1963. Commander George Toll was on Midway Island, looking out into the endless Pacific, wondering if his exile was worth it all. He had just been transferred from his minesweeper assignment. At sea his skipper had been puzzled by his assignment to nonmedical duties, but a set of top-secret orders, opened only after the second day out of Pearl Harbor, had indicated that the doctor was involved in some experimental psychological training mission. The orders had been signed at Bureau of the Navy level and were not to be questioned. No one was to inquire about the pathologist's duties other than to monitor his official activities and to deny him shore leave regardless of the circumstances. His senior officer was a twenty-two-year career man who had seen crazy assignments come and go, never fully knowing their significance or actually caring. If it was a Navy order, it was to be followed to the letter, and follow it he did. So did Commander Toll, astronomical sightings, data collection, and all. After a few months of isolated self-study he generated an interest in the stars, and overcame his bitter loneliness and the rejection by fellow officers. Agency Fahey never showed up, and as far as Toll could tell—his quarters were never searched. He had transferred the dance card to a plastic envelope sealed with airplane glue, and had carried it in the bottom of a large-sized jar of shaving cream. Tiny marks made on the surface of the shaving cream told

him it had not been tampered with throughout the entire
voyage in Alaskan waters.

As Fahey had predicted, the transfer to Midway was
timed so perfectly that it seemed a deprivation rather than
an escape. To make matters worse, he was forbidden to take
any of his star charts or notebooks in which he had detailed
his observations of the northern skies. Luckily no one denied him his personal effects or his shaving kit.

There was a small dispensary on Midway, staffed by a
medical corps lieutenant, who initially thought Dr. Toll
was his long awaited replacement. The base commander
quickly extinguished the lieutenant's hopes and told him
not to associate with the pathologist under any circumstances. He too had received a sealed letter from BURNAV
identifying Toll as a trainee for some top-secret mission
related to the space program. The base commander had
previously been involved in the recovery of the capsules
released on signal from the new satellites that orbited the
globe, photographing every village and tree below it. The
capsules were designed to sink if not rescued promptly,
and the contents were never viewed directly by members
of the pickup crew or anyone on board. These spy films
were new to the base commander, but then so was much
of the modern Navy. He knew nothing of satellites, nu-
clear-powered ships, or international politics. The man-
agement of personnel affairs on Midway, the logistics of
refueling, and the maintenance of the nine-thousand-foot
airstrip were his only responsibilities. If the Navy wanted
to use his isolated beach for some hush-hush training
mission for a pathologist/spy, it was none of his business.

Dr. Toll had heard about Kennedy's death from a Marine sergeant, who was pointing out the areas from which
a small garrison had defended the main island against the
Japanese invasion in December of 1941. The Marine had
not been told that Dr. Toll was off limits, and after ob-
serving the pathologist capture and measure starfish from
the lagoon, assumed he was a medical scientist on some
kind of research duty. The starfish study had been the
product of both boredom and psychological self-defense.
Toll had discovered that staying busy kept him sane and
found the transition from stars to starfish absurd and reasonable at the same time.

He tried to imagine the parade in Dallas and the book
depository from which the shots were fired. Newspapers
and magazines arrived later to fill in the details he had

been unable to invent in his own mind. From a professional point of view he was unable to understand why the President's body had been abruptly transported to Washington for the autopsy, and why a panel of experts from prominent medical examiners' offices had not been assembled to investigate the wounds. Later he would find that the whole pathological world shared his dismay and that this failure would cast doubts on the Navy autopsy and the conclusions of the Warren Commission for years.

As the President was being buried at Arlington National Cemetery, a Navy plane touched down at Midway and discharged a lone civilian passenger. He wore a hat that looked out of place on the hot, coral island, and carried a blue briefcase. There were agents making similar calls all over the world and each of them was grim—smiles that day were confined to isolated offices in Cuba, China, and the Kremlin.

"You're Commander George Toll?" the man asked as the pathologist walked into the poorly lighted Quonset hut. The civilian sat at a desk in the center of the empty hut and glared at the doctor over the top edge of a packet of letter-sized pages bound in a plain blue folder. It was marked "Restricted Information—Need to Know Only."

"Yes, sir," Toll said correctly. He had instantly sized up the civilian as one of Fahey's men.

"Sit down, Commander." The agent nodded toward the only other chair in the room. It faced the table but was separated from it by an unfriendly ten feet.

"Thank you, sir." The pathologist sat stiffly. He wore regulation khakis and tried not to perspire in the uncomfortable heat. There was a small fan in one of the windows but it was too far away to do any good. The agent appeared maddeningly cool even though he did not remove his jacket or loosen his plain dark tie.

"I have been sent out here to ask you some questions, Commander." The agent looked at Toll for a moment and then resumed his inspection of a document in the folder.

"I was not in Dallas on Friday," Toll said. He was not smiling.

The agent looked up angrily from his folder and slammed it shut in front of him. "Do you think this is some kind of morbid joke, Commander?" he shouted.

"No, sir," Toll said, surprised at his own meekness. He had not intended his remark as a morbid joke. He was simply angered by this intrusion into his life and into his sanity by another representative of Fahey's cloak-and-dagger world. They had brought him to sustained anger at Bethesda, to despair and back off Alaska; now, thousands of miles into the Pacific, they had the balls to interrogate him about the death of the President.

. The agent reached into his left armpit and took out a snub-nosed .357 revolver. He leveled it at the pathologist and flexed his jaw. "These are dangerous times, Commander. *Very* dangerous times. There is confusion at several levels in Washington, and no one is sure about anything. Do you read me?"

Toll looked at the weapon and tried to swallow. This was madness. He didn't even know the civilian's name. He had never seen the man before and no identification had been offered. He had been summoned from his isolated quarters by a Marine bearing a sealed envelope from the base commander. No explanation had been given. His orders were to report to this particular hut without delay. He had responded, thinking it was another scene in his humorless odyssey. But the muzzle of a revolver was more than he had anticipated.

"Make no mistake about this, Commander. I am fully authorized to shoot you in the face if you make one false move. Is that clear?" The agent's face was smooth shaved and a single rivulet of sweat rolled down his right cheek, announcing that he might be human after all.

George Toll nodded and completed the swallow he had begun moments before. He moved his hands very slowly from his lap to the edges of his chair and gripped the sides of his seat. The agent continued to glare at him for several moments before he put the gun on the table and reopened the folder. He read for a moment before he spoke again.

"Have you ever been to Parkland Hospital?"

"No, sir."

"Do you know Lee Harvey Oswald?"

"No, sir."

"O. H. Lee?" The agent referred to the name Oswald used to rent a room in Dallas weeks before.

"What is the Fair Play for Cuba Committee?"

"I don't know, sir."

"Who is Jack Ruby?"

"Who, sir?"

"Jack Ruby," the agent snapped impatiently.

"I don't know, sir."

"What is a Mannlicher-Carcano?"

"A what, sir?"

The agent glared at the doctor from behind the folder. "You heard me. You either know what it is, or you don't."

"I don't." His answer was a fraction of a second too quick.

The agent covered the revolver with his hand. "Piss me off. Just piss me off, will you?"

"I don't know what a Manchester-whatever-it-is, is," Toll said firmly.

The agent nodded and resumed his questions. He went through the names of every doctor who was on duty at Parkland Memorial Hospital the previous Friday. Toll denied knowing any of them. Jesus, he thought, these were the doctors that tried to save the President's life, for Christ's sake. What would it matter if he had known any of them? Did this insane agent think it was a *medical* conspiracy to assassinate the President?

The agent questioned Toll on every phase of his medical training. Who had he known in med school? Who did he serve his internship with? Where was his residency? Where had he received his training in gunshot wounds?

The questioning went on for hours. The agent had finally removed his hat, loosened his tie, and, in the end, taken off his jacket. He wore a holster under his left arm and a thin leather strap across his chest to hold it in place. His face was perspiring heavily and his shirt was soaked through as the sun left the sky, darkening the room. At last he had reached the end of his folder and his questions. He stood up, jammed the revolver in his holster, and put on his jacket.

"Return to your quarters, Commander," he ordered. "I have no further questions."

"Yes, sir. Thank you, sir." Dr. Toll was wet with perspiration. His mouth was bone dry and his throat ached. This could not be happening, he told himself. This is a nightmare and I'll wake up on that damned minesweeper in a few minutes.

"You are to speak to no one about this interrogation. Do you understand?"

"Yes, sir."

"No one." The agent motioned the pathologist toward the door with a casual flick of his hand.

Toll stood up and wondered for a moment if he was supposed to salute. He turned sharply and walked out of the Quonset hut without looking back. The warm Pacific breeze felt welcome by comparison with the hot, stale air in the hut. He marched along the gravel walkway to his quarters and felt the anger rising within him. Without shame he allowed tears of bitter frustration to run down his cheeks. In a moment he broke into a run and found his room. He slammed the door behind him and beat on the wall above his bed with clenched fists that cracked the plasterboard and made his knuckles bleed. Then as if possessed by an uncontrollable force he rushed to his shaving kit, took out the jar of shaving cream, and threw it against the wall above his desk.

"Enough!" he screamed as he collapsed on his bed in utter exhaustion.

An hour later as he slept heavily, almost in coma, a Navy plane roared down the runway, circled the field, and headed east for Pearl Harbor, its civilian passenger busily making notes in his blue folder.

Toll slept through till morning, his deep sleep a refuge from his anxieties. He awoke at daybreak, his emptiness reminding him he had skipped dinner. He stared at the ceiling of his room and tried to put the agent's interrogation in perspective. He was sure they didn't really consider him a suspect in the presidential assassination. It had to be a continuation of Fahey's psychological warfare. There was no other reason for the frightening question-and-answer session in the Quonset hut. Or maybe there were agents all over the world asking questions of all sorts of suspects. The fear of an international conspiracy was real. Nobody knew who was involved in the Dallas incident, but everyone had a theory. Toll's mind was alive with these conflicting thoughts. He knew he was a target for the CIA but he didn't know why they wanted to involve him in the death of the President.

He suddenly remembered the dance card and the smashed jar of shaving cream. He leaped from his bed and looked at the wall above his desk. The shaving cream had stuck to the wall and formed a small, white volcano from which white soapy lava and fragments of blue glass streamed downward to a mess on the inner edge of the desk. The jar lid was still closed around the broken rim, and the glass fragments glinted in the early-morning light from the window. He carefully reached into the pile of shaving cream and extracted the small plastic envelope without cutting his fingers. His knuckles were sore but the bleeding from them had dried during the night. The dance card was intact.

He wiped the shaving cream off the plastic envelope with a corner of his bath towel and studied it as he sat on the edge of the bed. He had kept it safe from "them" for over two years! He knew that sooner or later one of Fahey's men would look in the right place at the right time and the ball game would be over.

Toll's khaki uniform stuck to him uncomfortably. He had sweated in it the afternoon before and slept in it all night. His body begged him to take the damp, wrinkled uniform off and to shower. He put the dance card in the middle of the bed and unbuttoned his shirt. His flat abdomen glistened in the morning light. As he began to unbuckle his pants, he suddenly realized what he must do.

A half an hour later he looked like a Navy officer again. Showered, shaved, and wearing a clean uniform, he entered the small medical facility the Navy provided for the men on Midway. It was smaller than the student health building at an average midwestern university, but it was adequate. The normal complement was a doctor, three corpsmen, and two orderlies. There were no female nurses on the island. The Bureau of Personnel had considered that too dangerous. Put a couple of women with a few hundred men on a speck of coral in the middle of the Pacific and trouble would inevitably follow, they thought. The theory had not been tested, but so far the involuntary celibacy had worked.

It was still very early. The medical crew was busy with breakfast in the tiny snack bar attached to the dispensary. As usual there were no patients in the few beds supplied for minimal illnesses. Anyone who became seriously ill was air-evacuated to Pearl for treatment.

Dr. Toll walked up to the side door as if he had business there. The base commander had not forbidden him to enter the dispensary, but had instructed the young lieutenant in charge not to associate with the visiting pathologist. The lieutenant was a short-timer from the Berry plan and couldn't care less about the Navy. For him every day was one step closer to getting out. He didn't argue with the base commander about whom to treat and whom to avoid.

Toll eased the door open and let it close silently against the weight of his hand. The light conversation and the clinking of silverware against crockery told him what was going on down the hall. He needed only a few minutes to search the emergency facility. He quickly selected a few items from the drawers and shelves and stuffed them inside his shirt. The material made him look a little lumpy, but he was confident he could make it back to his quarters without attracting anyone's attention. He made it to the dispensary door as a corpsman came out of the dining room.

"Can I help you, Commander?" the corpsman asked. He was about twenty and looked sixteen.

"No. That's all right. I banged my knuckle on a clam-shell and just wanted a Band-Aid." He showed his hand to the corpsman for an instant and then waved it in the air to show that the injury was not serious.

"Yes, sir. Did you find what you needed?" The corpsman knew Toll was a doctor and gave him instant professional courtesy. Staff doctors were allowed to steal aspirin, Band-Aids, and small quantities of medical alcohol without question.

"Yeah. Everything's fine. I'll take care of the scratch at my quarters," Toll said as he left. "Say hello to the lieutenant for me."

"Yes, sir, will do." The corpsman watched the pathologist walk away from the dispensary and envied the intrigue surrounding the commander's hush-hush assignment. There were several screwball theories about what Commander Toll really did down there by the beach, but this particular corpsman thought it had to do with radiation effects on the marine life. He knew nothing about marine biology, atomic energy, or Pacific geography. For him it was sufficient to know that an island called Bikini was out there somewhere, and that an atom bomb had been exploded on it years before.

"Watch out for infection, Commander," he shouted pleasantly. "Those clamshell cuts can get bad in a real hurry."

Dr. Toll waved a note of thanks without looking back, and returned to his quarters. He locked the door and pulled the blinds. He unbuttoned his shirt and put the stolen items on his desk. Some of them were wrapped in small paper bundles designed for autoclaving. He took the mirror off the wall behind the dresser and propped it up on a chair in front of his bed. He then removed the rest of his uniform and examined himself in the mirror.

He moved to the tiny bathroom after gingerly scooping a little of the smashed shaving cream into his fingers, avoiding the fragments of glass. He applied the soapy cream to his abdomen and smeared it around like a cross between a fraternity joke and an autoerotic game. He changed blades in his aging Gillette before he stroked it across his abdomen, rinsing it under the hot water tap as necessary. It was a slow, careful shave, suitable for surgery.

The doctor dried himself with a fresh towel and resumed his seat on the edge of the bed. He inspected his abdomen in the mirror before cleaning the area again with Betadine solution, using a slow, continually expanding spiral. The iodine solution soaked through the four-by-four compresses he used as disposable scrub sponges and colored his fingertips brown.

He unwrapped a small glass beaker and almost filled it with seventy percent alcohol. That percentage was more germicidal than absolute alcohol and for that reason was kept in great quantities in the dispensary. The cocktail parties that it provided were considered an unofficial bonus. Toll picked up the dance card, still encased in its plastic envelope, and dropped it into the alcohol. He swizzled it with his finger and left it to soak. Luckily it was not leaking and small remnants of shaving cream rose to the surface as the card turned slowly in the solution, unseen germs dying by the thousands.

Then on the desk near the bed, he partially undid the sterile packages, taking care not to touch the inner wrappings or the contents. He opened the package marked "Xylocaine—2%" and peeled the metal cap away from the rubber tip. He inserted the neck of his 10 cc syringe into a small needle and pushed some air into the little bottle of local anesthetic. The air made the withdrawal of the clear liquid easier, compensating for the vacuum his syringe created. He placed the syringe on a sterile towel and pulled on his rubber gloves. With gloved fingers he could now complete the unwrapping of the instruments without contaminating them. He cut the suture packets with a pair of sterile scissors, dumped the wet threads on the towel, and peeled the aluminum foil from his scalpel blade before he changed his surgeon's gloves again. His operative tray was complete. He was ready for the most important surgical procedure he would ever attempt.

He glanced around the room. The shades were drawn, the door was locked, and the desk lamp had been adjusted to an appropriate tilt. It was not the main operating room at the Mayo Clinic, but it would have to do. He stood in front of his mirror and tried to see the right lower quadrant of his abdomen. The angle of vision seemed poor, causing him to sit down again without much improvement. There didn't seem to be a perfect position, so sitting would be as good as any.

Toll picked up the syringe and squirted a fine stream of Xylocaine into the air. It was a needless precaution to remove the tiny amount of air that filled the hollow needle. He pointed the needle at his own abdomen and took a deep breath. Self-injections become commonplace for diabetics and drug addicts, but he was neither of those.

The needle entered his skin with a small, sharp pain. He pushed the plunger of the syringe to raise a thin line of weals, deadening the nerves of the skin and allowing him to thrust the needle deeper into the skin and subcutaneous tissue. He moved the needle in several directions beneath his skin, and after a few moments the syringe was empty. The Xylocaine took effect almost immediately. The anesthetic blocked the conduction along the tiny sensory nerves that normally reported pain from their endings in the deeper layers of the skin and rendered them useless. Toll knew the anesthetic would wear off in a little while. He had no time to waste.

He put the syringe on the sterile towel and picked up the scalpel and blade. The gently curved blade slid easily onto the handle and snapped securely in place. Facing him, it had a more menacing look than it had in its package. As he approached his own skin, the light from the desk lamp glinted from its razor-sharp edge like a diamond on a woman's hand. He paused for a moment, wondering if this was the ultimate madness. Then, gritting his back teeth in spite of his internal promises to remain calm, he incised his own skin. The wound was extended to three inches and soon became deep enough to expose the underlying fat. His red blood trickled toward his right leg and scrotum, reminding him that the experience, while temporarily numbing, was very real.

He severed a minor skin artery in the incision and frowned as the blood spurted in a tiny pulsing jet onto the mirror in front of him. It was annoying, but not life threatening. He had been able to control the venous bleeding with compresses, but this one required a ligature. Toll picked up a small hemostat and snapped at the little artery, grabbing it on the third try. The clamp dangled from the edge of his incision like a strange piece of costume jewelry as he cut a generous piece of suture and made a simple overhand knot around the curved tip of the instrument. He pulled it snug and released the clamp, backhanding it awkwardly. He put it back on the sterile towel ready to use if he accidentally cut another vessel. Looking downward toward his body wound, he was unable to see these small blood vessels until cut. He then repeated his knot on the cut artery, pulled it tight, and cut the excess ligature with his scissors.

Toll then reached under the skin edge with a pair of curved forceps and carefully began separating it from the fascia which covers the abdominal muscle layer, creating a small pocket. A surgeon would have described his actions as blunt dissection, but to Toll it seemed like self-mutilation. He controlled the bleeding with firm pressure on a short stack of compresses and reached into the beaker for the dance card. He shook the excess alcohol from the plastic envelope and carefully inspected it for leaks. The plastic would remain inert, but the card itself, if allowed to contact his body fluids, would set up an inflammatory reaction that would turn into a massive abscess in a few days. An infection that serious would certainly call for medical attention, and require disastrous explanations. He could not afford either of these.

The envelope slipped easily into the subcutaneous pocket he had made in his abdominal wall and disappeared. Toll had been careful to stay above the muscle layer, so he knew there would be no communication between the skin pocket and the rest of his belly. Then with a sharp, curved needle already permanently attached to the sterile suture material by the manufacturer, he began to sew the wound closed. He made a reasonably neat row of stitches, tying and cutting each of them as he proceeded along the wound, closing the middle first, and then the ends. The surgery was over. The dance card had found a permanent home.

Dr. Toll maintained manual pressure on the wound long enough to minimize any postoperative bleeding. Local swelling and the sutures would control the bleeding after that. Bandaged and covered by a clean shirt, he would be able to ignore the small hematoma that formed in the wound as silent testimony to his inexpert surgical technique. In a few days his body would resorb the hematoma and the wound would heal.

Later, with his gloves and equipment wrapped in a pillowcase, he would bury the package somewhere along the beach like an abortionist hiding the evidence of his

crime. When the wound had healed, he removed the
stitches with manicure scissors and breathed his first sigh
of relief since acquiring the clandestine card in Key West.
The information would now be safely hidden from Fahey
and his men wherever he went. To all outward appearances Dr. Toll had simply had a routine appendectomy,
even though his medical record denied it.

15 In 1965 Fahey sent an agent to Midway with an offer for George Toll. He said that two years on a coral island where six-month hitches were considered hazardous duty was enough. The doctor, Fahey said, could end his exile by joining "the boys" who were enjoying a little tea party in the Dominican Republic. Bygones would be bygones, the agent promised. This time the CIA was playing it all above board. They not only had the President's permission to be visible in the struggle, but also his direct orders to keep the Dominican Republic from going Communist in the wake of continuous political turmoil. General Rafael Trujillo, a longtime dictator of the half-island in the Caribbean, had been assassinated and replaced by Juan Bosch in 1962, who, despite his early support from the United States, could not hold the government together. A military coup in 1963 replaced Bosch with a faltering three-man civilian junta led by a local Austin Motors distributor. Bosch's supporters staged a small revolution in the spring of 1965 in an attempt to oust the junta. Had the activities remained that internal, few in the Western Hemisphere would have cared. But the local Communists, assisted by political supporters on nearby Cuba, saw the rebellion as an opportunity to take control. Two Communist islands in the Caribbean were more than Kennedy had bargained for, and a Communist Dominican Republic was more than Lyndon Johnson would tolerate. He had reacted to the open shootings in downtown Santo Domingo by sending twenty-one thousand troops including the Marines, and also the FBI, twenty-four agents strong. The use of the FBI was an unusual but typical Johnson move.

The new chief of station in Santo Domingo was a career CIA officer named David Prexton. He had been transferred for the assignment from Mexico City, where his careful espionage activity had won him a fine reputation with the

135

Agency. Prexton was not the only new appointment made at the CIA headquarters in Langley, Virginia. John McCone, who had briefly taken over after Allen Dulles's resignation, was replaced by Admiral William Raborn, a Polaris missile expert with little or no experience in espionage. Nonetheless Raborn had President Johnson's confidence, and after the Bay of Pigs fiasco White House support was as important as code books or hidden radios.

James Fahey's sudden assignment to Santo Domingo had come directly from Langley. The transfer gave him a big opportunity to further his career in the Agency. His operation at Key West had gone smoothly enough, even if the Bay of Pigs hadn't. So far the dance card incident had been kept relatively quiet by Fahey and his subordinates. The attempts to get it back had been left to them alone, with unquestioned cooperation from selected people at the Bureau of the Navy. In Santo Domingo, Fahey saw a chance for distinguished service, leading no doubt to a promotion, perhaps to chief of station somewhere. The possibility of the dance card's disclosure now took on a more ominous meaning for him. Dr. Toll's secret information thus became less of a security breach in the Cuban operation and more of a career threat to Fahey himself. The transfer of this recalcitrant Navy pathologist from his isolation on Midway to the confusion in Santo Domingo was a masterful move, Fahey had convinced himself.

George Toll had had enough of Midway and the Pacific, anyway. He had classified and reclassified seashells and other marine animals until *he* almost believed the validity of his assignment there. His abdominal wound had healed well and would pass for a bona fide appendectomy anywhere.

Officially Toll was given TAD in Santo Domingo as special assistant to the naval attaché with Ambassador Ellsworth Bunker. The CIA used Bunker's office to cover many of their activities in the Dominican Republic and one more ghost assignment was hardly noticed. Fahey had engineered the transfer papers himself. With Washington giving a green light for the whole spectrum of CIA activities in the Dominican Republic, the Navy raised no questions about individual transfers.

Downtown Santo Domingo was still burning when Toll's plane touched down at the airport. U.S. Navy ships stood offshore and several helicopters were parked on the polo field near the Hotel Embajador. Fahey had sent a car for the pathologist, and an agent to clear him through the checkpoints along the sixteen-mile ride downtown. There was sporadic gunfire between the government troops and the rebels, although both sides were careful not to fire on the U.S. Marines guarding the embassy and the hotel. Their official mission was to protect American civilians and property rather than engage directly in the rebellion.

Toll sighed with relief when he saw Marines in full combat uniforms. At least the American presence was no secret. During the flight from Midway he had almost convinced himself that Fahey was going to ask him to repeat the Key West autopsy trick and hide any Americans who had been killed in Santo Domingo.

The car stopped at the sandbagged front entrance to the American embassy. The agent got out, opened the door for Commander Toll, and showed a card to the armed Marine. The Marine looked at the card, glanced at their faces, and passed them through the entrance without delay. Inside it was a madhouse. There were temporary duty people from State, USIA, FBI, CIA, and a half dozen other agencies, each trying to follow loosely coordinated orders from Washington. Crates of C rations were stacked along the corridors and dozens of newsmen scurried about, interviewing anyone they could buttonhole and generally making asses of themselves. Typewriters and Teletypes clattered in every room and alcove available, while men in uniform or civilian shirt-sleeves rushed from office to office in an endless stream of paper shuffling calculated to keep parent agencies in Washington instantly informed. To add to the bedlam, President Johnson chose to serve as Top Desk to much of the activity, issuing sudden orders and making impossible demands for data night and day. He was determined that Santo Domingo would not be another Bay of Pigs, even if he had to run the show personally. Total lack of expertise was no deterrent to Lyndon Johnson.

The agent escorted Commander Toll to a tiny office in the basement of the embassy. There were maps of the city and the surrounding countryside on every wall, obviously hung with great haste and frequently overlapping. It was as if a new edition had been thumbtacked over the previous map whenever a more urgent problem had to be considered. A stocky, middle-aged man stood facing one of the maps, his back to the door. Even before the man turned around to acknowledge Toll's arrival, the pathologist had recognized him as James Fahey.

"Ah, Commander Toll," Fahey said lightly. He extended his hand and managed a reasonable smile. "It's been a long time."

"Yes," Toll said flatly. "I've been away." He studied Fahey's face for a moment, hoping to gauge the agent's true attitude. The stone face gave nothing away. The handshake was firm but not friendly.

"So I understand." Fahey motioned the other agent out of the room. "But I'm sure you realize now how necessary it all was."

"All I know, Mr. Fahey, is that for the past four years you've kept me either freezing my ass off in the Arctic or sweating to death on a beach full of starfish while your goons continued to hound me for information I do *not* possess."

"It's taken me a while, Commander Toll, but I've finally decided to believe you."

"Believe me?" Toll asked skeptically.

"Yes. I'm willing to accept the fact that you do not possess the information concerning our little activity in Key West I once thought you did." Fahey raised his eyebrows, inviting the doctor to join his apparently lighter mood. "The dance card, I am convinced, simply does not exist."

"Then why...?"

"Why did I send for you? Simple—I have a medical problem here and you can be of some help to me. Besides, I thought you needed another chance to 'come back,' as it were. To redeem yourself."

"Redeem myself? From what? I haven't done anything!" Toll protested.

"Of course, Doctor. I can see that now. But there are many people in the Navy and in the CIA who by now assume you must have done something bad to merit your recent treatment. And since you wish to stay in the Navy, I thought you deserved an opportunity to regain your reputation."

"Why here? Why Santo Domingo?"

"For the moment this is the only action we have to offer you. Of course, we have station assignments all over the world, but somehow I did not envision you as a covert agent. You're more of a man of action."

Toll glanced at the maps on the wall and then renewed his study of Fahey's eyes. "What have you got in mind? Some sort of a field hospital assignment? I'm a pathologist, you remember, not a surgeon."

"No, nothing like that, Dr. Toll," Fahey said, leading him to a map of the area. "We have a 'communication problem' with one of the rebel leaders." He pointed to a section of the map that meant nothing to Toll.

"Where do I come in?" Toll asked. "I don't even speak Spanish, let alone understand who's who in this fight. I wouldn't know a rebel from a loyalist, or whatever you call them."

"Your assignment does not require military expertise or detailed information about local government affairs, Doctor. It is far more human than that. And incidentally, the rebel commander speaks fluent English. Columbia-Presbyterian, 1952."

"Columbia-Presbyterian? What the hell does that mean?"

Fahey smiled gently. "The rebel is a doctor, Doctor. He took some of his training at Columbia-Presbyterian Medical Center and returned here to practice." He shrugged and shook his head as if he too did not fully appreciate the rebel doctor's involvement in the local rebellion.

"So? What's he got? Some kind of medical-military secret you want me to steal from him?"

"No. Nothing like that. All I want you to do is to find him and offer him an opportunity to return to the States, settle down in south Florida or somewhere, and practice peaceful medicine with the full blessing of the United States government."

Toll squinted at Fahey as if the agent had suddenly lost his mind. "Would you run that by me again?"

Fahey put his arm around the pathologist and led him closer to the map. "We are here as advisers. Get it? We are not involved in this rebellion at all. Okay. But that is not enough to satisfy Mr. Johnson. He wants us to stay uninvolved, look tougher than hell so they won't jump any American property, and straighten the whole thing out, restoring the government to anybody but the Communists."

"Uh-huh."

"So, armed with that simple presidential mandate, we have resorted to certain other methods to achieve our goals."

"Such as?"

"Such as—we have identified selected personnel on both the rebel side and the government side, without whom this whole uprising will go to hell in a handbasket." Fahey released his brotherly hug on Toll and walked along the map, dragging his hand across it as if to collect the key personnel in one handful.

"And you're going to assassinate them, one by one, thereby ending the war," Toll supplied.

"Oh, dear me, no, Dr. Toll." Fahey looked offended. "If we killed them, they would become heroes to the local people. The men who killed Trujillo are still considered national monuments, even though they fear for their lives from some of the old dictatorship. Killing these assholes is the last thing we want to do."

"So what *are* you going to do with them?"

"We are going to buy them, Commander Toll, buy them—with hard, American dollars, and with new American cars, and with houses in Miami or ladies in New York, and with phony appointments to semi-official agencies in Washington, and God knows what else."

"That's the craziest thing I've ever heard of," Toll said.

"Then tell it to LBJ. We have already talked to General Wessin and made him an offer to leave the country."

"General who?"

"General Wessin y Wessin. He's the leader of the government forces. We've made a similar offer to Colonel Caamaño one of the rebel leaders. If we can get some of these bastards to get the hell out of here, things will settle down in a hurry."

Commander Toll ran the plan around in his mind for a few moments. Apparently Fahey was serious. It all sounded insane, but if it came from Washington, who was he to question it? They didn't teach international politics in medical school.

"Where does the rebel doctor fit in?" Toll asked.

"Dr. Rojas is a close friend and adviser to one of the top

rebel leaders. The general looks to Rojas for confirmation on anything that sounds American. I guess he figures that since Rojas studied in New York, he knows more about Yankees than anyone else on his staff. And maybe he's right, because so far Dr. Rojas hasn't taken the bait. We can't get close enough to his mind to convince him of the payoff plan."

"And you figure if another doctor talks to him, he'll come across," Toll said.

"You've got it. Is it a deal?" Fahey extended his hand like a used-car salesman.

Toll hesitated for a moment and then shook Fahey's hand. "A deal."

"Good. It's all arranged. You'll meet Dr. Rojas later tonight behind rebel lines. I'll have an agent take you to him, without your uniform, of course."

"You don't waste any time, do you?" Toll said. "But this is the only uniform I've got until they bring my bags from the airport."

"Never fear, Doctor. We have everything you need for your little mission." He patted the pathologist on the shoulder but somehow failed to reassure him.

Fahey had arranged for Toll to be housed at the Hotel Embajador with most of the other Americans. It looked like an armed camp rather than a plush hotel. No one felt safe in their suburban houses and American businessmen had moved their families into the hotel joining the men from the various agencies LBJ had sent in. Many of the Americans had shipped their families home earlier, but the rest, confident that the rebellion would be brief, had packed them into the few available rooms at the hotel to wait it out. With U.S. Marines camped on the lawn and helicopters in the tennis courts, it seemed safe enough. Besides, Johnson had made it clear that a mass evacuation might be interpreted as a lack of faith in the local government. From the safety of the White House LBJ had ordered them to be heroes.

Toll's room was not much larger than a broom closet. There was a sink in the corner, but no bath or toilet. The bed was a folding cot and a crate served as both table and chair. Fahey had provided him with some casual civilian clothes and had told him to meet the agent who would drive him into the rebel zone at sundown outside the hotel.

The schedule gave the pathologist less than half an hour to change out of his uniform and report. The plan seemed crazy enough, but if it would get Fahey off his back, he was willing to go along with it. He was confident that with a little luck he would be able to persuade this Dr. Rojas to accept Fahey's bribe.

Toll took off his shirt and glanced at the scar on his abdomen. The dance card had rested comfortably. If the plan with Rojas worked, Toll could reverse the surgery and remove the plastic envelope. He scratched the scar comfortingly and put on the pants and shirt Fahey had provided. The clothes were a little large and the pants puckered at the waist as he tightened the narrow belt.

The tall agent who had driven him in from the airport was waiting in a Jeep in front of the hotel when Toll came out the door. The Jeep had been "demilitarized" by painting out the Army serial numbers and the U.S. insignias. It reminded Toll of something out of National Guard surplus.

"Do we have to go in a Jeep?" Toll asked.

The agent looked at the vehicle apologetically. He wasn't fond of the damned thing either.

"I mean, it looks so military," Toll added.

"I think that's all there is, sir. But if you'd like me to check with Jim..."

Those damned first names again, Toll thought. He wondered why Abbott and Costello were the only one with last names.

"It will do," Toll said, climbing into the Jeep. "What's *your* name, by the way? Pete? Or Charlie? Mike? You didn't have one on the way in from the airport."

"I wasn't authorized to give a name at that time, sir," the agent said, easing in behind the wheel.

"And now?"

"Now it's Juan."

"Okay, 'Juan.' That's as good as any. Where are we bound for?"

"The destination will be disclosed on arrival, sir," the agent said. He put the Jeep in gear and it leaped forward, demonstrating his unfamiliarity with the vehicle. "Sorry," he said.

The car slipped past the Marine checkpoint with only a wave of the hand offered as clearance by the driver. The

Marine gave a halfhearted salute in return. Apparently he wasn't interested in departures from the hotel. Arrivals were held to tighter identification.

The tall agent drove down the main corridor that separated the rebel zone from the parts of the city under government control. The truce zone was recognized by all sides, since each of them needed access to the general hospital and other public facilities without constant dispute. With no one in total control and with nobody absolutely sure who would win, this no-man's-land agreement made life easier.

The cathedral and the Plaza de la Reforma flashed by in the twilight. Burned-out cars decorated the streets and bullet holes in buildings became more frequent as Juan guided the Jeep through the outskirts of the city. They quickly entered the deeper recesses of the war zone. Armed men wearing pieces of surplus uniforms could be seen on street corners and in doorways. Toll tried to remain unconcerned, but the appearance of these rebels made his palms sweat and pulse quicken. He glanced at Juan, who seemed preoccupied with street signs and the stick shift.

A couple of rights and a few lefts down narrow streets, and they were forced to stop at a military checkpoint. Juan produced a folded letter and offered a curt explanation in fluent Spanish. Toll's high school course did not permit him to follow the conversation, but the return of the letter and a wave of the guard's carbine told the story. As they cleared the roadblock, another armed guard placed a green sticker on the left headlight of the Jeep and impatiently urged them on.

"Communists?" Toll asked.

"Probably," Juan replied. "At least they are not loyalists or Bosch troops." He unbuttoned his jacket and moved the flap of his coat over the butt of a .45 stuck casually in his belt. Fahey had not issued a weapon to Dr. Toll, but as a medical officer he was not used to wearing one anyway.

After a mile or so the houses became more squalid and frequently lacked doors or windows. Despite the warlike atmosphere and the darkness, children played in the grassless yards and corner cantinas flourished. Some of the houses had electric lights and a few of them had ragged curtains. Civilians casually mingled with armed rebels and women stood on corners offering themselves to anyone with part of the price. Politics was not their game. Alarmingly beautiful as teen-agers, and old before their time as young mothers, the girls knew their opportunity to make a profit was brief with or without the *revolución*.

Juan took one more left turn and entered a short, narrow street badly in need of repair. It was lined by one-story commercial buildings that opened into the thoroughfare by overhead steel doors, padlocked at the bottom. Inside they contained automobile repair shops, retail outlets, industrial supplies, and machine warehouses. They had been faced inward for security and some of the doors led to comfortable courtyards and sometime the homes of proprietors.

The building at the end of the block faced a small, barren park exhibiting a central gazebo as a forlorn monument to Trujillo. A few faded placards decorating its sides promised a better life for all under the late dictator. The Jeep pulled up in front of the steel door and beeped three times. Juan flipped on the parking lights and waited, one hand on the wheel and the other on the .45. Toll looked up and down the short street. Deserted, it was by contrast more threatening than the busier neighborhoods they had just left.

A clanking sound came from inside the building and the door began to rise. Dim lights half-lit the empty, garagelike main room, but did not illuminate the dark corners. Juan inched the Jeep inside and shut the motor off as a man in his late twenties approached them from the left. He wore mismatched khakis and carried a bolt-action rifle looking like a relic from the Spanish Civil War. His complexion was dark and the dim light bouncing off his features gave mute testimony to his mixed ancestry. He puffed and chewed on a long unlit cigar as he inspected the letter from the driver. He returned the letter to the agent and used his rifle to motion toward the rear door leading into the courtyard beyond.

Juan acknowledged the unfriendly gesture by shutting off the Jeep and getting out. He had covered the .45 with his jacket again, although the bulge was obvious. Toll joined the driver at the rear door and waited for the guard to open it. The courtyard had once been a well-kept garden with small palm trees in the corners and bromeliads growing on corkboards wired to the stucco walls. A fountain, now dried up and overgrown with weeds, occupied the middle of the garden. A headless statue of some forgotten saint blessed the opposite end of the courtyard and, on better days, provided a resting place for birds.

The guard motioned them to wait as he walked to the door of the living quarters beyond the courtyard and knocked on the small door. He seemed unconcerned by the two visitors and had not spoken to either of them since their arrival.

"La caseta de Rojas?" Toll whispered to the driver.

"Qui sais?" Juan said humorlessly.

Toll looked for a smile but the driver and the guard looked straight ahead. The agent's gun hand remained open, the fingers poised at the hemline of his jacket. The door opened and a carbon copy of the first guard looked out from a brightly lighted room. A few Spanish words were exchanged before the inner guard looked at the two Americans. He nodded his head and disappeared inside the house, closing the door behind him. The courtyard seemed darker than before, their eyes slightly blinded by the brighter lights inside the dwelling.

Toll shifted his weight from foot to foot as he waited for the guard to reappear. His mouth begged for a cigarette to lessen the anxiety. Juan seemed tense and it was too dark for Toll to see if the agent was sweating. He wasn't. The door opened again and the guard beckoned the two Americans inside. The outside guard made no attempt to enter.

The doorway opened into a well-kept modest home with tile floors and Spanish colonial furniture. Above a heavy oak table in the entranceway there was a wrought-iron light fixture suspended by a heavy chain, like an electrified wagon wheel. The walls were smoothly plastered and small framed pictures of old men in black suits hung formally along one side. The house was totally silent and cool as they entered, their heels snapping on the hard floor and echoing against the walls.

The guard led them down a short hallway toward a half-opened door. He paused, knocked on it gently, and waited for permission to enter.

"Come in," a voice shouted in English. The accent was heavy enough to be noticed in only two words.

The guard pushed the door open and motioned the Americans into a small room. A Spanish-looking man sat alone at a heavy wooden desk, working on some papers and smoking cigarettes. He was in his late fifties and wore a khaki shirt with epaulets. The shirt looked a little small for his slightly obese body and perspiration had previously dried at the armpits, leaving concentric white lines of salt. The man was not as darkly complected as the guard outside, but he was probably a mestizo. He did not wear glasses, but when Toll and Juan entered, he looked up at them, head slightly downward, as if peering over his spectacles. He was smooth shaved except for his luxuriant black mustache and he wore his thick, dark hair combed back like an old Brylcreem ad. He waved the Americans toward the two chairs in front of the desk, ignoring the guard.

"I am Juan," the tall driver said. He did not offer his hand and took the closest chair. "This is Dr. George Toll."

Toll took the initiative and stepped forward to shake the man's hand. He wondered why, amid all the secrecy and phony first names, *he* had been correctly introduced. The man behind the desk accepted the handshake firmly and did not smile.

"Con mucho gusto," he said. "I am Dr. José Manuel Rojas-Guzman. Board eligible in general surgery and thoracic surgery. I did my residency at Columbia-Presbyterian in New York. I am happy to see you." He released the pathologist's hand and resumed his seat behind the desk.

"I'm glad to meet you, too, Dr. Rojas," Toll said. He had instant skepticism about middle-aged doctors who announced themselves as board eligible instead of board certified. It usually meant they had finished the residency but failed the specialty examinations.

"A man downtown told me to expect your visit," Rojas said, settling himself more comfortably. He took the still burning cigarette from the edge of his ashtray, flicked the ashes, and took a deep, backhanded drag. He butted the cigarette before he finally exhaled the smoke. "There is a representative in your organization called Fahey?" Rojas continued.

"Yes, I've met him," Toll said.

"So have I, Dr. Toll," Rojas said. "He is a most intriguing

man, to say the least." He threw a glance at the tall agent but received nothing in return.

"I'll have to agree with you, Dr. Rojas," Toll said. "Mr. Fahey is very intriguing." If Rojas only knew the half of it, Toll added mentally.

"He has a way of involving himself in many affairs of my country."

Toll nodded his head. "These must be difficult times for the Dominican Republic."

"Yes," Rojas agreed. "Some of us hoped we would have an opportunity to solve these problems among ourselves, but your President Johnson seems to have other plans."

Juan shifted his weight in his chair, unbuttoning his coat for comfort, again exposing his pistol. Dr. Rojas must have seen the weapon, but he showed no interest or alarm. Evidently the doctor felt secure with his guards stationed so close by.

"I'm not sure I understand every detail of President Johnson's plans," Toll offered neutrally.

The rebel doctor seemed to be a man who did not waste time on small talk and zeroed in on an introduction to the bribe offer without delay. "Mr. Fahey has made certain unusual offers to me," Rojas said. He reached into his shirt pocket and extracted another cigarette without showing the package. He lit the cigarette with a battered lighter, giving Toll an awkward pause to fill.

"I'm not sure I know all of the details of the deal Mr. Fahey offered you either, Dr. Rojas, but I understand I have been sent here to reassure you, as a fellow physician, that you have nothing to fear."

Rojas puffed on the cigarette and looked at Juan, searching for a change of expression on the agent's face. Juan's face said nothing.

"Perhaps *I* am confused," Rojas said.

"Oh? How so?" Toll asked.

Rojas placed his fingers against each other in front of him and held his head at an acute angle to allow the smoke to curl up his cheek, away from his right eye. "Because I know of no reassurance I need from you, Dr. Toll."

Toll glanced at the stone-faced agent on his left, but received no more from him than Rojas had. "Y'know," Toll continued, "Mr. Fahey thought you might feel more comfortable with his offer if you heard another doctor tell you that everything would be comfortable for you in Miami and that the opportunities for practice there would be quite good." Toll gave Rojas a small smile that was intended to be friendly.

"Miami? Florida?" Rojas asked. "What are you talking about? We are here to talk about something you have that belongs to Mr. Fahey. Something called 'the dance card'?"

Toll felt the blood drain from his face. He stared at Rojas in disbelief. The whole world had suddenly turned upside down. He glanced around the room. The guard in the corner had not changed his position. The agent to his left was carved in stone. Rojas appeared serious but not threatening.

"I don't know what you mean," Toll said. His smile felt phony and began to collapse.

"The dance card, Commander Toll," Rojas added without moving. "Mr. Fahey wants the dance card. And he has promised me certain support in my efforts to resolve my country's problems if I assist him in its recovery."

"Fahey promised you...?"

"A simple trade, Commander Toll," Rojas said. "We need additional ammunition and supplies and Mr. Fahey has them." He spread his hands, palms up in front of him. "I help him and he helps me."

"But this is ridiculous," Toll said, looking back and forth between the rebel doctor and the implacable agent. "If I had such a card—and I assure you that I do not—do you think I would be so stupid as to bring it here with me?"

"No, not really," Rojas said. "Fahey thinks you have hidden it somewhere. He told me he has attempted to persuade you to disclose the location of his 'dance card' but has been unsuccessful so far."

"I cannot give him what I don't have," Toll said firmly.

"Perhaps, Dr. Toll, Mr. Fahey's methods leave something to be desired," Rojas said. He puffed on his cigarette and took it out of his mouth just as the ashes fell on his shirt. He did not bother to wipe them off.

"Fahey made me a prisoner of the Navy," Toll said. "But no card was produced."

"He was restricted by certain formalities and circumstances," Rojas said. "We, on the other hand, are not so handicapped." He snapped his fingers and the guard went immediately to a cabinet attached to the wall near Rojas's desk. He opened the double doors of the cabinet and switched on a small light inside.

"You may not be familiar with these instruments in *your* practice, Dr. Toll," Rojas said, turning to admire the contents of the cabinet. Inside hanging from hooks on the walls of the cabinet were wires, coils, alligator clamps, and several small black boxes with dials. To someone else it could have been a ham radio kit, but Toll recognized the tools as equipment out of a physiology lab. He had seen similar instruments before, long ago in medical school. He had seen them used to stimulate cats and rabbits and frogs in neuromuscular experiments. He suddenly felt his skin crawl. Rojas snapped his fingers again and the guard handed him a coil of insulated wire with a clamp at each end.

"Evidently Mr. Fahey did not tell you that I am what you might call the 'interrogation officer' for captured enemy personnel." He held the wire in one hand and fondled the alligator clamp with the other. "I think you can see how cooperative one of these captives becomes when I attach this small clamp to his scrotum and the other to an electrical source?"

Toll was unable to swallow. Rojas was the torture doctor for the rebels. Or was it for the government forces? How could he be sure? He had read about the tortures used by Latin American agents to obtain political confessions and other useful information. The newspapers had claimed these methods were widespread in Chile and Argentina. Victims had described the pain as unbearable. With wires attached to various sensitive parts of the body, the operator, if he were skilled enough, could regulate the voltage to maintain pure pain and still not kill the victim until he was ready. In the end the victim would promise everything and do anything to get them to stop.

"Does Fahey know about this?" Toll demanded.

"Mr. Fahey has personally requested my services, Commander," Rojas said. He snapped the alligator clamp open and shut in front of Toll's face. "Your weak American system does not permit him to employ 'effective' interrogation methods, and I am delighted to be of some small service to him."

Toll knew he was trapped. The thought of his penis

receiving painful shocks through the alligator clamp made him want to vomit. He visualized a laboratory or prison cell somewhere beyond the wall behind Rojas. There had undoubtedly been many more victims before. He knew if he told them where the dance card was they would get it and kill him. Fahey would remain safely insulated from the whole incident. He would claim that Toll had been sent on a dangerous mission and had simply failed to return. Hell, Toll thought, Fahey would probably send his name up for the Navy Cross!

His decision was instantaneous. He wheeled to his left, grabbed the .45 from Juan's belt, cocked the hammer, and shot the guard in the chest. The man collapsed against the cabinet as Juan rolled to the floor defensively and Rojas reached for his desk drawer. Toll pulled the trigger again and the automatic responded with a roar. The tall agent's head half exploded as the heavy-jacketed bullet crashed through his skull. Toll turned the gun on Dr. Rojas and almost shot him before he recognized him as an exit visa.

"Freeze!" he shouted at the rebel doctor. Rojas obeyed instantly. He brushed his hands back from the desk drawer and slowly raised them above his head.

"Don't shoot me," Rojas pleaded. He looked toward his dead guard without turning his head. "We can make a deal."

"The deal is, I get out of here. Get up from that desk and walk very slowly to the door." Toll knew the outside guard must have heard the shots. He expected an entire army to burst through the door at any second. Rojas obeyed silently and came around to Toll's side of the desk.

"Open the door—slowly," Toll ordered. He stood behind Rojas and leveled the pistol at the back of the doctor's head, using two hands for stability. Toll wasn't used to big military weapons, and the gun felt heavy and awkward. Rojas carefully reached for the doorknob. "You need me to escape from here," he warned.

"You are going with me," Toll said. "Tell the guards to put their weapons down and let us out of the garage."

"*Sí*," Rojas stammered.

"And tell them in English."

"They do not understand English."

"They will when they see this forty-five at the back of your head."

Rojas opened the door slowly. His eyes were wide with fear. He expected one of his inexperienced guards to shoot both of them any moment.

"Don't shoot—it is me, Rojas!" he shouted.

In the courtyard the outer guard, still alone, froze in his tracks and stared at his leader emerging from the house as a prisoner. He may not have followed the English words, but the situation was obvious to him.

"Tell him everything is all right," Toll barked. "Tell him we're going to see Fahey."

"He doesn't know Fahey."

"Tell him anyway. In Spanish. Let him figure it out. But if he makes one move toward either of us, you're a pile of brains and bone."

Rojas snapped orders at the bewildered guard in machine-gun Spanish. Whatever he told the guard, it resulted in a dropped weapon, a door suddenly opened, and the man spread-eagled himself on the garage floor near the Jeep.

"Get in and drive," Toll said.

The rebel doctor obeyed instantly. Toll took the passenger seat and held the muzzle of the .45 against the doctor's ribs.

"Where are we going?" Rojas asked as he backed the Jeep into the street.

"To Port-au-Prince," Toll said.

"Haiti? By car? Through the mountains? It's not possible," Rojas protested.

"It's possible and you are going to do it." Toll pushed the gun further into the doctor's ribs for emphasis. "Or else you're a dead man."

"The road from Santo Domingo to the Haitian border is very poor, Dr. Toll. But after that it is almost non-existent."

"Once we're inside Haiti, I won't care about road conditions. I'll walk to Port-au-Prince, if necessary." Toll opened the glove box of the Jeep and felt for a road map, but there was none. "How far to the border? " he asked.

"About a hundred fifty miles, more or less."

"Then let's get going. I want you to drive slowly and carefully past every roadblock and checkpoint until we are in open country. And let me tell you something right now, 'Doctor'—if anyone tries to stop us, you will get the first bullet. I've got nothing to lose."

Rojas nodded compliantly and headed down the narrow street, operating the American Jeep more smoothly than Toll had anticipated. Rojas navigated the streets with familiarity and ease, beeping the horn at occasional pedestrians along the way. He avoided many of the checkpoints leading into the city and casually talked their way through the few that forced them to stop. The Jeep was full of gas, and even on Dominican roads there was a good chance of reaching the border. Crossing it would be another problem.

16 The Dominican countryside was unexpectedly quiet. Local radicals who held any opinions about the government had rushed to Santo Domingo to take sides and join the fighting. The *campesinos* remaining in the small towns knew little about the political philosophies that fed the rebellion and cared even less. For them life in the country was continuous hard work and poverty, regardless of who was in power. It was farm work from sunup to sunset, punctuated by an occasional bottle of poor rum and briefly comforted by mechanical sex with their wives.

Dr. Rojas knew the road to San Cristóbal and beyond. He had toured the countryside for the National Ministry of Health, surveying malaria for the World Health Organization. Nothing beneficial had come from the survey, of course. The funds had been diverted into the pockets of high government officials and false reports of mosquito control had been forwarded to Geneva.

"Drive right through the town or I'll blow a hole in your liver," Toll said as they approached San Cristóbal.

"But there may be additional checkpoints," Rojas protested.

"Talk us through them." Toll recocked the .45 to emphasize the order.

"You expect too much, señor."

"Not if you want to stay alive, Dr. Rojas."

As the road narrowed, the Dominican doctor slowed the Jeep to enter the city. There were 100,000 people living there, and from day to day few of them knew which faction of the government was in control. San Cristóbal would have to follow Santo Domingo regardless of the outcome. Local politicians and junior military leaders knew they had to emerge from the rebellion on the winning side. The game of watching and waiting became the only one in town.

There were people walking along the streets, and small restaurants were still open although the nightlife was not particularly festive. Small groups of men in nonmilitary khaki huddled outside tiny bars, comparing the events of the day. A few cars moved along the street, but traffic was minimal. On side streets flatbed trucks showed the remnants of vegetable crops brought to town that day for sale. Some of the farmer's children and often the farmer himself, now half-filled with rum, could be seen sleeping on or under the trucks, waiting for the return of the rest of the family.

There was no formal military checkpoint in San Cristóbal. A few armed policemen, looking like National Guard in U.S. surplus uniforms, leaned casually against the doorway of the local jail. Their rifles were stacked on the sidewalk in front of the station. The men seemed more interested in their cigarettes and jokes than in the unmarked American Jeep passing by with two men in it.

"I don't think they know there's a war on," Toll said.

"They don't," Rojas replied. "Whatever happens, they will still be policemen. Their superiors may be replaced, but not them. They are too small to rise and fall with politics." Rojas glanced at the first group of policemen and nodded pleasantly to them as they passed. As a rebel he was not sure how they would respond to him either. Some questions were better left unasked.

"Maybe they're just too smart to be involved with politics, and don't know it," Toll suggested. He glanced over his shoulder to satisfy himself that the cops had stayed where they were. Evidently no one had been sent from Santo Domingo to follow them. Even if word about the shootings had reached Fahey, Toll reasoned, he would not suspect an escape via Port-au-Prince. Toll anticipated that when the CIA agent was found dead at Rojas's house, a security watch would be set up at the waterfront and the airport in Santo Domingo. But even in that effort Fahey would have to be cautious, since he could not fully disclose his true relationship with Rojas. It would have to be an agent hunt all the way, with Fahey fully in charge. The only thing Toll could expect was the unexpected.

Following the route toward the Haitian border, Rojas turned left at the provincial soccer field and stadium and headed west out of San Cristóbal. It had rained earlier that evening and the road to Azua and Neiba was slippery with a light film of mud that flew up behind them in a fine mist. Potholes were frequent and some of them still contained rainwater, splashing onto the vegetation along the narrow road as the Jeep bumped along, barely maintaining forty miles per hour. Isolated villages appeared and disappeared suddenly as they drove by, scattering pigs, children, and chickens without warning or injury.

Rojas chain-smoked cigarettes until he ran out. He crumpled the package and threw it into the ditch.

"Will you let me stop and buy more cigarettes?" he asked.

"Sure. Stop at the next Howard Johnson's."

"There will be a small cantina near Lake Enriquillo," Rojas said, ignoring the American's desperate humor.

"Some kind of a resort?"

"People come here when it gets too hot in the city. They build *casetas* around the lake. Mostly business people from Santo Domingo."

"How far is the border from here?" Toll asked. He strained to look ahead of the lights into the rural darkness but saw nothing.

"Twenty—maybe thirty miles. No one will be there. The cantina is a little closer." He pointed upward toward the low mountains rising in front of them against the starlit sky.

"Isn't the border patrolled?" Toll asked incredulously.

Rojas shrugged. "Maybe so. Maybe not. Sometimes the Haitians close the entire border for weeks—months, even. Sometimes they move their border station several miles in from the boundary. You can never tell. They are all *loco*." He spun his finger around his ear to illustrate Haitian sanity.

"Then how do you get back and forth between the two countries?" Toll asked.

"Not by road. On the other side of the mountain, señor, is a jungle of Creole niggers. We don't want any of them. We sell them some goods we produce, but we send it mostly by boat. Except sometimes the Americans and the Germans in trucks."

"Why Americans and Germans?"

"They're stupid enough to do such things, señor. They

plan their trade routes in offices in New York and Frank-
furt."

"What about the Dominican side of the border?"

"If you are leaving the Republic, you will have no trouble. At least no trouble in times of peace. Now, who can
tell?"

"Will they want to see papers?"

Rojas laughed. "Perhaps your release papers from the
mental hospital. Their job is to keep the Haitians from
coming *in*. No one cares who goes out."

They came to the eastern edge of Lake Enriquillo. Now
and then a fragment of moon looked out from behind broken clouds and sent a silver ribbon across the dark waters
of the lake. The lake was far bigger than Toll had imagined. There were no lights on the opposite shore, and only
scattered cottages along the road. Rather than a popular
resort, Toll thought the lake area should be classified as
a wilderness.

The road curved around a hidden bay and came to a
tiny settlement. Rojas slowed the Jeep to crawl. Music
came from a small radio on the bar in the cantina and
escaped through the open windows. Inside six or seven
men drank beer from tall brown bottles and exchanged
laughing obscenities with the bartender. There were two
women in the place, but no one seemed to pay any attention
to them. When the time came, they would dance or go to
bed as ordered. In the meanwhile they drank silently at
tables somewhat apart from the rest.

"Cigarettes, señor?" Rojas pleaded.

Dr. Toll looked at the cantina and then at his weary
driver. There were no soldiers or cops on the street. As far
as Toll could see, he was the only armed man in the village.
He did not believe that for a moment, of course, but at
least there were no other guns in sight.

"Yeah, okay," Toll said, motioning toward the cantina
with his pistol. "But no funny stuff. I'll drop you in there
just as fast as I would in Santo Domingo. And I'll bet those
characters inside won't even give a shit if I do." He put
the .45 under his belt and pulled his shirt out to hide it.

"The people of this village care nothing for the *revolución*, señor," Rojas said contemptuously. He parked the
Jeep in front of the cantina, turned out the headlights,
and waited for Toll's permission to get out.

Toll turned to the rebel doctor and stared at him silently for a moment. "I have heard what you and your butchers have done to your political prisoners. You're even less than a criminal to me, Rojas. I would shoot you without hesitation if you gave me the chance. When a man uses his medical knowledge to do such horrible things to another human being, he is less than an animal."

"In difficult political times, Dr. Toll, we do what we must do. It is not always pleasant. At this time in my country there is no end in sight. Only a continuous struggle. And I am caught up in it." He shrugged his shoulders to demonstrate his helplessness.

Dr. Toll glanced at the cantina again. The interior looked safe enough. The revolution could have been on another continent.

"Cigarettes and that's all," Toll said, reaching for the doorpost to get out of the Jeep.

"A whiskey for our dusty throats would be good medicine," Rojas bargained.

Toll thought of a shot of Scotch rolling down his throat and sighed to himself. "One," he said, holding up a finger. "And you do the ordering. In Spanish. But remember, if you so much as make me nervous, I will shoot my way out, and you're first."

"Dr. Toll," Rojas reassured him, stepping out of the Jeep and adjusting his khaki shirt, "there is no misunderstanding between us. You have the gun, so you are in charge."

"Remember that and you'll walk out of this bar in one piece." Toll motioned toward the cantina and waited for Rojas to cross in front of the Jeep. He patted the butt of the .45 beneath his shirt as a demonstration to both of them.

The door of the cantina was blocked open by a large mahogany carving of an old farmer's head. Three worn steps led up to a tiny porch. There was sand on the steps and no railing. The cantina was dimly lighted by overhead bulbs hanging on fraying covered wires. The bar itself was less than ten feet long and had been made of lumber better suited for the construction of shacks. There were four or five small tables in the room and wooden chairs were scattered around loosely. One of the women cradled her head in her hands at the table farthest from the bar while the other one ran her finger around the rim of her empty glass.

The men stood at the bar in two small groups. The bartender shifted his attention rapidly from one to the other—arguments generate an electricity that can be felt in the air, regardless of the language.

The men at the bar turned toward the door as the two doctors entered the room. Conversations ceased immediately. The seven *campesinos* sized up the two strangers with cautious silence and squinting eyes that reminded Toll of an inevitable scene in every old Western movie. The difference was that the men were not wearing ten-gallon hats, spurs, or six-shooters and there were no horses tethered outside.

"Buenas noches," Rojas growled. He glanced at the first two men and then tactfully returned his gaze to the bartender where it belonged. Toll followed him to the bar without speaking.

"Bueno," the bartender said. He made a lazy circle on the bar in front of Rojas with a filthy rag that served as a towel.

"Whiskey," Rojas said, almost in Spanish. The universal word became Dominican for a moment by intonation.

"Para dos?" the bartender asked.

"Sí." Rojas threw a five-peso note on the bar and casually turned to survey the other men, his slow movements giving each of them an opportunity to turn back to the bar. The conversations started again but in subdued tones.

The bartender brought tall glasses without ice and poured a religiously measured shot of Scotch as Rojas studied his face. It was obvious to Dr. Toll that something about the bartender disturbed Rojas. Whatever it was did not show on the bartender's face. He was in his early thirties, slightly built, clean shaven, and deadly serious. His skin was olive dark and his hair was smooth and black. He was a true Dominican, blending his African and Spanish ancestry handsomely, with an arrogantly proud attitude that gave little and defended instinctively. His customers showed more of their black heritage, and because of it remained farm laborers—their racial characteristics, while not a source of overt prejudice, was an essential element in every job selection and in social achievement. It was a subtle fact accepted by everyone and thought about only at the university, where it mattered the least.

Rojas continued to stare at the barman as he reached

for his drink. Then, raising the glass, he turned toward Dr. Toll and offered a silent toast. Toll looked into the rebel doctor's eyes and found it difficult to see an enemy. Rojas was, without doubt, a ruthless man; in victory, Toll thought, such men became national heroes, while in defeat they are war criminals.

Suddenly, from beneath the bar, the barman raised a sawed-off, double-barreled shotgun and jammed it against Rojas's chest. The toast ended in midair, the doctors staring at each other but not drinking.

"I know who you are, you bastard," the barman said in Spanish. "You are the animal that tortured my brother before they shot him like a dog."

"No!" Rojas pleaded. "It was not me. I have no interest in the *revolución!*"

"You are a supporter of the Fourteenth of June organization!" the barman shouted angrily.

Toll looked at the man to his right and felt frightened. The .45 in his belt pressed against his sweating skin. A farm worker had quickly produced a small hooked knife designed for banana cutting, but perfect for tearing throats.

"No! You are mistaken," Rojas pleaded. "I am a follower of Juan Bosch! He has returned to become our president."

"Marxist pig!" the barman growled. He pushed the muzzle of the little shotgun further into the doctor's chest. Rojas held his glass in the air, the Scotch quivering in the bottom, echoing the tremor in his hand.

"I am not a Marxist," Rojas pleaded. "I hate Castro. I know nothing about the Fourteenth of June organization." The name commemorated an anti-Trujillo invasion by a force from Cuba in 1959. They had been defeated, but had remained as the most radical of the antigovernment forces in the entire Dominican Republic.

"You Communists will destroy us all," the bartender said. He glanced at Toll to make it clear he included both of them in his condemnation.

"I am an American," Toll blurted. He was not sure the announcement would do him any good, but the situation could hardly get worse. He expected to be shot or stabbed any moment anyway. If he was to be killed in an obscure Dominican bar, he reasoned, it might as well be as an American, and not as a Communist from Cuba.

"Un americano?"

"He is a doctor assigned to the American forces in Santo Domingo," Rojas explained quickly. "We are on a secret mission together."

The barman looked at Toll for a moment. "Is this true?" he asked in acceptable English.

"You speak English!" Toll said, obviously relieved.

"A little."

"Thank God," Toll said. "We are not on an assignment together. This madman tried to torture me for information."

"With his electric wires?" the barman sneered.

"Yes, but I killed his guard and took him prisoner. I am trying to get to the Haitian border."

"The Americans asked me to work on him," Rojas said. "He has information the CIA wants."

The barman spit on the bar in front of Dr. Rojas. *"That* is for the CIA," he said. "They are no better than the Cuban Marxists."

"They have hunted me, señor," Toll said. "They turned me over to this madman Rojas!"

"Is this true?" he demanded of Rojas.

"The leader of the CIA sent him to me. They were willing to exchange guns and explosives for the information." Rojas felt the sweat of his hand against his Scotch glass.

"I can prove who I am," Toll said. "In my wallet. My ID cards."

The barman uttered a throaty Spanish command to the man with the banana knife, and the wallet was quickly yanked from Toll's back pocket. The search also uncovered the .45. The farmer grabbed the pistol and placed it on the bar in front of the bartender. The barman did not seem surprised that Toll was armed. The farmer opened the wallet and dumped the cards onto the bar. The barman quickly picked through the cards until he came to a Navy ID bearing Toll's photograph, fingerprint, and rank.

"You are from the United States Navy," the barman announced, reading the card. "A commander?"

"Yes, I am a Navy doctor," Toll said.

"But the CIA is trying to kill you?"

"The CIA are only gangsters," Toll bargained. "They do not represent the American people. They are international criminals. The U.S. Navy refuses to cooperate with

them. That is why the CIA wanted me tortured or killed."
Toll was telling the barman everything he wanted to hear
as rapidly as he could get the words out.

"Why do you want to go to Haiti?"

"I have important information about the illegal activities of the CIA in the Dominican Republic. I must get it
back to Washington. My only hope is to escape through
Port-au-Prince. The CIA controls the airport in Santo Domingo."

"But your new President, Johnson—" the barman continued, "he has sent many American Marines into Santo
Domingo."

"They are infiltrated by the CIA," Toll explained. "I
cannot trust any of them. I must report to President Johnson myself."

The barman looked at the Navy pathologist as he
weighed the story. In the Dominican Republic intrigue
and distrust for the government was the norm.

"And what about this pig?" he said, nudging Rojas with
the shotgun.

"I needed him to show me the way to the border," Toll
said contemptuously. "He is nothing to me. I intended to
kill him as soon as I reached Haiti." He startled himself
with the announcement. In fact, he had been unsure how
he would get rid of Rojas.

The bartender offered a small smile and then glared at
Dr. Rojas. "We will save you the trouble."

"You must take me back to Santo Domingo," Rojas
pleaded. "I can get you much money for my safe return.
The government will pay you well for me."

"You will be returned," the barman told him in Spanish.
"But first you will enjoy some of the electrical tricks you
played on some of our compatriots."

"No!" Rojas screamed.

"And then we will dump your dead body on the steps
of the cathedral with your penis stuffed down your throat!"
The barman snapped orders to the farmers and they instantly obeyed. Two of them grabbed Rojas by the arms
while a third searched him thoroughly. The man with the
curved banana knife held it under Rojas's nose and twisted
the blade menacingly.

"We will take you to Haiti, Dr. Toll," the barman

said, returning the .45. "It is not far away and we know the places to cross without being seen."

"By the Haitians?" Toll asked.

"No. By the Dominican guards," the barman said. "The Haitians will not care if you enter their country. They are too poor and too stupid to care who crosses their border. But we can never trust our own border guards." He leaned closer to Toll as if to share an intimate fact. "They are the government."

Toll stared into the barman's eyes and nodded his head gravely. He might as well have been talking to a moonshiner in the mountains of western North Carolina.

"We will keep the Jeep," the barman said. "The trip to the border will be safer in my truck."

Toll recognized that this was not the time to claim color of title in the Jeep. At the moment, he would have been willing to part with the presidential limousine.

"There will be reprisals if anything happens to me," Rojas announced confidently.

The bartender put the shotgun away and came around from behind the bar. He stood very close to Rojas without speaking. Then suddenly he kneed him in the groin. Rojas screamed in pain and doubled up on the arms of the two farmers holding him.

"They will declare it a national holiday when I roll your head across the Cathedral Plaza!" the barman snarled. "Throw him in the Jeep," he ordered. "And if he moves, break his legs and arms. But save the neck for me." The barman ran the side of his rough farming boot along the front edge of Rojas's shin and crunched it on his instep. The rebel doctor screamed again, much to the delight of the farmers.

"No más," Rojas pleaded.

"Take him to the farm near the mountain," the barman said. "Tie him to the tree in front of the barn. I will be back to kill him myself after I show the American doctor to the border."

The word *truck* barely described the ancient machine behind the cantina—it was the oldest vehicle Toll had ever seen outside an antique-car museum. The bartender put his big hand on Commander Toll's shoulder. "My name is Antonio," he said. He smiled and exhibited his strong, white teeth.

"My name is Toll," the doctor said, holding out his hand and accepting a firm handshake.

"*Dr.* Toll," Antonio said proudly.

"Yes, that's true," Toll said. "I am a doctor." He withdrew his hand and wondered why the bartender was still smiling. Had it all been a trick? he wondered. Had this violent tavernkeeper offered his help simply to steal the Jeep? Toll had heard of tourists in Bogotá being killed for their wristwatches or their shoes. How much more valuable would an American Jeep be to these isolated farmers? He felt his throat thicken and he found it hard to swallow.

"The priest in my school said I should become a doctor," Antonio said expansively. "Only the smartest ones can become doctors. But there was no money and there were many children in my family." He shook his head sadly and lifted his shoulders, accepting his fate anew.

"Your country sends many of her doctors to the United States for specialized training. I knew some of them when I was a medical student."

"Who?" Antonio asked excitedly.

"I cannot remember their names, Antonio. It was a long time ago and I was only a student." He saw disappointment appear on the Dominican's face in the dim light from the open door to the cantina. "But they were very smart doctors," Toll added quickly. "Very smart."

The smile reappeared on Antonio's face. "The priest was right," he announced after a moment's consideration. "Only the smartest students can become doctors."

"You would have made a good doctor, Antonio. I am sure of it."

The bartender looked at Toll for a moment and narrowed his eyes to concentrate on that assessment. Then, apparently agreeing with the Navy doctor, he nodded his head vigorously and slapped him on the shoulder again.

"Come," Antonio said. "We have many miles to go before Port-au-Prince." He motioned Toll toward the passenger seat of the truck and climbed in behind the wheel.

"Port-au-Prince?" Toll asked. "You're taking me all the way to the city?"

"Why not? It would be a long dangerous walk from the border. More than forty miles!" He started the ancient truck with a practiced combination of secret adjustments of choke and accelerator. The machine sputtered twice and then responded with surprising smoothness.

"But you may have trouble with the border guards," Toll offered gently. His fears had left him and he began to feel slighty embarrassed by the barman's generosity. He knew he would be unable to repay the man's kindness.

"We will not see any border guards tonight," Antonio said.

He threw the truck into gear and roared onto the road in front of the cantina. The Jeep had already left and there were no other lights in front of them.

"We will take a road known only to the local farmers. It is used to sell vegetables and meat to the Haitians."

"But it crosses the border?"

"Of course. But it avoids the formalities of customs and taxes. The Haitians use it too. Many of them come over to work in the fields, planting and harvesting."

"Illegal aliens?"

"Legal—illegal—those are words for government men and lawyers to speak. Here in the mountains of Hispaniola there is only hard work to do and hungry mouths to feed." He reached under the seat of the truck and found a corked whiskey bottle. He pulled the cork with his teeth and handed the bottle to Dr. Toll.

Toll looked at the brown bottle for a moment and took a generous swig. It did not seem fitting to be shy. The liquor burned and grabbed his throat like gasoline as his brain raced to identify the mysterious liquid. He swallowed hard and repressed his cough as he handed it back to the driver.

"Local rum," Antonio explained after a long pull on the bottle.

"I'm glad to hear it," Toll said, grinning and releasing his cough. "For a moment I thought I was poisoned."

"Have another one. Maybe you will be," Antonio joked. He passed the bottle to the American and handed him the cork. Toll took another sip but made it look like a generous swallow. He feigned his appreciation of the Dominican's hospitality as an unsatisfied but grateful lover fakes an orgasm.

The town disappeared in the darkness behind them. There was no other traffic even though this was a main road to the border. The road seemed less and less used and potholes became more frequent. Antonio skillfully dodged most of them, but in others the large hard tires of the old truck smashed to the depths and challenged the axles to break under the impact. Toll had already concluded there were either no springs to worry about or that they had long before worn out.

About five miles from the cantina Antonio turned off the pavement onto a narrow dirt road almost obscured by brush and overgrowth. In some places grass grew in the middle of the road. There were no directional signals, traffic signs, or vehicles to observe them.

"The farm road?" Toll asked needlessly.

"Sí. But not so late at night. The farmers use this trail to cross into Haiti in the mornings. They get an early start to make the market in Port-au-Prince." Antonio had been smoking a Monte Carlo as he drove along the dirt road. The hot end and the wet end had become almost one before he threw it out the nonexistent window of the truck.

"The border is close by?"

"Just over that hill," Antonio said, pointing to his left. The road had been climbing into the mountains ever since they had left the cantina, but now the incline became steeper. Pine trees had replaced the tropical growth of the lowlands and here and there exposed rock formations peeked out from the thick, grassy carpet covering the mountain.

"They have no patrols in this area?" Toll asked. He reminded himself of old Nazi movies with border guards and snarling dogs on leashes searching for partisans in the hills.

"No. The Dominican guards are paid a small amount every month by the local farmers, and the Haitians, whenever they watch the border at all, are grateful for the food that comes in to be sold in the market."

"Then why do you not drive over the mountain on the main road?"

"That would be an insult to the guards. It is their job to prevent such activity. So if the farmer drove his cart beyond the checkpoint, he would have to be arrested." He pointed at the unobstructed and unimproved road in front of them. "This way they know nothing about it and are not embarrassed."

Dr. Toll nodded as he considered the practicality of the

peasants' solution to a border problem that confounded both governments.

"Then why do they bother having border checks at all?" he asked.

"To tax the Germans and the British. Importers bring big trucks over with washing machines and farm equipment. Sometimes too many Haitians want to come in to find work. Mostly to give somebody a government job as a border guard. Who knows?" he concluded. He reached for another cigarette and offered one to Toll. The American had smelled the previous cigarettes and was not enticed to try one. He half-turned to look downhill from the open doorway of the truck. The hillside quickly fell away beneath them into the darkness below. There were few landmarks to distinguish as they rattled along, slowly climbing the shelf road.

"How far to the border now?" Toll asked.

"Who knows? We may have already passed it. On this road it makes no difference."

"But we won't stay on this old road all the way to Port-au-Prince, will we?"

Antonio emitted a short laugh. "This road is only to get us around the border check. We get back on the main highway in a few miles." He pointed absently up the road in front of them. "Of course, from there it is a Haitian road." He made a face to show how little he thought of the Haitian highway maintenance.

"And then?"

"And then it's across the high plain around the salt lake and down the last mountain to Port-au-Prince. If we are lucky."

Toll turned to study his face for a moment. "What do you mean, if we're lucky?"

"We have no vegetables or animals to sell in the market. We may look suspicious."

"Suspicious to whom?" Toll asked, basking in the confidence Antonio had inspired in him.

"The Tontons Macoutes," Antonio said dryly.

"The who?"

"Duvalier's men," Antonio explained. "You have heard of Duvalier? He's a doctor too."

"Papa Doc! I read about him in *Time* magazine. He's the president, right?"

"El Presidente!" Antonio snorted derisively. "No chance! He is a dictator!" He spat onto the hillside outside his side of the truck.

"Is he dangerous?"

Antonio turned to look at Toll as if the American were the most uninformed man in the world. "Like Trujillo." He drew his finger across his throat and emitted a rasping sound.

"And who are the Tontons?"

"They are Duvalier's private army of gangsters. They do not wear uniforms, but they carry guns."

"What do they do?"

"They kill people. They collect money from the people for Papa Doc. They do whatever he wants."

The truck had reentered the paved road, such as it was. The terrain was flatter now. Beyond them lay the great salt lake, forty miles long with seashells and coral as living testimony to its oceanic origin. The water was more brackish than saline and because of it few fish found it a hospitable place to live. But if the fish didn't like the water, the crocodiles did and grew to fourteen feet, feasting on the ducks, the egrets, and each other.

The highlights of the tropical night sky bounced softly from the surface of the placid lake, even without a moon. The land was suddenly a desert as Antonio rattled the truck out of the pine forest and around the near edge of the lake.

"Bonita, no?" Antonio asked, pointing at the lake.

"Fantastic. What's it called?"

"The Haitians call it Etang Saumâtre, but it's good for nothing. It is too salty. On clear days the lake can be seen from Port-au-Prince, but it does not look real. It is ... how you call it?"

"A mirage?" Toll offered.

"Yes, a mirage. From the city it looks like a vision. But it is real. And worthless. Like most of Haiti." There was no tone of concern or prejudice in the driver's somber evaluation of the black republic.

Toll watched the lake pass by in silence and wondered why this country had been plagued with so much misery, misfortune, poverty, and disease. Even much of its geography had been a cruel joke to the men who tried to colonize it. Ninety-five percent of its four and a half million people were of African descent, imported as slaves by the French to work the rich soil along the malarial lowlands. With them the slaves imported yaws, a crusty nodular and ultimately destructive disease of the skin and bone which managed to infect seventy-eight percent of the entire population by 1915 and had spread to the rest of the West Indies and Central America. The Spanish colonists brought smallpox and, with it, wiped out the Indian population of the island they named Hispaniola. In exchange the Indians gave them syphilis. The mosquitoes provided yellow fever to ravage the remaining colonials while the black slaves were often immune. For the survivors there was widespread typhoid, malaria, tuberculosis, and hookworm. Had Columbus known what a pest house this half of the island was to become, he might have chosen to bypass it altogether.

Far beyond the lake to the south, La Selle, Haiti's highest peak, reached toward the nighttime sky. It rose some eight thousand feet and offered its slopes for wild strawberries to grow in the chilly air. Few Haitians ever saw those slopes, except at a distance from their cramped squalor. The cool highlands and mountain retreats were reserved for the *Elite* and the foreigners who could afford the expensive hotels the wealthy had built there.

The road curved toward a mountain pass and showed signs of improvement as the two men approached the hotel area around Furcy and Kenscoff. Affluent residences and mountain retreats began to appear along the road now dotted with women walking toward Port-au-Prince with baskets or bundles balanced on their heads.

"The market."

"At this time of night?"

"To be there at daybreak," Antonio supplied. "They will walk all night."

"What will they buy?"

"Not buy. They will sell a banana or a carrot. Maybe a chicken. Then they will walk home again. They have nothing else to do. Except have babies and starve and die."

Dr. Toll turned to look at several of them as they passed. His heart went out to them. Old before they reached their mid-twenties, their bodies exhausted from childbearing and disease, they shuffled on bare feet along dusty high-

ways to barter for existence in a city unable to sustain its
own burgeoning population.

"But have they no doctors or medicines to help them?
What about the children?" Dr. Toll wondered aloud.

"Medicine costs money," Antonio explained. "And even
though Papa Doc was a country doctor himself, he does
nothing to bring new doctors into this terrible country. It
is hopeless." Antonio shrugged and spit again into the
road, ignoring the women and their burdens.

"Someone could build a hospital for them," Toll suggested.

"Albert Schweitzer," Antonio said, pronouncing the
name badly.

"Someone like that."

"No. That is the name they gave to the hospital the
Americans build in Deschapelles."

"What Americans?" Toll was interested now.

"I do not know, Dr. Toll. All I know is some Americans
came and built a hospital to treat the poor. It may be closed
now. I have not been there to see for myself."

"Where is this place?"

"Deschapelles? It is two or three hours north of Port-
au-Prince, or so I am told."

"Can you take me there?"

Antonio drove several miles in silence and brought the
truck to a halt just outside Pétionville. He held the steering wheel with both hands and stared straight ahead into
the darkness beyond the headlights as he spoke. "Dr. Toll.
You have been a very fortunate man tonight, so far. You
arrived at my cantina in the company of a traitor to my
country and we did not kill you. You told us you were
trying to help us and I believed you. My country is at war
with itself. There are a few men that I can trust outside
of my own village these days. The United States has sent
soldiers and spies to interfere without knowing which side
does what. We can accept that because many days we too
do not know which side we are fighting on. I offered to
bring you to Port-au-Prince because you could prove you
are a doctor in the American Navy. Doctors are not soldiers
and they do not kill people. That is good. But now you talk
of Deschapelles and the American hospital. You can go
there if you want. And you can find your own way." He

turned to face George Toll. There was neither anger nor fear in his face.

"I don't think I understand, Antonio."

"I have come a long way to bring you close to Port-au-Prince because I thought you were helping *my* people. If I drive any closer to the city, I will risk arrest by the Tontons Macoutes. I have come far enough. I have helped you a little, I think. But I care *nothing* for these Haitian pigs."

Toll caught on quickly. He was being dumped and there was nothing he could do about it. He knew Antonio was right. The Dominican had problems enough of his own. It was time to get out of the truck and join the silent parade into town. He offered his hand to the driver.

"I am grateful to you, Antonio. I will never forget you." Toll stepped out of the truck and stood facing the driver across the seat.

"Give me your gun, Dr. Toll."

"My gun?" Toll instinctively felt for the .45 in his belt.

"If the Tonton find you with a gun, they will kill you without question."

"Without a gun I am helpless," Toll pleaded.

"Without your gun you have a chance." The driver held out his hand expectantly and waited as the doctor thought it over.

"I . . ."

"Give me the gun or I will drive to the Pétionville police and tell them you took me prisoner."

"But they would not—"

"They will believe me, Dr. Toll. They see me come by here often, bringing fruits and meat to the market. *You* are the stranger."

Toll hesitated and then slowly lifted the pistol from his belt. He paused for a moment and weighed the chances he would have if he shot the Dominican and stole the truck. The plan was hopeless. He handed the gun to the driver and tried to smile.

"Thank you, Doctor. Now give me your money." The driver had turned the pistol on the doctor. His jaw was firm and his eyes had become narrow. "These are difficult times for all of us."

Toll reached into his pocket and produced a small packet of American dollars. He hoped it would satisfy the man. The Dominican accepted the money without inspection and nodded slowly. Toll reached toward his rear pocket, slipped his wallet out, and handed it over. The driver opened the billfold with one hand and fished into the money compartment with his finger. Satisfied there was no more money, he returned the wallet to Toll.

"You keep the cards and your identification. You may need it—to carry out your mission." Antonio put the truck in gear and held in the clutch.

"Antonio, I don't understand you, but I am still grateful. You are right. I will need my identification to get to Washington."

"*Sí*. Good luck. And besides, I would not like to be caught with the cards of an American doctor in my truck. It would be difficult to explain—even to some idiot Haitian." He laughed and released the clutch. The truck leaped forward, spinning Toll aside.

Toll watched the Dominican disappear down a side street ahead. There was no doubt Antonio knew where he was going. Since Toll did not, he knew it was time to get out of the area in a hurry.

17

The feeling of being alone can come on suddenly or emerge slowly like the smallest gnat entrapped in the hairs on the back of the leg—denied at first and then acknowledged with an insistence that is overwhelming. Commander Toll felt the loneliness amid the line of native Haitian women as soon as the truck had departed.

After walking for about twenty minutes, he saw the entrance to a stately residence, enclosed by a high wall. There were no guards at the entrance and, conforming to Duvalier's power rationing, no post lights to welcome the visitor or to identify the occupant. Its stature and wealth suggested to Toll it was one of the expensive resorts Antonio had pointed out to him on entering the town. Toll debated with himself as he walked along the edge of the long, winding driveway toward the large stone house that occupied the top of the hill. He argued that a straight approach to the front door would no doubt bring a butler who, when he heard the visitor speaking English with an American accent, would call the owner. The back door would lead only to the servants who would assume he was a hitchhiker or a beggar and reject him before he had had an opportunity to explain.

Toll walked as quietly as he could without appearing to be sneaking along. It was still quite dark and the details of the mansion could not be seen clearly, although Toll estimated there had to be twenty to thirty rooms in the three-storied structure. The grounds were well kept and the grass was cut to golf course precision. Whoever lived there had money enough to employ full-time gardeners, Toll reasoned, although by Haitian standards such services might be cheap. Toll pictured the owner as a wealthy import-export representative, who would speak French but understand English. Toll knew his opening lines would have to be direct and yet free of any hint of danger. He

172

would have to demonstrate need without appearing desperate. He decided to tell the man that he was an American separated from his traveling group and robbed by three black men down the road. If the man bought his story, Toll would ask him directions to the Hôpital Albert Schweitzer and claim that was where his group had gone. This would give him an opening to say he was a doctor, thereby disarming the owner even further. With a little more luck, Toll convinced himself, he could expect the wealthy owner to have one of the servants drive him to the hospital. Toll would ask the man not to mention his impromptu visit or to report the robbery to either the Haitian or American authorities, since it would only serve as an embarrassment to the church that supported the hospital. The owner would, of course, accept this reasoning, and Toll's illegal status in the country would remain undetected. Toll couldn't find a flaw in his smooth scenario and began to walk a little more boldly toward the door.

There was a single small light over a large brass plate to the right of the massive double doors at the entrance. The house was totally silent. No dog growled, no man grunted, as Dr. Toll stepped confidently onto the big front porch, oblivious to the click of his own heels on the polished stone, and reached for the bell. Somewhere deep within the entranceway a rich set of chimes began to work its way through the assigned notes, Toll ignored the first notes but with the striking of the fourth, fifth, and sixth notes in rapid succession, the tune challenged Toll's mind with an insistence that approached panic. The doorbell was playing "God Bless America"!

Hard footsteps approached the door from within. A chain was unhooked on the inside of the door with bold authority. Another clack released a bolt mechanism and the door was thrown open with military precision. In the doorway stood a United States Marine in full uniform.

"Yes, sir!" The Marine insisted rather than asked.

Toll looked at the brass plate again and forced his eyes to focus on the lettering despite the dim lighting. The sign said, "Embassy of the United States of America."

Toll looked at the big Marine for a moment and said nothing. He felt like a fly on the edge of a giant web. He did not want to meet the spider inside.

"Scuza," Toll said, bowing slightly and reaching for an

unfamiliar accent. "Dis is da 'talian consulate, no? I'm-a-want-a see da man about-a some papers and-a—"

"*This* is the United States embassy," the Marine announced in a withering tone that simultaneously reaffirmed the Monroe Doctrine, the Bill of Rights, and, for all he knew, Tippecanoe and Tyler too. The Marine, twenty-seven years old, with medals and a Purple Heart, was from Topeka, Kansas. He had never heard an Italian accent outside of the movies and a televised ad for frozen pizza. And while he was willing to give his life in an attempt to save the ambassador from an armed attack by terrorists or to rescue the secret code books from a raging fire or assume any other heroic role his fantasies identified, he had no time for this idiot.

"... an' I'm-a-need a stamp or someting like-a dat on da paper da man at da refinery give me to bring to—"

"The consulate of Italy, sir, is located in Port-au-Prince. The Italian consulate will open for business at oh-nine-hundred, sir. Thank you for calling." The Marine closed the door on the still jabbering Toll with visible discourtesy and with no offer of additional help.

Outside the door Dr. Toll sighed the deepest sigh of his life, glanced at the heavens, and returned to the highway.

By daybreak he had reached the squalid outskirts of Port-au-Prince. The affluence of the hills near Pétionville was quickly swallowed by abject poverty and slum. Gone was the cool mountain air and the scent of flowers; it was replaced by a heavier air that spoke of pigs and garbage and diesel and industry. The native housing testified to ingenuity rather than design, with mismatched boards scavenged from other structures crudely nailed together. Deeper into the city, toward the magnificent but underdeveloped harbor, the architecture exhibited an additional schizophrenia. Scattered throughout was a hodgepodge of Chinese pagodas, Indian mosques, and ugly Victorian structures. Some of these served as dwellings for the international population that tolerated the hot, dirty downtown, while others became offices for aggressive tradespeople from around the globe.

Toll felt increasingly uncomfortable in Port-au-Prince. If challenged, he knew he would be unable to convince any of Duvalier's men of his mission or of his innocence. Papa Doc's hold on the presidency was based in terror and strong-arm tactics enforced by several thousand Tontons Macoutes who were either blindly loyal to him or quickly eliminated. He paid them "personally" with funds expropriated from the general treasury and used them to extort citizens and foreign businessmen alike to feed his coffers. Between Duvalier and his henchmen there was, at best, a delicate balance that would in time crumble and fall. But for the moment their terrifying presence, heightened by their Baron Samedi appearance—business suits, snap-brim hats, dark glasses, and automatic pistols—was sufficient to keep the public at bay.

Toll wished it was as simple as buying an airline ticket under an assumed name and flying to Miami; but he had no exit documents and he knew that an extremely burned Fahey would have every airport and harbor covered. His disappearance from Santo Domingo would be more than Fahey could stand. Even worse, Toll was now AWOL, and would be the object of a naval search as well. He had no doubt that when captured, he would be turned over to Fahey's men for "further questioning." Toll knew then that his escape from Santo Domingo had destroyed whatever security he had enjoyed as a naval officer. He was, at last, totally on his own.

He spent most of the day carefully wandering around the city, avoiding everyone and trying not to think. The American tourists wore flowered shirts and carried cameras around their necks as an international sign. They also were seldom alone and carried straw shopping bags stuffed with ebony carvings and native paintings. Toll longed to ask for their help, but could not risk their willingness to become involved in his plight.

Toll made his way toward the municipal market. It was a teeming center where everyone was overwhelmed by the pungent odors that wafted from the stalls vending fish, chickens, leather goods, straw baskets, and overripe fruits. For Toll its crowd provided a margin of safety—he assumed that the Tontons Macoutes and the CIA would seek better-smelling assignments.

He paused now and then among the rows of stalls to inspect the goods on display, shaking off the anxious salesperson with a dispassionate shake of his head. The questions and sales pitches were in Creole, which Toll found totally baffling. At the end of a third row there was a stall that sold candles, lanterns, and oil lamps as substitutes for General Electric. The proprietor was obviously not Haitian. Neither was his only customer. Dr. Toll watched them from a short distance as they debated the price of a thick, squat, yellowish candle the young white woman held in her hands. She examined it like an entomologist on a field trip. From across the crowded aisle Toll could not hear what they were saying, but the Armenian shopkeeper bobbed and shrugged, offering other candles and smiling widely beneath his black mustache. The woman was in her thirties and was dressed in a coarse but comfortable white dress. She was not pretty, but compared to the Haitian women of the marketplace, she became better looking every moment as Toll continued to watch her. It may have been her ankles, a little too slim for the white shoes she wore, or maybe it was her blond hair, cut short against the heat and held back along one side to show her delicate ear. Or maybe it was the fact that she was unmistakably white while the shopkeeper was olive and everyone else was very black which kept Toll's eyes riveted on her. He watched her reject two more candles before he knew that some sort of contact with her had become unavoidable. She had turned and had seen him across the aisle, a little closer than before, standing in front of a shop filled with grotesque brass utensils from India. With his back turned toward the metal merchant and his gaze fixed on the activity in the candle seller's shop, it was clear to the woman that this strange white man was interested in her. She allowed their eyes to meet a moment too long before she abruptly turned to the candle man and began to search her black shiny handbag. The Armenian smiled in anticipation of a sale.

Toll threaded his way across the aisle to the candle stall and stood near one of the low, boxlike counters. He appeared to be examining one of the candles. The shopkeeper spotted him instantly.

"Une chandelle?" he asked in a heavy, non-Gallic accent.

"Oh—no—thank you," Toll said. "I was just looking at your fine products."

The woman caught the English words instantly. She stared at the doctor and their eyes met for another moment before she spoke.

"Some of them are quite lovely," she said to Toll. She smiled at him disarmingly. She wore no makeup and looked quite attractive in a plain and wholesome way Toll found appealing. There was something in her attitude that Toll found more than friendly. She could have been one of those people who come to the door on Saturdays to quote the Bible or who stop travelers in airports to give away poorly printed cards promising eternal life. Her eyes held more than a sparkle or a gleam. In them there was an undeniable fervor. He fought an impulse to back off.

"What are they for?" he asked, searching for something to say.

"Why, to light up the room, of course," she said simply.

"You're an American," Toll said, unable to identify her flat accent.

"Yes, I am. And so are you, I gather."

"Yes, I'm from..." He caught himself at the last moment. "...the Midwest." It would not be smart to give away too many facts to an American woman he knew so little about. His affair with Pam Fisher at Bethesda had taught him that.

"Really!" she responded, coming closer and holding out her hand. "I'm from Ohio, originally."

"And what are you doing here?"

"In Haiti?" She threw her head aside slightly as to identify the whole country at once. "I live here now. This is my life's work." From her enthusiasm there was no mistake she meant it to be an announcement of more than just work. It was obviously a vocation.

Toll took her hand and shook it gently. Her hand was not as soft as he expected and her arm was wrinkled from the sun. The shopkeeper busied himself with an impromptu rearrangement of some fat candles in another box.

"I've been here for several years," she continued, slowly withdrawing her hand. "I work at the hospital with the others. My group is called the Disciples of God, although there are others at the hospital too. It's more or less a mixed group, you might say."

"You're a nun?" he asked without challenge. Her coarse white dress did not look like a classical nun's habit and there were no Christian emblems on it that he could see.

"No, Mr....ah..."

"Anderson," Toll supplied.

"Mr. Anderson. My name is Barbara Collins. And I'm not a Catholic nun. As I said, I am a member of a small group called the Disciples of God. We came here from Ohio to join the work started by Dr. Mellon. You've heard of him?"

He shook his head gently. "No, Miss Collins, I'm afraid I haven't. Excuse me."

"Oh, that's quite all right, Mr. Anderson. We are, after all, not here for fame or glory. We are only here to serve." She made the announcement in such a simple way that it was impossible to doubt her.

"And *whom* do you serve?"

"These poor Haitians," she said, sweeping her hand toward the crowd in the market. "I'm a nurse."

"Is your hospital in Port-au-Prince?"

"No. The hospital is in Deschapelles, about three hours from here, near the Artibonite Valley." She gestured to a place somewhere far beyond the candle shop.

A chorus of bells rang in his ears. He suddenly knew that she was not an agent planted by Fahey, not a vacationing schoolteacher, not a tourist looking for a willing male to satisfy repressed midwestern desires. She was an angel, appearing to whisk him off to the Albert Schweitzer Hospital! His heart quickened with excitement. At last he knew where he could hide for a while and forget about Fahey and his relentless search for the dance card.

"Could you...take me there? To the Albert Schweitzer Hospital?" he asked. "I would like to see your work."

She looked at him with ever brightening eyes. She had been prepared to accept the unexpected gifts God sent her way. "Would you really like to see our hospital?" she asked.

"Very much," Toll said, taking her hand again. "I don't know how to explain this exactly," he stammered, hoping to sound genuine, "but it is as if I were suddenly... suddenly..."

"Called?" she supplied excitedly.

"Yes! That's it! It's as if I were being called. Somehow I think you understand, Miss Collins." He squeezed her hand gently but not sensuously.

"The station wagon is just down the street," she said. She made no attempt to take her hand back. "Let me pay for these candles and I will be ready to leave."

"Are the candles for your religious ceremonies?" he asked.

She laughed a little and withdrew her hand to fumble with her purse. "No, Mr. Anderson, nothing quite so romantic. We simply have no electricity in many of our cabins and candles are cheaper to buy in the market than they are to make. The people in Deschapelles are so poor they have nothing to spare and no way to make candles or lamps."

"I'll carry them to the car," he offered, feeling a little awkward.

"That's very kind of you, Mr. Anderson. Will you be able to stay overnight at the hospital? There will be no way back before tomorrow."

"Perhaps longer than that," Toll said, picking up the box of candles.

"God will show us," she said.

Toll was not convinced that God saw them get into the station wagon, but the Tontons Macoutes on the corner did.

18 The drive from Port-au-Prince to Deschapelles was dreary, and because of the poverty-stricken areas through which they passed, Dr. Toll became increasingly depressed. The people who inhabited the Artibonite Valley, the region surrounding the Albert Schweitzer Hospital, could have quadrupled their incomes and still have remained destitute. In their struggle for bare existence they had stripped the land of natural resources, destroyed the forests, and triggered massive erosions that scarred the hillsides. The ragged little plots from which they attempted to coax vegetables mocked them while malnutrition shortened their lives to an average of less than forty years. Disease triumphed in the wake of malnourishment, and the people flocked to the American hospital and its invariable welcome, regardless of their inability to pay. Few of the patients were able to offer money although some brought a chicken or a piece of crude handicraft as an offering. Too often the pig or chicken tendered as payment was equally in need of medical care and infested with parasites, making its value as food somewhat dubious.

The hospital had been founded by William Larimer Mellon in 1947 after he had read a magazine article about Dr. Albert Schweitzer. Like Schweitzer, who gave up a distinguished career as a musician and theologian to begin his medical studies in his forties, Larry, a grandnephew of financier Andrew Mellon and heir to part of the Gulf Oil fortune, gave up his string of Arizona cattle ranches and became a physician. Mellon financed most of the hospital construction out of his personal fortune and continued to reach into his pocket to make up the difference between the mounting costs of medical care and the pitiful contributions the natives could afford. Over 250,000 people inhabited the Artibonite Valley and Mellon's hospital was their only medical facility.

As a physician himself Papa Doc had looked away when malcontents within his central government urged him to close or nationalize the American hospital. He knew he would never match the service provided by the dedicated staff of the Hôpital Albert Schweitzer, nor could he hope to come up with the half-million-dollar-a-year deficit to run the place. Begrudgingly tolerant of the Mellons' efforts to treat the sick, Duvalier offered little support.

Barbara Collins ran the history of the hospital by Dr. Toll with obvious pride and flawless detail. She had apparently found her life's work at last. She had come from a moderately wealthy manufacturing family and lived with a spiritual dissatisfaction for years until she was introduced to an active church and through them to the medical mission in Haiti. She had not embraced the same denomination Schweitzer or Mellon had, but the hospital colony was receptive to several different Christian denominations. The common ingredient was dedication, self-sacrifice, and love of life.

Toll was afraid to tell her about his plight and decided to maintain his identity as Mr. Anderson throughout the trip. His simple curiosity about their work was sufficient for her. As far as he could tell, she had no interest in politics, Haitian or American. Wild stories about the CIA and Fahey would certainly seem inadequate when compared to God's work.

They arrived at the Hôpital Albert, as many of them called it, at dusk. Nurse Collins pointed out several of the more prominent buildings, all hand-constructed of native stone and painted white against the tropical sun, before showing him to a small wooden structure that served as guest quarters for visiting missionaries and doctors. The permanent medical staff was small, but from time to time other physicians came from Europe and the United States to donate a few months, cleansing their souls and slightly improving the native health.

Toll found his room simple but adequate. There was a bed with clean sheets, a small writing desk, and a King James Bible. The building had been designed for four visitors, but he was the only guest.

After sunset Toll could see the flickering lights from campsites that native families had set at the edge of the hospital grounds. They came to stay near a loved one who

had been admitted as a patient, or to be first in line when
the clinic opened in the morning.

The sight of the bed reminded him he had not slept
since he had left Santo Domingo. He slipped off his shoes
and stretched out on the sheet. He slept so soundly he
didn't hear the aged black woman enter his room with a
tray of sandwiches and the pot of tea Nurse Collins had
thoughtfully sent over to him.

The next day the sun streamed in through his window,
dazzling the white, smooth walls and illuminating the
native painting of Christ that hung opposite the bed. The
artist had made Jesus look part Creole and the colors were
garish, but the traditional peaceful expression had been
captured. Toll felt uncomfortable in his clothes and wished
he had taken his shirt off before going to sleep. He found
the shower and survived the shock of the cold water and
strong soap that stung his skin, reminding him of hospital
disinfectant. As he lathered his abdomen, he paused to
finger the appendectomy scar. As usual there was no sign
of inflammation. The dance card rested comfortably in its
subcutaneous vault. Still alone in the guest quarters, he
padded back to his room, wrapped in a coarse towel. As
he opened the door, he recognized someone else had been
there. The untouched tray had been replaced by a small
pot of coffee and a croissant with honey. He was very
hungry and consumed the roll in two bites as he poured
the coffee. Behind the pot there was a simple white a card
that said:

> Good morning. God loves all of us.
> The director would like to see you
> in his office at your convenience.
> Building three, first floor.
> Barbara Collins, R.N.

Toll shook his clothing before dressing, hoping to make
them less uncomfortable. Out of habit and paranoia he
checked his pockets and found everything intact. He
wasn't sure if he was expected to make the bed, but he
smoothed the sheet anyway. He would later find that
housekeepers were one of the few categories of workers
that were never in short supply at the hospital. Many of

the native women contributed housework in lieu of other payment for treatment given to their children or husbands.

As Toll emerged from the guesthouse, he saw a small crowd of Haitian women standing near the entrance of a long, low building that served as the screening clinic. Many of the women held babies in their arms and chattered in Creole as they waited. A black woman in a white uniform seemed to be taking their names and other information on a clipboard. The women were young and underfed and all the babies looked sick. Toll continued to watch them as he walked into the central area of the hospital compound. The grounds were well kept and flower gardens gave the place a pleasant appearance; no doubt the male counterpart of the voluntary housekeeping.

At the far end of the lawn there was a gleaming white chapel. The front doors were open and it was evident a service had ended only a short time before. Inexplicably, Toll felt an urge to enter the place and say some sort of a prayer for his safe deliverance from Fahey, but he repressed it and continued to look for building number three.

To the right of the chapel, halfway down the quadrangle, there was a rectangular building that would have to be the administrative offices. The doorway led into a spacious foyer with mahogany furniture, tile floors, and portraits on the wall. On the opposite wall hung the obligatory portrait of Duvalier, with long black formal coat, thick glasses, and a myopic, porcine expression that seemed all too appropriate. Toll paused to look at the pictures before he approached the offices along the short corridor. A bilingual sign identified the second office as that of the director. Toll's knock was answered by a pleasant male voice from within.

"Entrez."

Toll opened the door slowly and politely. "Excuse me," Toll said, "I believe the director would like to see me?"

A man in a white clinical uniform stood up from behind the desk and smiled widely. He was older and darker than Toll had expected. He did not fit the image Toll had mentally prepared for an heir to the Gulf Oil fortune. This man looked like a foreign graduate serving his residency in any city hospital in the United States.

"Come in, Mr. Anderson," the man said, extending his hand and coming around from behind the desk. The hand was thick, blunt, pink-palmed, and moist. He was unpretentious and cordial. Toll guessed his age to be fifty and his national origin one of the Latin Americas.

"Miss Collins sent you our customary invitation with your breakfast, but I'm afraid she did not know Dr. Mellon had to leave the hospital on urgent business. I am Dr. Arturo Fuentes. I am the assistant director." He shook Toll's hand warmly and directed him to a heavy wooden chair in front of the desk.

"Bill Anderson," Toll said, retrieving his hand and returning the smile.

"I hope you slept well, Mr. Anderson." Dr. Fuentes returned to the high-backed swivel chair behind the desk.

"Very well, thank you."

"We all rest from time to time," Fuentes sighed. "But the work here never ends. You have visited us before?"

"No, Dr. Fuentes. This is my first visit. You seem to have established a wonderful hospital."

"The hospital owes its existence entirely to Dr. Mellon and his generous wife, Mr. Anderson. Without them there would be nothing here."

"Miss Collins told me their story as we drove here from Port-au-Prince," Toll said. He glanced around the room and recognized many familiar medical titles on the bookshelves. Along one wall there were photographs of young men and women in white coats.

"She is a very dedicated woman," Fuentes said.

"From Ohio," Toll recalled. "Where are *you* from, Dr. Fuentes?"

"Originally from Nicaragua, but now I consider myself a child of God and a citizen of the world. And you, Mr. Anderson?"

He paused for a moment, aiming for consistency. Fuentes had no doubt already talked with Nurse Collins. Toll had kept his conversation with the nurse light and noncommittal, and Fuentes seemed friendly enough; still, it was time to be careful.

"I'm also from the Midwest," Toll said. "From Indiana."

"Indiana!" Fuentes repeated. "I have never been there myself, but I have always been interested in the car races they have there each year."

"Have you spent some time in the United States, Dr. Fuentes?"

"I completed my residency in internal medicine at Georgetown University Hospital. In Washington, D.C.," he added for clarity.

The mere mention of Washington, D.C., caused Toll to double his guard. Thoughts of Fahey and his devious Agency raced through his mind. He had heard the CIA had programs at some of the major universities to identify dissident foreign students and to cultivate some of them as informants or unwitting agents when they returned home.

"That's an excellent school," Toll commented flatly.

"You're familiar with Georgetown?"

"No, not really. As a matter of fact I'm not very familiar with Washington, except what I read in the papers. Too many politicians." He smiled to make the remark sound as casual as possible.

"Politicians are everywhere," Fuentes agreed. "And I'm afraid your Washington officials do not confine their interests to the United States."

"That's for sure. Have some of them visited this hospital?" Toll wished he had a cigarette to puff in a nonchalant manner, but none had been offered and there were no ashtrays in view.

"We get American visitors frequently, Mr. Anderson. Many of them are doctors who come to work with us for short periods of time, but every American government official who visits Port-au-Prince comes to see us or expresses some interest in our work. I think they get questions about us from their constituents. We are very well known in some circles, you see."

"I gathered that from Nurse Collins," Toll said. "But tell me, Dr. Fuentes, these American doctors that come to work. Are they sent here by some organization, or..."

"Usually, yes. But sometimes we are blessed with a doctor on his vacation who simply walks in, likes what he sees, and volunteers his services. We take help from anyone."

"And they practice medicine here? There is no problem of a license or credentials?" Toll asked without sounding alarmed or too interested.

"Mr. Anderson," Fuentes began, "look around you. This is Haiti's Artibonite Valley. Who would concern himself with formalities if the volunteer was competent and willing to work?"

"That's interesting," Toll said. "I, too, find myself fascinated by your hospital. I had hoped to meet Dr. Mellon and discuss working with you for a short time."

"Oh? You have medical training?"

"No formal training, of course," Toll said. "I mean, I am not a doctor, or anything like that. But I have worked in hospital laboratories as an assistant."

"You're a technologist?" The doctor's eyes displayed sudden enthusiasm and Toll recognized it.

"Not a *registered* technologist. Not ASCP, you understand. I worked in small hospitals and for a while thought I would like to pursue more formal training, but circumstances did not permit it." Toll knew the ASCP registry was too easily checked, even from a remote village in Haiti.

"Keeping laboratory personnel is always a problem for us here," Fuentes sighed. "We offer a very small salary and our equipment is never up to date. I'm afraid the laboratory people are easily bored."

"I'd like to see your lab," Toll suggested.

"You would? It's very small, but I would be happy to show it to you," Dr. Fuentes said, rising from his seat. "On the way I'll show you the rest of the hospital."

"I hope it's not too much trouble, Doctor."

Dr. Fuentes paused at the doorway. "Mr. Anderson, we are proud of this little hospital. We enjoy every opportunity to show it to visitors. We owe much of our support to visitors who return home and continue to think about us."

"I'm not much of a potential donor," Toll said.

"That remains to be seen, Mr. Anderson. If you are as familiar with laboratory work as I hope you are, your arrival here will be considered nothing less than heaven sent."

"Do you have a pathologist?" Toll asked casually.

"Not full time. We have periodic visits from some American pathologists and we operate our lab with technicians. As a matter of fact we have only two native lab assistants at the moment." Fuentes ushered Toll out of the office and down the corridor toward the front door.

As they walked along the well-swept sidewalk toward the tiny lab building, both of them offered silent thanks to God, but for entirely different reasons.

"Well, Dr. Fuentes," Toll said as they reached the lab, "I've never thought of myself as a missionary, but I'm sure you'll find me competent in the lab. Who knows? Maybe this will turn out to be one of my more interesting vacations."

"Oh," Fuentes commented pleasantly. "You're on vacation." He was apparently relieved to get the information.

"Yes—from my hospital job. You didn't ask me about that."

Fuentes looked into his eyes and adopted a serious expression. "Mr. Anderson, there are some questions we have learned never to ask. Where a man is from exactly, why he is here, and if he is married. In those respects we are similar to the Foreign Legion."

Toll smiled gently. "I think we're going to get along just fine, Dr. Fuentes."

19 It took George Toll only a few weeks to whip the laboratory into shape. It suffered from small hospital syndrome: a lethargic attitude that creeps into the thought processes of the medical staff and from there percolates to all personnel levels until everyone is convinced that nothing can be done to improve the situation. Unfortunately small hospital syndrome is not isolated to small hospitals.

The lab at the Hôpital Albert Schweitzer was as well equipped as any isolated American hospital of comparable size. It offered CBC's, blood chemistries, urinalysis, basic serology, standard bacteriology, and a mechanism for tissue examination. Without a permanent pathologist daily microscopic examination of surgical tissue was seldom available. Specimens were either shipped out or else diagnosed by the surgeon according to gross appearances alone. Toll would have to be very careful not to appear too knowledgeable.

Thérèse and Marie, the two Haitian lab technicians, were dedicated to their jobs and could have functioned as lab assistants anywhere. Thérèse had received part of her training in a French-Canadian hospital outside Montreal and had considered joining the Grey Nuns until she became pregnant by one of the orderlies. She had spontaneously aborted and had returned to Port-au-Prince in personal disgrace. She had told only her confessor about it, but the experience had been enough to make her reconsider her vocation. She came to the Hôpital Albert with deeply rooted guilt and thereafter applied all of her energies to the penitential service to the sick. She was in her early thirties and her dedication far exceeded her technical abilities.

Marie was locally trained. She was forty-eight and had wanted to be a nurse, but had proven to be too unreliable. At times her calculations of medical doses were downright dangerous, and she often neglected to notice changes in patients' symptoms. As a result she had been "promoted" to the laboratory and confined to dipstick urinalysis and elementary hematology. In that capacity she became significantly less of a threat to the patients.

The technicians accepted Mr. Anderson and his knowledge of laboratory procedures without question. They spoke almost no English, and since Toll's French was less than poor, they conversed only in labese, a technical language of chemical symbols, technical directions, and metrics. This inability to communicate socially made it easier for Toll to maintain his anonymity and to remain on a high professional plane with the two women despite daily contact. In a matter of a few weeks the medical staff was pleased with Toll's improvements. A few of them had attempted to pry into his past as they offered praise for his work but avoided further inquiry when answers were vague or withheld.

Fuentes had moved Toll from the guest quarters to a tiny cabin that was once occupied by an Irish priest who had come originally to help but who had found greater comfort in his personal supply of whiskey than in patient contact. The cabin had been built especially for the priest since he did not mingle well with the others, and after his departure for British Guiana it had remained empty. It suited George Toll perfectly.

Barbara Collins saw Mr. Anderson as a gift from heaven and asked no questions. At first she saw him only as a child of God, but later she found he was a man. She often brought him little things, like a flower for his desk, or an extra piece of cake from the kitchen in the late afternoon. Barbara usually offered to take him on her trips into Port-au-Prince to pick up supplies, and after a few weeks Toll had accepted. The ride had provided him with an opportunity to get away from the hospital for the day and to chat pleasantly with another American. In Port-au-Prince, while she busied herself with her errands, he looked around the city. He gradually became more relaxed around the ever present Tontons Macoutes. He tried to look European, had only shrugged whenever asked directions by a tourist. He would have continued to go regularly to Port-au-Prince with Barbara if she had not taken him to the airport one day, without warning, to pick up two American doctors from California.

They had come to perform volunteer orthopedics for a couple of weeks, and their small talk on the way back to the hospital had almost given Toll a stroke. They had brought steel hip prostheses, recovered at autopsies in the States, to replace tubercular joints in children, and were excited by the opportunity to do the cases. Toll didn't know either of them, but his anxiety hadn't escaped Nurse Collins's attention, and she skillfully intervened when he awkwardly tried to answer their questions with meaningless but consistent answers.

When the orthopedic men left to return to the United States, Barbara came to his cabin late in the evening.

"I am sorry those orthopods made you nervous," she said. "It was all my fault. I should have told you they were coming."

"Why? I have nothing to hide."

She smiled sweetly at him and sat on the edge of his bed. "You do, but whatever it is, it's none of my business."

Toll searched her face for a challenge. There was none there. She was sitting close to him, closer than ever before.

"I would never do anything to hurt you, Bill." Her face was no longer that of a missionary nurse. She was a woman at last.

"Barbara, I..."

She silenced him with a sudden passionate kiss that told him why she had come to the cabin. He put his arms around her and held her close. It had been so long since he had held a woman. He wanted her desperately. She yielded to him with an open hunger that matched his own. Without speaking, they fumbled with each other's clothes until, still kissing, still touching with trembling hands, they lay together, naked and unashamed. Barbara's needs cried out from years of repression as she climaxed again and again beneath him. He bit his lip, denying himself to make it last, the sweat rolling down his face and dropping on her like exotic perfume. Suddenly, when he knew he could stand it no longer, he arched his back, held her tightly, and emitted a long, aching cry as he burst inside her. Her passion doubled in generous response as she tried to take all of him, forever. It was as if there would never be another chance. His body begged him to stop for that peace that follows orgasm, but his passion drove him on, matching her hungry movements until without warning she began to twitch and to emit a different sound. She tried to call out to him, but her speech was slurred and her face was drawn to one side.

"My God, Barbara, what is it?" He rolled to one side, panting and still erect.

"My arm—my leg," she lisped, obviously frightened.

He looked at her frantically for a moment, wondering if she had had a stroke. "What do you feel?" he asked.

"My arm, Bill. It tingles. It's numb." She tried to open her eyes widely but the lids responded unevenly.

Toll's anxiety was suddenly replaced by a devilish grin. "I know what you need," he said, getting up from the bed. He went to the desk and pulled out the lower drawer.

"Bill!" she slurred. "I'm afraid!"

He was still laughing when he came back to the bed carrying a paper bag. "Here," he said, "put this over your head and breathe deeply. You're hyperventilating."

In an instant she knew he was right. She had blown away the carbon dioxide in her blood and gone into tetany. After a few minutes of rebreathing her own expired air inside the paper bag, she felt fine and began to laugh.

"You need to make love more often," he suggested. He dropped the paper bag on the floor and cradled her face in his hands.

"We both do," she said.

"We will," he promised.

"But the others can never know." Her eyes registered her concern.

"It will be ours alone." Toll held the nurse close to him again and looked at the wall behind her. Her breasts pressed against his chest. She felt good in his arms. She had taken him a million miles from Fahey, but now he was back. Somehow, he vowed, he would keep her from them. There would be no more Pam Fishers, no matter what it took. He knew he could never share his problem with Barbara Collins without sharing the danger.

"Bill," she said softly on his shoulder, "I don't know why you came here, but I'm awfully glad you did."

"I came because I came."

"It's more than that. But I promise I'll never ask."

Toll felt her tears on his back. He held her tightly

against him and did not look at her face. "Maybe someday
you can know," he sighed.

In the morning before dawn she slipped out of his cabin
and took the long, safe way to her own quarters. They had
begun to share something and she wanted to make it last.

The director of the hospital, Dr. Mellon, remained in
the United States for several months for postgraduate
training. By the time he returned to Haiti, Toll had weath-
ered in at the hospital and Fuentes was able to offer to
the director his own theories about Anderson's shy behavior. Fuentes had decided Mr. Anderson had been the
victim of a terrible personal tragedy or a disappointment
in love. Fuentes suggested that if Anderson wanted to be
left alone, it was a small price to pay for his outstanding
skills. The director had happily agreed. For the first time
the lab was performing accurate cardiac enzyme studies
and the new quality-control program had raised everyone's
confidence in the routine tests.

As the months slipped by, Toll became increasingly
comfortable with his new home. No one bothered him, and
when American doctors visited the hospital, he was never
introduced or forced to participate in the small social
events held in their honor. His isolation had been accepted
by the whole staff.

The *revolución* in the Dominican Republic had re-
solved itself, reducing the CIA threat to Toll. The news of
America's problems trickled in with understandable delay,
and was generally ignored by the medical missionaries.
Toll followed some of the events in newspapers and magazines left by visitors and wondered what it all meant.
There was racial unrest in many of the American cities
and people died in flaming riots in a place called Watts.
The war in Vietnam escalated again and again while college students clamored for its end or Lyndon Johnson's
head, or both. The United States sent astronauts closer
and closer to the moon and the Israelis shot up the Arabs
in a six-day war. Hijackers diverted airliners and terrorists blew up airports as the world watched and worried.
With that much unrest, Toll began to see the Albert
Schweitzer Hospital as more than a refuge from Fahey
and the CIA. It had become a haven from an insane world.
The widespread desertions from the American armed

forces and the draft-card burners helped Toll see his own absence from the Navy as less important. He began to convince himself that no one would maintain sufficient interest in his disappearance to continue the chase. Soon, he hoped, the Bay of Pigs would become a distant memory in the minds of a few thousand Cubans in Miami. With a little luck Fahey might even forget the dance card.

Toll was, of course, totally wrong. Fahey had been transferred to the Latin American desk in Washington, and since Toll's escape from Santo Domingo, not one day had passed without his face appearing in the agent's mind. For Fahey, Toll represented a continuing threat, a nagging embarrassment. Toll's image invaded his dreams, diverted his thoughts, and gnawed at his peace of mind like a cancer. He subtly and habitually included the doctor in all of his plans and, whenever it was safe, added his photo to official searches for other subjects. Instinct had told him Toll was still alive, and logic had convinced him he was no longer in the Dominican Republic.

For the first several months Fahey was sure Toll had not risked a return to the United States—AWOL from the Navy, a fugitive from the Agency, with no family and few friends, Fahey knew Toll would have no place to hide in the States. Central America or Mexico, Fahey assumed, or perhaps one of the smaller islands in the Caribbean. Wherever he had fled, Fahey vowed from his desk in Washington to wait and watch. He knew Toll would evaluate the political climate until he felt it safe enough to come home. And then, by God, Fahey promised himself, Toll and the dance card would be his!

Meanwhile, George Toll built up quite a library of classics in paperback, which he read and reread. He had found an inner peace in his voluntary isolation, which he guarded jealously: visitors, other than Barbara, became intruders, and all signs of his early feelings of loneliness vanished. The dance card and the CIA were always just beneath the surface of his consciousness, however, and sometimes when Steinbeck or Hemingway or Faulkner failed to hold his attention, he found himself wondering how long he could hold out. He often wanted to reopen his appendectomy and destroy the dance card, but he knew that would not solve his problem. His problem was Fahey, and Toll had no way of knowing where in the world Fahey might be, or even if he still existed.

The bright, unrelenting Haitian sun rose to fill another humid morning. The seasons were blurred by the tropical setting. As usual he got up before his alarm went off. The birds and the insects had already begun their chorale, and from the sunlight streaming in from the window, Toll knew the day would be hot until the afternoon rains came to cool another unblemished evening.

He showered quickly and dressed in a clean shirt and a pair of simple white duck pants the hospital had been happy to supply him. Fuentes had feared Mr. Anderson might feel too clinical in whites, but they reminded Toll of his naval uniform and he was happy to wear them.

Toll walked to the staff dining room and took his usual seat. A pleasantly formal black man brought him coffee and began to prepare a soft-boiled egg without comment. There was seldom a variation in Anderson's breakfast requests. Dr. Fuentes had already finished his plate of rice, black beans, and bits of fried sausage and egg. Toll had forgotten the Spanish name for the mixture long before the unpleasant flavor. Breakfast with Dr. Fuentes was one of the few social contacts Toll permitted himself.

"Bonjour," Fuentes said. His French was not much better than Dr. Toll's, and the greeting had become a small joke.

"Buenos días," Toll returned.

"A good night?"

"As usual, thank you."

"We will have interesting visitors today," Fuentes announced, swirling the coffee in the bottom of his cup.

"Oh? Americans or Tontons?" Toll asked lightly. In fact, Duvalier's men seldom visited the hospital despite their harassment of every other enterprise in the country.

"No, nothing from Papa Doc, thank God," Fuentes said. "And by the way, some say he may have had a heart attack..."

Toll commented silently with eyes and mouth.

"...I wouldn't mind if the old bastard died, but you know what would follow," Fuentes continued.

"Chaos."

"At best. No, the visitors today may be of particular interest to you."

"Why?" Toll nodded his appreciation to the steward for his egg already carefully cracked along the tip, protruding from the porcelain cup. He inserted the tip of his knife into the crack and began to incise the top portion of the shell like a neurosurgeon entering a patient's skull. Fuentes studied Anderson's deft moves with an appreciation undiminished by its daily performance.

"Because..." Fuentes said absently and slowly, more concerned with the removal of the egg shell than with his own words, "they...are...American...pathologists."

Dr. Toll stabbed his knife through the opposite side of the shell with uncharacteristic clumsiness. Fuentes frowned in disappointment and returned his attention to his coffee.

"Path—" Toll began before catching himself. "Oh," he added calmly. "That's nice. Where are they from?"

"Several places, I understand. They are a committee from the International Association of Pathologists. Do you know the organization?"

"University types mostly," Toll said, resuming his careful attack on the egg with a tiny spoon. "What do they want with us?"

"Something about tropical diseases or parasites, I don't know. They sent several letters to Dr. Mellon."

"Funny, he never mentioned it," Toll said nonchalantly.

"Since when have you cared who visits us, or who doesn't?" Fuentes asked with a chuckle. "You hardly ever show up to meet them. The director probably assumed you would not give a damn."

"Oh, I suppose he is right. But if they are Americans, I might know one or two of them." Toll inserted a small piece of butter and waited for it to melt on the still intact yoke.

"Maybe so. Would you like to see the list of their names?" Fuentes reached into the pocket of his white clinical jacket and handed Toll a folded letter.

Toll took the letter, opened it casually, and read it as he massaged the melting butter into the egg.

Dear Dr. Mellon:

This is to confirm the visit of the subcommittee on tropical medicine and parasitology of the International Association of Pathologists. As we have indicated previously, our inspection will have to be brief due to other commitments in Central America and in the Caribbean area. The Association is gratified by your offers of hospitality and I personally look forward to the opportunity to visit your outstanding hospital and to meeting you. As you know, part of our function is to identify and evaluate the nominees for our annual award in the field of tropical medicine research. I would be remiss if I did not mention that you are on this year's list.

Accompanying me will be Dr. Claude Poliak of the University of California, Dr. Joseph Burton from the Miami Institute for Tropical Medicine, and Dr. Henry Robinson from Emory.

None of us has visited Haiti before and we are looking forward to it. I will call you from Port-au-Prince when we have completed formalities there with the United States Consulate and representatives of President Duvalier.

Sincerely,

ALLAN WATKINS, M.D.
Associate Professor of Pathology
Duke University Medical Center

Toll put the letter on the table and repeated the names in his mind. Offhand, he did not recognize any of them. He had never studied at California, the Miami Institute, Emory, or Duke, but he knew how the professional pathologists liked to shift around, assuming new positions to raise their academic status and rank. It was entirely possible he had met one or more of them in a medical meeting, or in the service. The thought was upsetting, but he was determined not to show it.

"Know any of them?" Fuentes asked absently. He had hardly expected a lab tech like Anderson to know any of these pathology professors.

Toll shook his head slowly. "Can't say that I do." He poked at his egg and tried not to tremble. "When did you say they were coming?"

"About eleven. Miss Collins is picking them up at the airport now. They called from Port-au-Prince last night." Fuentes stood up and dabbed his mouth with his napkin.

"Well," he added, "I have to prepare some case files for our distinguished guests." He threw his eyes at the ceiling to show he was not really impressed.

"And I guess I'll clean up the lab a little. They will probably want to see it," Toll replied.

Dr. Fuentes smiled warmly. "How could you make it any better, Mr. Anderson. You have already reached perfection. At least for us."

Toll nodded with feigned impatience to dispose of the compliment. All he would need would be for one of those pathologists to recognize him and Fuentes would know why he had done such a good job with the lab.

"Encore du café, Monsieur Anderson?" the steward asked, offering the pot.

"No, thank you, Jean-Paul," Toll said absently. He rose from the table, his egg only half-eaten. "I am needed at the laboratory."

"Oui, monsieur," the steward said. He watched Toll leave the dining room, glanced at the egg, smelled it, and shrugged helplessly.

20 Toll hurried to the laboratory, examined the incoming blood and requests, and sent Thérèse to collect another sample on two patients. She had brought back the originals in the wrong tubes, allowing the blood to clot, making them unsuitable for the tests ordered. Marie had already started on the several small bottles of urine submitted for routine analysis. Toll spent several minutes flipping through the lab slips and was pleased to see that no tests had been requested that would require his personal attention.

"When you get the urine tests logged in, Marie, you may start on them alone. I am going to be out of the lab for a while this morning," he announced.

"Pardonnez-moi, monsieur?" she asked simply.

"Commencez. Start in. Get it?" He augmented his French with a few gestures toward the appropriate reagents.

"Ah, oui," Marie said, confused but smiling.

"There will be visitors," he said pointing to the clock on the lab bench near the microscope. "American doctors." He spoke slowly and slightly louder than he would have if Marie had understood English.

"La Visite?"

"Oui. Four American doctors." He circled his index fingers in front of his eyes and scanned the lab like Rommel surveying the African desert.

"Ah, oui!" she acknowledged.

"I must go and meet them," he said, shaking hands with himself and bobbing.

Marie shook her head. "H'okay," she announced confidently.

Toll gave the woman a little smile and walked out of the lab building. The lab was too conspicuous and too isolated to provide him with the slight advantage he needed.

He wanted to observe the four pathologists on arrival before they had a chance to see him.

He walked toward the center of the campus, still wondering where he should go. Suddenly a bell rang out from the abbreviated church steeple.

Toll confidently turned toward the chapel. He knew the director would not offend four visiting pathologists by presenting the chapel first and there was no chance the iconoclastic Fuentes would ever enter the door. The morning services had just finished, leaving the chapel empty for the rest of the day. The front door faced the main quadrangle, with the Administration Building in full view. The chapel would be perfect, he decided. He walked toward the building slow enough to allow stragglers to leave.

The chapel was moderately dark and seemed cooler than the other buildings. He saw no one inside as he closed the door quietly behind him. The chapel was carefully nondenominational, although the services were basically Christian. There were no crosses or stained-glass windows and the altar area was adorned only by a simple lectern. The services were not the bell-ringing, incense-burning sacrifices the Haitians preferred, but the presence of God could be easily imagined by the participants. If it provided nothing else, the simple chapel offered a quiet place apart from the medical activities for a moment of peace. Albert Schweitzer had awakened a reverence for life in the staff and to follow that simple belief, religious ritual was unnecessary if not repugnant.

Toll walked along the side aisle toward the main front door, avoiding the wooden chairs the founder provided instead of pews. According to his calculations it would be less than half an hour until the station wagon arrived. The inevitable greetings would take several minutes and that would give Toll time enough to evaluate the visitors.

He waited quietly, half-crouched behind the partly closed door, and studied the front of the Administration Building. After several minutes Fuentes came out, looked around, glanced at his watch, and went back inside. Toll was not the only one growing impatient. A fly whined above his head and took the hint to explore elsewhere when Toll swatted at with his hand. Around the hospital campus he could see the usual coming and going of staff and prospective patients. In most respects everything

seemed normal, with every promise of being as boring as
the day before.

Suddenly the station wagon pulled up in front of
Administration. Barbara got out from the driver's side as
Fuentes came out to open the rear door. Four men got out
of the car, each dressed in tropical suits, shirts open at the
necks, none wearing a hat. All but one man was white.
They each seemed to be over forty and one was probably
beyond sixty.

Hands were shaken and every face had a smile as introductions and greetings were exchanged with Fuentes
and Mellon. Toll wished he could hear what they were
saying, but the chapel was too far away. It was close
enough to see their faces, however, and Toll was relieved
he did not recognize any of them.

Suddenly Toll felt a hand on his shoulder. He stood up
quickly and faced the hospital chaplain.

"A moment of personal reflection, Mr. Anderson?" the
chaplain said. The man was seventy-five and had spent
most of his life in a small Baptist church in South Carolina
before retiring to the Hôpital Albert.

"Oh, hello, Mr. Cameron, I was just..."

"It's all right, Mr. Anderson," the chaplain said sooth-
ingly. "Every man must find a comfortable place for his
own conversation with God."

He glanced at the floor near Anderson's feet to see if
there might be some lost object the lab tech was searching
for. Cameron had known one old woman who preferred to
pray in a closet, but this was the first time he had seen
a man kneeling behind the front door of a chapel.

"I was just about to leave and my shoe felt loose," Toll
offered weakly. He did not know that Cameron had been
watching him for over five minutes before he decided to
say hello.

"I see," the chaplain said softly. He glanced out the door
and saw the visitors entering the Administration Building
with Dr. Fuentes.

"Some friends of yours?" he asked.

Toll glanced at the visitors and then at the chaplain.
"Not exactly," he said. "Dr. Fuentes said they were visiting
American pathologists and I—"

"And you are avoiding them."

"Well, not *avoiding*. I mean—"

"Let's just say you don't choose to rush out there and join the welcoming committee." Cameron smiled to show he was not attacking.

"I'm not much for visitors."

"I've noticed that, Mr. Anderson. Whenever someone shows up, you seem to have other things to do." He held up his hand as Toll tried to reply. "But don't misunderstand me, Mr. Anderson, there is nothing wrong with that. You have your reasons for not wanting to mingle with our visitors and I respect them. You are among friends here and as long as you are happy doing the Lord's work, you may do it in your own way. I may not understand fully, but I am sure He does."

"That's not it at all, Mr. Cameron. I've just never felt comfortable with strangers. It takes me a while to get to know someone."

"You've been with us quite a while, Mr. Anderson, and I do not know you yet." Cameron raised his eyebrows and waited, having scored a point.

Toll knew he was being backed into an intellectual corner. Soul searching with this retired minister could be very dangerous. For all Toll knew, this old fart had spent a year writing home to his cronies in the States, trying to identify the mysterious Mr. Anderson. A chill went up Toll's spine. Could it be that this kindly, old South Carolinian was one of Fahey's plants? He studied the old man's face. It seemed so kind, so seasoned, so devoid of threat.

"What's wrong, Mr. Anderson?"

"There is *nothing* wrong, Mr. Cameron," Toll said sharply. "I just thought I might know one of those American pathologists and I wanted to check them out. Before I surprised him with a big hello."

Cameron frowned, unconvinced. He glanced at the visitors, now on their way into the Administration Building. "Who are you, Mr. Anderson?" he asked firmly.

"I'm William P. Anderson from Indianapolis, Indiana. That's who I am, Mr. Cameron. Is that all right? Is that good enough for you?" Toll was losing his cool and he knew it. He struggled with himself to regain his balance.

"Please, Mr. Anderson," Cameron said, putting his hand on the pathologist's arm. "Forgive me, I didn't mean to pry."

"Dr. Fuentes knows my story, Mr. Cameron. *He* understands why I am here. If you have to know more about me, go ask him."

"Please, Mr. Anderson, I—"

Toll pulled his arm away from the old man. He had succeeded in reversing the tension. Now he had to solidify the advantage.

"And now I am going over to the Administration Building and surprise my friend. You want to come along?"

"No," Cameron said softly. "You go ahead. I'll get a chance to meet them all later. It's time for you medical people to talk together." He patted Toll's arm approvingly. It was apparent the old minister felt guilty about his inquisition.

"Good," Toll said strongly. "If they stay long enough, I'll introduce you around." He walked boldly out of the chapel and marched toward the Administration Building without looking back. He was sure Cameron was watching, giving him no opportunity to avoid the big front door. With a little luck the pathologists would already be in the director's office.

If Toll had had an eye in the back of his head, like some ancient animal, he would have seen the aged chaplain turn toward the altar of the church and bow his head in a genuine petition for forgiveness. He had spent a lifetime trying to be charitable and he had fallen again.

Inside the foyer of the Administration Building the four pathologists listened quietly as Fuentes explained each of the paintings on the wall. The black pathologist seemed fascinated by the formal portrait of François Duvalier, who had risen from a simple country physician to become the ruler of an entire nation. It was not much of a nation, but Dr. Henry Robinson was impressed. He too had overcome the odds and had gone from a poor beginning to play football for Ohio State while getting his bachelor's. He had then worked his way through Meharry Medical School, before finishing his pathology residency at NYU. The offer of an academic position at Emory had followed when his research team had identified an obscure brain disease. He took a pay cut to accept the teaching position in Atlanta, but as one of the first blacks on the pathology staff, he knew he had to do it. He had accepted the position not only for himself, but for the others who would come after him.

The doctors and Nurse Collins stood chatting pleasantly and sipping cool lemonade which the steward had provided for their arrival. It was a moment for trivia and banality, with everyone glad to make the acquaintance of the others, and four of them wishing they could use the bathroom. Toll paused at the front door, glanced back at the chapel, and entered the Administration Building. His entrance surprised Barbara and obviously pleased Fuentes.

"Ah! Mr. Anderson," Fuentes announced. "Come and meet our distinguished visitors."

"This is Dr. Watkins," Fuentes said, introducing the group's leader. "This is Mr. William Anderson, our laboratory chief and compatriot of yours."

"I am pleased to meet you, Dr. Watkins," Anderson said. He studied the pathologist's face for a moment and then quickly glanced at the others. There were no signs of recognition from any of them.

Barbara watched the introductions from just behind the group. She remembered the orthopedic surgeons and how uncomfortable their visit had made Bill feel.

"Hello, Anderson," Watkins said. "It is nice to meet you. Where are you from?"

"Indiana." He shook Watkins's hand and was passed to Dr. Poliak without delay.

"This is Dr. Poliak from the University of California," Watkins supplied. Poliak smiled with even white teeth gleaming from the opening of his full jet black beard and mustache. At thirty-nine Poliak was in good physical condition—tall, lean, athletic, and tanned the way every Californian is supposed to be.

"Hi," Poliak said. "How's it going?" He released Anderson's hand, pleased but not concerned by the meeting.

"And this is Dr. Burton from Miami," Watkins continued. Burton was shorter than the others. His sandy hair was dry and disorganized from the ride.

"Dr. Burton," Anderson said, rushing the handshake. Burton had been talking with Nurse Collins and seemed anxious to return to a point he had been making about native Haitian art. He knew nothing about Haitian art. He had only read about it on the plane. Toll's eyes met Barbara's over Burton's shoulder. She searched his face for any sign of a problem, but there was none. He was glad to see there was no message for him in her eyes.

"Dr. Robinson," Fuentes announced, presenting the last visitor to the lab tech, "this is William Anderson. We are quite proud of him and his accomplishments."

"I'm very pleased to meet you, Mr. Anderson," Robinson said. "You run the lab here?" His dark brown eyes narrowed slightly as he evaluated Anderson. He was tall and poised, a caricature of Paul Robeson with a deep voice but with a rasp that predicted he smoked cigarettes heavily.

"I'm pleased to meet you, Dr. Robinson," Anderson said. There was something in the black man's face that was vaguely familiar.

"Where did you say you were from?" Robinson asked, releasing Anderson's hand.

"Indiana. A small town outside of Indianapolis," Anderson said cautiously. Had he really met this man before? He hadn't met many black pathologists. He searched his memory to review the faces dimly stored there. None came up for positive identification.

"Really? I'm from Ohio originally. I spent some time in Indianapolis in my younger days," Robinson said. "Have we ever met before?" The others had returned to their own conversations with each other. No one but Robinson seemed interested in William Anderson.

"I don't think so, Dr. Robinson," Anderson said. "I moved away from Indiana right after finishing high school."

"Where was that?" Robinson asked lightly.

Toll thought for a moment. These were the fatal details he had managed to avoid at the hospital. Even Fuentes seemed interested in the answer. There was no way to avoid it.

"Woodrow Wilson," Anderson said hopefully. He was counting on the fact that most large cities had a Woodrow Wilson High School.

Robinson shook his head slowly. "I can't say that I have ever heard of it." He smiled widely. "But then there's a lot of things I haven't heard of. How long have you been here?"

"It's more than two years now, isn't it, Mr. Anderson?" Fuentes said.

"Something like that," Toll mumbled.

"He has literally rebuilt our little laboratory," Fuentes added proudly.

"That's wonderful," Robinson said. "I'd like to see it."

"The lab?" Toll asked.

"Yes. I've spent a lot of time in small hospital labs over the years. At least I did before I took the job at Emory. Black hospitals have never been known for their large, automated laboratories, if you know what I mean."

"Many of them are very efficiently run," Toll said, smiling slightly for the first time since he had entered. He knew he was nervous but he hoped it didn't show.

"Gentlemen," the director announced loudly, "bring your drinks. We will continue our meeting in my office." As the group turned to leave the foyer, Robinson held Anderson by the elbow.

"Dr. Watkins," Robinson said, "if you don't mind, I'd like to skip the meeting in the director's office and visit the hospital lab with Mr. Anderson. I am sure it will be very instructive."

Robinson said nothing until his group had disappeared into the director's office. Then, still holding Anderson by the elbow, he guided him toward the outside door.

"Now tell me what this shit is all about," Robinson said sharply.

"Pardon me?" Toll said, pulling his arm free.

"Come on, man. There is only the two of us out here. Clue me in. What the hell is going on?"

"I'm afraid I don't—"

"Look. I don't remember your name, but I never forget a face. I saw you at Bethesda in '61."

Toll stopped abruptly and faced Robinson. He could not recall meeting the man before. But after so many years how could he be sure?

"You were in the Navy?" Toll asked, his pulse racing.

"No. Air Force. But I was sent to the AFIP for a special course and they didn't have room for me at Walter Reed. I bunked at the naval hospital at Bethesda for a month. I saw you there. I am sure of it."

"And?"

"And you weren't any lab tech then, *Doctor*."

"Keep walking, Dr. Robinson. Let's stay out in the open away from everyone. I am not sure who I can trust anymore."

"You can trust me. I don't give a hot flying damn why you're here. I'm just curious why they all think you're some kind of a lab tech. Hell, man, you're a pathologist like the rest of us. Aren't you?"

Toll nodded slowly. A denial would only excite Robinson's curiosity further.

"Can I give it to you straight?" Toll asked.

"There is no other way I'll take it."

"I'm hiding."

"Obviously. But why?"

"I am AWOL from the Navy." Toll waited to see Robinson's reaction. None was visible.

"So what's new? The papers say we've got a whole division living in Toronto. A lot of people feel pretty strongly about the mess in Vietnam." Robinson's tone was soothing and unconcerned.

"It's not Vietnam."

"So you hate Navy food or something?" He smiled, and his bright teeth shone from his dark, smooth face. Robinson was a handsome man with rugged features, and an early touch of gray at his temples made him look even more distinguished.

"I had a problem with the government. There's really nowhere for me to go."

Robinson stopped, put both hands on Toll's shoulders, and looked deeply into his eyes. "Look, man," he said softly, "I'm no fan of the federal government either. After Selma and Watts and the assassination of Martin Luther King, I am ready to tell the feds to kiss my black ass. So go ahead and level with me. If I can help you, I will. You can count on it."

There was nothing ungenuine about Henry Robinson that Toll could see. His eyes had narrowed and his lips became hard as he spoke Martin Luther King's name.

"Sounds like you got a hard-on for the government too, Dr. Robinson."

"FBI, mostly. And by the way, it's Robbie."

"My name is George Toll." He held his hand out and shook Robinson's for the second time. This time it felt sincere.

"Okay, George, now what did the bastards do to you?"

The two pathologists wandered around the hospital grounds, staying out of earshot of patients and staff. Toll knew it was too dangerous to tell him everything, but he also knew if he lied to Robinson and got caught at it, the pathologist might blow the whistle on him when he got back to the States. Toll's only hope was to level with this man, trust him, and hope like hell he would be sympathetic. He told Robinson about the Bay of Pigs and the dance card, but not about the fake appendectomy. Somehow he felt too vulnerable. Too alone. Too naked to tell it all. He had to keep something for himself.

They came to a stone bench beneath a giant banyan tree and sat for a moment as Robinson lit another cigarette.

"You mean the CIA has been hounding you all over the place to get this information back?" Robinson asked. He seemed convinced and amazed.

"Uh-huh. And now I think they will kill me if I show up with or without the dance card."

"You may be right. They're capable of anything. You have the dance card with you here in Haiti?"

Toll felt a chill come over him. Was Robinson a plant? Was he sent by Fahey to sucker him into some kind of an admission? How had Fahey found out he was at Albert Schweitzer? Fuentes? Barbara? Had they gotten to her like they did with Pam? His mind was spinning with suspicion and confusion.

"No, not here," Toll lied. "I have it somewhere in the States with instructions to turn it over to *The Miami Herald* if anything happens to me."

"Why the *Herald?*"

"They have a big interest in the Bay of Pigs, even now. Miami is crawling with Cubans."

Robinson nodded gravely. "But what about you, George? What are you going to do, rot down here until they forget about you?"

"They'll never forget about me, Robbie. It's just a matter of time. Sooner or later somebody—like you—will spot me and turn me in and that will be that."

"Hell, *I'm* not going to turn you in. I'm on your side."

"But what do you expect me to do? Hop a plane back to Washington and tell the President all about it? Shit, he'd just stick me in Portsmouth and throw away the key."

"But there are extenuating circumstances, George. Maybe I could—"

"No, you're not going to get involved. It's enough if you just keep all of this quiet. I couldn't ask you to do more than that." Toll watched the black pathologist drag the last few milligrams of smoke and tar from his cigarette before lighting another. Most of the pathologists had stopped smoking when the cancer studies came out, but Robbie had not been one of them. Not even for a day.

"I want to help," Robinson said firmly.

"I wish there was some way you could."

"There *is* something," Robinson said slowly. "It just might work."

"What?"

"In a couple of months—I'll get you the exact date—there is a joint meeting of the ASCP and the CAP. It is going to be in Atlanta this year. At the Regency Hotel."

"And?"

"And you could show up as an assistant researcher to the paper I'm presenting on parasitology. And then—right out of the blue—you shock the asses off of them by telling your whole damn story." He spread his arms wide and searched Toll's face for approval.

"You mean in the middle of the meeting? Just like that?"

"It would work. I'm sure of it."

"And once it was out in the open, the CIA boys couldn't touch me."

"You'd be in every newspaper in the country."

The suggestion increased Toll's confidence in Robinson. One of Fahey's men would never have suggested a sudden public disclosure in the middle of the pathologist's meeting.

"I like it, Robbie. It just might work." Toll was beginning to see a way home at last.

"Can't you see their faces when you come out on the stage on the middle of my asshole paper on microfilaria and tell a whole ballroom full of pathologists how you faked the autopsies from the Bay of Pigs?" Robinson rubbed his hands together, obviously delighted.

"If you'll help me with this, Robbie, I'll never forget you."

"I've always believed that pathologists are the bottom line. When it comes to telling the truth about a patient's disease, or his treatment, who else can we depend on but the pathologist?"

Toll nodded. "You're right, Robbie, we may be all there is left."

"You know, if I'm going to sound convincing when I get back to Watkins and his Boy Scout committee, you better give me a tour of your lab." He stood up and reached for another cigarette.

21
It was several weeks after the pathology group left Haiti when Toll heard from Robbie again. His message came in as a note attached to a color brochure. In it Robinson said he would write a formal request to the hospital, urging them to send Anderson to the meeting. The paper on microfilaria, he claimed, would give the hospital an opportunity to display its work to several thousand pathologists from all over the world. Toll looked at the date on the brochure. He would have sufficient time to make the necessary arrangements, assuming they would buy him a plane ticket. The hospital had a limited travel budget, usually reserved for senior medical personnel. The meager honorarium Fuentes had arranged for his lab work provided Anderson only with personal items. By being frugal, he had accumulated only a few hundred dollars, which he kept in a box in his room. Being a volunteer at a religious hospital was not a get-rich-quick scheme.

Toll spread the announcement on his desk in the lab. The topics ranged from new methods for doing blood chemistries to papers on experimental cancer in rats. Speakers were scheduled from American, Canadian, and European universities and medical centers. For many pathologists the meeting would be a time to get away from their hospital duties and to enjoy Atlanta's fine restaurants. For others it would be an opportunity to talk about research problems with other experts. Some of those would have to be content with hamburgers in the hotel's coffee shop.

Thérèse and Marie were obviously curious about the color brochure on Mr. Anderson's desk. He seldom looked at nontechnical material in the lab. They hoped that at last he was planning a vacation. He had not been away for longer than a day since he had come there.

Thérèse cleared her throat to announce the arrival of Dr. Fuentes in the lab.

"Good morning, Mr. Anderson," Fuentes sang pleasantly. "I missed you at breakfast."

"Good morning, Doctor," Toll said, glancing up from the brochure. "I was not very hungry. I had coffee here."

"Jean-Paul had an egg selected for you."

"He spoils me," Toll said, smiling.

"You deserve to be spoiled." He glanced around the lab approvingly. The ladies, not yet spoken to by the assistant director, did not look up. *"Bonjour, mesdemoiselles,"* he said officially.

"Bonjour, docteur," they chimed.

"I see you have an announcement on the pathology meeting in Atlanta," Fuentes said.

Toll glanced at the folder on his desk and nodded happily.

"I received similar material this morning from Dr. Robinson."

"Oh? You intend to go?" Toll asked.

Fuentes shook his head and feigned impatience with the absurdity of the question. "Not on your life, Mr. Anderson. I would find nothing fascinating about a hotel filled with pathologists. It is you who are going."

"Me?" Toll thought it safer to seem surprised.

"The International Association of Pathologists has asked the hospital to send you to the meeting to assist in the presentation of a paper on microfilaria."

"Dr. Robinson was impressed with the slides we had here. He said he would like to present some of them to his colleagues, but I—"

"Then it's Atlanta! For you and for the hospital." Fuentes was impressed and proud.

"But how—?"

"The hospital will make all the arrangements." Fuentes smiled broadly and rubbed his hands together with delight.

Toll frowned. "There may be a problem," he said.

"How?" the deputy director asked.

"My departure papers. I have been here a long time now, and I no longer have one of those exit cards."

Fuentes pouted and thought about the problem for a moment. "We could get you a new one," he announced.

"That would require a Haitian government form and some kind of an explanation. I've been here too long to have the Duvalier government asking questions."

"You have some personal reason for not wanting to be photographed or fingerprinted, Mr. Anderson?" Fuentes asked softly.

"No, not at all," Anderson replied confidently. "It's not my photograph or fingerprints that bothers me, it's Papa Doc."

"You're in bad favor with the Haitian government?"

"Probably," Toll said.

Fuentes stroked his chin with long, soft fingers as he considered the problem.

"I know a man in Port-au-Prince who has been a friend of ours for a long time."

"And?"

"And for a small fee he could be persuaded to provide you with an authentic exit card. Authentic enough to get you out of Haiti, but of course there would be no official records."

"A fake?"

"Call it what you wish, but here the government records are so hopelessly confused that your quiet departure will hardly be noticed. No one will care, I am sure."

"What about the 'small fee'?" Toll asked. Even with his meager savings from his hospital stipend, he could not afford a bribe.

"Fifty dollars," Fuentes whispered, "and I will see to it that the hospital takes care of it. This hospital has to fight for every honor it gets, no matter how small. A chance to be recognized by the national convention of pathologists is a great opportunity for us. The director has almost insisted that you go, but he does not want to force you. That is why he sent me over to talk to you."

Toll stared at Fuentes for a moment. There was no hint of duplicity in the man's face.

"It's a deal," he said. "When can we see your friend in Port-au-Prince?"

"Tomorrow," Fuentes said. He smiled broadly and pumped the pathologist's hand. "I will drive you into town myself. I'll make the arrangements and you will have your exit card."

At dinner in the staff dining room Toll quietly signaled to Barbara. After dark there was a gentle knock on his cabin door.

"Come in, Barb," he said, glancing beyond her to make sure she was alone. They had met regularly since the first time and both of them were happy to keep the affair quiet.

She closed the door and kissed him. "What's this about a trip to Atlanta?"

"Well," he said, holding her close to him and smiling, "the pathologists invited me to participate in a paper and Fuentes came up with the money."

"You deserve it. The hospital's got to be proud to see you on the program." She moved into his room and flopped into his desk chair, a caricature of an exhausted nurse.

"It's all about parasites," he said.

"I wish I could go," she replied.

Toll came close to her and kissed her gently on the forehead.

"Not if you wanted to come back," he sighed.

She turned in her chair to look at him. "Bill. Of course I would come back. This is my life's work."

Toll walked to the window and looked out between the curtains. He wanted to tell her the whole story. He wanted to announce they would both go and never come back. "Barbara, I've been happy here," he said without facing her.

"This is the true way to happiness, Bill. Doing good for others who need it so badly. Our work here is much more than just the practice of medicine."

"It is for you, Barbara," he said, turning from the window. "I've known that from the beginning."

"And for you too, Bill. We don't know why you came here, but you've found peace with us, and that's important. Don't you feel it?" She got up from the chair and stood close to him, her arms around his waist.

"I know. But for me there have been several reasons for staying. Especially you."

"And when you get back, we'll be together again." She put her head on his chest and held him a little tighter.

"Like before?"

"No. I've thought about that, Bill. It's time we told the others, if they don't already know."

"You think they do?"

"Maybe Fuentes," she said. "He smiles at me a lot lately."

"Maybe it's because you look happy."

"I am, Bill. You make me happy."

"I want to make you happy, Barbara. I need to make you happy."

She felt his grasp tighten around her. It was somehow different. "Bill," she said softly, looking up at him. "What's wrong?"

"There's nothing wrong."

"There is, Bill. I can feel it. It's the trip, isn't it?"

He looked away from her for a moment. God, yes, he thought. It's the trip. It's them. It's Fahey. Was there any way she could understand? He wanted to tell her so badly. He needed to share.

"Barbara, I..."

"Bill, come here," she said, pulling him toward the bed. "Be with me. Be part of me."

"Barbara, I can't. I'm..." His words dissolved into her eager approach. She knew he was troubled and reached for an intimacy that would solve all problems, at least for the moment. He collapsed onto the bed, his eyes hidden behind his hand. He knew he was ready to crack and knew he couldn't. Not now. Not this close to the resolution of his problem. He had found a way out. He had to take it.

"Shhh," she said, unbuttoning his shirt. "Not now. Whatever it is." She found his chest and let her hands run across it, touching him, wanting him.

"I'm going to come back for you, Barbara." He felt himself responding to her touch. "No matter what you hear while I'm gone, I'll be back."

"We could be happy here, together," she said. "Fuentes will let you run the lab as long as you want."

He tried to imagine Fuentes's surprise when he came back, not as Anderson the lab tech, but as George Toll, pathologist. "I'll bet he will, Barbara."

She moved closer to him and kissed him on the cheek. "I want you," she whispered.

"You'll have me," he promised.

* * *

Toll had always been under the impression that Dr. Fuentes did not drive, and the trip into Port-au-Prince almost proved it. Toll hung on all the way until noon, when the station wagon entered Port-au-Prince. The streets were crowded with tourists and tradesmen. As usual the natives ignored them both. Some of the streets were jammed with farm carts while others, lined with expensive shops, were almost empty. Fuentes made a right turn onto one of those quiet, narrow streets and humped a rear wheel over the curb with a tooth-rattling crunch. There was a small bookstore in the middle of the block. Fuentes pulled up in front and shut the engine off. The station wagon blocked more than half of the street, but Dr. Fuentes did not seem concerned. He was confident the "Hôpital Albert Schweitzer" sign on the front door would protect them from traffic tickets.

"This is the Bibliothèque Desuss," Fuentes explained needlessly. The sign over the door said the same thing. "Emile Desuss deals in rare books, expensive prints, and the odd piece of sculpture."

"And questionable documents?" Toll quipped.

"But only of the finest quality," Fuentes said, opening the door.

A small bell on a long, arching spring announced their arrival and reminded Toll of a bakery shop in his childhood. The bookstore was lined with shelves of leather-bound volumes, except where wall space had been cleared for fine European prints and framed fragments of historical documents. The place was empty and quiet—more museum than shop.

Emile Desuss sat at his rolltop desk in the rear, a crook-necked lamp illuminating the lower half of his face. He was in his sixties and had a red face dotted with acne scars. His upper teeth protruded, forcing his mouth to hang open slightly and making him lick the saliva frequently from his lower lip. His eyes bulged from sockets that seemed too small to hold them and his tiny, beaklike nose barely supported his thick glasses. The acne had driven the fat from his cheeks, giving him a drawn and sinister appearance. Desuss knew he was not handsome, and as a result he had always retreated from women, remaining unmarried. He stood up as Fuentes entered the shop.

"Bonjour, Docteur Fuentes," Desuss announced, coming forward to greet the two men.

"In English, please, Desuss," Fuentes said, pulling Toll by the arm. "This is my good friend, Mr. Anderson. He has done marvelous things for our little hospital. He is an American."

Toll held out his hand on cue and met the bookman halfway across the store. "How do you do?" Toll said.

"Enchanté," Desuss said, shaking the pathologist's hand and for a moment ignoring Fuentes's request to speak English. "How may I help you?"

"We need one of your special services," Fuentes supplied. He took his turn shaking Desuss's hand, lingering longer over the formality than Toll had.

"Oh? A rare edition perhaps?" Desuss asked. His eyes met Fuentes's and an instantaneous message was exchanged.

"None of your dusty books, Emile," Fuentes said. "Mr. Anderson needs a small document from you."

"Surely not a health card," Desuss said, enjoying his little remark.

"An exit permit," Fuentes said flatly.

Desuss withdrew his hand and studied Toll for a moment, nodding slowly. Fuentes had never brought him an embarrassment before and there was no reason to think this would be the first time.

"It could be arranged," Desuss said quietly. "It would take some time, of course."

"Today," Fuentes said. He reached into his pocket and produced fifty dollars worth of Haitian gourdes. He held the bills across his chest in full view of the bookseller.

"Am I permitted to inquire into the rest of the problem?" Desuss asked, taking the money and stuffing it into his pocket.

"No," Fuentes said. "But you have my assurance there is no criminal difficulty. Mr. Anderson needs to catch a flight to the United States without delay." He paused for a moment as Desuss looked at Toll again.

"Well, I—" Desuss began.

"The director requests it," Fuentes added.

Desuss nodded again. The bookman's mother had been treated at the hospital before she died of congestive heart failure. The favor was owed. "Come into the back room," he said. "Give me a moment."

Fuentes ushered Anderson beyond the desk and into the cluttered back room as Desuss placed a small sign in the front door, indicating he would be back in half an hour. After locking the door, he joined the two men in the room.

"Now, Mr.—" Desuss said, opening a low cabinet and taking out a thin folder of government forms.

"Anderson, William P.," Toll supplied.

"We will need a thumbprint." Desuss opened a drawer in an ancient desk stuffed with papers and books and took out a small, inked stamp pad.

Toll glanced at his thumbs and shrugged at Fuentes. There was an "oh, what the hell look" in Toll's eyes. He had come this far and there did not appear to be any graceful way out.

"They insist on the thumbprint and the photograph because you have been here longer than six months," Fuentes said. "The weekenders from the cruise ships get temporary permits, but one of those would never get you on an airplane after all this time. You wouldn't be on any tourist lists."

"Where is he entering the United States?" Desuss asked, pulling an ancient camera on a tripod out of a closet.

"Miami?" Fuentes asked Anderson.

"As good as any, I suppose," Toll agreed.

22 The thumbprint and photograph were examined with only routine interest at the data desk of the CIA attaché in Port-au-Prince. There had never been any trouble at the Albert Schweitzer Hospital and the face named Anderson did not match any of the files at this relatively obscure post. It took the CIA man in Haiti the usual four or five days to transmit a routine copy of the phony exit card to Washington. The only message received in return was to notify Fahey by phone when the date of departure was known. A check of airline reservations provided this information without the slightest difficulty, as the airlines routinely supplied the U.S. embassy with this semipublic information. The Agency had great confidence in the expertise of Emile Desuss and the incompetence of the Haitian immigration service. There was not the slightest doubt Toll would make the plane or that the Haitians would let him go. Like a spider guarding a giant web, Fahey played the waiting game; and with a little help from Air France his long-sought-after prey was about to fly in.

Dr. Fuentes and Nurse Collins delivered Mr. Anderson to the airport in Port-au-Prince at 9:00 A.M. the following Tuesday. He had gathered his slides and reports on the rarer cases of parasitic diseases from the laboratory files and packed a single suitcase with his few personal belongings. The director had wished him a safe trip and presented him with several hundred American dollars for expenses. Everyone on staff at the hospital was proud of him and Mr. Cameron promised he would offer prayers for a safe trip. As the station wagon left the main gate, Toll felt a twinge of remorse for the true motives that made him go. He had found friends and peace at the Hôpital Albert and quietly renewed his vow to return.

The Immigration man stamped the exit card and dropped it into a slot on his high desk. He scratched the name, "Anderson, William P." on a cheap paper form, blurred the lower right corner with a rubber stamp, and entered his own initials. By then he was looking beyond Anderson at the next departing tourist.

"Have a nice trip," the official said without sentiment.

"Thank you," Toll said, and stuffed the Haitian departure slip into his ticket envelope before joining the line for baggage inspection. As he waited for the perfunctory search of his few clean shirts and his briefcase, he casually glanced around the area. No one else seemed interested in his departure. Fuentes and Collins had waved and gone to the observation deck, confident that everything was all right. The Tonton Macoute assigned to the airport was more interested in his own fingernails than the tourists in the area. Toll began to feel comfortable amid a sea of straw hats, flowered shirts, and ebony souvenirs. So far, he thought, his luck was holding.

Flight 350 departed at 11:45, on time for a change. The inflight service was a typical mixture of nonchalance and haughty disdain calculated to make each American passenger vow never to fly Air France again while at the same time feeling curiously satisfied.

The plane arrived before two at Miami International and the passengers and crew were herded along a corridor to Immigration, a section of the terminal separated by a series of doors. The crowd eventually entered a large room and began to line up in front of the small glass booth maintained by the U.S. Public Health Service. A white-haired man in a maritime uniform worked his way along the line, inspecting the standard yellow folders in which immunization records were recorded. Since Flight 350 had arrived from Martinique, Guadaloupe, and Haiti, the PHS officer demanded proof of smallpox vaccination within the previous three years. Toll had not anticipated this particular challenge to his reentrance into the United States. Typical of doctors, neither he nor Fuentes had given it a second thought. Both of them knew there was no smallpox remaining in Haiti. In time the Public Health Service would come to the same conclusion and dispense with this formality, but that was years away. For the time being it was produce the card or be evaluated for vaccination and quarantine. Toll's heart began to pound as the officer approached.

"Health card?" the officer demanded.

Toll smiled self-consciously and reached into his inside jacket pocket as if by some hygienic miracle, the card would be there. He produced the small form the Haitian official had stamped at the airport in Port-au-Prince.

"No, sir, the yellow card," the PHS officer said. "The International Immunization Record." The officer wore collar insignia of lieutenant commander, indicating he held the PHS rank of assistant surgeon. The Public Health Service, the oldest medical organization in the United States government, could be identified by the caduceus and anchor on the sleeve and the thin red stripe in the gold band on the cap.

"I've had all my shots," Toll said, fumbling through his pockets.

"Yes, sir," the officer said, glancing impatiently along the line behind Toll. "We are only interested in your smallpox vaccination record at this time."

"Smallpox? But I..." Toll continued to fumble.

"A formality, I assure you, sir. You are an American?" So far his expression had not changed from official boredom. For a man of his age and rank this assignment was obviously a bureaucratic mechanism to move him to Miami while he completed his thirty years toward retirement. The position could have been filled by an intelligent clerk, but World War II had left the Public Health Service with a surplus of commissioned medical officers and an inadequate number of hospital assignments. As a result many of them spent their last days performing menial tasks that would have driven younger doctors into civilian practices.

"Yes, of course I'm an American," Toll said hopefully. "I was born in Indiana."

"Why were you in Haiti?"

"I was working at the Albert Schweitzer Hospital," Toll said. "With a church."

"You're a physician?"

Toll hesitated for a moment.

"No. I'm a laboratory technologist."

The PHS officer looked at Toll and nodded. "The clinical lab?" he asked.

"Yes. I ran the hospital lab for the past few years. Have you heard of the Albert Schweitzer Hospital, sir?" Toll hoped a casual conversation might soften the man's official demeanor and get him waved through.

"Oh, yes. We need more of that kind of thing around the world. I spent many years as an internist with the Indians in the Southwest. I can appreciate what you were up against." The PHS officer seemed interested in Toll's medical experiences, but was distracted by the growing impatience of the line of tourists. He glanced at his watch. "I'll tell you what," he continued, "take this blue card to the Immigration desk and wait for me there. I think we can work something out for you." He smiled for the first time since confronting Dr. Toll. He knew his job was an inconvenience, but he was too mature to be a pain in the ass as well.

"Thanks," Toll said, picking up his briefcase and moving toward the other line. So far, so good, he told himself.

The U.S. Immigration and Naturalization Service had constructed a series of small glass booths open at either end, in which the reviewing officer and the traveler could face each other. Toll approached the booth marked "U.S. Citizens" and waited for a woman in front of him to clear. The government had placed a blue line on the floor in front of the booth, limiting the interview to one person at a time. Toll displayed his phony papers confidently—the Immigration Service seldom asked for strict proof of citizenship and most Americans returning from vacation couldn't prove it anyway.

The booth cleared and Tool stepped in. He handed his white declaration card to the officer and said, "Good afternoon," hoping to disarm the man with a pleasant remark.

"How do you do?" the officer grunted. He took the declaration card and looked at the name, flipping the pages of his Service Outlook Book to the A's. The book was as thick as a Manhattan phone directory and was looseleaf for frequent updating. "You have come from Haiti?" the officer said, running his finger down a column in the book.

"Yes. From the Albert Schweitzer Hospital."

The officer's fingers stopped on a name. The Service Outlook Book was kept on a slanting stand so a traveler in front of the desk could not see the pages. Toll studied the officer's eyes as he read the name and the comment at the end of his finger. There was a slight frown from which the officer immediately recovered. He looked at Toll and gave a small smile.

"You are William P. Anderson?" he asked blandly.

"Yes, sir."

The officer's foot slid onto a button on the floor and pressed it. There was no sound and his expression did not change. He placed the declaration card on a stack with several others and nodded at Toll. "Everything seems to be in order," the officer said. "You may proceed to Customs and be prepared to open your luggage when requested."

Toll looked at the Immigration man for a moment. There was something plastic about the man's smile, but not an overt threat. Toll looked around quickly. No one else seemed to be watching him. He felt slightly anxious, but he had made it. He was almost home.

At the next table the Customs inspector asked him to open his suitcase, but seemed disinterested in the contents when Toll's clean shirts and underwear came into view. He was similarly unconcerned with the scientific reports in the pathologist's briefcase. For a moment Toll wondered if these officials were always this lax. He could have been a dangerous international spy, he told himself. And they had simply waved him through! How could they represent the security of the United States? How could...?

"Mr. Anderson!" a voice shouted, interrupting his mental critique just before he reached the exit. He turned and looked for the caller.

"Mr. Anderson!" the voice said again. It was the Public Health officer. He held a finger in the air and rushed toward the pathologist. "A moment please."

Toll sighed and put his suitcase down. Was his entrance about to be blocked by his failure to be vaccinated?

"Yes, Doctor?" Toll said glumly as the PHS officer approached.

"You may need this," the man said. He held a yellow card in front of him. "Your immunization record. You must have left it near my desk. The PHS officer smiled and half winked.

"I don't understand," Toll said softly.

The PHS officer glanced around quickly and saw they were relatively alone. "My own church has often sent donations to the Hôpital Albert. They have been proud to help other such charitable activities around the world. Under different circumstances I might have enjoyed a medical missionary assignment too, but that was not my fate, so perhaps in this small way I can think I have been of some help too."

Toll looked at the card again and then at the PHS doctor. The man had the same look Toll had seen so often in Barbara's face.

"Thank you, Doctor," Toll said. "I will remember your kindness."

"God bless you," the man said. He grasped Toll's arm for a moment and then turned away to return to his duties. He had violated the regulations he had sworn to enforce, but in his heart he knew he had done no wrong and he was pleased.

The Public Health doctor's help made Toll's hopes soar to new heights. He took the immunization card as a sign his journey to Atlanta would be blessed with good luck. He picked up his briefcase and left the federal area to arrange his flight transfer. As he walked toward the Eastern Airlines counter, his steps felt energized and his heart felt lighter. He could not prevent a smile from splitting his face. In his happiness he failed to notice Agents Hardy and Clyde following him at a safe distance. They were both dressed in business suits and Clyde carried an attaché case. They, too, were happy.

Fahey had kept them in the area for two days, waiting for the silent signal from the Immigration officer's foot switch. For both of them Toll's peaceful arrival was the end of a long search. With Dr. Toll once again in sight, they could look forward to the recovery of the dance card and with it an end to departmental persecution under James Fahey.

On the flight from Miami to Atlanta Toll had a window seat, and half-turned in it to watch the beauty of Biscayne Bay slip beneath them as the big jet took off. For a seat companion Toll had drawn a woman from New Jersey who tried to start conversation by producing snapshots of her new granddaughter, recently born in Miami Beach. Toll grunted a few unencouraging responses before busying himself with the medical reports in his briefcase. After a few moments the grandmother abandoned her attempts and began to flip through the airline magazine.

Agents Hardy and Clyde had split up to cover the tourist section more effectively. Hardy sat several rows behind and to the left of the pathologist while Clyde sat to the front. They were confident that Toll had no idea he was being followed.

It was almost 5:00 P.M. when the jet touched down at Hartsfield International Airport. The traffic rush out of Atlanta was in full swing, jamming the southbound expressway, but leaving the inbound route almost empty until the following morning. Agent Clyde preceded Toll to the baggage area and waited inconspicuously as Hardy trailed the pathologist from the landing gate. Halfway to the main terminal Toll stopped at a wall phone unit and dialed a number from a folded piece of paper in his shirt pocket. The phone was answered on the third ring. The voice was deep and formal. "Dr. Robinson," it announced.

"Oh, Dr. Robinson, this is Bill Anderson. From Haiti?" The pathologist paused, but not long enough to allow a reply. "I'm in Atlanta. I'm glad I caught you at Emory. I was afraid you had already gone home."

"Bill! I was beginning to wonder whether or not you were going to show. How was the flight?"

"No problems. Immigration was a breeze. Do you want me to meet you somewhere?" Toll asked, tapping his foot against his briefcase.

"I've made reservations for you at the Hyatt Regency downtown. I think it would be best for you to take the limo directly there and check in. I hope you don't mind that I can't pick you up at the airport," Robinson said. "I've got a meeting."

"I understand. Do you want me to call you when I get there?"

"I'll be out of touch, but I will check with you tomorrow before the afternoon meeting. My paper is at two. Maybe we could get together for lunch."

"Sounds good to me. I brought the parasitology reports just in case you wanted to include any of that material in your part of the paper."

"That's not a bad idea. It might look better for you if you ever have to justify the trip to your friends in Haiti. No use burning all your bridges."

"Yeah," Toll agreed, "but I think my part of the speech will take care of that."

"You don't think anybody in Washington knows you're here, do you?"

Toll glanced around automatically. There were no suspicious characters in view. There was only one average white male trying to squeeze the sports statistics out of the afternoon paper. "Not a soul, Dr. Robinson. I'm home free thanks to you."

"Tomorrow then, Bill. We'll work out the details for your bombshell. I'm going to love this."

"Me too. It's been a long time coming."

"I hope it all works, Bill. I'll call you tomorrow." Robinson hung up without further comment. There was nothing in his voice to alarm Dr. Toll. Everything seemed to be going according to plan.

Toll picked up his briefcase and proceeded to the baggage area. His suitcase was being carried along the conveyer belt like a passenger on a silent merry-go-round. He grabbed it, gave the attendant the claim check from his ticket envelope, and headed for the limo departure area. He bought a ticket to the Regency and boarded the repainted city bus for the seven-mile ride downtown. Behind him Clyde sat quietly, his eyes riveted on Toll's head as Hardy got into a cab. Hardy told the cabdriver he was tailing his girl friend and a man and that he wanted to follow the airport limo downtown. The cabdriver, intrigued by the romantic story and impressed by the ten-dollar tip paid in advance, was happy to cooperate.

At the Hyatt Regency Toll was awestruck by the immense lobby that stretched upward, unobstructed, to the skylight. Hundreds of balconies ringed the twenty-six floors above him, many with hanging gardens. For a moment Toll became a typical tourist as he watched the light-studded glass elevators rise and fall along the massive columns supporting their silent mechanisms.

"Checking in, sir?" the doorman asked.

The doorman picked up the bag and led the doctor to the registration counter across from the Kafé København. Apparently most of the pathologists attending the meeting had already checked in. There were no lines at the desk.

"I believe I have reservations," Toll said to the desk clerk. "Anderson? William P.?"

The clerk punched a few buttons on his computer console and read the little TV screen silently. "Yes, sir, I have it. Room two-six-ten." He produced a small card and slid it across the polished countertop toward the pathologist. Toll looked at the card for a moment, scanning it for questions he might not want to answer, filled it in with his hospital address in Haiti.

The clerk spun the card around, read it quickly, and, apparently satisfied, put a key in the bellman's outstretched hand. "Twenty-six ten for Mr. Anderson," he announced. "Have a pleasant stay with us, sir."

"Thank you," Toll mumbled. The bellman had already taken the bags toward the bank of elevators. A small group of people stood chatting and laughing near the elevator doors, waiting their turn. Toll glanced at a few of them before turning his attention toward his shoes. When the elevator arrived, the bellman skillfully blocked the door with the bags and motioned with his head for Toll to get in before everyone did. Only one couple managed to join them. The elevator rose quickly, leaving the dazzling lobby beneath them and evoking the inevitable gasp from the female passenger. The lobby became the size of a living room when the elevator stopped at the fifteenth floor to discharge the couple, and the size of a postage stamp at the twenty-sixth.

"Yours is over here, sir," the bellman said. He led him to room 2610 and opened the door. It was a beautiful suite facing the street and was tastefully furnished. Toll walked to the window and looked out over the city as the bellman went through the pretip routine, adjusting the lights and thermostat. He placed the bags on a low stand and stood in the middle of the sitting room, waiting for Toll to notice him.

"Will there be anything else, sir?" he asked, smiling.

"No. Thank you very much." Toll handed the man an American dollar, knowing he expected more. "Are you sure this is the right room?"

The bellman looked surprised. "Yes, sir. Twenty-six ten. Is there something wrong?"

"No. I guess not. It's just that I didn't expect a suite."

"I could check it for you, sir, if you wish." He took a few steps toward the phone.

"No. That's all right," Toll said. "I'll call the desk and if it is not correct, I'll make arrangements to move."

"As you wish, sir. Call us if we can be of any help whatsoever." He put the key on the writing desk and left, closing the door behind him.

Toll walked to the door and slipped the night bolt. He

turned, gave the sitting room the once-over, and walked into the adjoining bedroom. There was a large double bed and new bedroom furniture. A second full bathroom opened into the bedroom and in the opposite wall there was a door apparently into the next suite. Toll entered the bathroom, swept the shower aside, and then paused to look at himself in the mirror. "Calm down, George," he said aloud, "you're almost there." He left the bathroom a little slower and checked the rest of the suite beginning with the connecting door. He was alone. He walked to the phone in the sitting room and dialed the reservation desk. It was promptly answered.

"This is William P. Anderson at twenty-six ten," he announced. "Would you check my reservation please?"

"Pardon me, sir?"

"My reservation. I'd like you to check it. The room is much larger than I expected and I wanted to make sure there is no mistake before I unpack."

"Yes, sir, just a moment."

Toll looked at the prints on the wall as he waited. They were of better quality than he would have expected to find in a hotel. The whole arrangement looked quite expensive. "This has got to go for a hundred bucks a day," he mumbled aloud and underestimating the price.

"Mr. Anderson?" the clerk said, returning to the phone.

"Yes."

"I've checked your reservation and there is no mistake. The suite was booked for you by a Dr. Henry Robinson and payment has been arranged through the International Association of Pathologists. Is that not correct?"

Toll paused for a moment and smiled for the first time since entering the hotel. "Why not?" he asked.

"Pardon me, sir?" the desk clerk asked.

"I said, that's fine. Thank you. And, clerk?"

"Yes, sir?"

"I'd like to order a drink." Toll began to loosen his tie. The time had come to relax.

"Yes, sir. Simply dial room service. They will be glad to accommodate you."

"Okay, thanks," Toll said, hanging up the phone. Toll spun around twice in the middle of the room, his arms outstretched, and collapsed onto the sofa. For the first time in many years he felt happy.

23

The commentator on the television set folded his hands, framed for a full head-and-shoulders shot, and intoned, "And that's the evening news tonight. Join us again tomorrow." Credits began to roll across his expressionless face, but Toll was not reading them. In fact, he had missed the newscast entirely. He came out of the bathroom, wiping his face with a towel. He was dressed in a pair of dark trousers but no shirt. He stroked the side of his face, pleased with his fresh shave. He glanced at the TV for a moment as a knock sounded on the door. He left the bedroom, crossed the sitting room, and unbolted the door. When the door opened, Hardy and Clyde stood there, dressed as bellhops. In front of them there was a mobile cart with metal covered serving dishes. Toll paused for a moment, perplexed.

"Room service," Hardy said. He began to push the cart into the room.

"But I didn't..." Toll backed away slightly, letting the men enter.

"Mr. Anderson?" Clyde said, shutting the door. He held a restaurant tab in his hand and seemed to be checking the name.

"Yes, but—I don't understand," Toll continued. Hardy pushed the cart toward the little table in the sitting room as Toll padded behind him in bare feet. Behind him, Clyde flipped the door bolt closed. When he turned around he held a .357 revolver and pointed it at Toll's back.

"Shall I serve dinner now, sir?" Hardy asked, removing some of the metal covers. He was still facing the table.

"Dinner? Who...?" Toll turned to face Agent Clyde. His next question died in his throat when he saw the gun. "What the—?"

"Easy," Clyde advised. Hardy turned from the table, drawing his own gun from beneath his jacket.

"No one needs to get hurt," Hardy said.

228

"Who are you guys?" Toll asked. "Is this a stickup?"

"Something like that, Dr. Toll," Hardy said. He cracked a tiny smile that lasted only a second.

"Fahey," Toll said softly.

"The dance card, Commander Toll," Hardy said. "This time we intend to get it."

"What...?" Toll said, raising his bare arms slowly above his head. He watched Hardy's eyes drop to his belly and focus on the upper half of his appendectomy scar and then return to his face.

"Hand over the dance card and we'll disappear into the night and leave you with your pathology playmates," Hardy said.

"Like nothing ever happened," Clyde added. He stepped quickly into the bedroom and reappeared in a moment. "He's alone."

Toll backed slowly to the sofa and sat down. "Do you mind?" No one knew what was beneath the scar, Toll assured himself. He had to believe that.

"Not as long as you keep your hands in sight," Hardy said. "Check him, Clyde." Clyde put his gun on the table behind Hardy and then ran his hands over Toll's legs and ankles. Satisfied the doctor did not have a gun, he backed away and looked around the room. He spotted the two bags on the luggage stand and went over to them. In an instant he had the briefcase opened and the papers removed. He rapidly looked at each of the papers before dropping them on the floor in a pile.

"We can go easier on you if you tell us where it is," Hardy said. He moved slightly backward and to his left, still keeping the gun on Toll, as he took a few French fries from a plate and stuffed them into his mouth. "The food is for real," he said. "Want some?"

He shook his head. He hadn't eaten since the snack on the plane but his appetite had vanished. He glanced at Agent Clyde, who had begun to search the suitcase, tearing the pockets off the shirts and running his fingers along the seams.

"How did you find me?" Toll asked.

"I don't know how the Agency located you, Commander Toll," Hardy said, sitting himself comfortably in the over-stuffed chair opposite the sofa. "We picked you up in Miami."

"Then you knew about Haiti?"

"We were told you would be on Air France from Port-au-Prince," Hardy admitted smugly.

Toll mentally retraced his exit from Haiti and his entrance into the States at Miami. Robbie! Good old Dr. Robinson and his phony concern about the federal government and their involvement in Martin Luther King's assassination.

"What have you got on Dr. Robinson?" Toll asked bitterly.

"*Henry* Robinson?" Hardy asked. "Why nothing, Commander. For a while we thought he might have been involved, but you're too careful a man to trust your precious dance card to a man like Robinson. He's liable to be picked up leading a march into some southern state capitol. Far too risky."

"Then who?"

Hardy smiled smugly again. More than the assignments themselves, Hardy enjoyed the cat-and-mouse games it afforded him with contacts. It gave him great pleasure to show captured subjects how clever his Agency really was. Without some disclosure the activity was too sterile to satisfy him completely.

"Have any trouble with Immigration?" he asked coyly.

Toll's mind flashed to the Immigration officer and then to the helpful Public Health Service doctor. He nodded resignedly. "You mean, the doctor from the PHS?"

Hardy shook his head slowly. "He's a little too half-baked for us, Dr. Toll. I think he's better suited for the Indians. As a matter of fact we don't find many of those PHS types suitable for our kind of work. We had them as doctors for the Agency for a while, you know. But they're too happy being bureaucrats."

"So the Immigration guy was one of yours," Toll said.

Hardy nodded happily. "We took him off the job right after you were cleared for entry. He's probably back at a desk somewhere in Langley."

Clyde had turned his attention to Toll's shaving equipment in the bathroom. He squirted the pressurized shaving cream into the sink and shook the can next to his ear before dropping it into the wastebasket with a clank. He inspected every toilet article in the doctor's shaving kit and dumped them on the bathroom floor before returning to the sitting room.

"Nothing yet," Clyde announced.

"Go slow, Clyde," Hardy said. "We've got plenty of time. The doc's speech isn't until two tomorrow afternoon."

Toll frowned. "How did you know about my speech?"

"Shit, man, you're on the program," Clyde said. "Something about some kind of screwball worms in the blood? I looked it up. Hell, I might want to hear about that stuff myself. I didn't know you could get worms in the blood!"

"I imagine there is a lot of 'stuff' you don't know about," Toll said with contempt. He had classified Clyde as a man easily disliked, and the ransacking had done nothing to redeem him.

Agent Clyde stiffened at the pathologist's remark. He took a quick step toward Toll and backhanded him across the face. The doctor's head snapped toward his shoulder with the blow and he started to get up.

"Hold it!" Hardy said, pulling Clyde away from Toll and sticking the .357 in his face. A small trickle of blood appeared at the corner of Toll's mouth as Clyde walked angrily to the window and looked out. He was a slow learner and he knew it. He made up for his mental abilities with blind obedience and unquestioned loyalty. Hardy knew what Clyde was capable of and moved in to protect the pathologist.

"Keep that goon away from me," Toll said through his teeth, oblivious to the muzzle of the gun in his face.

Hardy lowered his voice to a near whisper. "Don't lean on Clyde, Doctor. He's an animal. And a damn good one too. I don't want to see you get hurt when you don't have to."

Toll looked at Hardy and followed his eyes. He glanced at the other agent near the window. The man was overcoming his rage, but with great difficulty. Toll quickly decided he had some kind of a pathological personality and to leave him alone.

"Okay," Toll said gently. "I'll behave."

Hardy smiled and relaxed. He turned to his easy chair and lowered the gun. "Tell Clyde you're sorry, Doctor. He's sorry, Clyde. He'll tell you. Won't you, Doctor?"

Toll tried to assess the two agents. They were obviously dangerous men, with Clyde considerably less predictable.

If they were only hit men from some casino, they'd be dangerous enough; but as federal agents wrapped in the flag and convinced of their own patriotism, they were far worse. God only knew what Fahey had told them about the significance of the dance card. At best they had been probably informed Toll was a traitor or a counteragent. Either way he would be expendable in their eyes.

"I'm sorry, Clyde," Toll said. "I didn't mean anything."

Clyde turned from the window, smiling. He was like a small boy who had won a point. Say the right thing and it all got better.

"I only said I'd like to know about them worms in the blood, Doc."

"We call that filariasis, Clyde," Toll said gently. "If you're really interested, I could show you some of the reports I brought with me for tomorrow's speech. They are diseases spread by certain kinds of mosquitoes."

Clyde quickly warmed to the invitation. Toll realized he'd have little trouble diverting this simple agent with a gory description of the skin ulcers produced by the migrating larvae of tropical worms, or the elephantiasis that caused a man's scrotum to enlarge to wheelbarrel proportions.

"Tell him about it, Doc," Hardy said. "The door is locked and you wouldn't stand a chance running from dear old Clyde here." He got up from his chair and replaced the gun in his belt. "In the meantime I'll give this set of rooms a good going-over." He produced a switchblade knife from his pocket and released the spring, snapping the long, gleaming blade into place. Then without comment he began to dissect the chair with surgical precision.

Hours later sunlight streamed into a hotel room reduced to rubble and piles of upholstery stuffing. The furniture in both rooms had been cut to shreds and thoroughly searched. The pictures on the wall had been smashed and sliced. The carpet had been torn up in strips and the drapes had become rags. By contrast, in the corner of the room, at the bar, there was a neat pile of medical reports and several anatomic diagrams over which a tired instructor and his fascinated student continued their review of every pathological condition Toll could think of. During the night Clyde had allowed the doctor to get dressed and together they had filled an ashtray with cigarette butts until all of them were out of smokes.

"Tell me about that cancer of the penis again, Doc," Clyde pleaded, childlike. He picked through the pathologist's diagrams again until he found the one he liked. It showed a grotesque, ragged tumor totally engulfing the head of a penis. Toll had made all of his drawings as brutal as he could, successfully distracting the agent while his partner conducted the fruitless search.

"I told you about that cancer three times already, Clyde," Toll said wearily. "You don't want to hear about that again." He yawned in spite of his efforts to appear wide awake and interested in his medical topics. He was buying time and he had to keep at it.

"Yeah," Clyde agreed, dropping the penis drawing on the bar. "I guess you're right. Tell me about something else."

"Like what?" Toll asked absently. He watched Hardy slit the towels open one by one and drop the strips on the bedroom floor.

"Like how you take out the appendix," Clyde replied.

Toll's attention snapped back to Clyde's face.

"Yeah, Doc," Hardy said, standing in the bedroom door, his knife blade gleaming in the sunlight. "Tell him about the appendix." There was a cruel smile on Hardy's face.

"But I'm not a surgeon," Toll protested.

Hardy moved across the room with his knife, the frustration of his search written all over his face. He was unhappy in defeat.

"I had a sister who had them taken out," Clyde said absently.

"Had what taken out, Clyde?" Toll asked, still staring at Hardy's knife.

"Her appendix," Clyde said. "She had them taken out when she was a kid."

"The appendix is an 'it' Clyde, not 'them,'" Toll said carefully.

"All the same, Doc, I'm interested," Clyde said.

Toll forced himself to look at Clyde's face instead of the knife. Beads of sweat formed on his brow and his left eye began to twitch.

"Maybe we could take out Clyde's appendix," Hardy said. "You'd know how to do that, wouldn't you, Doc?"

"Sure, Hardy. I could do that." Toll forced a smile. "Is that all right with you, Clyde?"

Clyde grinned for a moment and then turned to face Hardy and the knife. The smile died as quickly as it was born. He knew it was a joke, but it made him nervous anyway.

Toll caught Hardy staring into Clyde's eyes. Hardy was squeezing the maximum out of the joke at Clyde's expense. Hardy enjoyed playing with Clyde's anxieties.

Suddenly the phone rang, interrupting the three-cornered stare. "Hold it!" Hardy snapped. "Give me a chance to get to the bedroom phone. You watch him, Clyde." He held the knife in the air and showed it to Toll again. "Watch what you say, Dr. Toll."

The phone continued to ring until Toll picked it up on a nod from Clyde. In another room Hardy eased the receiver off the hook and quietly released the button.

"Anderson," Toll said flatly.

"Oh, Bill," the voice said. "This is Robbie. Did you have a good night's sleep?"

"Yeah, wonderful," Toll said.

"Good. I just thought I'd check with you this morning. Everything set for this afternoon?" The black pathologist's voice was filled with morning enthusiasm.

"Everything is set as far as I'm concerned," Toll said, looking at Clyde. The agent's expression remained firm.

"When can we get together?"

"Anytime you want—the sooner the better," Toll blurted. In his mind he could see Hardy frowning in the bedroom.

"How about twelve thirty?" Robinson suggested. "We could have lunch."

"Breakfast would suit me better," Toll replied. He saw a public meeting with Robinson as a way out of his imprisonment in room 2610 and had nothing to gain by a delay.

Clyde waved his hands, relaying a negative message from Hardy. Toll looked at the wall in front of him, trying to ignore the excited agent.

"There are some committee meetings I can't get rid of," Robinson said. "It will have to be lunch, but we'll have plenty of time."

"It's my slides," Toll said quickly. "They're a little confused and I thought you could help me straighten them out." Clyde moved toward the pathologist threateningly.

"With what you've got to say, the slides won't make any difference," Robinson chuckled. "All you've got to do is to get up there and tell them the whole story. You don't need slides for that." He laughed, enjoying what was to come later that afternoon.

Toll realized he had taken Robinson as far as he dared. He couldn't afford to have him disclose the real subject of this talk. If Hardy already knew what they were up to, it wouldn't make any difference. But if he were still in the dark, there was a chance.

"Okay then, Dr. Robinson, call me around noon or twelve thirty and I'll meet you in the lobby. You're right. We'll have time enough to get it together then." He hung up quickly as Clyde grabbed his shoulders and spun him around.

Hardy came into the sitting room on the run. "You almost blew it, Dr. Toll," he said. He had put the knife back into his pocket.

"Well, it's true," Toll minimized. "I'm already a wreck from staying up all night and I *do* need help organizing my talk." He hunched his shoulders to look innocent.

"You damn near got him up here, that's what you did," Hardy scolded. "That wouldn't have been smart."

"What's the difference?" Toll asked. "He's going to find out about you guys sooner or later."

"We'll see about that," Hardy said. He turned to Clyde. "Unlock the door, Clyde. It's time for all of us to get the hell out of here."

Toll looked a little shocked. Whatever trouble he was in, he was better off in the room. If they took him out of the hotel, Robinson would never find him.

Toll hesitated for a moment. "Can I take a leak first?"

"Yeah," Hardy said, "but be quick about it."

The agents waited in the sitting room as Toll walked to the bathroom. He knew he only had a minute or two. He flushed the toilet for background noise and used a sliver of hotel soap to write "2506" on the mirror. He knew it wouldn't be much of a clue if it were found at all, but a longer message might be discovered by the agents before they left. The code number for the Brigade would have to do.

He returned to the sitting room, still zipping his pants. "Where are we going?" Toll asked.

"We've got someone who wants to see you," Hardy said.

"In Atlanta?"

"Yeah," Hardy admitted. "In Buckhead. We've got a safe house there. And if you cooperate, no one will get hurt."

"But my speech."

"You'll be right back. Now get moving," Hardy barked. He took his gun out of his belt and held it level with Toll's abdomen.

"Who's going to be there? Fahey?" Toll asked, moving toward the door.

"If you don't stop talking and move out of here nice and slowly, I'll make you another scar on your belly to match the one you've already got."

Clyde held the door open as the other two men stepped into the corridor. Sounds of early risers drifted upward from the lobby below them. Many of the conventioners had already finished breakfast and were wandering around the lobby, waiting for the first meeting to begin. It was almost nine o'clock.

The corridor stretched all the way around the top floor like a giant square, ringing the sheer drop to the lobby. Only the elevator complex interrupted it, high above the registration desks. In the corners the architect had built emergency stairwells, spiraling downward to the ground floor with locked doors preventing reentry at any other level. Once into the emergency staircase a man could run down and down, round and round, until he entered the lobby. But inside there would be no chance for help. No screams would be heard and a wounded man might not be found for hours. Toll glanced at the exit sign near his room and prudently decided against a sudden dash into the unfamiliar stairs. He knew he would be safer in full view of as many people as he could find. The agents would have to walk him through the lobby and the crowd might produce a familiar face. He walked slowly with them toward the elevator bank. There was no one else on the twenty-sixth floor anywhere. The agents had buttoned their bellhop jackets over their guns, but all three men knew how quickly they could be produced.

They were halfway to the elevators, Toll in front, the

agents behind. No one spoke. There was nowhere else to go. Suddenly Toll remembered the slides and the medical reports on the bar in his room. He stopped in the middle of the corridor and turned.

"Wait a minute," he said, facing Hardy.

"What now?" Hardy said.

"The maid is going to think all hell broke loose in that room and call someone to clean it up."

"So?"

"They'll throw out all my medical reports and slides with the junk you spread out all over the floor. Let me go back and get them. It will only take a minute."

"No way, Dr. Toll," Hardy said. "We've got a date with the man and he don't like to be kept waiting."

Toll's expression turned hard.

"But Dr. Fuentes and the rest of the people at the hospital in Haiti had nothing to do with all of this," Toll pleaded. "Let me at least get those reports and have them sent back to them. They're good people!" He tried to force his way between the two agents, but Clyde grabbed him by the neck and the arm. The agent was incredibly strong and Toll began to gasp for air.

"The dance card, Dr. Toll," Clyde grunted. "That's what this is all about. Nobody cares about your stupid medical reports."

Toll summoned all of his remaining strength and spun himself and Clyde around, crashing first against the wall and then into Hardy. He brought a foot up sharply into Hardy's abdomen, doubling the man over in pain. At the same time he twisted free from Clyde's neck hold and tried to run. The agent did not let go of the pathologist's arm and was dragged along for a few steps, off balance and stumbling. Then, partly regaining his balance, he pulled the doctor backward, forcing him onto the railing. The ants in the lobby saw none of the struggle so many floors above them.

Toll brought his free hand around as hard as he could and smashed Clyde on the right side of his head, causing little damage, but instantly enraging the man. Clyde hit Toll in the stomach with his other fist and grabbed him around the neck again. He held him against the railing and began to choke him. There was a wild, enraged look in his eye, like that of a wounded animal. In an instant he had both hands around Toll's neck, forcing him backward over the railing until only the pressure of their two bodies kept the pathologist from falling into the lobby below.

Hardy quickly recovered from the kick and grabbed Clyde from behind, pinning his arms on his chest, but the stranglehold continued.

"Stop it, Clyde," Hardy shouted, struggling with his partner.

Toll's lungs screamed silently for air and his heart pounded in his chest. He reached helplessly for the man's face and tried to pry the viselike fingers from his throat.

Clyde suddenly twisted to free himself from Hardy's grasp and the three of them crashed against the railing once more. The two agents grabbed each other for balance when for a moment it seemed as if they were all going over the side. Hardy backhanded the edge of the railing and grabbed Clyde by the front of the coat, but the frightening moment forced Clyde to release his grasp on Commander Toll's neck.

Totally unbalanced when released, Toll tumbled almost gracefully over the railing, a caricature of a diving champion executing a near perfect back dive from a high platform. The fall into the lobby was completely silent and the crash of Toll's body onto the floor could barely be heard by the two agents above him. They looked over the railing hopelessly and then pulled back out of sight when a waitress in the Kafé København dropped her breakfast tray onto a customer's table and screamed. She had witnessed her first jumper.

24 "This is the well-developed, well-nourished body of a white male, symmetrical in all areas, possessing four limbs and moderately obese. There are no visible tattoos. There is, in the right lower abdominal quadrant, an old, well-healed oblique scar measuring approximately four inches in length. The head is covered by moderately short brown hair. There is a prominent area of abrasion covering the right-frontal forehead, with obvious fractures of the skull beneath it. This fracture area is externally compound and through an area of laceration in the tempero-parietal area on the right side of the skull, brain tissue and blood exudes." Dr. Twig Stanton spoke into a microphone that hung above the dissection table, activated by a foot switch under the table. The morgue assistant, Bubba Hutcheson, had already looked the body over, but knew that it was not his job to supply the description in such an unusual case.

"The eyes are blue, the sclerae white, and the conjunctivae are injected. The pupils are dilated bilaterally. The nose is deformed to the left, and probably fractured. There is a slight amount of blood in the nose and mouth, now coursing backward along the left cheek. The face is otherwise free of wounds. The mandible and maxilla are fractured. The dentition is that of the decedent and shows normal repair. No dental chart is prepared at this time." Dr. Stanton reasoned that the fingerprints would be sufficient to confirm the identification with the doctor's naval records. He hated to make dental charts anyway. The jaw was usually firmly set by rigor mortis, requiring him to break it or cut through the cheek. Sometimes he could pry the mouth open and look at the teeth with a curved dental mirror, but slicing the cheek gave better exposure. He stepped on the foot switch again.

"The neck is well developed and exhibits superficial abrasions bilaterally, overlying the external lines of the sternocleidomastoid muscles and measuring approximately one by three centimeters. They are oriented medially and slightly downward."

He paused in his dictation to glance at his assistant. "If I hadn't seen this body on the floor of the hotel lobby myself, I would wonder about his being strangled." He pointed at the neck abrasions.

"You think somebody helped him off the twenty-sixth floor, Doctor?" Hutcheson asked.

"This case has a lot of loose ends, Bubba. Nothing would surprise me."

"Well, I never got tied up in the body cooler before," Bubba said. He rubbed his wrist as he reminded himself of the ordeal.

"Whoever those guys were, Bubba, they certainly knew what they were after. They cut the pockets out of this doctor's clothes like a couple of street robbers rolling a drunk."

"I wonder what they took," Hutcheson said.

"I suspect that they missed whatever they were looking for, Bubba."

"Why do you say that?"

"Elementary, Dr. Watson," the pathologist quipped in his best British accent. "They cut *all* of Dr. Toll's pockets. Now, it is improbable that the thing they were looking for was in the very last pocket they cut and they would have ended their search if they found it sooner. Since they cut all the pockets, my bet is that they struck out. Like it?"

The morgue assistant nodded his head and smiled. "Yeah, Dr. Stanton. I like it. It makes sense."

Stanton looked at the body for a moment. "Did you shoot a set of X rays, Bubba?"

"Uh-huh. Do you want 'em up on the view box?"

"Any bullets?" the pathologist asked.

"Not in the head, chest, or belly," the assistant said. He scurried to the darkroom just off the main morgue and shouted, "But he's got one hell of a busted neck."

"I imagine he does, Bubba. Twenty-six floors can have that effect on a fella." He examined Toll's hands and fingers as he waited for the assistant to return with the X rays. There were no "defensive" wounds on the forearms or palms, and none of the knuckles were scraped. The left index fingernail had been torn to the quick, leaving tiny residual wisps that told the forensic pathologist it was recent and suggested a struggle.

"Here's the pictures of the head and neck," Hutcheson said, snapping the films onto the view box. "No bullets." The skull showed a massive eggshell pattern and the upper cervical spine exhibited a fracture/dislocation at C-3.

Dr. Stanton glanced at the assistant and then at the body. There was an well-healed scar at McBurney's point, characteristic of an appendectomy. He returned his attention to the X ray of the abdomen. The view included the tips of the hipbones, and the lumbar vertebrae appeared as gray building blocks, stacked one above the other in the middle of the film.

The pathologist walked to the morgue desk and punched the intercom button.

"Yes, sir?" the upstairs secretary answered.

"Did Detective Baines call or show up with any of the medical records on this case?" Stanton asked.

"No, sir. Not yet."

"Let me know when he does, will you? He said he was going to call someone in Washington and get it read to us over the phone."

"You want one of our investigators to get it from him, Dr. Stanton?" she asked. The medical examiner's office maintained a small team of investigators to dig up information concerning their cases. They were usually recruited from the list of retired policemen. A police background was good experience for a medical examiner's investigator. He had to be professionally nosy, uncover the decedent's secrets, and yet appear unobtrusive to the family and the police.

"No, not yet," Stanton said. "I'll wait for Baines to show up." He clicked the intercom off and returned to the body. He moved his hands along Dr. Toll's upper chest, pressing in to gauge the resistance.

"Are you ready to open him, Dr. Stanton?" Bubba asked, tugging on the cuffs of his latex gloves to work a wrinkle out of one of the fingers.

"I guess so," Stanton said. He accepted the heavy-handled scalpel from his assistant and made the first cut on the chest. Making the first incision was a ritual with him. He was not one of those pathologists who stayed in his office while the assistant did all the dissection in the

morgue. But Hutcheson worked compatibly and skillfully
with his boss. Whenever the pathologist reached into the
field, he would carefully withdraw his knife. Not cutting the
boss was a good way to stay on the job, he often remarked.

Dr. Toll's chest was filled with blood on both sides. The
impact had fractured his ribs and driven several jagged
ends into the spongelike lung tissue. The internal blood
loss was as effective a hemorrhage as it would have been
had it bled outside his body. Juries often had difficulty
understanding that. In the average juror's mind there was
no such space in the chest and even if there were, it was
hard to see how blood in this area would be "lost." It was,
after all, still in the body.

Bubba reached into the chest and pulled the left lung
free. "Be careful of those broken ribs, Doctor," he warned.
His gloved fingers had already found several sharp edges.

"Let's get a blood alcohol on this man before we remove
any organs, Bubba."

The assistant dropped the lung into the bloody pool
within the chest and picked up a large plastic syringe from
the dissection stand. He attached a number 19 needle and
slipped it into the aorta just above the heart. He pulled
back on the plunger, and blood bubbled into the syringe.
When he had taken about 15 cc's, he removed the syringe
and pushed the needle into a rubber-stoppered test tube
containing a small amount of sodium fluoride as a pre-
servative. He wrote George Toll's name, the case number,
and the date on the label to identify the specimen through
the laboratory. Stanton ran a blood alcohol on every suicide.

With the blood sample secured, Stanton began the sys-
tematic removal of the heart, lungs, and abdominal organs
as Bubba aspirated the blood from the chest with a plastic
tube connected to the water faucet beneath the table. The
vacuum carried the blood into the drain with sucking
noises that often made visiting policemen wince.

"Fractured his liver and his spleen," Stanton remarked
casually as he removed these organs.

"Broke his pelvis and his back too," Bubba said, pointing to an obvious fracture at T-11.

"We can't assume all these injuries were caused by the
fall," Stanton said. "He could have been stomped before
he went over the railing. It would be almost impossible to

distinguish abdominal injuries from a kick from those due to the fall."

Stanton put each organ in the weighing pan that hung above the dissection table and gave Hutcheson a chance to record the weights in grams before placing it on the cutting board. The organs showed normal weights for a man of that size and age. Some pathological conditions cause the organs to become larger or smaller, heavier or lighter, harder or softer than normal, and such observations are traditional in an autopsy report. In Dr. Stanton's morgue they were never omitted.

The pathologist continued his recorded description as each body area was explored and dissected. He had described the lacerations in the lungs caused by the broken ribs. He had mentioned the minimal coronary arteriosclerosis. He had noted the fractures of the liver and the spleen, and had recorded a contusion of the left kidney with a small amount of right peri-renal hemorrhage.

"The esophagus is intact and empty," Stanton droned into the microphone. "The stomach is distended by a few hundred cc's of air but contains no recognizable foodstuffs. The gastric mucosa is arranged in delicate folds and shows neither ulceration nor hyperemia. The duodenum and remainder of the small bowel are unremarkable. Tan, pasty, well-digested material is noted in the small intestine. The appendix is present and unremarkable. The large colon exhibits soft brown feces in the distal and...and..."

Hutcheson sensed alarm. "What's wrong, Dr. Stanton?"

"That's funny," the pathologist said, pointing to the junction of the small and large intestine. "He has an appendix!" He held the little organ in his fingers. Its resemblance to a worm had given it its name: the vermiform appendix.

"But he has a scar," Hutcheson protested.

The pathologist returned to the right lower abdominal wall and inspected the scar. He flipped this half-dissected portion of abdominal wall over in his hands and inspected the inside. The internal surface was smooth. The abdominal incision, whatever its purpose, had never penetrated the entire abdominal wall!

Stanton handed the edges of the abdominal skin flap to Bubba to hold while he carefully reopened the surgical scar at McBurney's point with his scalpel. The scar tissue cut with more resistance than normal skin, but parted beneath his blade. Beneath the fat and above the muscular layer of the abdominal wall, he encountered a sealed plastic envelope. It was only partly transparent, having become somewhat cloudy from the body's defense mechanisms.

"What is it, Dr. Stanton?" Bubba asked, his eyes wide with excitement.

"Damned if I know, Bubba," the pathologist said. Stanton freed the plastic envelope from the skin fat and the connective tissue with his gloved fingers. He looked at it briefly, turned it over to inspect the other side, and then held it up to the light. "There's something inside," he said softly.

The pathologist placed the plastic envelope on the cutting board where it was wet but clean. With his scalpel Dr. Stanton cut the edge of the envelope along one entire side. He raised the edge with a rat-toothed forceps and squeezed the envelope between his thumb and forefinger, causing it to bulge open.

"There's a card in here with writing on it," he announced. Dr. Stanton had discovered the dance card.

"But why would anyone want to..." Hutcheson's voice trailed away as he watched the pathologist dry his gloves carefully and remove the damp, fragile card from its plastic pouch. Stanton took the card to the morgue desk, placed it on a clean sheet of white paper, and slid it into the brighter light of the desk lamp. He read the card silently, trying to find some meaning for the names and the other words present.

After a few moments he said, "This has got to be what those goons were after, Bubba."

The assistant had remained at the side of the corpse, burning with curiosity, but trained well enough to know he had not been invited to inspect the card at the desk.

"This card has information on it that is probably secret and none of our business. I want to keep this quiet until I can find out what it all means and what to do about it," Stanton said.

"Yes, sir!" Bubba said. Hutcheson had handled sensitive evidence in many of Atlanta's murders for years and could be trusted.

Stanton stood up, removed his gloves and apron, and

put the dance card in his shirt pocket before washing his hands. "Give me about five minutes, Bubba, and then tell Libby I've gone over to the medical library at Grady Hospital. Tell her I want to look up a rare disease." He walked toward the morgue door.

"I'll tell her," Hutcheson said, looking a little bewildered.

"And you can release Dr. Toll after you've sewn him up," the pathologist said, leaving the morgue.

Hutcheson shook his head slowly and began to pack the dead pathologist's internal organs into the abdominal cavity. He picked up the small glass jar of formaldehyde and wrote the autopsy number on its label. Small pieces of Commander Toll's internal organs selected by Dr. Stanton swirled in the liquid, which served to harden and preserve the tissue. He wondered if Dr. Toll had ever heard his boss's definition of a pathologist. "A pathologist," Dr. Stanton would remark when asked, "is the doctor who tries to get as many people as he can into little glass jars before they get him into his."

25 Shelby Baines half-rose from his seat in the Sundial Restaurant, high atop the Peachtree Plaza Hotel, as Dr. Stanton approached the table.

"I was just fixin' to come over to the M.E. office when you called," Baines said. "When you told me to meet you up here, I thought you had flipped your lid. But you're here, so I guess you know what you're doin'."

"Been up here before?" Stanton asked. He turned to look out over the panorama of downtown Atlanta and the surrounding countryside from the seventy-third floor.

"Once. Just after it opened," Baines said. "I came up here with the hotel manager. His security people wanted us to be familiar with the place in case they had a big holdup or something crazy, like a sniper."

"I called you from Grady Hospital because I knew that I could lose anyone on my tail inside that madhouse."

"That's for sure. I get lost every time I go over there. A thousand beds in one big hospital," Baines said. "But why do you think you were being tailed?"

"Oh, hell, Shelby, I don't know. I didn't want to take any chances. Not after what I found."

Detective Baines responded to the pathologist's hushed tone, and leaned forward. He was about to encourage the doctor to share his discovery with him when a waiter arrived.

"Would you gentlemen like a cocktail before I bring the menu?" he asked stiffly.

"Just coffee," Dr. Stanton said, dismissing him without a glance.

"I'm very sorry, sir. We do not serve 'just coffee' in the Sundial." He made the doctor's order sound like something contaminated.

Detective Baines glanced at the waiter impatiently and flipped his ID folder out of his inside coat pocket. The gold

246

badge flashed in the sun for a moment as the waiter's eyes widened to match. "Bring us two coffees, will ya?"

"Yes, sir. Right away," the waiter said.

Baines threw a contemptuous glance in his direction as he left. "Asshole," he sighed.

"I suppose they have to keep the price up just to pay for the ride," Dr. Stanton suggested.

"They can keep their goddamned ride," Baines said. "Seventy-three goddamned floors on the *outside* of the building? And in a glass elevator? No, thanks! Next time you call me, let's eat at McDonald's, or someplace civilized."

"I knew we'd be safe up here, Shelby. I'm sorry if the ride gave you the willies."

"Safe from what?" The detective looked around the revolving restaurant, sizing up the other patrons as mostly tourists.

"I'm not sure, Shelby. I think I've stumbled onto something big. It was in that jumper from the Regency."

"*In* him?" Baines asked in a half-shouted whisper. He lowered his voice again and pointed his finger at the pathologist accusingly. "Don't tell me. He was a mule and you found his gut full of condoms stuffed with heroin. Right?"

The waiter arrived with the coffee and arranged the cups in front of each man with agonizing care. Baines continued to stare at Dr. Stanton until the waiter had gone.

"Wrong," Stanton said.

Shelby Baines collapsed in his seat with mock defeat. "My big diagnosis," he moaned, "and I blew it. Okay, what then? A suicide note?"

"Better than that, I think," Stanton said. He looked around the room slowly, causing Detective Baines to join him.

"What is it, Doc?" Baines asked quietly and seriously. "Somebody muscling you?"

"No, nothing like that, Shelby."

"Doc, you just say the word and point the bastard out to me and I'll take care of him."

"It's not like that, Shelby, but thanks." The doctor reached across the table and patted the detective on the arm.

"Hey, Doc. Anything. Anything at all. We go back a long way." The detective had already decided the pathologist had gotten himself into a gambling debt or else a prostitute had picked him up and was threatening disclosure.

"Shelby, you said this pathologist was ex-Navy?"

"That's the way we got it. That other squirrel from Iowa or Idaho started us on that track and it turned out to be right."

"How about his service records?"

"They're being sent in," Baines said. "But in the meanwhile I had the highlights phoned ahead. They don't like to do that, but if you lean on 'em..."

"Uh-huh." Dr. Stanton was familiar with the detective's leanings.

"But there wasn't nothin' special about him, Doc. The Navy said his medical history was negative. I mean, he wasn't a mental case or anything like that. They said he'd been around the world, though." He shook his head slowly to register his amazement.

"Did they say anything about any secret assignments?" Stanton asked.

The detective looked at the pathologist and smiled superiorly. "Now, Doc—if the assignment was secret, do you really think they'd tell me?"

"I don't know, Shelby. You have a way of prying secrets out of lots of people before they know it."

The detective raised his eyebrows playfully. "Well," he drawled, "there was one peculiar thing the clerk told me."

"Like what?" Dr. Stanton slipped his hand inside his coat and lightly fingered the dance card in his shirt pocket. He had still not made up his mind to show it to Shelby Baines. Before he did that, he had to know what the detective knew.

"The Navy clerk said that there was a notation on his folder to forward all information received at Central Filing to a Washington phone number. She also allowed that was mighty peculiar. She said she never did see any notation like that on anyone's service record before."

"Did you get the number from her, Shelby?"

"Does a bear shit in the woods?" The detective reached into his pocket and took out a small spiral notebook. He flipped it open and turned the page around to face the pathologist.

"I'm sure you've already tried this number," Stanton said.

"All I got was some guy who confirmed the number and said somebody made a mistake giving out his home phone. He says he don't know nothing about any pathologist or anything about the U.S. Navy."

"Did you get his name?"

"He didn't want to give me his name, Doc, and at that distance I figured what the hell. If he didn't know nothing about the Navy, what do I want to pester him for?"

"What did you tell him?" Stanton asked cautiously. He took a sip of his coffee and tried to seem unconcerned.

"Nothing specific. Of course, he wondered what the call was about when I began to ask him about Dr. Toll, but that's all."

"You, ah ... left him your name," Dr. Stanton suggested. "I mean, in case he wanted to call you back with any information that might come in?"

"Sure. I gave him my Atlanta P.D. desk number. But I don't think he'll know any more later about this case than he does now. It's just a government foul-up. He doesn't know Dr. Toll or anything about him."

"Shelby," Dr. Stanton said softly. "I think you're one of the best homicide detectives in the Southeast."

"Aw, Doc ..."

"No, I *mean* it, Shelby," the medical examiner persisted. "But you may have more to learn about the United States government and some of its cloak-and-dagger departments."

The detective looked around with slight nervousness. "What cloak-and-dagger?"

"You remember those two guys that were eyeballing the scene at the Regency when we first examined Dr. Toll's body?"

"Yeah?"

"Those must have been the same guys who came over to the morgue, tied up my assistant and the ambulance drivers, and cut up Toll's clothes. But whatever they were after, I'm convinced they didn't find it."

Baine's eyes widened in disbelief. "They were after something in the doctor's room at the Regency too. They made one hell of a mess out of the place." He blew on his coffee and sipped it across the surface.

"Okay." Stanton used his fingers to tick off the points as he made them. "They ransack the doctor's room, push him off the balcony, and come over to cut up his clothes."

"Push him off the..."

"Well, okay," Stanton admitted, retracting one of the points already scored on his fingers. "Maybe he fell during the struggle. Maybe he jumped to get away from those two goons. Oh, hell, maybe it's a straightforward suicide, like we thought. But in any event it didn't make sense to me until I did the autopsy."

"Why? What's he got?"

"He had some kind of a list or code or something sewn inside a pouch of surgical plastic in his right lower abdominal quadrant."

"His where?" Baines began to explore his abdomen with his free hand to orient himself to the medical examiner's description.

"Under the skin. Just about where your appendix is," Stanton explained. He watched approvingly as the detective felt for McBurney's point.

"Under the skin!"

"Uh-huh," Stanton agreed. "And he still had his appendix. So somebody went to a lot of trouble to put it in there and make it look like an appendectomy."

He reached into his pocket and produced the dance card. He looked at it for a moment and then slid it across the table toward the detective.

The detective stared at the little card and squinted. *"This* is the thing you found under the guy's skin?" He winced as he said the words, telegraphing the contamination he associated with autopsies.

"You can see a list of names clearly enough," Stanton instructed, pointing at the column to the left side of the card.

"Uh-huh. But what's the other stuff. Some kind of code?"

"More or less. It's medical shorthand. A pathologist would use words like those to describe conditions he might find in an autopsy. Basically they're diagnoses. Look at this one," he said, pointing to the words beside the first name. "It says, 'GSW-neck.' That's got to be a gunshot wound of the neck."

"Okay?"

"And the word next to that?"

"It says . . . 'impaled fence post.'"

"Right. I figure that was another diagnosis to cover the first one."

"To cover?" the detective asked. "Why would they need cover?"

"Who the hell knows, Shelby? But if you'll look at the rest of the list, you'll see that all the names have a military-type injury in one column and a cover diagnosis in the other."

The detective took a moment to check the pathologist's hypothesis and found it to be correct. "Look at this one," the detective said. "The cover diagnosis says 'car wreck.' Why do you suppose this Dr. Toll had the card?"

"Beats the hell out of me, Shelby. But it was there, and it's hard for me to believe that those two guys weren't after it."

"They must have known he had it with him." Baines pushed the card toward the pathologist and wiped his hands on his jacket. It was still something from a dead body and no amount of intrigue would change that. "Do I get a copy?"

"Do you think you should?"

"Why not? It's evidence, isn't it?"

"Technically I guess it is, Shelby. The only thing is— I'm not sure what it's evidence of."

"Well now, Doc. You yourself said it might be a homicide. I guess that makes your little card material evidence. Right?"

"Oh, I can't argue that point with you, Shelby. It's just that if this card is really as hot as I think it is, it would not be wise to let anyone know we found it."

The detective stroked his chin and thought for a moment. "That makes sense," he said. "But if it is that hot, it might be better to keep it in more than one place."

"Would you be willing to keep it out of your report for a while, Shelby? The longer we keep it quiet, the better chance we'll have of finding out what it means before somebody tries to take it away from us."

"You wouldn't want to just call the FBI?" The detective

shook his head as he spoke, indicating he didn't think much of his own idea.

"Not yet, Shelby. We've got to assume the information has something to do with the federal government. I mean, look—it's got a military-type wound for every one of these guys, and Dr. Toll was in the Navy. That makes it government till proven otherwise.

"Before we give it to anybody, I think we've got to try to find out which part of the government it belongs to, and who was trying to steal it out of a pathologist's hotel room."

He looked the detective straight in the eye for a searching moment. "Do we have to tell them, Shelby?"

"You're playing with fire, Doc." He swirled the remnants of his coffee in the bottom of the cup.

"And?"

"Aw, shit, Doc. I'll go along with it if that's what you want."

The pathologist smiled and put the card back in his inside pocket. Baines looked at Stanton and then glanced around the restaurant as the waiter approached with the coffeepot.

"More coffee, gentlemen?" he asked. His tone was not friendly. There was a line waiting for tables, and cops or no cops, the waiter was not happy about two men tying up a table without ordering lunch.

"No, thank you," Stanton said. He knew Baines would stick it to the snooty waiter if he got the chance. It was time to move on. "We've got to be going," he added, standing up.

"I'll take the check," the detective said, eyeballing the waiter.

"Let it be our pleasure, gentlemen," the waiter said, eyeballing the detective.

Dr. Stanton watched the electric silence between the two men for a moment longer than he intended. It was instant animosity. The pathologist threw himself into the static. "C'mon, Shelby, we've got work to do for the citizens on the street."

Baines continued to stare at the tuxedoed waiter as he reached into his pocket and slowly pressed a dime onto the spotless tablecloth. The waiter rolled his eyes toward the sky, spun around, and marched off.

"Fag," Baines said softly.

"C'mon, Sam Spade," Stanton said.

"Christ," the detective sighed. "I just remembered about that damned elevator. How many floors?"

"Seventy-three." The pathologist could not repress his smile.

"And every one of 'em on the outside of the building. What was the guy who built this place? A sadist, or something?"

26 Ed Adams came out of the Hyatt
Regency meeting room, a little
more upset than when he went in.
The lecture, scheduled for 2:30
P.M., was listed in the program as
"Histopathology of the Liver in
Response to Selected Medications." Dr. Adams worried
about patients' reactions to drugs and had sent in a reservation. Unfortunately the speaker originally listed in
the program had failed to arrive from the National Institutes of Health and had sent his dull, mumbling research
assistant to deliver the paper. The NIH "patients" that
practical Ed Adams had hoped for turned out to be isolated
rat liver slices and the medications were all in the experimental stages. At the end of this lecture Dr. Adams was
more convinced than ever that national medical meetings
were a total waste of time.

His meeting with his wife, Maude, was prearranged.
Neither of them drank, so a rendezvous at the Clock of
Fives or the Parasol in the lobby of the Regency never
entered her mind. In fact, not much ever entered Maude
Adams's mind except thoughts about her husband, his
practice, small-town civic activities, and food. At 3:35 P.M.,
in the lobby of the Hyatt Regency, food won out. She was,
as Ed expected, seated comfortably in the Kafé København,
the hotel's interpretation of a sidewalk restaurant, eating
a sweet roll with a fork and waiting for the tea to ooze out
of the bag into her cup of tepid water. Maude had reminded
the waitress to bring "boiling hot water," but the girl was
strung out from the cocaine party she had attended the
night before and couldn't care less.

Ed gave his wife a peck on the cheek before she knew
he was there, and sat down. He put his tape recorder, 35
mm camera, program, and ballpoint on the table and
picked up the shiny menu.

"How did it go, dear?" Maude asked.

"It was a lot of nonsense. That's what it was," Ed said,

still looking at the menu. "Rat livers and experimental leukemia drugs!"

"Sounds *very* impressive," she cooed, poking at the softened butter pat with the edge of her fork.

"I don't see many rat liver biopsies in Poplar Bluffs, Maude."

"Were the slides pretty, dear?"

"Not worth wasting film on, if you ask me. I don't know why, in God's good name, they ask these foolish research peop . to come to meetings like this to talk about their government-sponsored laboratories and the federal rats they feed all kinds of impractical drugs to, just to see if—"

"Dear—" Maude said, touching him on the arm.

"—they turn belly up or all their hair falls out, or—"

"Dear—"

"—they develop tumors of the bladder after a carload of saccharine and—"

"Dear!" she said more pointedly. "They are paging you over the loudspeaker." She pointed into the lobby and cocked her head to one side to improve her hearing. He waited with her for the next announcement.

"Dr. Adams. Dr. Edward Adams, please. [pause] Contact the registration desk in the main lobby for a message. [pause] Dr. Edward Adams." The paging was done by a female voice, devoid of all regional accent, and flat as a board.

"You paged," Ed explained impatiently at the registration desk. "You just paged my name over your blessed loudspeaker." He threw his arm toward the rest of the lobby to help the clerk understand.

"Oh, yes, sir, Dr. Adams," the young man said. "There was a call for you to meet Dr. Berglund at his car on the second garage level."

"At his car?" Ed asked. "Dr. Berglund from Mayo Clinic?" Dr. Adams had, of course, heard of Nels Berglund through his writings, but he had never met the man.

"I don't know, sir. I took the call and a Dr. Berglund— He said he was from Rochester, Minnesota, if that's any help?"

"Yes, yes, that's him."

"Well, he said he wanted Dr. Edward Adams paged and to tell Dr. Adams that he had slides for him. But he said he couldn't wait, and for Dr. Adams to meet him by his car in space number G-eleven in the second-level garage as soon as possible."

Ed Adams frowned and ran the situation through his mind rapidly. His logical explanation was that there was another Dr. Edward Adams registered at the Hyatt Regency for the pathology meeting, and that he would turn out to be Berglund's research assistant.

"Do you have another Edward Adams registered here?" the pathologist asked.

"Another, sir?" The young man flipped his Cardex rapidly. "No, sir. Just one. An Ed Adams, M.D., from Poplar Bluffs, Ohio."

"Iowa," Ed corrected gently.

Dr. Adams walked to the escalator and took it down to garage level. G-11 was in the far corner. There was a beige Mark IV Lincoln in the space. The engine was running and the lights were on. Ed Adams concluded that Dr. Berglund was really in a hurry. He felt better about having responded to the page. Perhaps he could pick up the slides from him, locate the right Ed Adams, and help them out. He opened the passenger side door and looked in.

"Dr. Berglund?" he said, smiling broadly and extending his hand. "You won't believe this, sir, but I'm Dr. Ed Adams. I heard you page for your associate, but I thought I could be of help."

The big man at the wheel reached across the seat, took Ed Adams's hand, and yanked him into the car. At the same time, another man came up from the floor in the backseat and put the muzzle of a snub-nosed .357 against the pathologist's head.

"No trouble, please, Dr. Adams," the man in the back said softly.

Adams became very still and listened to his heart rate quicken. "I haven't got much money on me, but you can take it all," he said.

"We're not after your money, Doctor," the man in back said. "We want you to sit there like a normal human being while we drive out of this hotel. Do you understand?"

"But my wife is upstairs, and—"

"You'll be back, Dr. Adams. You will not be harmed if you cooperate. We have to talk to you."

Adams resigned himself to his captive status, arranged himself in the car and shut the door.

"We're going to drive out of here like three close friends, Dr. Adams," the driver said smoothly.

"But I'll have a gun on your back every inch of the way," the man in back added. "And this magnum will go through the seat like tissue paper. Get me?"

"Where are we going? Why are you doing this? Who are you?" Ed Adams asked rapidly.

The car rounded the pillars with low-pressure squeals and wound its way up the concrete ramp to exit on Ivy. The driver paid the parking ticket while the man in back sat close to Dr. Adams's head and purred safe instructions to him. Adams, facing forward, sat as quiet as a statue and dared not to swallow.

Ivy, a one-way street heading north, paralleled Peachtree. The Lincoln turned left into the traffic. A MARTA bus in the next lane gave the Mark IV a dominating blast on the horn and forced it to turn left at the corner, less than half a block away.

"Shit!" the driver said angrily at the bus. "That rotten son of a bitch!"

Dr. Adams did not speak or move. A series of kidnappings in Europe on the news had caught his attention over the previous few weeks, but he was not a wealthy industrialist. The Palestinian terrorist shootings flashed through his mind, but he dismissed the idea as ridiculous. Ed Adams had never had a controversial political thought in his life.

Hardy turned another left onto Peachtree and slowed for traffic. The turn put them in front of the main entrance to the Hyatt Regency. Dr. Adams sighed and turned to look at the hotel as the Lincoln waited for the light to change. Maude was standing outside the main entrance talking to the uniformed doorman. Without thinking, he reached over and leaned on the horn. The result was not a friendly beep, but a long, penetrating blast that continued until Hardy could pry the doctor's fingers off the steering wheel while Clyde applied a hammerlock on his head.

The horn blast evoked furious fist shaking from the driver in front of them as he moved with the traffic. It also made Maude Adams and the doorman look into the street and observe the commotion in the Lincoln. Almost not believing, she recognized her husband as the car leaped away with a squeal.

Clyde reached over the seat and grabbed Ed's necktie. He pulled it over the doctor's left shoulder and relaxed his hammerlock.

"That was a dumb thing to do, Doctor," Hardy said, urgently cutting into traffic and skipping his left turn toward Ivy Street. He continued south on Peachtree past the Plaza Hotel and Davison's Department Store before he turned right.

"Where are you going?" Clyde asked.

"I'm just getting the hell off Peachtree, after that little demonstration," the driver said. He continued past the statue of Henry Grady toward the Omni.

"Relax," Clyde said. "Who do you think noticed? There are two million people in this city. Somebody blows a horn every goddamned minute."

"Just the same," Hardy said. "I don't like it. Let's play it smart. Maybe our cover has been blown and there's somebody waiting for us in Buckhead."

"So?" His partner's anxiety made Clyde search the streets for any sign of the unusual.

"So we junk the Buckhead meeting and get the fuck off the street," Hardy said decisively. He pulled the car into the motor entrance of the Omni International and stopped before they got to the doorman.

"What's the play?" Clyde asked.

"A public place," Hardy said. "A nice safe public place." He noticed the congestion in the doctor's face. "Ease up a little, Clyde. You're going to give him a stroke."

Clyde let the necktie go and put the gun in his coat pocket.

"Now listen to me, Dr. Adams," Hardy said through his teeth. "That was your first mistake, and you're only allowed one. My partner has his gun on you right from his pocket. I've got mine on the other side. We're going to let these turkeys park the car while we walk calmly upstairs into the Omni Hotel. You get it?" He paused for a silent nod from the doctor.

"And then what?" Clyde asked as Hardy moved the car toward the door, following his own instructions.

"And then we walk into Bugatti's like three normal businessmen and order dinner," Hardy said.

"Bugatti's?" Clyde blurted. He bit his lip at the slip and wished Hardy had not turned to glare at him, making it worse.

"Exactly," Hardy said, apparently remaining calm. "Who would look for us there, if in fact anyone were interested in our whereabouts?"

"How 'bout our old friend in the black suit?" Clyde asked.

"He ought to be in Atlanta by now. I'll give him a call and ask him if he wouldn't care to join us."

"And stick him with the check," Clyde added slyly.

The three men got out of the car. Hardy tossed the keys to the Omni doorman and waited for him to get behind the wheel. "Doctor, you may never know why, but let me assure you—we are authorized to kill you, if necessary." The agent and the pathologist exchanged an eyeball-to-eyeball look that made believers out of both of them.

They entered the motor lobby and waited impatiently for the elevator. They said nothing more as they rode one floor to the plush Omni International Hotel lobby and stepped onto the deep carpet. Hardy paused for a moment and then stopped a passing bellhop. "Bugatti's?"

"Over there, sir," the bellhop said, pointing toward the far end of the lobby and a dimly lit passageway. "But it is not yet open," he added, glancing at his watch.

"Not open?" Hardy asked, obviously disappointed.

"No, sir. Not until six thirty," the bellhop said.

"What now?" Clyde asked. "You want to take him into a bar and wait for the restaurant to open?"

"I don't drink," Dr. Adams said self-righteously.

"No. Too risky," Hardy said. "Let's see if the old man is in."

"He's staying *here?*" Clyde asked. He gave the opulent lobby another once-over.

"Hell, yes, he's staying here," Hardy said, lowering his voice. "The Navy and the Jesuits travel first class."

"What's the Navy got to do with this?" Dr. Adams asked quickly. "I'm an ex-Navy man myself."

"Uh-huh," Hardy said, looking at the row of housephones along the wall. "Watch the doctor, Clyde. I'll check on our friend upstairs."

The two men watched him walk to the phones and pick

one up. He was far enough away that they could not hear him speak.

"What's this all about, anyway?" Dr. Adams demanded.

"Security," Clyde said softly.

"Security, my foot. If this is some kind of damned fool FBI stunt, my congressman will hear about it first thing in the morning. And let me tell you, he's influential down there in Washington too. Been there through three administrations. Why, there's nobody that he doesn't know. In fact, he's been—"

"Did you get him?" Clyde asked as Hardy returned.

"Yeah. He's here," Hardy said, "and madder than hell about us bringing the doctor here. He wants it to go his way, every time. Couldn't care less about how tough it gets on the streets."

"Ivory tower," Clyde said derisively.

"It goes back a long way, Clyde," Hardy agreed. "You know these Kennedy appointments." He suddenly remembered Dr. Adams. The doctor was so retiring it was easy to forget him, even when he was present.

Suddenly a swarm of little boys, ages seven to nine, ran into the lobby from the activity section of the Omni. They carried ice skates in their hands, or around their necks on the laces. They shouted and laughed wildly as they pranced ahead of a bewildered nun.

"Boys!" she shouted in a high-pitched voice that failed to carry very far. "Boys! Stay together. Do not run! Come back here and form a line." She shrugged helplessly at the three men as the last of her babbling brood engulfed them and ran on. Her habit whistled slightly as she scurried by. "Excuse me, gentlemen. It's been a *very* long day for them on the Land of Green Ice."

Parochial-school instincts were triggered subconsciously in both agents, who nodded respectfully as they paused to let the nun pass. They watched silently as the thundering herd headed for the elevator to the motor lobby and pushed the down button several hundred times.

Hardy turned to Clyde with a benign look on his face. In a moment they realized they were alone. Dr. Adams had quietly slipped away into the crowd.

"Son of a bitch!" Clyde said, looking around the lobby rapidly. "He's gone!"

Hardy looked in the opposite direction with no better luck. They ran toward the entrance to the main Omni. Inside, the two stories of shops and restaurants babbled with people. The entrance from the hotel lobby opened onto the second floor. The ice-skating rink lay below them, filled with children and adults skating counterclockwise to recorded music. Towering above them were the many floors of the hotel, the office complex, and the Mad Mad World of Sid and Marty Kroft. The two men paused for a moment in front of Givenchy's boutique and looked over the entire scene. There were hundreds of people in view, but not one of them was Ed Adams.

At that moment Dr. Adams, breathless and frightened as a hunted rabbit, huddled in the back of a bazaar filled with ornate brass artifacts, and begged the alarmed Pakistani proprietor to hide him and call the police. The storekeeper at first thought the sweating pathologist was a robber, but then decided he was drugged, crazy, or both. He was happy to oblige with a call to the Atlanta P.D. Memories of his own persecution in Bombay at the end of the British rule made him halfway sympathetic to the frightened Iowa doctor. He let Dr. Adams hide in his tiny storeroom until Detective Baines arrived fifteen minutes later.

"This is my day for crazy calls from the Adams family," Baines said as he gently opened the storeroom door. He had learned not to surprise or challenge frightened men.

"Oh, Mr. Baines," Adams said, "I'm so glad to see you." He glanced appreciatively at the storekeeper. "This man let me hide till you got here."

"Your wife was phoning me from the Regency at the same time you called," Baines said. "What's this about your being kidnapped?"

"It was awful," Adams said. His lower lip began to quiver slightly. "They were government men. And they said they were authorized to kill me. Is Maude all right?"

The Pakistani businessman quietly decided all governments are the same.

"Who were they, Dr. Adams? Your wife is fine. I sent a man over to the Regency to stay with her until we got there." His sentences ran together in an excited string.

"I don't know who they were. They were named Hardy

and Clyde. And they said some friend of theirs was staying at the hotel."

"At the Regency?" Baines asked.

"No. *This* hotel. *Here.*"

"The Omni?"

"Yes. They called him on the housephone, but he must have been upset that they brought me here. He told them to take me to a 'safe house' in a place called Buckhead. Do you know where that is?"

"Buckhead is a fashionable section of Atlanta," the Pakistani supplied proudly.

Baines looked at the shopkeeper for a moment and assumed he lived there, in one of the posh apartments along East Paces Ferry Road. Pakistani shopkeepers could afford to live there. Atlanta detectives could not.

"Are you sure they said 'safe house'?" Baines said, pronouncing the words with clinical precision.

"Safe house. Yes, I'm sure of it. Why?"

"It's a...government term," the detective said, eyeballing the Pakistani. The businessman took the hint and moved to the front of the store, leaving the two men alone.

"I thought they were FBI, but they said something about the Navy, so I'm not too sure," Adams said. He mopped his brow with a crumpled handkerchief and stuffed it into his pocket.

"Why Navy? Why FBI?" Baines asked, bunching words again.

"They *looked* like FBI. Y'know. Big, Anglo-saxon, dark suits, that sort of thing? But they said something about the Navy and the Jesuits traveling first class."

"The who?" the Georgia detective asked.

"The Navy and the Jesuits. That's a Catholic religious order," Dr. Adams explained. "They run places like Notre Dame University."

"Oh," Baines said, not really comprehending. He knew even less about Notre Dame than Adams did.

"Nothing like this has ever happened to me, Mr. Baines. In fact, nothing ever happens to me, and that's the way I like it. Now at this pathology convention I run into a man I haven't seen in years, and he turns up dead—a suicide no less! Then these two guys hold a gun to my head and talk craziness about the government and the Navy, and all..."

"It will be all right, Dr. Adams," Baines said, calming him. "We'll figure it all out. Do you think you'd recognize those two men if you saw them again?"

"I'm positive I would, sir, but I'm not going out looking for them. Once is enough. This time they're liable to kill me. And I wouldn't even know what for."

"How did they get your name?" Baines asked.

"Damned if I know. I was paged at the hotel—"

"Your wife told me that."

"—and I thought it was a chance to meet Nels Berglund and—"

"Meet who?"

"Nels Berglund. He's a well-known pathologist from the Mayo Clinic."

"In New Orleans?"

"No, Rochester, Minnesota," Adams supplied, a little offended by the detective's ignorance of American medical facilities. "But when I got to the hotel garage, these two men grabbed me and pulled me in the car. A big one—a Lincoln, I think."

"Did you see the license plate?"

The pathologist shook his head. "No, I guess I was too excited about meeting Dr. Berglund. I just didn't—"

"Well, Dr. Adams!" Twig Stanton said, stepping around the opened storeroom door and interrupting them. He glanced at Shelby Baines and nodded hello. "What sort of a pathology seminar did they schedule for you here?" The medical examiner laughed a little to lighten the moment, but it didn't work.

"Oh, Dr. Stanton. I'm glad to see *you*," Adams said. He grabbed Stanton's hand and pumped it. "How did you get here?"

"*I* called him," Baines said.

"But why?"

"I also thought your abduction was possibly linked to the dead pathologist." He glanced at the medical examiner. A slight nod told Stanton that he had not discussed anything important with Dr. Adams.

"After all, you identified him," Stanton said. "You may be the only one who can help us." He fingered the edges of the dance card in his pocket and wondered if he should have left it at the office.

"Me? How?"

"Point out the two men to me," Baines said.

"But they tried to kill me."

"Look," Stanton said reassuringly, "Detective Baines has men all over the place by now. Whoever those two guys were, they are not going to attack you in the middle of the Omni. All you've got to do is point them out. The police will do the rest."

Adams was either challenged or reassured by these words from another pathologist. He agreed to accompany the medical examiner and the detective to the second floor overlooking the skating rink and to study the crowd for any glimpse of the two agents. As they left, Ed Adams promised himself once again that, accreditation or no accreditation, this would be his last pathology conference away from home.

27 Room 1540 at the Omni International Hotel overlooked the indoor skating rink. It was approached, as were all of the rooms in the hotel, by a glass-in elevator that rose from the lobby on the outside of a massive concrete column. The room was expensive, the appointments were plush, and the perfumed soap had *OMNI* etched into its side.

A quiet man with a gray Hemingway beard looked out the window and wondered about the few hundred skaters below him. He saw the whole structure as a monument to frivolity and wondered if it was solvent. It wasn't, but it was too far in debt to fold.

The man was dressed in a black suit and a full Roman collar. He fingered a vial of nitroglycerine pills and squinted as he searched the crowd below for a glimpse of Hardy or Clyde. Ordinarily he would not appear at a scene. As an executive he was good: assigning a specific task to competent agents and then staying out of their way. But this operation was different. It was the end of a long and difficult responsibility given to him by a president he respected. As far as he was concerned, the dance card was the last problem. With the recovery of the dance card his promises to JFK would be fulfilled.

He continued to scan the crowd. At the far end of the rink, leaning over the railing on the second floor, just outside Reggie's English Pub, he spotted the two agents. It was apparent they were searching the crowds, sometimes pointing in opposite directions and then rejecting these choices with violent head shaking. The man in the window fumed with anger and frustration.

Then as if by appointment the agents pointed toward the far end of the second level, an area the man upstairs could not see from his window. They began to run through the crowd. The man adjusted his Roman collar, turned from the window, and left his room. Alone in the elevator he plummeted toward the lobby, stopping only on the sixth floor for an obese, well-dressed woman to get on. She carried a tiny dog that glared at the priest with unmistakable distrust while soaking up the inane cooing of its mistress with sensuous appreciation.

"Reverend?" she said distantly, greeting the priest.

"Madame?" he asked in return. The woman, a southern fundamentalist, associated his demeanor with Catholicism in general and grunted smugly to her dog.

The elevator opened into the lobby and the woman got off. Annoyingly, she paused at the door, trapping the priest briefly, before moving on.

The priest half-trotted toward the skating rink. The lobby exit came out on the second level above the ice. According to his mental calculations he had found the right corner. He could only hope the agents and the man they had excitedly pointed at were still there. Faces and bodies squeezed by quickly, giving the priest only a moment to glance at each of them.

Three men that he did not recognize suddenly appeared in front of him and stopped. Dr. Stanton acknowledged the priest's collar with a courteous nod. It was obvious that these men were also searching the crowd. To the priest they could have been three businessmen late for a meeting. To them he was a priest on an unannounced mission. Then without comment the men passed by each other and hurried on in opposite directions.

The priest continued to sweep the oncoming faces for the two agents. Suddenly, out of a knot of shoppers, Clyde and Hardy appeared, brushing by him on the right.

"We found him," Hardy puffed aloud. He threw his eyes toward Dr. Adams and the other two men.

"Found whom?" the priest asked Hardy. He turned to face the same direction as the agent. The agents looked at the bearded priest for a moment and then recognized him.

"The old doc that identified Toll's body," Clyde added, surprised to see the man in the Roman collar.

"But—" The priest tried to gather more details as the agents rushed on.

"He's right up there, and I think he's alone," Hardy announced. In his surveillance he had evidently not identified Shelby Baines or the medical examiner with Dr.

Adams. For agents with as much experience as Hardy and Clyde, that was unforgivable.

"Be careful," the priest warned, "he's liable to..." The two agents had slipped into the throng. He knew he would not be able to hold them.

Several feet in front of him, Hardy reached Dr. Adams. The pathologist stood between Stanton and Baines. All three were looking in the opposite direction and did not see the agents approach. Hardy reached for Adams but missed with the first try. The second time he managed to grab him by the right elbow. The doctor spun around, gasping in terror as he recognized the agent.

"Doctor, please," Hardy said, "I only want to—"

"It's him!" Dr. Adams shrieked. "He's one of them!" He wrenched his elbow free and cowered toward Detective Baines.

Baines's instincts were instantly triggered, and his right hand flashed beneath his coat, producing his snub-nosed .38. Hardy's brain registered "Russians" while Clyde's said "international terrorist." Hardy's .357 appeared from his shoulder holster in a flash, with Detective Baines a split-second quicker. The .38 went off with a roar just before Hardy's weapon fired. The agent grabbed his chest, lurched into some bystanders, and fell over the railing onto the ice-skating rink below. Dr. Adams yelled in pain and spun around into the wall. A woman screamed as the crowd recoiled a step or two from the shooting.

"Police officer!" Baines yelled, pointing his gun at Clyde's belly.

"Federal agent!" Clyde countered. He pulled his gun off target and expected a bullet to crash through his liver any moment. It was like watching a school clock tick to the hour and waiting for a bell that would never ring.

"I'm hit," Dr. Adams groaned. He slid down the wall, leaving a bloody smear, and slumped into a heap on the floor. Hardy's bullet had crashed through the outer edge of Dr. Adams's shoulder, tearing a groove in the right deltoid muscle and opening a small artery. Blood gushed from the wound, soaking his jacket sleeve, and seeping between the fingers of his left hand as he tried to apply pressure. Dr. Stanton immediately bent over him, trying to help.

"What the hell is going on here?" Dectective Baines

shouted at Clyde. He pointed his .38 at the middle of the agent's sweating face.

"I'm a federal agent," Clyde puffed. He let his revolver drop to the floor.

"You're almost a dead man," Baines said through his teeth. He glanced at Dr. Adams and instantly returned to the agent. "How bad is Adams hit, Doc?" he asked the medical examiner.

"It's just his arm, I think, Shelby," Stanton said. He unbuttoned Adams's coat and looked him over for a chest or abdominal wound. There was none. Dr. Adams was conscious—but obviously in a state of emotional shock. His lower jaw quivered like a man coming out of ice cold water.

"Let's see the ID," Baines snarled at Clyde. "Slowly. Or I'll blow your brains all over the skating rink."

Agent Clyde reached toward the left breast pocket of his jacket. His movements were careful and slow. His gaze was fixed on the muzzle of the detective's gun and the cold eyes behind the rear sight. The agent took out a small black folder, opened it, and held it in front of his neck. Detective Baines quietly appreciated the professional movement that let him read the ID card and still maintain his on-target position. The card identified the man as CIA.

"Is this one of the guys that grabbed you, Doc?" Baines asked.

Dr. Adams looked at Clyde over Stanton's shoulder. "He's the one from the backseat," he blurted. "He's the one who stuck the gun against my head."

"You sure?" Baines asked.

"Positive," Adams said. He struggled to get up but Dr. Stanton held him down.

"But there's two of them," Adams persisted. "Where's the other one?" His eyes searched the nearest bystanders.

"He went over the rail," Baines supplied, indicating with his head.

"I'll take a look at him," Stanton said. "You'll be all right," he reassured Dr. Adams. "Just hold this handkerchief tight against the wound. We'll get a Grady ambulance up here for you in a few minutes."

"Be careful, Twig," Baines said. "That guy is armed and wounded."

"Or dead," Clyde said grimly.

"If we're lucky," Baines agreed. "He's got to be some kind of a maniac."

"He was a dedicated federal agent," Clyde said.

"Not when he pulls a gun on me, he ain't," Baines said. "What the hell were you guys after, anyway? What's Dr. Adams got you're so all fired interested in? Drugs?"

"We are *not* DEA, sir," Clyde said, apparently offended. "We're CIA."

"Yeah, well same difference to me," Baines sneered. "A fed is a fed. Who gives a crap who signs your paycheck. You're all a bunch of assholes."

"We had our orders," Clyde said.

Dr. Stanton stood up, careful not to get between Baines and his prisoner. "I'll go check on the other guy, Shelby. What's his name?" he asked the captive agent.

"His name is Hardy," Clyde said.

"What's his whole name, dummy?" Baines said, still pointing the gun.

The agent stared at Detective Baines without flinching. "His name is Hardy," he repeated slowly. The two men continued to stare at each other without yielding.

"Anyway, I'll check him out," Dr. Stanton said.

Dr. Stanton nodded, glanced at Adams once more, and slipped into the crowd. The bystanders parted to make a path for him as if he were contagious. He found the spiral staircase to the lower level and scrambled down. At the second turn he could see another knot of people gathered at one end of the rink, just below Baines. The tightness of the crowd told him the object of their curiosity was a body. After hundreds of homicide scenes the medical examiner could almost smell a death crowd.

"Let me through, please," he said to the outer fringe of the crowd. "I'm the medical examiner."

The crowd parted reluctantly, as if unwilling to yield their positions for the rest of the show. With effort Stanton emerged into a small clearing. Agent Hardy lay faceup on the ice, his shirt soaked with blood and his head cradled in the lap of a bearded priest. The agent made sticky bubbles through the blood oozing from a bullet hole in his chest. His eyes were rolled back and his lips were very pale. The priest wore a purple ribbon over the back of his neck. One end dangled onto the agent's bloody shirt as he mumbled the prayers for the dying. Stanton slid in next

to the priest and touched one of the agent's eyeballs. There
was no corneal reflex.

"...*absolvo ab omni peccati...*" the priest droned softly.

"Last rites?" Dr. Stanton asked.

The priest nodded without breaking his rhythm.

"Good," Stanton said, "because he's dead." A small gasp
came from the nearby crowd at the doctor's announcement.

"You're a doctor?" the priest asked.

"Yes, Father, I'm the medical examiner."

"For Atlanta?" The wrinkles at the corners of the
priest's eyes danced slightly, indicating he might have
been pleased.

"Right. Metropolitan Atlanta." Dr. Stanton stood up
and looked at the lifeless form on the ice beneath him.

"A robbery?" the priest asked.

"Something like that, Father." He looked at the second
floor above him and saw Detective Baines looking down.

"You all right?" Baines shouted.

"Yeah. Everything's okay down here," Stanton shouted
back.

"Is he dead?" Baines asked.

Stanton nodded his head and held out his right hand,
thumb down.

"There'll be a couple of officers down there in a few
minutes," Baines said. "I used the security guard's radio
up here."

"Good," Stanton said loudly. "After all this I need a
break."

"I'm sending Dr. Adams to Grady Hospital from up
here," Baines yelled.

"Is the doctor seriously hurt?" the priest asked solic-
itously.

"He took a bullet across the arm," Stanton said, demonstrating on his own body. "He'll be okay once they get
him to the E.R."

The two uniformed officers emerged through the crowd
of bystanders as promised. One of them brought a hotel
sheet and spread it over the agent's body.

"You can move him to the morgue when the ambulance
arrives for Dr. Adams," Stanton told the nearest cop. "I'm
sure it will be all right with Detective Baines." The officers
nodded and one of them took the inevitable notebook out
of his pocket. He glanced at his watch and began to write.

"I wonder if I could have a word with you privately, Dr....ah," the priest said softly.

"Stanton. Twig Stanton," the M.E. supplied.

"Dr. Stanton? I think I've heard the name."

"Oh? Where?" Stanton asked skeptically.

"I'm not sure," the priest said, "but probably in relation to your business rather than my own." He smiled coyly.

Stanton thought about the priest's remark for a moment and returned the smile. "You're all right, Father..."

"O'Connell."

"Most people would be pretty shaken up by the scene of a homicide."

"Well, Doctor," the priest said slyly, "if a priest and a pathologist can't maintain good spirits in the face of death, who can?"

"C'mon, Father," Stanton said, taking the aged priest by the arm. "I'll buy *you* a drink."

"Best offer I've had all day," the priest said lightly.

Stanton caught the eye of the officer nearest to the body. "Tell Detective Baines I'll be in Burt's Place if he wants me." He threw his eyes toward a well-known bar above them.

"Or even if he doesn't," the priest added, smiling. They started through the crowd and Stanton detected a grimace on the man's face.

"Are you all right?" Stanton asked.

"Just a little angina."

"Got something for it?"

"Nitro. I'll be all right when we sit down and have our drink."

"We'll walk slowly," Stanton assured him.

"Thank you, Doctor." The priest mopped his brow with a gray crumpled handkerchief. Stanton vowed that if the Pope ever called him for advice he would tell him to issue a clean, well-pressed handkerchief every day to every priest. Just as Conrad Hilton would do for all his employees.

The two men walked across the ice, excusing themselves through the crowd. Some of the people were on skates, but everyone just stood around silently, awed by the fascination of homicide.

They arrived on the second level almost in front of Burt's Place, a popular bar and restaurant done in turn-of-the-century junk, with a caricature of the owner on the door. The priest paused for a moment, catching his breath. He fumbled for a nitroglycerine pill in his left coat pocket.

"Let's wait a moment, Father," Dr. Stanton said. "We can sit right here and rest until you're feeling better."

The man shook his head and placed the tiny pill under his tongue with trembling fingers. "There's no time," he said. "There's a lot for us to talk about."

"Father," Stanton said, touching the priest's arm gently, "I'm a pathologist. I know about these things. Our drink will wait."

"But I cannot," the man said. His sense of urgency and disregard for his own well-being urged the medical examiner on. Inside the bar Dr. Stanton found an empty table and assisted the priest to a chair. He sat across the table from the old man, studying his face for signs of a heart attack. It was clear the priest was uncomfortable, but he was not pale or sweating. He seemed stronger than Stanton expected for a man with angina.

A girl in a scanty costume rushed to take their orders.

"Chivas on the rocks," Stanton said.

"Spanish brandy," the priest sighed. When he said it, it sounded like a medicinal.

"Y'mean like Courvoisier or Christian Brothers?" the girl asked nasally.

The priest shook his head, refusing both, but then wiggled his gnarled hand at the girl to indicate he'd changed his mind. "Courvoisier will do fine," he said weakly. He turned to Dr. Stanton again as the girl departed.

"I knew a priest in Tampa who used to drink only Felipe II or Carlos Primero," Stanton said lightly, still worried about his companion's health.

"He was either a smart man or Spanish," the priest quipped. His ability to compete despite his chest pain forced the pathologist to admire the old man.

The girl quickly brought the drinks and put them on the table. Stanton raised his glass in a silent salute to his own survival and took half the Scotch in the first gulp. The priest trembled his snifter to his lips and took a meager sip.

"Dr. Stanton," the priest began, placing his brandy on the table and dabbing his mouth with the napkin, "it is my impression that we may have a mutual acquaintance."

"Who might that be, Father O'Connell?"

The priest squinted at the medical examiner before looking over his shoulder, as if to assure himself there were no eavesdroppers.

"Commander George I. Toll, United States Navy Medical Corps." He folded his hands in front of him to watch Stanton's reaction.

Stanton was stunned. He stared at the priest for a moment and then finished his Scotch without speaking.

"Dr. Toll, I believe, was found dead in the lobby of one of your downtown hotels," the priest continued.

"I know the case," Stanton said. He tried not to sound shocked.

"I was sure you would."

"Why is that, Father?" Stanton asked.

"Because he had some information that belongs to me. Very *secret* information. Information of vital importance to the security of the United States itself." The priest had lowered his voice to a rasp. The light from the red cocktail candle flickered eerily across his face, making him appear suddenly grotesque.

"What...information?" Stanton whispered. He jiggled the ice in his glass nervously.

"The dance card, Dr. Stanton. The dance card." He lifted the corner of his table napkin and showed the pathologist the muzzle of a .38 caliber derringer.

28

Baines turned Agent Clyde over to another detective for transportation downtown and further questioning. Clyde protested that the APD was interfering with a vital government investigation, but Baines assured him he would have the opportunity to clarify all that with the captain. Shelby Baines was reluctant to turn loose any man who had pulled a gun on him, no matter who he claimed to be.

At the same time, he supervised the removal of the dead agent's body from the ice, and ordered Dr. Adams transported to Grady Memorial Hospital. As a courtesy to the frightened Iowa pathologist Baines requested a police car for Maude Adams to join her husband in the E.R. There would be time for him to question Dr. Adams and his wife later.

Baines spoke briefly to the sergeant in charge of the crime scene and walked across the ice toward Burt's Place. A cabaret like Burt's Place did not often attract a career detective like Shelby Baines unless he had someone under surveillance and the visit became unavoidable. He was quite aware there was nothing more obvious than a plainclothes cop sitting in a bar, not drinking.

He found Stanton and the priest at a table near the door as soon as his eyes adjusted to the dim light. There were glasses in front of each of them but they were not drinking. In fact, neither of them spoke as he joined them.

"My name is Detective Shelby Baines," he drawled, dragging up a chair from an empty table nearby. He held his hand out to the priest as he sat down.

"I am Father O'Connell," the priest said. "Excuse me for not shaking your hand. Under the circumstances you will understand."

Baines shot a glance at Twig Stanton and assessed the pathologist's serious expression. "What's going on here?" Baines said quietly. He was professional enough to sense when one man had the drop on another, but he was trained to remain calm and to underreact.

"I want you to remove your gun from your holster, Mr. Baines, and to put it under your napkin, slowly and quietly," the priest said, exposing his weapon.

"What the hell is this?" Baines asked through his teeth. He slipped his revolver out of his holster and eased it under the napkin. The double muzzle of the little derringer looking at him told him it was a large caliber and not to be fooled with.

"Just my job, Mr. Baines. You'll understand soon enough," the priest said softly.

Dr. Stanton studied the priest's eyes again. They were less serene than he expected, and his beard was well trimmed. When they had entered the bar, Stanton had detected the slight aroma of Brut cologne on the priest's face but had not been concerned. The gun had come as a complete surprise, even for a "modern" priest.

"A holdup is now a priest's job?" Baines asked.

"This is not exactly a holdup, Mr. Baines," the priest said.

"Then what 'exactly' is it, Father O'Connell?" Stanton asked.

"It's a matter of national security, as I told you. Now if you will be so kind as to hand over the dance card, Dr. Stanton?" He held his other hand out expectantly. On the fourth finger there was a plain gold ring with an onyx stone.

Detective Baines's expression changed slightly at the request. He quickly recovered his poker face and avoided a glance at Stanton.

"Even if I knew what you were talking about, Father O'Connell, what makes you think I would have it with me?" Stanton asked.

"You autopsied Commander Toll," the priest explained. "If you found the dance card, you probably recognized it as something important. At least I presume a man of your intelligence would infer its importance from the unprofessional commotion that our two inept agents caused looking for it." He smiled again and wiggled his hand insistently.

"So?" Stanton asked. He had decided that despite his age the man had a brilliant mind, whoever he was.

"So I conclude you would not trust the dance card to

anyone else. At least not yet. For a day or so I would expect you to carry it around and maybe show it confidentially to a friend?" He glanced slyly at Baines but the detective's poker face held.

"You could be wrong," Stanton suggested.

"It's possible, Dr. Stanton, but neither you nor I are paid to be wrong," the old priest said.

"Or scared," Stanton added.

"Besides," Baines said, "you wouldn't actually shoot us right here in the middle of a public bar, would you?"

"In a minute and without the slightest hesitation," the priest said calmly.

"I'm not Catholic, you understand," Baines continued, "but I always thought priests and nuns took vows to avoid sin and violence."

"True enough, Mr. Baines," the priest said, "but not when they are on government service." He reached into his side coat pocket with his free hand and produced a folded piece of paper. He slid it across the table to Dr. Stanton. "Read it," he told the pathologist.

Stanton unfolded the letter and immediately recognized the seal of the President of the United States. The letter was handwritten on expensive bond paper, but it did not look new. He glanced over the top edge of the letter at the priest, and used his eyes to ask permission to share the message with Detective Baines. A nod of the priest's white head told him it was all right. Stanton leaned toward the detective and unfolded the lower third of the stiff paper. The two men squinted to focus on the message in the dim light of the barroom. The candle, flickering inside its ruby red glass jar covered by plastic netting, was in fact a hindrance rather than a help.

"'TO: Reverend Terrence O'Connell, S.J.,'" Stanton read in a low voice. "'FROM: The President. SUBJECT: Special Assignment.'" Stanton stole another glance at the priest before continuing. "'Accept my gratitude for your efforts in my behalf to date. I appreciate your candor in disclosing the existence of the clandestine notes removed from the scene of your recent activity. I cannot understate the need for the urgent recovery of this information. You have my complete confidence and authorization to take *whatever* steps *you* deem necessary to recover the notes identified as 'the dance card.' All military and federal per-

THE DANCE CARD 277

sonnel reviewing this document are hereby commanded to give you complete and unquestioned cooperation." Stanton paused at the signature and date. He was dumbfounded.

"Signed?" the priest prompted.

"By John F. Kennedy," Stanton stammered. "And dated April thirtieth, 1961."

The priest paused for a moment to let the two men comprehend the message. He knew they never would, completely.

"Could be a fake," Baines suggested softly.

"But you'll never get a chance to find out, Mr. Baines," the priest said. He moved the derringer an inch closer to the pathologist and held his other hand out for the return of the letter. He folded it with one hand and slipped it into his coat pocket.

"And those two agents?" Baines asked.

"Bunglers," the priest sighed. "Faithful servants over the years, but at best bunglers. I'm happy they didn't shoot you."

"That's two of us," Baines agreed. "What kind of kooks do you have in this church of yours?"

"Alas, they were not really members of my flock," the old man admitted. "They were servants of Caesar rather than Christ, you might say." He smiled at his own remark.

"I've got one of them downtown," Baines bargained.

"So do I," Stanton added.

"But there are many more, gentlemen," the priest said simply. "Agent Clyde will be free before you get back to your office, Mr. Baines. And as for Agent Hardy... well, they all know they are expendable. It comes with the job." He reached across the table and casually collected the detective's .38, napkin and all.

"Heroism is not confined to federal agents," Baines said firmly. He ground his back teeth together and produced small ripples in the muscles of his jaw.

The waitress showed up but was waved away by the priest before she could ask about more drinks. She had served businessmen in heavy discussions before. She knew they would end their conference and get drunker later.

"You're quite right, Mr. Baines," the priest said. "You could make your move toward me, force me to shoot both of you, and make it slightly more difficult for us to recover the dance card from Dr. Stanton. You could be a hero—

briefly—but you'd be a long time dead, and you'd never know for what. Now, that's not very smart, is it?"

"Smart or not, it might be my job," the detective said.

"Cool it, Shelby," Stanton purred. "This whole mess is bigger than we are and I think Father O'Connell is playing it straight. I'm not saying we'd agree with the whole thing if we knew every detail, but under the circumstances I think we'd better cooperate."

"There's two of us," Baines said confidently. "We could take him."

"But not without getting shot, Shelby," Stanton argued sensibly. "Besides, if that letter is real, I'd like to help Father O'Connell out. JFK would like that. Wherever he is now."

"We all know where he is," the priest said softly.

"And I'm not ready to join him. Not yet," Dr. Stanton said. "Watch me carefully, Father." He reached into his right pants pocket with exaggerated slowness and took out the dance card. He pushed it across the table toward the priest.

"Is that card really this important?" Baines asked.

"*We* think so," the priest said, covering the card with his hand.

"All you feds are crazy," Baines snarled.

"You may be right as rain there," the old man agreed. He glanced at the dance card and smiled to himself. "Oh, God," he purred ecstatically, slipping the card into his jacket pocket. "Tell me," he said to the pathologist, "where did he hide it? We looked everywhere for years."

"In him," Stanton said.

"By Him, and with Him and in Him . . ." the priest mumbled almost to himself.

"Pardon me?" the doctor asked.

"Nothing. Where, in him?"

"Sewed under his skin," Stanton explained. "The scar looked like an ordinary appendectomy."

The priest nodded appreciatively. "Probably did it himself. We checked everybody else he ever knew, for God's sake." He palmed the derringer into his coat pocket and kept his hand there. He stood up and slipped the .38 under his belt with his other hand. From the bar it would have looked like he was only adjusting his pants, but no one was watching.

"How does it work from here?" Baines asked, frustrated and angry.

"It's simple," the priest said, pulling at his Roman collar uncomfortably. "You two stay here for fifteen minutes and I make my getaway."

"You'll never get out of the Omni," Baines growled.

"Ah, but you see, I will," the priest said confidently. "I owe that to dear Mrs. Adams."

Stanton and Baines exchanged quick unbelieving glances. Maude Adams? A woman that benign was involved? The homicide detective scolded himself for misjudging her character so badly.

"Yes, Mr. Baines," the priest explained. "I arranged to have her picked up at the Hyatt Regency. She thinks the man who came to get her is a policeman, of course, but by now she may know the truth."

"A hostage," Baines grunted.

"Insurance," the priest said. "You stay here for fifteen minutes and she goes free." He looked into the faces of each man once more and nodded, apparently satisfied. He walked toward the door and turned to face the table once more before leaving. "Be smart," he added, "and everybody will stay alive." He stepped out of the restaurant, turned right, and disappeared among the people passing by. He walked more briskly now, apparently not bothered by chest pains any longer.

Baines began to fume at the table. He watched the armed priest make his escape and was angry about his inability to prevent it. Shelby Baines was not a good loser. In fact, he could not tolerate losing at all. He started to get up from the table. Stanton reached for his arm and grasped the sleeve gently.

"Take it easy, Shelby," the pathologist said. "That guy is not some nervous amateur. If you jump him too quickly, some innocent people are liable to get hurt."

Baines looked at the medical examiner and knew he was right. "As a matter of fact, Doc, you might be one of them. It wouldn't be fair to risk our best medical examiner for some crazy fed, whatever he's after."

"Thanks, but I wasn't thinking of myself, Shelby. We just don't know how big this whole thing is." He paused to let the impulsive detective consider his words of caution.

"Yeah, Doc, I guess you're right."

"Give him his couple of minutes. What can it hurt to be safe?"

Baines nodded heavily and sat down again. For the time being it looked as if the feds were winning. He was willing to bide his time, but not for very long.

After a few yards the priest's pace became hurried, but he did not run. He detoured through the bazaar and rushed toward the motor lobby of the hotel. He no longer looked like a man with angina. He pushed the elevator button and stood patiently until it arrived. He had the nerves of a man who could defuse a bomb.

The elevator arrived and accepted him. He was relieved to be alone in the elevator and rode it to the fifteenth floor. When the door opened, he sprang out of the car with a light step that belied his apparent age. He walked to room 1540 and opened it with a key. The sign on the door knob still said "Do not disturb." Inside, he leaned on the door with a sigh of relief and self-satisfied grin. After a moment he pulled the Roman collar off and walked toward the dresser. He put the derringer and the detective's .38 on the dresser. He knew the revolver would be too big to conceal if he got into trouble later. He quickly took off the black suit coat and threw it on the bed. Then, reaching behind his back with both hands, he watched himself in the mirror as he untied the black rabat and slipped the vestlike garment off. His T-shirt was damp with perspiration.

The man leaned closer to the mirror and began to pick at his gray beard just below the ear. At first it resisted him, but then started to come loose. He winced as he inched it free along his left cheek. He repeated the operation at the right sideburn and finally pulled it free of his chin and upper lip. The face was smooth and slightly red from the spirit gum that had held the false beard and mustache in place.

He looked at himself in the mirror for a moment. He was obviously pleased with his accomplishment.

He rubbed his face to remove the small pieces of spirit glue that remained on his chin and undid his pants. He stepped out of the black trousers and shoes with one continuous movement and went to the closet. Removing the clothes he found hanging there, he quickly dressed in a light blue sport coat, a deep red sport shirt, yellow Palm

Beach slacks, and brown and white loafers. The outfit would have made any professional golfer wearing it proud to be seen at Pinehurst.

He transferred his own pocket contents from the black suit to the new outfit and opened the door to the bathroom. The lights were on and it looked empty. Then from behind the shower curtain a series of grunts and muffled cries began to fill the room. The man threw the shower curtain back in one sudden movement.

"We made it, Father O'Connell," he said. He looked at the aged Jesuit in the dry tub. The priest was tied in a sitting position, his hands behind him and his mouth tightly bound with adhesive tape.

The man tugged the tape from one side of the priest's face. The Jesuit began to sputter and complain as soon as his mouth was free.

"You're a diabolical man, James Fahey," he gasped, trembling with rage and infirmity.

"We all must do what we must do, Father O'Connell," Fahey said. "Here, try one of these." He held a tiny white tablet in front of the priest's face and helped his trembling tongue work the nitroglycerine into his mouth. The Jesuit ceased struggling against the ropes that bound him and savored the relief that came as the tablet dissolved beneath his tongue. The anger in his eyes melted briefly to gratitude.

"I had to take a couple of the damned things myself to make it look good," Fahey said. "I'm glad they help you, because they didn't do a thing for me."

"They would if you had my coronaries," O'Connell said. He looked at Agent Fahey with disappointment. "Why did you do this to me?"

"I had to. We had only a slim chance of finding these two idiots of mine and interviewing this Dr. Adams they found. I was afraid your heart wouldn't take it." He paused for a moment and offered the priest a shrug. "Am I forgiven?"

"That depends," O'Connell said. "Did you find Dr. Adams?"

"Uh-huh," he grunted slyly.

"And he knew about the dance card?"

"I don't know. He got shot."

"Shot? Sweet Mother of God," O'Connell said. "Who shot him?"

"Hardy. He never did have any brains."

"Agent Hardy? And himself? How is he?"

Agent Fahey lowered his eyes and waited for a more serious expression to appear on his face. Father O'Connell's commitment to the dance card project had never been a joke. His devotion to John Kennedy had never wavered in spite of criticism over the Bay of Pigs and later the assassination. "He's dead, Father O'Connell," he announced grimly.

"May he rest in peace." The priest sighed genuinely. He reflected a moment on how difficult the scene with Dr. Adams must have been. He wondered if he could have prevented the violence if he had been there instead of being held prisoner in a bathtub.

"An Atlanta detective named Baines dropped him when he made a grab for Dr. Adams," Fahey explained.

"Was anyone else hurt?"

"No. Just Adams and Hardy. The doctor will be all right. It was just a nick in the arm."

The Jesuit lowered his eyes and tried to accept another failure on the long, frustrating road toward the recovery of the secret information. "We'll never get the dance card now, Fahey. It's all over. Take these damned ropes off me."

Fahey put on a devilish smile and reached into his pocket. With maddening slowness he produced the dance card and dangled it in front of Father O'Connell's face. The old priest stared at it with disbelief before tears came to his eyes to blur the image.

"My prayers have been answered," he said. "It's been so long. So terribly long." He looked at Fahey and let the tears fall on his wrinkled cheeks without shame.

"Yes, Father O'Connell. And I'm sorry it had to turn out this way for you. Years ago it wouldn't have mattered if you had come along, but now, with your heart and all..." Fahey returned the card to his pocket.

The priest nodded his head and recovered his composure. "I understand, James. I'm an old man. I can't keep up anymore."

Fahey wiped the priest's eyes with a bathroom Kleenex and threw it into the toilet. "The information was too important to take chances, Father. I had no choice. I had to tie you up here and keep you quiet until I found this Dr. Adams. For all we knew, he could have been the one who kept the dance card for Commander Toll for all these years."

"Did he?"

"No. Dr. Toll had it sewn into his skin somewhere. It looks like Dr. Adams had nothing to do with it."

"Then where did you get it?" O'Connell asked.

"From the medical examiner, Dr. Stanton."

"He knew Dr. Toll?"

"Only after he died. Stanton recovered the dance card from Toll at the autopsy."

"And he *gave* it to you?" the priest asked. He wiggled around in the tub to adjust his cramped, tied body.

"Just like that!" Fahey smirked, snapping his finger. "Of course, my .38 derringer helped to persuade him." He patted his coat pocket reassuringly.

"You didn't shoot him too!"

"*I* didn't shoot anyone, my dear Reverend," Fahey said self-righteously. "My role in this whole painful mess has been to track down a card containing information of dubious present value in order to put to rest questionable rumors about an operation that ended as a fiasco." He shook his head painfully. "And they call that government service."

"When President Kennedy asked for our help, James, he didn't set limits." The old priest wiggled again to find a more comfortable spot on his bony frame. "Be a good man now, and untie me. My arteries are too old to stay tied up in a bathtub." In his pleading O'Connell was unconsciously doing an acceptable impression of Barry Fitzgerald.

"I'll tell you what I'm going to do, Father O'Connell," Fahey began. "We came down here together and I'm forever in your debt for calling before you left Washington. Getting the dance card back meant almost as much to me as it did to you."

"I promised the President."

"And so did I, Father, although I admit my allegiance to the Agency sometimes outruns my loyalty to the temporary occupant of the White House."

"In the end it's the same."

"Oh, you may be right," Fahey said. "But we all have

to have our priorities. And mine at this moment are centered around safe transmission of this goddamned dance card back to headquarters. There are still some people up there who want to see it for themselves before they dispose of it."

"And you want to be there to get the credit for its recovery," O'Connell added.

"Well, I think that's only fair. I mean, after all I've been through over the years chasing after Toll..."

"...and taking all that criticism for letting it get loose in the first place..." O'Connell chided.

"Et tu, Brute?" Fahey said, looking wounded. "So you see? The importance of the card leaves me no choice than to inconvenience you a little while longer."

"You're going to leave me *here?*"

"Only for a little while, old friend. The Atlanta Police Department will be all over the place by now, searching the hotel for an old bearded priest with a heart condition."

"Bearded?"

"A touch of theater. I couldn't resist it," Fahey said, posing. "Nobody will be looking for a middle-aged Florida golf enthusiast with a youthful step and a clean-shaven face."

"You figure they'll jump all over me the minute I walk into the lobby," O'Connell theorized.

"Uh-huh. They'll assume the beard was a fake. And that black suit is all you've got to wear. I'm glad we are about the same size."

"I've got some other clothes in my bag," O'Connell protested.

"Correction, Father. By the time you get free from those ropes, you will discover that in Atlanta, you have only one Vatican-approved black suit and Roman collar to your name. I doubt you'll want to ride a glass elevator to the lobby in your underwear. And by that time I'll be long gone."

"They'll be looking for you too."

"How could they? Clyde won't talk. You're the only other person who knows I'm here." Fahey was obviously pleased by his plan.

"I don't think I'll ever be able to get free of these ropes," O'Connell said. He strained at the bonds to prove it.

"Probably not," Fahey agreed, "but the maid will find

you soon enough when I reverse the tag on the doorknob to read 'make up this room immediately.'" He paused to give the priest a chance to follow the plan. "You like it?"

"What do you expect the maid to think when she finds me here?"

"Who knows? Robbery? Extortion? Some rabid anti-Catholic Ku Kluxer? Explain the thirty-eight on the dresser to her. Think up something exciting, Father. It'll be all yours. And I'm sure you won't want to tell her the truth and blow the whole thing. Your loyalty to Kennedy's ghost will keep you from doing anything foolish."

Father O'Connell thought for a moment and then resigned with a nod. "It's your ball game now, James. Just do one thing for me before you go."

"What's that?"

"Put a couple of nitroglycerine tablets on the edge of the tub for me. I can reach them with my tongue, if I need one."

The agent took the pills out of the bottle and made a neat line of small white tablets along the edge of the bathtub. "Be my guest, Father," he said. "Take one as needed, and call me in the morning."

"Contact me when we both get back to Washington, James," O'Connell said, trying to make himself comfortable. "I want to be sure it all worked."

"It will work," Fahey said. "I'm sure of it. In spite of yourself, you'll be praying for me every inch of the way." He left the bathroom and gathered everything, except the priest's clothes and the false beard. He removed the tag from the priest's suitcase and carried it out the door. There was no one in the hallway. He planted the instructions to the maid on the doorknob, found the exit at the end of the hall, and walked down the stairwell to the street level. In the lobby he became another tourist, and left the suitcases near a potted plant. With a little luck he would find a street taxi willing to go to the airport.

29 At Burt's Place, Baines glanced at his watch. "That's long enough," he announced. "We've played their game and followed their instructions to the letter. Now it's our turn."

The detective got up and headed for the bar. The bartender surrendered the phone the instant the detective flashed his badge.

Baines dialed the Atlanta Police Department and was quickly put through to Communications.

"This is Detective Shelby Baines," he announced hurriedly. "I want you to raise the officers at my homicide scene at the Omni and tell them to seal off the exits to the street."

"You want them to stop everyone?" the communications sergeant asked formally.

"Everyone going in or out of the whole Omni complex. And I want them to be on the lookout for a priest with a gray beard."

"A priest, sir?" the sergeant asked, astonished.

"Yeah," Baines snapped, "a priest. Y'know—Roman collar, black suit? All the good stuff."

"Yes, sir."

"He's about six feet and I make him to be in his early fifties. It's hard to tell with the beard."

"Yes, sir."

"But they are to stop everyone else too—men, women, and children. I want a bottleneck. Got it?"

"Yes, sir. Men, women, and children." The radioman did not sound convinced.

"And then send twenty more men over here to the Omni. I'll meet them at the Marietta Street exit and take charge."

"Yes, sir."

"The priest is to be considered armed and dangerous, and—"

"Pardon me, sir?"

"Armed and dangerous," Baines repeated impatiently. "He's got a gun. And *that's* armed and dangerous."

"Yes, sir."

"And that's not all, Sergeant. I also want you to send a squad to the airport and stop everyone with a gray beard or anyone in a priest's suit, bearded or not. Got that?"

"Men, women, and children at the airport too, sir?"

"No, Sergeant. Just men out there. But at the Omni I want *everyone* stopped. It'll add to the crowd and confusion. I think he's still inside."

"Do I tell them the nature of the offense, sir?"

"Tell them to stop him on suspicion of murder," Baines said. "I'll take full responsibility."

"Yes, sir," the radioman said, gaining confidence in the scheme.

"And one more thing..." Baines paused, hesitating to make the next request.

"Sir?"

"Tell the captain to send me another loaded thirty-eight. Mine is in the priest's pocket."

There was a stunned silence. The radioman found the last remark impossible to believe. Shelby Baines was, after all, the homicide chief.

"Got all that?" Baines snapped.

"Yes, sir. Is that all?"

"No—call Homicide and tell them to hold the federal agent they picked up over here. I want him kept for me, no matter *who* comes to spring him?"

"*Who*, sir?"

"Never mind, Sergeant. Homicide will know who I mean. I don't care if the whole damned FBI shows up to get him out. I want him held until further notice." He glanced at Dr. Stanton, who had just joined him at the bar.

"What about Mrs. Adams?" the medical examiner asked.

Baines thought for a moment and then put his hand over the phone. "That's a chance we'll have to take, Twig. If they got her, they got her. But I think the priest was bluffing about Mrs. Adams."

"You may be right, Shelby," Stanton said, "and I don't think he was a priest at all."

"Why not?"

"Because he smelled of Brut after-shave and he wore a ring. Priests don't wear rings."

"They don't?" Baines asked, searching his shallow Baptist memories for nonexistent shreds of ecclesiastic trivia.

"Not unless they're bishops."

The detective thought about that observation for a moment and nodded appreciatively, removing his hand from the telephone mouthpiece. "Good thought," he said.

"Pardon me, sir?"

"Nothing," Baines said. "Get right on that stuff, Sergeant. Every second counts. And send a car over to the Hyatt Regency to pick up a Mrs. Maude Adams."

"Mrs. Maude Adams?" the sergeant repeated.

"Right. Her husband, Dr. Ed Adams, is already en route to Grady with a flesh wound to his arm and—"

"Mrs. Adams was picked up already, sir."

"By who?"

"Unit two sixty-five, sir. They just cleared the ride to Grady a few minutes ago. They're not code three. They're not running blue lights or a siren."

"Are you sure?" Baines asked.

"That's affirmative, sir. I logged the ride myself."

"And the unit is being driven by one of *our* officers?" Baines persisted.

"Sir?" The communications sergeant found himself asking "Who else?" but swallowed the remark.

"Skip it, I've got to go." Baines slammed the phone down and grabbed Stanton by the arm.

"Where to?"

"The Marietta Street exit. And stay the hell out of the way. We don't want you getting shot." They headed for the door and had almost left when the waitress ran up to them.

"That'll be three-fifty," she said.

"I'll get it," Stanton volunteered. "You head for the exit. I'll meet you down there." He reached into his pocket for the money as the detective left and ran through the crowd.

"Three-fifty out of five," the girl said mechanically.

"Keep it," Stanton said. He tried to follow the detective through the crowd, but quickly lost sight of him. The homicide detective's advice to stay out of the way stuck in his mind—he'd had enough guns and shooting for one day.

Stanton walked toward the hotel lobby, feeling a little weak. The excitement of the shooting and the confrontation at Burt's Place had pumped enough adrenaline into his bloodstream that he now felt shaky on the withdrawal. He crossed the carpet of the hotel lobby, intending to use the motor-level exit as a safer route to Marietta Street and Detective Baines.

There was a moderate crowd in the lobby. It was not elbow to elbow, but the rush of people hurrying to go places caused them to jostle each other frequently. Dr. Stanton's mind was captivated by the sight of the dead federal agent on the ice and the bizarre confrontation by the man dressed as a priest. It had been a unique day. He began to lose track of himself in the crowd and become a little careless, bumping first into a loud fat lady with a small, pale child in hand, and then into a middle-aged man who was in a hurry.

"Excuse me," he said to the man.

"Sorry," the man returned.

Their eyes met for a moment of déjà vu. Stanton squinted to focus his attention on the man. He found the man's eyes very familiar but the face was not. The man was about five feet nine and was about fifty.

The man looked at the medical examiner and gasped inaudibly. The doctor was immediately familiar to him. He had just held a gun on him at Burt's Place. He took a quick reading of the pathologist's eyes and decided Stanton had not yet recognized him. It was apparent the pathologist was curious, but he had not yet tumbled. Fahey fought his rising nervousness. He knew he was looking at Stanton too intensely and for too long. The pathologist's subconscious drive to make sense of the recognizable bits of information pouring into his professional brain emerged at the conscious level the same instant his nose identified the Brut.

In an instant he put it together. Stanton's imagination hung a gray beard on Fahey's smooth face, and a Roman collar around his neck, completing the suspect's picture.

"You!" Stanton stammered.

"Excuse me, sir," Fahey said brusquely. He sidestepped the pathologist and slipped behind two children carrying skates. He refused to be recognized and knew his escape hinged on his ability to ignore the pathologist. A confrontation would gain him nothing.

"You!" Stanton repeated after him. "You're the priest!" He ran his hand across his own face as if to feel for a nonexistent beard.

A fiftyish and dumpy woman nearby looked at Stanton curiously and then glanced at Fahey as he merged into the crowd. She didn't see any priest and wondered if Stanton was drunk.

"Come back!" Stanton shouted at Fahey. The agent paid no attention. The pathologist thought of Shelby Baines and his roadblock at the Marietta Street exit. There was no way back through the crowd to summon the detective without losing Fahey. Stanton knew he would have to follow the agent by himself. He glanced to his left and saw the woman still staring at him. She had dismissed her diagnosis of drunkenness and now considered him crazy.

"Lady!" Stanton shouted at her across several unconcerned people. "Go to the Marietta Street door and tell Detective Baines that Dr. Stanton found the priest!" He waited for a moment to see if she comprehended any of that.

The woman's mouth was open and her lower lip tried to form a word or some sort of sound. No noises came out.

"Lady! Do as I say!" Stanton insisted. "I am Dr. Stanton, the medical examiner."

After a moment the woman nodded compliantly and rushed off toward the area he had indicated. Stanton stood on his tiptoes in an effort to see over the crowd, but it was almost hopeless. Fahey had faded into the mob and was quickly escaping. Stanton knew Baines could not have blocked the rear doors by then. The medical examiner's heart quickened with excitement. The only link between the dance card and its true meaning was slipping away. Stanton quickly overcame his reluctance to be involved further. He knew if he lost Fahey, it would be all over. He plunged into the crowd and elbowed his way toward the rear doors.

The southwest corner of the Omni opened into a courtyard adjacent to the sports arena. It was the home court of the Atlanta Hawks and the home ice for the Flames. Neither Stanton nor Fahey had been great fans of professional basketball or hockey but evidently the people in the crowd between the two buildings were. Lines had formed at the several ticket booths in the courtyard. Fans who already had tickets were filing through the entrances into the big arena. Above the center door, in lights, it said, "Flames take on the Flyers."

Stanton burst out of the hotel, breathless and excited. He had hoped to see Fahey running across an empty parking lot and was dismayed to encounter another big crowd—this time, hockey fans.

Fahey pushed his way to the front of the shortest line, ignoring the remarks from the other fans as he bought a ticket in the reserved section. For a moment the ticket booth hid him from Stanton's view as the frustrated pathologist swept the crowd for any glimpse of the agent. Fahey reasoned that the exits to the Omni complex were more likely to be covered by the police, if, in fact, Baines had sounded the alarm. He could not be sure if Stanton was still after him or whether he had abandoned the chase. There was no longer any doubt in his mind that he had been spotted. Cover blown, he needed the sanctuary of a crowd. A pro hockey game would do perfectly.

Fahey emerged from the shadow of the ticket booth and headed for the nearest entrance. He walked slowly, head down, apparently busy with the details on his ticket. Viewed from the Omni exit, he was almost impossible to distinguish from the other popcorn-eating fans who had come to watch the Flames pound Philadelphia into sports oblivion. Hockey fans in general got no Brownie points for good behavior, and this group was no different from the average. They represented organized mass hysteria, willing and ready to become an angry mob at the drop of a puck. Upset, they could throw hand-warmed pennies or fresh octopuses onto the ice where they would flash-freeze and disrupt the game. Football fans were sane by comparison.

Dr. Stanton scanned the crowd once more. The pathologist employed a search technique usually reserved for Pap smears. He ignored the distracting details and forced his eyes to race, slightly out of focus, across the patchwork of faces, garments, and people, hoping his brain would halt his search when it recognized Fahey. Using a similar method, cytotechnology techs were able to screen without boredom hundreds of slides covered with thousands of epithelial cells from normal female cervixes. If they actually concentrated on each normal cell as it went by in the high-power microscopic field, nothing would get done. The faces in the crowd became normal cervical cells and Fahey the malignant cell.

His methodical surveillance soon paid off. He spotted the agent just as he handed his ticket to the gate attendant and entered the arena. Stanton knew that Fahey was both trapped and free inside the giant sports complex. It was big enough to hold a football field, although the stadium on the south side of the city made that type of production unlikely. For a hockey game it would seat up to seventeen thousand fans.

Stanton looked back at the crowd streaming from the Omni. Baines was not among the people pushing each other out of the hotel complex toward the arena. Stanton knew he had to keep Fahey in sight. The crafty agent would certainly cross the arena, locate an exit on the opposite side of the building, and disappear forever. The dance card and its explanation would exit with him. Going back for Baines was out of the question. Stanton felt like a new physician stopping at an accident and struggling to understand the Good Samaritan Law—he had no duty to act, but he had volunteered and now had to do a reasonable job. Anything less would make him negligent, if only in his own eyes.

The pathologist darted between the ticket holders and approached the gate attendant. He reached into his pocket and pulled out his identification folder. It showed him a younger-looking doctor in a white coat, and testified he was the Fulton County Medical Examiner. A gold-colored badge gleamed from the opposite side.

"I'm Dr. Stanton, the chief medical examiner," the pathologist explained.

"Is there a body in there?" the attendant asked, frowning over the ID card. He was in his late sixties and wore a black clip on plastic tie.

"Not yet," Stanton said. "I'm a little early."

"Because I always get notified on my walkie-talkie when they expect the cops or an emergency vehicle to arrive at my gate." The attendant was one of those retirees who, having been issued a uniform, suddenly became an officious expert despite his total lack of experience.

"I need in," Stanton said. "It's official business."

The guard smiled slyly, pegging the pathologist as another cop who didn't want to part with the price of a ticket. "Okay, Doc. But you're going to have to stand down by the ice at one of the corners. The seats are reserved tonight—"

"Yeah, okay, thanks," Stanton said, rushing by the attendant. He repressed the urge to call him an asshole. He slipped his ID folder into his pocket and again began to sweep the crowd for any trace of Fahey. The agent had disappeared. Hockey fans streamed along the outer concourse, munching popcorn, spilling beer, and bitching about the mustard dispensers that spattered onto the hot dogs instead of leaving a smooth trail along the center of the meat. Vendors hawked programs, pennants, and loyalty items to identify the real fans from everybody else. The true fans were those excited, overweight, middle-aged men who felt dignity was enhanced by an undersized hat that said "Atlanta Flames."

Stanton flashed his badge to the young man at the nearest portal and stepped into the arena. He was on an upper level and the concrete stairway to the ice stretched out before him like a runway to a giant white stage. Both teams were on the ice, and the organist sent enthusiastic music into the air as the officials made final checks at the scorekeepers' table. Someone somewhere adjusted the overhead lights to brighten the rink and soften the seating area. For Stanton, frantically sweeping the crowd from the entrance portal, the dimming was exasperating.

"The visitors' section is down there, sir," the portal boy said. He pointed toward the ice and hoped Stanton would move on, out of the way, and into his seat before the game started. There were only minutes left before face-off and the boy knew a last-minute rush of beer drinkers would be triggered by the sound of the national anthem. In school he had been taught to stand at attention for "The Star-Spangled Banner," but here he had quickly learned to stay out of the way.

"Thanks," Stanton said. He took a few steps toward the rink level and paused again. The arena was almost filled.

The faces became dots on a photograph enlarged beyond its capacity and made blurry by its graininess. He blinked and brought them back into focus. He needed a place to start.

30

Detective Baines had felt a great need to tell the insistent woman that he was really very busy and had no time for her problems. By pure luck Stanton had selected a woman whose compulsive behavior at home in Decatur had caused her beleaguered husband to banish her downtown "...for shopping, for sightseeing, for lunch, for *anything,* for Christ's sake." She had been bored with her exile until the medical examiner had given her an urgent assignment, however temporary.

"But he said he was a *doctor,*" the woman pleaded. She finally had Detective Baines's attention. "And, I think he must have been on drugs or something." The lady was convinced she was performing her civic duty.

Baines had a crowd on his hands. Reasonable people were complaining about being detained at the Marietta Street exit. The last thing he needed on his hands was another wacko complaining about her last doctor visit.

"Now, when did you talk to your doctor last, ma'am?" Baines asked wearily. His question was aimed at the woman in front of him but his eyes swept the screening activity near the door.

"Just a few minutes ago," she yelled, pointing into the Omni complex. "I just came from Rizzoli's Bookstore and..."

"Yes, ma'am." Baines was Joe Friday out of *Dragnet,* hoping his disinterest would show and drive her off.

"Well, he told me to go the Marietta Street exit and find Detective Barnes. Are you Detective Barnes?"

"It's Baines." Something at the checkpoint caught his eye. A young woman and several small children were trying to leave and an uniformed cop made her dig through her handbag to find an ID. "Let her go, Schneider," he yelled to the cop. He waved his arms to help move the woman and her brood out into the street.

"Tell me again lady, I'm listening." He leaned his face toward hers and squinted.

"This man," she began, her "one more time" tone showing badly, "got a hold of me in the Omni, and he said he was a doctor and he said to go to the Marietta Street exit and find Detective Barnes or something like that." Her compulsions were serving her well.

"Uh-huh." (Why me, Lord?)

"But he must have been on drugs or crazy or something. A man like that shouldn't be allowed to run loose in a public building."

"Yes, ma'am." (One more minute. That's all she gets.) "Did he assault you in any way?" (She's bananas.)

"Oh, no!" the lady said righteously. She shifted the unbuttoned edges of her light sweater across her flat chest, preserving every shred of decency.

"But you thought he acted irrationally?" She probably sends crayon letters to the mayor, he thought.

"Sure I did. I'm not stupid, you know. I know a priest when I see one," she said confidently. "I mean, I'm no Catholic or nothin' like that, but a priest is a priest."

Baines came alive. He grabbed the woman by the shoulders with both hands and stared into her widening eyes. "Tell me *exactly* where you saw him and what he said. He's not crazy. He's working on a very important case for us. Where was he?"

"Just beyond the bookstore."

"Rizzoli's?"

She nodded.

Baines shouted over his shoulder to the two plainclothesmen who had joined the officers at the exit. "We got him, Benson. You and Countryman come with me. He's headed out the back door towards the sports complex."

The three detectives hurried through the crowd around the public skating rink. Baines was worried about Stanton. The medical examiner was not combat trained and the agent seemed like an expert. Baines was unwilling to trade Stanton for some phantom fed on a hush-hush assignment. Despite his job, Stanton had often shown warm human qualities to Detective Baines and to other men on the police force. He'd explain medical things to him. He was down to earth with them. Other doctors, especially the young ones in white pants at Grady, treated them like dumb-ass cops, and some of them were, but Stanton always found time for each of them, especially Shelby Baines.

They rushed by the bookstore. Rizzoli's carried fine editions, expensive prints, and classical records. Baines had never been inside and probably never would.

"Where do you think they got to?" Countryman asked, slightly out of breath. He was a little overweight, mid-thirties, and wrinkled.

"If they made it out the back door, God only knows," Baines supplied, slipping by an old man with a shopping bag.

"Have we got anybody in the street?" Benson asked, also puffing, also pudgy, also wrinkled.

"By now we have," Baines reassured him. "I set it up when we secured Marietta Street."

"What if they're inside the game?" Benson added.

"What game?"

"Hell, the Flames are playin' the Flyers," Benson said. He wondered how anyone could not know.

Suddenly, on a tiny balcony that opened through sliding doors from one of the rooms on the fifteenth floor, a black housekeeper stood at the railing facing the rink and the crowd below. She resembled the Pope about to address the faithful in St. Peter's Square.

"God Almighty!" She shouted to the non-listeners below. She could have been an evangelist, but the panic in her voice gave her away. "Help me, somebody. Help me!"

The three detectives looked up instinctively.

"God," Baines said softly, "another jumper."

"No way," Countryman said. "Not a black female." His instant analysis was right. Baines mentally scored him a gold star for paying attention to Dr. Stanton's forensic lectures at the police academy.

"There's a *dead* man up here," the maid shouted. She turned to face the room again and put her hands to her face.

"Call it in," Baines said flatly.

Countryman reached into his hip pocket, under his coat, and pulled out a small radio unit. "D-two fifty-one," he said.

"Go ahead, Two fifty-one," the dispatcher responded.

"Relay to the special unit at the Omni—we've got a black maid on one of the upper balconies screaming about a dead man in a room. We can't cover it right now. We've got our hands full." He paused for a moment. "You copy?"

"C'mon," Baines said to his partners. "We've got enough to do without taking on some dead tourist. The unit will cover it."

The three detectives rushed toward the rear door. Baines assumed that since Stanton was not in the crowd, neither was the agent.

"Notify the street men to button up the exits from the sports arena. Tell 'em to stop everybody," Baines said over his shoulder.

"How about a description?" Countryman asked.

"The guy had a beard and a black suit when he left Burt's Place, but I'll bet you my ass he hasn't got either of them on now."

"So what does he look like, Shelby?" Countryman asked.

"Beats the hell out of me," Baines said. He reached for the exit latch on the main door leading from the hotel complex to the sports arena. "He's probably in his fifties, about as tall as I am, and a lot stronger than he seemed to be at Burt's."

"Why 'stronger'?" Benson asked, following Baines through the door.

"He was dressed like an old priest when he jumped Dr. Stanton and me. He tried to look aged and sick. He even took a heart pill in front of the doc, but the way he took off after he got the dance card makes me think the heart pain was all an act." Baines looked at the marquee announcing the hockey game. The roar inside the building let him know the game was in progress.

"You think he went into the game?" Benson asked.

"Wouldn't you?" Baines replied. "The cover would be perfect."

Countryman flipped his ID at the gate attendant. The old man reacted instantly and waved him through.

"They're with me," Countryman said, nodding toward the other two detectives.

"Sorry," the attendant said. "I've got to see it. House rules, Cops with ID's I pass, but they can't bring guests."

"Shit," Benson said softly as he produced his badge and held it close to the old man's face.

"He's just doing his job, Benson," Baines said. He

slipped his ID folder out of his pocket and showed the attendant the badge. "Have you by chance seen a Dr. Twig Stanton?"

"Who?"

"Dr. Twig Stanton. About my age. Maybe an inch or two taller. Hair starting to gray?" He ran his fingers along his temple.

"Could be most anybody," the attendant said.

"Uh-huh," Baines agreed. "I didn't think you'd know him, except he gets his name in the paper all the time. He's the Fulton County Medical Examiner."

The man's eyes opened almost as wide as his mouth. "Medical examiner?" he asked.

"Yeah," Baines said impatiently.

"He came in here a little while ago," the attendant said.

Baines sighed with relief. "Am I glad to hear you say that." He turned up to Countryman. "Up to now I had a horrible feeling in the pit of my stomach that said the lady who showed up at Marietta Street with Stanton's message was really another federal agent. I wouldn't put it past them bastards."

"Was there anybody with him?" Countryman asked.

"No," the attendant said. "He seemed like he was in a hurry, though. He went right in through one of the portals, I guess. At least he didn't hang around out here nowheres. But there weren't nobody with him, if that's what you mean."

"You've been a big help," Baines said. "Keep your eyes open, and if Dr. Stanton comes by again, tell him Detective Baines is looking for him. Got it?"

"You guys spread out," he ordered. "Keep your eyes peeled for anybody running or not looking at the game." He watched the two detectives depart into the crowd, fanning out to his right and left, before he started slowly down the aisle toward ice level. The game had already begun.

At the other end of the arena, halfway up behind the hometeam goal, Fahey assessed his choices. His ticket was for a seat at rink level but the crowd was thin down there. There were empty seats in the cheaper sections too, but none on the aisles. He would have preferred an inconspicuous aisle seat if only to sit down, like everyone else, and yet be in a position to get out in a hurry if he were spotted.

He was at a row halfway up from the ice. The crowd

was becoming excited. In the center of the row there were four unoccupied seats. The rows above and below the four vacancies were filled with yelling, cheering men waving paper cups of beer. Fahey stood in the aisle for a moment, looking alternately at the empty four seats and his ticket stub, as if confused by the number on it.

"Sit down, will ya, buddy?" a voice yelled from a few rows behind him.

"Yeah," someone joined in. "We came to see the Flames, not you."

"Sorry," Fahey mumbled. The complaints forced him to move. He desperately needed to be swallowed by the crowd. Edging into the row, he made small apologies to the five or six men seated between him and the four empties. One of them stood up as he bumped his way across the row but the rest only raised slightly in their seats, craning their necks to follow the game as he temporarily blocked the view. By then the game was in full swing. Fahey was not a hockey fan and wasn't sure which team were the Flames. The hometown roar of the crowd quickly told him who was who as a slapshot sailed over the goalie's head and slammed into the Plexiglas. The puck was immediately recovered behind the net and shot to the left of the rink as two players collided with such force that everyone could hear their bodies slam against each other and the boards. The impact brought most of the men in Fahey's row out of their seats, screaming and shaking their fists. Fahey, trying to look like one of the crowd, leaped to his feet and yelled at the players. The man to his left approved of his sudden enthusiasm with a wave of his beer. He nodded his head and smiled at the agent as they all sat down again.

"That Tebeau is one hell of a fine player, eh?" the man said.

Fahey thought he detected a faint Canadian accent. "He's the best," he agreed.

"Came here from the Rangers," the man said, concentrating on the game again.

"He does a great job," Fahey said, his voice trailing off to end the conversation.

Fahey began to scan the crowd for signs of Stanton or the police. There were three or four uniformed cops at the ice level, just outside the boards, to keep fans out. The cops were watching the game and not searching the crowd. Fahey's hopes continued to rise as he ran his eyes over the rest of the fans. Beer vendors and program hawkers and scattered fans kept walking up or down the aisles, but there was no Stanton! Fahey knew he had made it! He had apparently lost Stanton in the crowd. Or, he reasoned, maybe the doctor had gone back to get the detective. That had to be it. That meant the medical examiner and the cops would not be back for a while. There would be time enough to exit through one of the rear portals and find a safe way into the street. It would be safer to wait for the entire crowd to leave, he thought to himself, but that would mean an hour's delay, giving Baines enough time to cover all the doors. No, he decided, the escape had to be now, only a few minutes into the game.

The lighting above and behind Fahey's row was dim in contrast to the glare of the rink. Had Fahey turned to look high over his left shoulder, he could have seen Dr. Stanton making his way slowly down the aisle, inspecting the hundreds of faces right and left as he went.

Beyond the opposite goal and near the middle of the rink Baines, Countryman, and Benson moved down separate aisles, studying the fans, watching for unusual movements, hoping to flush the rabbit out of hiding and into a run. Countryman and Benson, not knowing what Fahey looked like, relied on their police instincts, hoping to spot their suspect by his suspicious behavior or when he ran.

Fahey looked up and down his row. He knew the man to his left would be annoyed if he asked them to let him out so soon, but an angry-looking fan occupied the next seat beyond the three empties to his right.

Fahey took his ticket stub out of his shirt pocket and studied it rather obviously, setting the stage for his move.

"Excuse me," he said to the man next to him. "I think I'm in the wrong row." He stood up as if to leave but the man did not budge.

"What the hell's the difference?" the man snapped, still watching the game. "A seat's a seat."

"But I'm supposed to be with some friends. I thought these four seats were ours."

"Oh, shit," the man moaned. He moved his knees to the

left, bumping the man next to him like a domino. "He wants out," he said, pointing at Fahey with his thumb.

"Out?" the next man asked, pained by the suggestion. "Out where? He just got here!"

"He's in the wrong row, Harry," the first man said.

"My ass," the other man said, half standing up as Fahey struggled by. "Why don't you come back and forth every five minutes?" he snarled.

"Sorry," Fahey said. He had made it to the third man, unfortunately, stepping on his toes as the man shifted to let him pass. The action on the ice produced a roar from the crowd and the fourth fan leaped up, spilling part of his beer on Fahey's sleeve. It was an exciting game and unthinkable that anyone would be leaving so soon.

"Look out, goddamnit," the man said, spilling more beer and shoving Fahey toward the aisle. The shove pushed Fahey into the man in the aisle seat, spilling popcorn onto the steps.

"Watch it, asshole," the man snapped. He stood up, sprawling Fahey into the aisle on his hands and knees. He felt the derringer shift in his coat pocket and covered it with his hand. He couldn't afford a gun clattering down the aisle in front of him, especially a derringer. Someone would think he was a madman and jump him for sure.

Saving the gun made him fall even more awkwardly into the aisle. He lunged forward, banging his knee on the step in front of him, and rolled toward his right, unable to prevent his fall without losing the gun.

The man in the aisle seat was standing by then. He was no longer as annoyed. Seeing Fahey fall made him offer his hand. The cheering crowd was standing too, but for a different reason. The Flames had scored.

"Are you hurt, fella?" the man asked. He grabbed Fahey's left arm and yanked him halfway to his feet before the agent could respond. The man was much bigger than Fahey and there was no way he could refuse the assistance. The man pulled Fahey by the arm and collar of his sport jacket, trying to keep him from falling farther down the steep aisle. The movements were clumsy and disjointed, causing Fahey to be lifted and turned over at the same time despite his own efforts to regain his balance.

As Fahey scrambled to his feet, readjusting the gun in his jacket pocket, he brushed off his knees and offered apologies. He did not see the dance card on the concrete floor near the aisle. It had fallen from his inside jacket pocket.

The commotion attracted Stanton's attention. He quickly moved down the aisle, covering the steps in twos. The man on the aisle had Fahey on his feet by the time Stanton came close enough to recognize him.

"O'Connell!" Stanton shouted. The pathologist knew the name was probably a fake, but it was the only name he had for the agent.

Fahey looked up the aisle and saw Stanton still several steps above him. The astonished doctor had paused and was pointing at the CIA man. Fahey wrenched himself free from the fan and began to run down the aisle toward the ice. The fan became even more confused by Fahey's reaction and stepped back into his seat, staying out of Stanton's way as the pathologist resumed the chase. Unknown to all of them, the fan had kicked the dance card under the seat, where it joined the popcorn, the beer cups, and the rest of the trash.

The commotion had attracted the attentions of Baines and his men from the other end of the arena. Baines immediately recognized Dr. Stanton and began to run down his aisle toward the ice. The detectives quickly followed him in their own aisles.

At ice level Fahey started to dash to his left, hoping to get to the end of the rink before Stanton caught up to him. The cop at the near end of the ice saw him run and shouted for him to stop as Stanton reached the lower end of the aisle. The policeman and the pathologist almost collided in the confusion, giving Fahey an additional precious second to outdistance the medical examiner. Then, at the end of the rink in front of him, Fahey saw Baines running along behind the visitor's goal. The detective had a gun drawn and it was obvious he was going to make it to the corner before Fahey could.

The agent stopped midway along the front row and looked both ways. They were closing in from both ends. He was trapped.

Suddenly he leaped onto the boards, caught the top of the Plexiglas with both hands, and began to pull himself up. The uniformed policeman drew his revolver and aimed, but was unable to fire when Stanton grabbed his wrist and began to struggle with him.

On the ice the action was confined to the home goal. The fans were on their feet, shouting, waving, oblivious of the chase below them and the man climbing the glass. The goalie blocked two quick shots in succession. The action behind the net was furious. The fans were becoming insane.

Baines reached Fahey's position in time to grab one foot, but not soon enough to hold it. The agent kicked his way free and threw his other leg over the glass. His only chance was to cross the ice and escape through the players' exit on the opposite side.

A Flames defenseman chopped at the puck with his stick, slamming the opposing player into the boards, to the delight of the fans. The puck slid along the boards in front of Stanton and the cop, still wrestling with the gun. A forward for the Flames followed the puck with sudden, savage instinct as a Flyer defenseman closed in rapidly to prevent him from breaking free. There was no one else between the Flames man and the Philadelphia goal except this single defenseman and the goalie. Each of them knew it was all or nothing. They skated toward each other with total abandon and slammed together like two locomotives as Fahey fell between them from the top of the glass. The sounds of the crash filled the arena and was followed by a stunned silence. The three men lay in a tangle of bodies without moving for an agonizing moment as fifteen thousand fans stood in total disbelief.

The referees hesitated for a moment, confused by the sight of a fan sprawled on the ice, before starting over to the men. Then, slightly dazed by the impact, the two players struggled to their hands and feet. The Flames player staggered to his skates and looked helplessly at Fahey, facedown and motionless on the ice in front of him.

In an instant Fahey was surrounded by the officials and players from both teams. A referee bent over him, holding his head with both hands as Baines rapped on the glass with the butt of his revolver.

"I'm Detective Baines—Atlanta Police," Baines shouted, holding his badge folder against the glass.

A Flames player saw the badge and pounded on the

referee's shoulder to attract his attention. The fans remained standing but there were no cheers or shouts.

Stanton and the policeman reached Baines's side as the referee turned from Fahey's crumpled form to face them.

"How is he?" Stanton shouted. "I'm a doctor."

The referee looked at the man outside the glass helplessly.

"He's dead!" the official said.

31 The naked body of Agent Fahey
lay on the morgue table, faceup.
His eyes and mouth were open and
one arm hung limp, the hand
pointing toward the floor. Stanton
and Baines stood at the middle of
the table, staring at the man without speaking. In the far
corner of the room three detectives gathered in a group
and talked softly as they compared their little notebooks.

Stanton shook his head slowly. "I don't understand it,"
he said finally.

"I went through every stitch of his clothes," Baines
mumbled.

"I'm sure he would have had it on him," Stanton said.
"It meant too much to him to trust it to anyone else."

"The priest sure as hell didn't have it," Baines said,
continuing to stare at Fahey.

Stanton looked at the table beyond the agent. On it
Father O'Connell lay in peace, his body covered with a
white sheet. The worry had disappeared from his face and
his eyes were gently closed.

"Have they finished searching O'Connell's room?" Stanton asked. There was no hope in the tone of his voice. He
knew the answer.

"My men searched that room as good as Fahey's boys
went over Toll's. We found the beard, but no dance card.
There was one peculiar thing, though."

"What's that, Shelby?"

"He had a printed mass card in his wallet. It said, 'Pray
for the twenty-five oh six' and it was dated April 1961."

"Could Fahey have passed the dance card to somebody
else? Somebody at the game, perhaps?" Stanton offered
lamely.

Baines shook his head. "If he did, why would he run?
No, Doc, he had it with him at the game, I'm sure of that."

Stanton nodded slowly. He sighed deeply and looked at
the ceiling light, trying to assess the confusing events of

the day. Suddenly his moment of silence was shattered by the bong of the intercom.

"Dr. Stanton?" the receptionist said.

"Yes, Libby?" Stanton replied without turning to look at the intercom box on the wall.

"Dr. Robinson from Emory is up here to see you. He says it is important."

Stanton and Baines looked at each other and lifted eyebrows.

"In reference to what?" Stanton asked.

"He says he knows something about Dr. Toll," the secretary supplied.

Baines held his hands upward in front of him. The gesture said, What next?

"Send him down, Libby," Stanton said.

"Who's Robinson?" Baines asked.

"One of the pathology professors from the medical school," Stanton replied. "He's okay. We don't agree on everything, but he's a good guy."

They turned to face the morgue door as Robinson entered alone. Baines made a small gesture to one of the detectives to tell him it was all right.

"Hello, Robbie," Stanton said. "You don't get down here very often."

"You're right, Twig. And that's my loss. I spend too much time in my ivory tower." Robinson walked to the morgue table and shook Stanton's hand. He glanced at Fahey's body without seeming to care, and then turned to Baines.

"This is Detective Baines," Stanton said. "Dr. Henry Robinson."

"Pleased to meet you, Mr. Baines," Robinson said, offering his hand.

"Likewise," the detective said. He had never met a black pathologist before and his face showed it.

"Libby says you knew Dr. Toll?" Stanton asked, breaking into the detective's stare.

"Well, I didn't know him as Dr. Toll, although I saw him some years back when we were both at Bethesda."

"You were in the Navy with him?" Baines asked.

"He was Navy. I was Air Force," Robinson said. "I was housed at the naval hospital. While he was there. In 1961 or so."

"How did you know he was here?" Stanton asked.

"He didn't show up for a speech we were supposed to deliver together this afternoon and I asked the hotel desk clerk about him. The police were all over me before I could cross the lobby. They told me he had jumped."

Baines nodded knowingly. "I staked out the desk and Toll's room after we found it ransacked," he said.

"Oh, they were courteous enough, Mr. Baines," Robinson said. "At least, after they found out who I was." He brushed his sleeve as if to remove a few unseen handprints on it. "They brought me over here."

"Good," Baines said. "What kind of a speech were you two going to give?"

"Actually it was a bit of a fraud," Robinson began. "On the program it said we were going to talk about some interesting cases of tropical parasitology, but Mr. Anderson here had a much bigger announcement to make."

"Anderson?" Stanton asked. "Did you call him *Mr.* Anderson?"

"That's the name he used in Haiti, the last time I saw him," Robinson said.

"And that's how he registered at the hotel," Baines said. He lowered his voice to a rasp. "Where did you see him in Haiti?"

"At the Albert Schweitzer Hospital," Robinson looked at Dr. Stanton for a moment and harvested a knowing nod before he continued. "Do you know Dr. Toll's story?"

"I'm not sure," Stanton fenced.

"I mean, are you aware he was being hunted by the CIA?"

Baines and Stanton exchanged glances. The detective gave a small, encouraging nod.

"You'd better tell us what you know about it first, Robbie," Stanton said. He glanced over his shoulder at the other detectives. "But keep it down."

Robinson came a step closer. "After I met him in Haiti this year, Toll told me the goddamnedest story about his involvement with the CIA and a cover-up of American dead from the Bay of Pigs invasion of Cuba."

Stanton's mouth fell open. "And?"

"And I invited him to come to the meeting in Atlanta to tell the whole world. We figured a public announcement would pull the CIA off his back and give him a chance to talk to somebody about his secret information before they could get to him."

"What secret information?" Baines asked.

"Something he called the dance card," Robinson said simply. "He said it would prove what he knew about the Bay of Pigs."

Stanton pointed at Fahey's body again. "Did you know this guy too?" he asked.

Robinson looked at Fahey and shook his head. "No. Who is he? A homicide?" He did not seem concerned.

"How about the other one?" Baines asked, pointing at Father O'Connell.

"Not him either," Robinson said. "Should I? Were they involved?"

"This one's a CIA agent and the other one's a priest," Stanton said.

"A priest?" Robinson asked.

"And maybe another agent as well," Baines added. "They were both involved."

"They were both after the dance card," Stanton said.

Robinson gave a slow, almost inaudible whistle. "And they were killed?"

"The agent died of a fractured skull," Stanton said professionally. "The priest had a heart attack. We found nitroglycerine tablets in his room."

"And the dance card?" Robinson asked.

"We thought you might help us with that question," Baines said gently.

"Me?" Robinson was slightly shocked at the question, "Hell, I never laid eyes on it. All I know about it was what Anderson, or Toll, or whatever his name was, told me about it. Frankly I was never completely convinced it existed."

"It existed all right," Stanton said. "I saw it."

"So did I," Baines said.

"But where's it now?" Robinson asked.

Baines pointed at Fahey. "This guy, the agent, took it away from us and tried to run."

"Did he kill Toll?" Robinson asked, puzzled by it all.

Baines shrugged heavily. "That's a good question, Dr. Robinson. I don't think we'll ever know for sure. A couple of his men tore up Toll's room, we think and—"

"—and searched Toll's body right here in the morgue," Stanton added.

"For the card," Robinson said.

"Uh-huh," Stanton agreed. "But they didn't get it. It was sewn inside him."

Robinson squinted for a moment and made a face that said he found it all hard to believe.

"And now nobody's got it," Baines said. "As far as we can tell."

"You mean, there's a chance the feds have it?" Robinson asked.

"A slight one," Baines admitted. "But I doubt it."

"Well, if the feds don't have it," Robinson asked, "where do you think it is now?"

Stanton glanced at Baines before attempting an answer. "My guess is that he dumped it somewhere inside the Omni."

Baines nodded slowly as Robinson swept his face for confirmation.

"Well, then," Robinson said, "it will turn up when you complete your search."

"I'm not sure it's all that simple, Robbie," Stanton said. "Where would we go from there?"

"What do you mean?" Robinson demanded. "Toll gave me the whole story about the Bay of Pigs. At least, he told me enough of it to make me understand how important it was to him. You can't just let it go now! Not just like that!"

"What else can we do?" Baines said, warming to Stanton's idea.

"Look, Robbie," Stanton said, "the government was after Toll because he knew too much and because he had proof. What do we have?"

"You've got *me*," Robinson said. "I could tell them everything I know. I could tell the whole world about the Americans killed in the Cuban invasion and what really happened to their bodies."

"And how would you prove it?" Baines asked. "You couldn't prove it if you had the dance card in your hand. The information was only names and diagnoses. They'd block us at every turn if we tried to check it."

"But Anderson...er...Toll said the card was the proof," Robinson said eagerly. "I could prove Jack Kennedy

lied when he said there were no Americans involved in
the Bay of Pigs."

"And that would get you one of two things," Baines
said. "You'd either be the next body on the slab, or the
first one locked up in the booby hatch. Without hard proof
you're nowhere."

Robinson looked stunned. He glanced back and forth
at the two men in disbelief. After a moment he nodded
slowly. "You really think it's that tough, huh?"

"Four men have already died over this dance card, Dr.
Robinson," Baines said somberly. "It's that tough."

"Four?" Robinson asked, glancing around the morgue.

"Another one of their agents," Stanton said simply.

"I shot him," Baines said.

Robinson stared at the detective again. He had never
met anyone who had actually shot and killed another man.
The admission began to make him see the gravity of the
situation.

"But if you leave the dance card somewhere in the
Omni, the feds might find it," Robinson suggested.

"That's the best thing that could happen," Stanton said.
"If they find it, they'll go home happy and leave us all
alone. If we go back and find it, they'll have to worry about
how much we know."

"And that might not be too healthy," Baines added.

Robinson looked at Father O'Connell's body for a moment and then at Fahey's open eyes. His lips mouthed,
"Four men..." but no sound came out. Baines and Stanton
gave him a moment to think it all through.

"If you don't mind, gentlemen," Robinson said, "I think
I'll go home and be sick."

"Do that, Dr. Robinson," Baines said. "It'll restore my
faith in humanity. I didn't think pathologists ever threw
up."

"By the way, Robbie, does the number twenty-five oh
six mean anything to you?" Stanton asked.

Robinson thought for a moment before he began to
shake his head. "We made a vaccine by that number a few
years ago, but otherwise it doesn't mean a thing to me.
Why?"

"Nothing," Stanton said. "Just wondering."

"I'll be in touch, Twig," Robinson said, patting the medical examiner on the shoulder. "I don't know how you stand

this job." He shook the detective's hand silently and walked toward the morgue door.

"You think he'll hold up?" Stanton asked, watching Robinson leave.

"Give him a while to think about it and he'll see he really has no other choice," Baines said.

"What about Dr. Adams?" Stanton asked. "Do you think he knows anything?"

"He'll be on the next plane back to Poplar Bluffs and I'll bet you my ass he never leaves Iowa again," Baines said, smiling a little.

Stanton stroked his chin and knew Baines was right. He had never known the crafty detective to be wrong before.

The phone rang, shattering their mutual silence. A detective in the corner picked it up and spoke briefly before hanging it up again.

"That was Headquarters, Baines," he said across the room. "The U.S. Attorney's Office just showed up downtown and sprung the fed."

Baines extended his hands in front of him and winked at the medical examiner. "That's the last we'll hear of *them*," he said confidently.

"Let's hope so, Shelby. We've got a pretty nice town here. I'd like to see it stay that way."

Detective Baines threw his arms around Twig Stanton affectionately. "How 'bout the homicide chief buying the medical examiner a beer somewhere?" he asked.

"Why the hell not, Shelby. Why the hell not?"